T0304822

THE LIGHTBORN

Tales of the Edge: volume 3

THE LIGHTBORN

Tales of the Edge: volume 3

Rebecca Zahabi

First published in Great Britain in 2024 by Gollancz
an imprint of The Orion Publishing Group Ltd
Carmelite House, 50 Victoria Embankment
London EC4Y 0DZ

An Hachette UK Company

1 3 5 7 9 10 8 6 4 2

Copyright © Rebecca Zahabi 2024

A CIP catalogue record for this book is
available from the British Library.

ISBN (Hardback) 978 1 473 23447 5
ISBN (eBook) 978 1 473 2340 5
ISBN (audio) 978 1 473 23451 2

Typeset at The Spartan Press Ltd,
Lymington, Hants

Printed and bound in Great Britain by Clays Ltd,
Elcograf S.p.A.

www.gollancz.co.uk

A mon père,
Qui ne lit pas de fantasy,
et pourtant m'a toujours soutenue.
Merci.

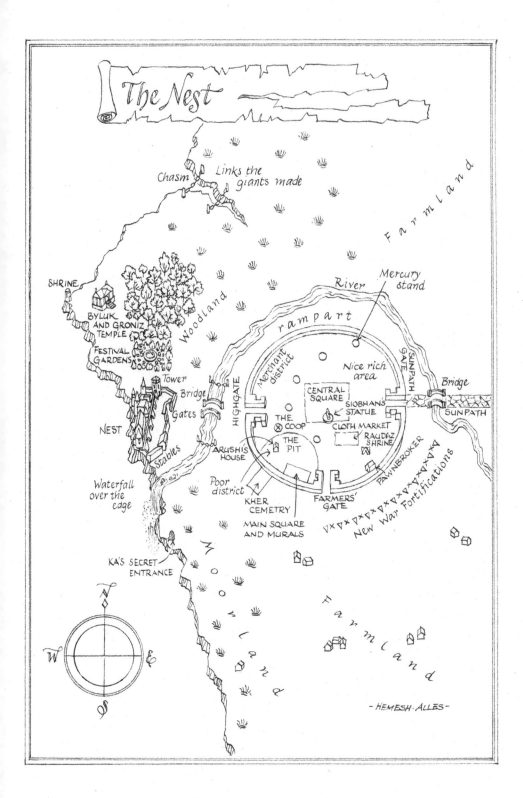

The Nest

Chasm

Links the giants made

Farmland

Woodland

River

Mercury stand

rampart

SHRINE

BYLUK AND GRONIZ TEMPLE

FESTIVAL GARDENS

Merchant district

Nice rich area

SUNPATH GATE

Tower

Bridge

Gates

NEST

HIGHGATE

THE COOP

CENTRAL SQUARE

SIOBHAN'S STATUE

Bridge

SUNPATH

Stables

ARUSHI'S HOUSE

THE PIT

CLOTH MARKET

RAUDIZ SHRINE

Waterfall over the edge

Poor district

PAWNBROKER

KHER CEMETERY

FARMERS' GATE

New War Fortifications

MAIN SQUARE AND MURALS

KA'S SECRET ENTRANCE

Moorland

Farmland

N

W

E

S

-HEMESH·ALLES-

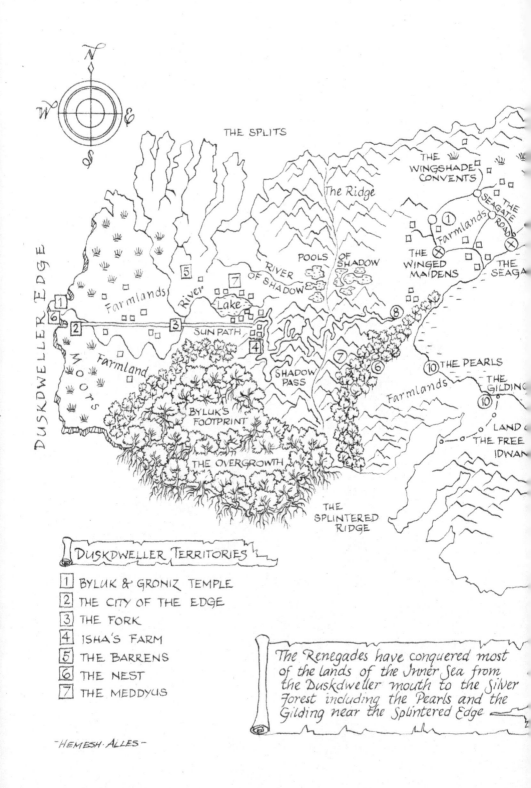

THE SPLITS

THE WINGSHADE CONVENTS

The Ridge

THE SEAGATE ROAD

① Farmlands

POOLS OF SHADOW

RIVER OF SHADOW

THE WINGED MAIDENS

THE SEAGA

D U S K D W E L L E R   E D G E

⑤ THE BARRENS

⑦ THE MEDDYUS

River

Lake

Farmlands

①
⑥
②
③ SUN PATH

④

Moors

Farmland

⑧

BYLUK'S FOOTPRINT

SHADOW PASS

⑦ ⑥

Farmlands

⑩ THE PEARLS

THE GILDING

⑩

THE OVERGROWTH

LAND
THE FREE
IDWAN

THE SPLINTERED RIDGE

DUSKDWELLER TERRITORIES

1 BYLUK & GRONIZ TEMPLE
2 THE CITY OF THE EDGE
3 THE FORK
4 ISHA'S FARM
5 THE BARRENS
6 THE NEST
7 THE MEDDYUS

The Renegades have conquered most
of the lands of the Inner Sea from
the Duskdweller mouth to the Silver
Forest including the Pearls and the
Gilding near the Splintered Edge

—HEMESH·ALLES—

THE FAITHFUL'S LONG ROAD
(PILGRIMAGE)

THE LAST SHRINE

Farmlands

THE SKY'S JAWS

THE UNGIFTED ALLIANCE

THE WETLANDS

HERE BE LIGHTBORNS

SUNRISER EDGE

SHADOW LAKE

THE BLACK BOGS

THE GAP

THE SAMUDRA CONVENTS

REDSTONE CONVENT

THE RED BELT CONVENTS

LOWTIDE PASS

THE INNER SEA

RAFTS OF THE SEAFARER KHERS (THE WATER TRIBES)

OVERTIDE

THE VELVET

REDGATE CITY

THE FRAME

HAWK'S CONVENT

PEOPLE'S PATH

Farmlands

PODGY HILLS

THE SUNLIGHT WEAVERS

Hills

THE HIGHLANDS

SUNRISER CONVENTS

① THE PROSPEROUS SQUARE
② SUVARN'S CHILDREN
③ THE HANGING CONVENTS
④ THE WOODLAND CONVENTS
⑤ THE EVERWARS CONVENTS
⑥ THE ROHIT PATRA
⑦ THE IMMORTALS' TRIBE
⑧ THE DUSKDWELLER MOUTH
⑨ THE SILVER FOREST
⑩ THE SEA'S CROWN

Chapter 1

Tatters stepped out of the prison and into the courtyard. He shielded his face with one hand, blinking, trying to make out shapes within the brightness. He rediscovered light. The pale stones reflected the sun, the blades on the weapons' racks burnt like fire. Passerine waited while Tatters tried to find his footing. He still felt sore, but the warmth of the sun thawed his muscles, lessened the ache inside his bones.

We survived, thought Lal. She was faint, still, in a corner of his mind, but gaining strength by the minute.

I missed you. And he'd missed the sun on his skin. He'd missed being alive.

'Keep moving,' Passerine instructed.

Had there always been this much noise – the voices of apprentices, the snorts and neighs of horses, the whistling of servants? Had there always been these smells – manure, sweat, mud licking at the soles of people's shoes, squelching underfoot? Tatters followed Passerine through the arches leading into the Nest; the shadowed interior was a relief for his eyes. There were kher guards lining the archways, and Tatters could only search vainly for the one kher he'd been trying to find since his first night in the cell. Arushi wasn't there.

They entered the circular hallway, girdled with steps on either side, leading to a towering balcony. Tatters recognised the inside of the Nest, but only as one recognises a place visited long ago, a memory already faded. He felt as if he had been gone years. Apprentices, mages, everyone seemed to follow him with their eyes, inquisitive, invasive. Robes that shouldn't have surprised him, deeply dyed blue, grey, and black, were the most luxurious pieces of clothing he'd seen in months. Faces that should have been familiar swam at the edges of his vision, but he didn't recognise anyone.

Passerine started up the stairs and, as stunned as if someone had punched him, Tatters followed. He made slow progress. He hadn't walked since he'd been flung in the cells – or only short distances, pacing the darkness. After a few steps, he was out of breath, his legs shaky beneath him. The giant staircase, despite the addition of small wooden steps, was hard work even for someone in good shape.

He was halfway up when he spotted Isha rushing down. She stopped in her tracks, staring as if he were a spirit risen from the underworlds.

'We thought you were dead,' Isha whispered.

I thought I was dead too, Tatters nearly answered. She hesitated, fretting, as if not sure whether to come closer or give him space.

Then suddenly, unexpectedly, she skipped the last few steps and hugged him. He nearly pulled back, out of habit, because no-one had tried to touch him with good intent since the lawmages had burst into his life. But she was warm, vibrant, with a broad hug that squeezed him tightly, with a heartbeat he could feel through her robes. Even the residual fleshbinding ebbed away when she held him. He was out of prison. This truth was sinking in. He squeezed back.

They stood for a while, neither of them speaking, and Passerine didn't interrupt. Isha broke off the hug first. Tatters noticed the wetness around her eyes; she turned away and wiped them on her sleeve. Happiness flooded her face.

'You seem well,' he said, because what else did you say to people? He watched Isha's full, asymmetrical features, and thought of Yua. Isha had a face no-one had ever tried to break. He could have cried, if he'd had any strength left.

They had drawn a small crowd, apprentices pooling around them at a safe distance.

'Go to the kitchens and see if they have any leftovers,' Passerine ordered, dismissing Isha. 'Bring the food to my chambers.'

Passerine placed a hand on Tatters, holding the nape of his neck in an iron grip. Tatters hadn't been expecting it; in any case, he was too weak to resist. Passerine held him firmly, as one would an unruly child.

'We can talk in private later,' Passerine said.

Isha nodded. It was only once she was headed down, out of sight, that Passerine dragged Tatters up the staircase, and there was nothing Tatters could do but follow. Students parted before them like reeds in a strong wind.

Passerine didn't let go when they reached the top of the staircase and turned into an inner corridor, nor when he arrived at the door leading to his chambers. He strode forward, Tatters stumbling beside him, and what stung most wasn't the pain, but the helplessness, the fact that this was it, he had run from the Sunriser kingdoms to the edge of the world, he had crossed the Shadowpass, he had tried his utmost to escape, yet he had been caught, and broken, again, again.

Passerine pushed open the door of his apartments and hauled Tatters inside. Then he turned gracefully, like a dancer, and slammed Tatters' skull against the wall. Head ringing, Tatters felt Passerine invade his thoughts – he was too shocked to react.

Hawk's advice sprung to mind. 'If you're going to mindbrawl

someone, bash in their heads first. It can't hurt.' Her raucous laugh. 'Well, it can't hurt *you*.'

Tatters struggled to regain focus, but his brain felt as if it had been splattered over the wall of Passerine's chambers. *He's going to kill me.*

Not on my watch, snapped Lal.

Passerine strode through his mind as it settled, as bookshelves and tables and scrolls sketched themselves in the imagined space, and Tatters barely had time to create a version of himself to face him down. Passerine didn't break his stride, but lifted a hand and grabbed Tatters' collar. In the real world, Tatters felt Passerine's long fingers around his neck. Both worlds melded, the real world where Tatters was pressed against the wall, his hair damp with blood, Passerine clutching his throat; and the mental landscape, a library of long-kept secrets, where Passerine was also gripping the collar, the cold of metal and the warmth of flesh mingling.

Passerine knew the collar wasn't active. He was trying to awaken it.

The collar lit up and started shrinking. Tatters found himself struggling for breath.

'I told you to come grovelling and that, if you didn't, I would find you,' Passerine said. His voice was stained with rage. 'Well, here you are. Did you think I'd forget? Did you think I'd ever forgive you?'

Tatters tried to push back, but Passerine was holding him fast. He must have writhed in the real world, too, because he felt Passerine's knee connecting with his stomach. He toppled over, but Passerine kept a firm grip on his bind, holding him upwards. All sensations were coming to Tatters sluggishly, and the shock of being hit landed well after the blow.

Lal appeared in the centre of his mindscape. The sound of

her voice seemed to echo across the lush chambers, as much as within the mental library.

Let go, she said.

'You realise you don't exist, don't you?' asked Passerine. His hands were hot around Tatters' throat. 'You're the projection of his guilt at having killed his sister.'

Lal spoke slowly, each word like a leaden arrow: *Let. Him. Go.*

While Passerine was distracted, Tatters kicked him. He managed to hit his shin hard enough that Passerine's grip around his neck slipped. But Tatters was weakened by hunger, sleeplessness, fear. His head was pounding, the ache worsening every time he moved. He didn't know where to run. As he hesitated, unsure if he should attack Passerine, leave the room, ask for a truce, the high mage lunged. Passerine was taller, with a broader build. When he hit, it was the sort of punch a soldier would have landed. Tatters found his legs couldn't hold him up. His knees buckled and he fell onto the cold stone. His vision was blurring too, maybe because of that first blow to the head.

'You destroyed everything we've ever worked for,' Passerine snarled. 'First you nearly destroy the Renegades, everything Hawk has ever achieved. Then you destroy my life's work. You ruin everything you touch.'

I have no idea what you're talking about, Tatters mindlinked, too winded to speak.

Passerine hesitated. 'What?'

He towered over Tatters. For a while nothing happened. Tatters was gasping for breath and trying to convince his legs to hold his weight, but he found he couldn't move them. Lal was inside his mind, guarding it, fierce enough that, for all his talk of her not being real, Passerine didn't try to invade. The collar glinted like a hoard of gold people would kill for.

Someone pushed the door open.

Passerine took a step backwards. Lal felt more relieved than Tatters would have liked as she retreated to the back of his mind.

'Get up,' Passerine said.

Tatters struggled to his feet, his breathing still laboured. On the other side of the door stood Isha, balancing a tray on one arm.

'I've got some bread, cheese, ham, and ...' She trailed off, taking in their expressions. Her eyes were soft, and the compassion within them would have warmed Tatters, if he hadn't been in Passerine's lair, if his collar wasn't still glowing with the aftermaths of mindlink.

'What in the underworlds is going on?' she asked, aghast. She pushed the tray onto the desk before hurrying to Tatters' side. 'Are you all right?'

I'll give you three guesses, snarled Lal.

Before he could answer, Isha rushed to correct herself: 'No, of course you're not, forget what I said, what I mean is ...' She trailed off, then turned to glare at Passerine. 'What were you doing to him?'

Although Tatters wouldn't have believed it possible, Passerine appeared uncomfortable. 'Tatters has a lot to answer for,' he said.

'I don't care!' The anger in her voice seemed to surprise even Isha. She straightened, chin high, fists clenched at her sides. 'I don't care what he did, or what you did, or whatever happened in the past. Look at him!' Tatters expected Passerine to shut her up, relying on his authority as a high mage if need be. But he stayed silent. Isha took a deep breath, her voice growing in strength with each word. 'Don't you get it? There's only us. If we don't work together, no-one can stop the Renegades. People have suffered, people have *died*, because you couldn't put the past behind and just talk. Do you know how much violence we could have avoided, if you'd only made the effort to talk?'

Everything was still. They watched each other like skittish animals who have yet to decide who is predator or prey. The room was vast, yet barren, with only a large, four-poster bed, a desk, two chairs. No tapestries decorated it. The stone walls felt as wispy as spiderweb thread.

'Thirsty?'

Tatters took time to understand what Passerine was saying. At first it sounded like a short bark.

'Thirsty?'

'Yes?' Tatters wasn't sure what he was agreeing to.

Passerine picked up an earthenware jug from the tray and poured water into a tumbler. He handed it to Tatters. Tatters took it. He drank. Silence stood between them like a fourth, uninvited guest.

Passerine opened his wardrobe. He took out a small square rag, which he wetted inside the jug. He handed the damp cloth to Tatters. Tatters took it, not knowing what he was supposed to do with it.

'Your head,' said Passerine.

Tatters lifted the rag gingerly, tapping at the side of his head with the piece of fabric, pushing his matted hair aside. Isha was watching him, chewing on her lower lip. When he went to rinse the cloth inside the jug, Tatters saw it was red. He touched his temples. He was bleeding. Lightly – nothing that would kill him. But he was bleeding.

Tatters pressed the sodden rag against the side of his head. He thought of Mezyan's words: *So you didn't make it, after all.* He went to sit on the bed. He felt sick. The shock of the last few days was settling in the pit of his stomach. Passerine's nose scrunched in distaste when Tatters slumped on his covers. Tatters half-expected Passerine to shoo him off the bed, but he let it lie.

'I agree with Isha.' Tatters would have liked his voice not to sound so frightened. 'Could we maybe not fight?'

We never did anything to you, said Lal.

Passerine answered in mindlink. *You have no idea what was lost because of you.* The sentence was heightened with impressions, faint sounds and smells – paper burning, a man screaming his throat raw, the embers flying out into the night. Books, Tatters realised. A bonfire of books and scrolls, curling and growing black as the words were lost to the fire.

Tatters didn't know what this meant but he felt, confusedly, that he should. Or that Passerine expected him to understand, at least.

Passerine sighed, as if making a difficult decision. 'Isha isn't wrong,' he admitted.

'I'm glad that's been established,' she said, her tone not quite light enough.

'I am not one of the Renegades anymore,' said Passerine. 'I won't bring you back to Hawk. We have common goals: we want to stop her.'

'You were always Hawk's second-in-command,' Tatters said.

'I was. I wanted...' Passerine cut off abruptly. 'It doesn't matter. I tried to avoid violence. It is no longer possible to avoid it. Either we fight Hawk, or we die.'

'Hawk has crossed the Shadowpass,' Isha interrupted. It should have upset Tatters more, but it was only one piece of bad news amongst others. Another pebble in a bag of rocks.

'If you don't pretend to be under my orders,' Passerine went on, 'you will be hanged, and me with you. I have risked my reputation by covering for you.'

Tatters nodded. He was unsure why Passerine had taken such a risk.

Because he thought he could control you, said Lal. *He hoped the collar would work.*

'If you are going to leave, I want to know,' Passerine went on.

'Will you help us, is what he means,' said Isha, her voice fierce. 'Will you stand by us, when our enemies come?'

Tatters wasn't sure he had much of a choice. 'Yes,' he said. 'I suppose so.'

Passerine rubbed the palms of his hands together, looking at nothing, avoiding their gazes. He seemed to be waiting for Tatters to add something. After a moment of silence, he got up.

'You can tell the servants to fill a tub of warm water,' he told Isha. Then, to Tatters: 'You need a bath.'

Isha hesitated, glancing towards Tatters. He nodded, because he didn't know what else to do. For now, he could cope with the menial task of keeping himself clean. Passerine went to fetch a black robe from his wardrobe and threw it across the bed. 'You can wear that.' Tatters didn't want to argue, even at the sight of a high mage's robe.

Isha should have left as soon as her master had given her an order, but she was standing at the door, as if uncertain about leaving them.

'Promise me you're not going to fight again,' she said.

Passerine crossed his arms in front of him. His long sleeves folded over like a bat's wings. 'I'll let him clean up in peace, if that's what worries you. I'll follow you out.'

She opened the door for him, and the high mage stepped out, with a meekness that baffled Tatters. It occurred to him that Isha wasn't scared of Passerine. And Passerine was, if still curt – he was always curt – indulging her somewhat. The authority he could have used to push her around and exclude her, he used to keep her included.

They both left, Passerine stiffly, not gracing Tatters with a farewell; Isha smiling his way, encouraging, obviously trying to convey support before she closed the door behind them.

This is how we go from runaways to slaves, said Lal.

* * *

Tatters bathed in the zinc tub the servants brought up. It was a relief to wash off the grime of the prison at last. His muscles relaxed in the hot water, and for the first time in months, he felt, if not safe, then calm. When he stepped out of the water it was brown, with scum floating on the surface, and no doubt grit settled at the bottom. The servants didn't comment.

He wore Passerine's black robe. It was too big for him. He folded over the bottom of the robe, asked the servants for thread and a needle, and adjusted the clothes to his smaller size. His fingers were sore and unused to this work. He had never been good at it in the first place; Lal had done it for them both when they lived together. He still swam inside the garment afterwards, and the fabric bulged in places. But it was clothing that hadn't been soaked in blood and sweat.

If it had been salvageable, he would have kept his old stana. It had been his first piece of dyed clothing. The servants took it away to burn it, then boiled the sheets he'd sat on and dusted the furniture. Tatters wasn't sure whether to feel insulted, or to revel in such luxury.

When the evening came, he was sitting at Passerine's desk, staring out at the sun setting over the Edge. On some level, Tatters knew he should be moved by the view. The winter lights were purple like a kher blush, with lines of pink streaking the clouds. The glinting sun caught the foam from the river, drawing a broken, unfinished rainbow arc. It was lovely. The colours were warm. Tatters felt cold.

He looked at his hands. He had scars around his wrists where the manacles had dug in for so long. They were thin lines, like bracelets, neatly printed in his skin.

The visible scars are always smaller, said Lal. It was a saying from the Meddyns fiefdoms.

Tatters closed his fist. When his muscles moved, the scars did too.

Passerine let himself in, the sound of his key preceding him. Tatters noticed for the first time that he'd been locked inside. He hadn't even thought of testing the door.

He expected Lal's *Maybe you should have*, but it didn't come.

Passerine locked the door behind him, but this time the key was on the inside. He briefly studied Tatters.

'That's better,' he said. He went to his wardrobe to change into a nightgown. Tatters looked away. He heard the rustle of cloth, the low rasp of Passerine's breathing. He hadn't shared space with other people in a long time. He remembered the Renegades' camp, where men changed, pissed, slept and ate together. Women too, although they sometimes went further into the woods when nature – or too much wine – called. He remembered, but only vaguely, what Passerine looked like, half-naked by the campfire, as he stitched back his shirt where it had ripped from the swing of a sword, his skin glistening in the dull light.

The memory prompted something unexpected: Hawk herself, laughing, resting a hand on Passerine's naked shoulder. Him glancing up and smiling with white teeth. A reminder of the intimacy they'd shared.

When Tatters turned around, Passerine was in bed, a candle next to him and a scroll across his knees.

'Where am I sleeping?' he asked.

Passerine shrugged. 'As you wish. The bed is big enough for two.'

Tatters didn't answer. He hated this forced closeness, when his instinct screamed to get as far away as possible from Passerine, when he knew that the man could, and would, be violent if he deemed it useful.

Passerine pulled the vellum closer to read. 'We have slept closer than this before,' he said, eyes on the scroll.

They had; they'd shared blankets thrown on the ground, travelling an uncomfortable land, piles of soldiers pressed together for warmth.

'When we were Renegades.' Tatters amended, 'When I was a slave.'

Let alone what happened years ago, said Lal. *What about what happened this afternoon, when he attacked you?*

Passerine let the vellum rest against his legs and deigned, at last, to look at Tatters. He held Tatters' eyes, his voice as deep and serious as an executioner's. 'I don't want to talk about it.' Then, without transition, he waved one hand towards the wardrobe: 'I have a travelling nightgown, if you wish.' He went back to his reading.

The idea of a bed – a mattress, a pillow with feathers inside, a proper cover – was hard to resist. Slowly, skittishly, like an animal unused to human contact, Tatters went to the wardrobe. He removed his robe and pulled on a nightshirt which fell down to mid-thigh. Passerine didn't look at him or say a word as Tatters slid underneath the covers. They didn't even touch – there was space enough. But Tatters still felt vulnerable. How could he sleep and be sure to wake up in bed, rather than bundled on a horse headed for the Renegades?

You can't be sure, said Lal.

He sat, hands crossed in his lap, tenser than he'd been in prison, where at least brutality was expected.

'I'm leaving in the morning,' he told Passerine at last.

After an uncomfortable pause, Passerine laid his scroll on his lap. 'Where will you go?'

Tatters felt sick. Although he was conscious the bed couldn't be moving, he felt as if it were rocking, floating on tumultuous waters. He had no answer.

So instead, he asked a question of his own: 'What made you think the collar would respond to you?'

Passerine watched Tatters for a long moment. The sun had set completely now. The chambers were dark, with only the white glow of the moon in the room, painting its angles grey and silver, and the candle, casting an orange light on Passerine's face. He had short hair, as always. Close shaven, as always. There was more grey in the black curls, but nothing else to indicate time had passed, that they had grown old.

'Hawk handed over control of the collar to me. I don't know how you could forget such a thing.'

Memories rose in Tatters like nausea, knotting his throat. *One day he will do something, something unforgivable, something you cannot overlook, and you will have to admit I was right, and you will hand him over to me.* Passerine's voice. The flickering of a campfire across his features. The primal, vicious way the collar had reacted to him, the first time Tatters had learnt of his presence in the Nest. *Come grovelling for forgiveness, and you might get it. But if you don't come, I'll find you.*

His head was spinning. He was forced to take deep breaths until the world stabilised.

'The Shadowpass must have had a price,' Passerine concluded. He rolled up his scroll, knotting a thread of leather around it to hold it closed. He placed it beside the bed, next to the candleholder.

'Why would Hawk do that?' Tatters asked.

Passerine shook his head slowly. 'Maybe you did well to forget. In a way, you can pretend you are not responsible for the deaths.'

Tell us what happened, Lal urged.

'I'll only say this: you nearly killed her. Even with the collar undamaged, you nearly murdered your master.' When Passerine spoke, his deep tone felt as vast as the plunge beyond the Edge. 'Which is why I know you're the one who can kill her.'

Tatters stared at his fingers, knotted on his lap. The scars on the wrists. The fine hairs on the back of his hands.

'If you want to flee, I can't stop you,' Passerine concluded. 'But you should stay.'

He leant over and blew out the candle.

* * *

It took time for Tatters to fall asleep. When he did, he dreamt. It was unpleasant because it wasn't his dream.

He didn't realise at first that it wasn't his. It was set in the Renegades' encampment, on the road, when they'd had enough people to attack convents. Horses tied to trees on the outside, tents borrowed from khers on the inside, soldiers strewn around half-dying fires, drunk on victory. He knew it was a dream when he spotted Lal walking beside him.

When he reached the edge of the camp, which had been set on top of a hill, he saw the city in the dip of the valley beneath them. High towers, domed palaces, the pier along the silvery lake. It was the convent of the Winged Maidens, the centre of the Wingshade world, which was rumoured to be paved with gold, brimming with treasures. But when Tatters had been part of the Renegades, they had never attacked the Wingshade stronghold.

'Ugh,' said Lal. 'I bet we're in Passerine's dreams.'

'Why are you here?' Tatters asked. 'Shouldn't you be having dreams of your own?'

She shrugged. A breeze lifted her heavy curls, unfurling them behind her like a banner. Red on black, when the Renegades' flag was black on red. She was wearing a shirt tucked into a pair of trousers and a leather jacket.

'I don't think they even made armour your size,' Tatters said, playfully tugging at the hem of her clothes.

'Not you again.'

They both turned. Passerine was walking up the slope towards them. He was holding a spear, the weapon he had favoured when warring with the Renegades. As he came closer, Tatters saw the tip was dark with blood.

'It was obvious this was going to happen,' Tatters said. 'We're too close.'

Passerine frowned. He seemed annoyed to see them there, although what this place meant to him Tatters could only guess.

Lal waved at the city of a thousand riches. 'Did Hawk's predictions go as planned, then?' she asked. 'Was it impossible to take without our help?'

'She didn't say it was impossible to take,' Tatters corrected. 'She said it would be a bloodbath.'

Lal shook out her hair. She was half Tatters' height, so light that he could have carried her on his shoulders. In all these years, she hadn't grown.

'Well?' she insisted. 'Was it?'

Passerine sighed through his teeth. 'Wake up. Leave this place.'

Lal gave him a wicked grin. 'It must have been pretty bad, if it still haunts your nightmares.'

Tatters was about to advise Lal not to antagonise Passerine too much – they were in his dreams, after all – but Passerine beat him to it. He brought his spear forward, the blade darting downwards, and pushed with both hands in one swift, cruel movement. Tatters felt the shock of the blade against his chest and woke up suddenly, in a cold sweat.

He could feel his heartbeat ringing in his ears. He pushed himself upwards, legs entangled in the sheets, struggling to catch his breath. It was pitch-black inside the room. By killing him, Passerine had forced him out of the dream.

The bastard, fumed Lal.

Tatters was tempted to poke Passerine's shoulder and forcefully wake him. He was snoozing peacefully, his arms tucked under his cushion, showing no signs that his sleep was troubled. Although Lal was all for getting into a fight in the middle of the night, Tatters decided against it. He forced himself to lie back down. He waited until his breathing was regular again. There was an ache in his chest, even though he knew it had to be phantom pain.

He tossed and turned before managing, at last, to fall asleep again.

When his dreams solidified, stopped following the uncoherent threads of unconscious sleep and became something more vivid, he groaned.

'Not again ...'

It was inside the Coop this time. He was seated at his usual table. Lal was slumped beside him, chin tucked in her hand, a chunk of bread, a breadknife, and some cold meats in front of her. She tore off a piece of bread and a slice of ham, stuffing them both inside her mouth.

'Your dream includes a sense of taste,' she said approvingly. 'I like it.'

'How do you know it's mine?' Tatters asked. He checked the room for Passerine. He couldn't be far – Tatters could practically smell him.

'It's yours,' Lal said. 'Why would Passerine dream of the Coop?'

Tatters had to agree with her. After his last awakening, he didn't particularly want to be run through with a spear again. He kept watching the room until at last he spotted him, a flash of black robes at the other end of the tavern, standing by the counter. Passerine had his back to them.

'He hasn't noticed us yet,' Tatters said, relieved.

Lal grabbed the breadknife. Before Tatters could stop her, she'd crossed the busy tavern, squeezing between the members of the crowd.

She waited until she was behind Passerine to say, 'Rise and shine!'

As Passerine turned to see who had spoken to him, she stabbed him, pushing the breadknife into his stomach with all her strength. People shouted and moved aside. Blood spurted as he tumbled off his stool, but his corpse never hit the ground. He disintegrated into dust. Lal gave the innkeeper the knife with a sharp: 'Clean it. And more cheese.'

She walked back to where Tatters was seated, smiling ear to ear. 'See how he likes it.'

But they didn't get to enjoy their Passerine-free sleep. Tatters felt someone shaking him and, messily, blinking, confused, he found himself back inside the chambers of the Nest.

'Do you think this is funny?' growled Passerine. All Tatters could see of him was the white of his eyes. It didn't make him any less threatening.

Tatters shoved him away. 'You're one to talk. You started this stupid feud!'

He pushed himself upwards. They both sat on their opposite sides of the mattress, not wanting to admit the other person had won. It was the most uncomfortable time Tatters had ever spent in such spacious chambers.

When Passerine spoke, his tone was as cold as the stone walls, as bleak as the starless night. 'Let's agree to ignore each other if we share our dreams again.'

'Agreed,' said Tatters.

Try me, said Lal.

They both shuffled to lie down. They listened to each other's breathing.

They didn't manage to sleep again.

Chapter 2

The next morning, Isha met up with Passerine and Tatters. Tatters was wearing a high mage's robe, which changed him in unexpected ways. It aged him; he blended in more. He didn't seem that different from the controlling mages who owned the Nest. Of course, he had the collar. Before it had been easily mistaken for something else, covered in grime and scraggy red hair. Now it shone like polished shackles.

She couldn't help noticing that he looked diminished. Before he had been wearing rags; now it was his soul, some core part of himself, that appeared threadbare.

When she was close enough, she realised it wasn't only Tatters who seemed worn. Passerine had a drawn expression that she had rarely seen on his proud face. Both men looked exhausted.

'May you grow tall,' she said, uneasy at how drained they both were. The unmistakable tightness of mindlink swathed them both, as if they were on the verge of fighting, or busy guarding their thoughts. Maybe both.

'May you grow tall,' said Passerine.

'May you grow tall,' Tatters repeated dully.

An awkward silence settled. There was a lot to talk about, but nothing struck her as relevant. Would Tatters be interested in the fact that Lady Siobhan had died, that Kilian had left Lord

Daegan, that Passerine now owned a district? Would he care about any of this?

'We're going to do some work,' Passerine said. 'Isha, gather the other apprentices.'

Tatters cocked an eyebrow at Passerine. 'You have apprentices? You hate teaching.'

When Passerine didn't answer, Tatters huffed. Isha didn't have much choice, so she answered that she would bring the apprentices to the usual training room.

It took time to gather everyone. The Nest was preparing for the second Groniz festival, also called the Homecoming – after bidding Groniz goodbye before winter, wishing her well while she lived in the underworlds, it was time for celebrations to greet her as she returned. The musty sheets stored in chests all winter were unfurled again for spring, as green banners were pulled up. The servants were also carrying yellow flags to represent Gelhwos, the ruler of all lightborns and bearer of light.

A number of maids were struggling with garlands of flowers; broad-chested young men were hoisting chandeliers to the ceiling; children carried baskets of candles. The smell of rose-scented wax permeated the halls. Isha found Kilian first, and together they scoured the Nest for Passerine's new followers, side-stepping piles of cut blossoms, ducking beneath wreaths being fastened above the arches.

As they entered the training room, there was more than one gasp of surprise. Whether people had heard of Tatters or not, they were surprised to see a collarbound. Adding to the mystery, wooden weapons had been piled against one wall: spears, clubs and swords, all roughly carved. Although they knew better than to ask questions, everyone stared expectantly, waiting for an answer.

'Come in,' said Passerine.

'May you grow tall, everyone,' said Tatters.

They cut a fine duo, despite – or maybe because of – the tension surrounding them. They both wore the same shade of black, but Passerine was taller, darker, and Tatters was smaller, leaner. The only touches of colour in their outfits were Passerine's belt and Tatters' collar. They stood poised as if about to lunge for each other's throats.

The followers piled inside the limewashed room. Two coats of arms decorated the walls: the painting of the castle with golden spires, the symbol of the Nest, on one side; and on the wall facing it, Lord Daegan's personal heraldry, wheat and coin being weighed against each other on golden scales. This was a recent addition. The yellow paint was still fresh.

'The war against the Renegades is going to require the Nest to be stronger, smarter, and more creative in its mindlink,' Passerine said. He had a way of filling space that made everyone fall quiet. 'Our magic, as it stands, is stale. I have brought a ... an experienced mage, who I hope will remedy that.'

Tatters took a step forward. A few people in the crowd, Isha noticed, such as Ninian and Kilian, didn't seem as keen as the others. Knowing enough about his arrest to be ashamed, they kept their eyes averted.

'I'm Tatters. Some of you might have heard of me, or seen me around.'

There was a brief, subtle exchange in mindlink between Tatters and Passerine. Isha didn't catch the message, but it was there, as clear as a scuffle, and Tatters' lips curled into a snarl.

'The lost property, finally found,' he said, as if answering Passerine, but not glancing back at the high mage. There was a coldness in him that hadn't been there before; a shard of winter. 'Yes, I'm a collarbound, and no, you don't get three guesses as to who my master is. To be honest, I'm not sure how much help I can be.'

'Apprentices will be ordained and sent to the Ridge. Mages who haven't gone already will be enlisted,' Passerine said, including everyone with a large sweep of his arm. His tone was matter-of-fact. 'If we cannot fight the Renegades, we will die.'

This was why people were here, Isha mused, rather than with Lord Daegan or more preeminent mages – because they thought they would find what they needed to win the upcoming war.

Tatters looked sceptical, but he only waved to the apprentices. 'Let's see what you guys can do, for starters.'

He organised them into groups of three. Two people were pitted against one, to create situations where someone was always at a disadvantage. The person by themselves had a weapon; in the group of two, one person had a weapon, one focused on mindlink.

'I'm going to give you some techniques to try.' He listed them off, shocking Isha with the variety of ideas. He talked about doubles, but also about thinking in a foreign language, or grounding the body in physical sensations so as to detach from the mindlink, to let attacks float through without landing.

Isha was offended. Why was he giving away their secrets, their techniques? How was she going to face other mages and apprentices if they knew her tricks? Even as she had the thought, she questioned it. If they couldn't challenge her, they wouldn't be able to stand up to the Renegades. Had she learnt to treat everyone like enemies? Maybe Tatters was right. Maybe sharing ideas was the way forward. Mages didn't need to be steeped in secrets; they could be allies too.

Tatters walked across the room, watching the fights as they took place, giving advice when necessary. He forced the apprentices to use physical strength, if only bashing the wooden weapons together for now, even as they mindlinked. He broke up the groups that had formed themselves amongst Passerine's followers. Isha never got to train with Kilian; she always found herself in front of a new face. She kept having to ask people for their names, and before she could introduce herself, she would always be dismissed by an 'I know who you are, Isha.'

I have to learn these people's names, she realised. *I have to learn their strengths, and weaknesses, and fears. We all have to learn how to work together, win together.*

'Those of you who can write, try to picture your thoughts in writing, as a narrative,' Tatters advised. 'Most people can't read – mages can, of course, but you won't be fighting mages.' He paused, thoughtful. 'If you have a bright idea, speak up. We're going to need all the help we can get.'

One young lawmage-in-training – someone who must have left Sir Leofric, Isha realised, to be able to join Passerine – shyly lifted her hand.

'Go for it,' said Tatters.

'We might be able to think in shorthand,' she said.

'What is shorthand?' asked Tatters.

She explained how scribes used a series of simplified symbols to replace letters. The lawmages relied on shorthand during court cases, to write down testimonies without pausing.

'And not everyone will know shorthand, even if they can read,' Ninian pointed out. 'It's reserved for the most esteemed scribes.'

'Find yourself an esteemed scribe to teach you, then,' said Tatters. Like all competent teachers, when he spoke, he had everyone's attention; when he joked, people laughed. 'Or those of you who know it already, get the others on board.'

As Tatters let them experiment, Isha felt the energy was better, charged. The room was humming with ideas about what could be done with mindlink. A few people were getting the hang of mindlinking with their eyes open, swinging their swords at the same time, and a few others garnered bruises. Something Isha had never witnessed before was happening: the mages were trying to share, rather than hoard, knowledge.

Maybe it was because Tatters was talented but not precious about his gift, which encouraged others to be the same. She wondered if Passerine even realised what Tatters was doing – he was creating a community where there had only been a crowd. Passerine worked alone; he would never have been able to forge such a sense of unity.

To her surprise, Tatters interrupted them.

'It's not good enough,' he announced. Everyone stared at him in shock. Isha had never felt a session go so well, yet have the teacher seem so despondent. The only person who wasn't baffled by Tatters' assessment was Passerine, who, if anything, seemed inclined to agree. 'We'll never make it in time. Hawk's been studying how to beat mages for nearly twenty years. What have we got? A couple of weeks?'

'We have to do our best with what we've got,' said Passerine.

'This is not our best.' Tatters clicked his tongue. 'The truth is, there's only one way to do this.'

The leeway for hope those few words left had the whole room hanging onto his words.

'The khers have to take part in our training.' He didn't blink or flinch. If he noticed the low muttering that rippled through the crowd, he ignored it. 'If the Nest can't include khers, we'll be slaughtered.' He paused, to let his words sink in, before concluding: 'And it'll be what we deserve.'

Isha sensed something fierce in him, like a rekindled flame, where there had seemingly only been ashes. She could taste his mind, as if the air were vibrating, trembling, like it sometimes does above a fire when it is too hot.

'Very well,' said Passerine.

Tatters didn't visibly relax, but his mind backed down. Everyone breathed in, as if the sour air had cleared.

'This will require going against the supreme mage,' warned Passerine.

'This is the only way we stand a chance of winning,' Tatters answered. His voice was filled with such certainty that it became contagious; Isha felt the minds around her aligning with him, agreeing. Believing. 'Let's start with the guard tower, see where that gets us.'

* * *

Everyone was forced to move aside for them. Servants who had been busy decorating scattered to the sides, put the gold-plated bells aside, tucked the baskets of seeds and dried rose cuttings between their legs. It was, Tatters realised too late, a show of power. He was trailing enough followers to threaten any coterie of mages, and rather than keeping to the shadows, he was parading them along the giants' balconies.

Passerine and Tatters walked through the Nest as if they were one entity. When one thought of lingering, the other was already slackening the pace; when one lengthened their stride, the other never fell behind. Tatters wondered how they did it. Maybe they were so acutely aware of each other that they could predict every move.

Which shows how on edge you both are, said Lal.

Together, Passerine and Tatters descended the main staircase. The hall was spread out below them, filled with a mush of grey and black robes. A long carpet, woven with deep blues and gold, which must have been brought out for the Homecoming festival, ran the whole length of the room. It dipped in the circle the giants had carved at the centre of the hall, then continued all the way to the foot of the stairs.

As they reached the rug, the crowd parted. A man was waiting with a patient smile, his fingers crossed and resting on his stomach. Despite his apparent cool, he must have rushed out of his chambers to block their way, hastily gathering followers, driven by a sense of duty, of fear. Of territory.

'Ah, Sir Passerine!' The stranger lifted one hand, nearly waved. One step behind him was Starling.

She narrowed her eyes at Tatters, but nothing else moved, neither lips nor eyebrows. Tatters couldn't tear his gaze away from her. She moved stiffly, in a plain dress threaded with gold down the wrists, to state her master was rich even though he liked his women modest.

Her master. It's the man who inherited after Lady Siobhan, thought Lal.

He was Kilian and Isha's master, as well. What is his name? Tatters took a while to place him. *Lord Daegan.*

Tatters couldn't help but notice the opal rings, the silver-rimmed cane, which was an uncomfortable reminder of Sir Leofric, the rich fabric of the robes stretching over a heavy gut. The fact that this man had built a cage to capture a lightborn.

Passerine was polite, non-committal. 'May you grow tall.'

'I see you've found a collarbound of your own,' said Lord Daegan. 'How ... convenient.'

Tension lifted in the air, created by men and women holding their breath, excitement boiling under their skin. The carpet was eerily like an arena, its square edges delimitating the area where the high mages glared. The atmosphere was tight as a bowstring; the only question was who would shoot the first arrow.

'And I'm told he is a mage too,' Lord Daegan continued. 'Not much use against a lightborn, I'm afraid.'

Somehow Tatters knew what was coming next.

'Tatters?' said Passerine. Tatters turned to him with a sense of fate unfolding. This was bound to happen, the threads of destiny woven as tightly as the gold around his neck. This had been going to happen from the moment Passerine laid eyes on him.

It's the collar, Lal whispered faintly, as if from far away. *Its hold is growing.*

'Alight,' said Passerine.

The order echoed a much older one, spoken years ago. This was why this collar existed. This was why he had put it on. This was the first order he had heard.

Tatters started running before he could quite decide to. He raced towards Lord Daegan and Starling and, when he was about to reach them, he jumped. He felt himself lighten, his flesh melting away, his soul burgeoning forth.

He alighted.

Then he was light, a red flash that flew past Lord Daegan, past Starling, and beyond. He curved upwards, stretching as he hadn't in years, shedding secrets as he arched towards the ceiling. He circled a pillar before gliding back down, landing in human shape, slicing the air as he shifted from red to black. The carpet was soft and bouncy under his feet.

Alighting filled him with adrenaline. His emotions were purer, sharper. He didn't even deign to look at Passerine when he asked, through gritted teeth: 'Happy?'

'Satisfied, let's say,' Passerine answered.

Starling didn't seem surprised in the least, but Lord Daegan's composure was shattered. The crowd was silent, but mindlink thrummed through the mages, the ominous buzzing of a hive. Tatters could practically hear the wild rumours as they grew around him with the speed of mushrooms sprouting overnight. One captured lightborn was news enough, and Lord Daegan had been displaying his catch throughout town. If the mages believed Passerine had owned, and not exploited, such an incredible advantage, they would be scraping frantically for what other revelations he might be keeping from them.

Not owned. Lal's voice. The alighting had done her good too. *He doesn't own you. He would do well to remember that.*

Temporary allies, prompted Tatters.

That still needs to be proven. But he felt her agreeing, begrudgingly.

Lord Daegan was fumbling for words. 'How... Where did you find a lightborn?'

'A sehwol,' Passerine corrected, although that was just semantics. To all intents and purposes, a sehwol differed from a lightborn only in that they weren't purebloods, or didn't live in the skies, or mingled with humans. In Tatters' case, all three.

A flash of green in the crowd. Sir Leofric moved like a snake closing in for the kill.

'Ah, the infamous collarbound who can fleshbind and mindlink.' He winked at Tatters as if they were old friends who shared a secret. 'Aren't you full of surprises?'

At the sight of him, Tatters tasted bile. Suddenly, unexpectedly, he could smell the stench of the prisons, as if he were back inside his old cell. He wondered if all these rich, scented rooms stank of fear and urine and death, and whether he was the only one to notice.

Lord Daegan's lips formed a thin line through which words escaped reluctantly. 'It is very lucky of you to have found a fleshbinding lightborn.'

'People make their own luck,' said Passerine.

Their words didn't quite reach Tatters. He was still focused on Leofric. It was insidious. When the lawmage spoke, his tone and his phrases never matched. He had a charming face, a coy smile, sweet, small movements of his hands and head. He brushed back his hair or touched his sleeves, and no-one seemed to notice the blood.

But the way he looked at Tatters right now – that was the look of someone who knew exactly the power he held. He wanted payment for the freedom he'd given.

'I don't believe in luck.' In Leofric's mouth, it sounded like a warning.

'Good friends are worth more than chance,' Passerine agreed smoothly. 'I believe we could achieve more as allies than as enemies.'

Lord Daegan said nothing. He watched Passerine intently, like cats do when hissing, claws sliding out of their paws, trying to decide when to go for the eyes.

'We could fight, and split the Nest, and whoever came out on top would have a hard time managing the Renegades.' Passerine knew how to hold an audience; his voice echoed across the hall. 'But I am not interested in fighting.' This did nothing to relax Lord Daegan's shoulders, or the grip of his hand around his malachite cane.

'Be sensible,' Leofric chipped in. 'Hawk has prepared for this day since before the Nest even knew to worry. Each time someone brings information from the Shadowpass, it's only to confirm they saw more horses, more soldiers, bigger numbers, a bigger encampment.'

Watching Leofric and Passerine at work was like watching two hunters herd an animal towards its death. It was skilful, but grim. The way they bounced off each other effortlessly turned Tatters' nausea into something worse, something deeper, which settled in his bones. Leofric seemed content. There were no traces of grime under his nails. The eyes he had cast, uncaring, over Yua's broken face – those were now sparkling.

It's too high a price to pay, Lal said. *We shouldn't ally with Leofric. We should die before that happens.*

'We could form a triumvirate,' Leofric went on, with the aplomb of a butcher removing skin from a carcass. 'We can rule the Nest, exceptionally, because of the upcoming war, as a group.'

'In exchange, I will teach your disciples how to defend against the Renegades,' Passerine went on. 'The three of us will make decisions, with Sir Leofric acting as the neutral party.'

Sir Leofric was grinning, from his slim red mouth to the slit of his green eyes.

At first, Lord Daegan didn't answer. Passerine and Leofric waited, patiently, for him to realise he had lost. The silence had turned to lead.

Now what? Tatters asked. Lal had no answer. It was too late to die. They'd have to live through this nightmare.

Beside her master, unaware of how much worse everything had become, Starling was glancing at Tatters, maybe trying to say something, through her eyes, if only show some concern. He couldn't hold her gaze. He could barely stand. He wanted to throw up, curl into a ball, and wake up only once the links keeping the Edge from falling had been broken.

Before Lord Daegan could speak, a small but bulky woman, unafraid of taller men, elbowed her way into their circle of conversation. She was dressed in an orange nasivyati, which echoed the henna in her hair. She was clearly a Winged Maiden; if the dyed hair hadn't given it away, the brooch at the front of her robes would have. It was wooden, in the shape of a bird, its eyes painted blue. No doubt the original had been far more precious, but this would do in times of hardship.

Unlike the Duskdweller mages, who politely stood aside and listened, biding their time, she forced her way closer.

'I will be a part of this conversation,' she hissed. 'If the Mad Sehwol is here, that changes everything.'

And here I was thinking things couldn't get worse, Lal said.

It didn't upset Tatters as much as it should have. He was beyond being upset for names long gone. He'd been called the Mad Sehwol, the Red Scourge, and many other unflattering names, while he fought for the Renegades. The names would stick again, no doubt, when he fought for the Nest. Maybe they would find new ones. The Butcher from the Sky, maybe. Shortcuts to say: the man who murders.

'Do you really think that's the Mad Sehwol, Lady Mayurah?' another Sunriser mage asked, a plump man, as pale as Tatters, with a strong Pearls accent. A kinsman, dressed in a fancy, flowing nasivyati, which he'd bleached but left undyed. He'd followed in Lady Mayurah's wake. 'I thought he was dead? The Winged Maidens claimed that death, as I recall.'

'That's irrelevant,' Lady Mayurah snapped.

'Quite the contrary, it's extremely relevant,' the man insisted. His voice was placid, yet too loud.

Lady Mayurah struggled to be heard. 'If that's the Mad Sehwol, his master has to be a Renegade!'

Her outraged tone was drowned by her companion's confident boom: 'If you claimed a victory against Hawk that never happened, we deserve to know about it.'

Leofric cut in, but his voice was lost to Passerine speaking over him, in Wingshade. The spell of silence was broken. The situation became more confusing as everyone suddenly decided to enter the conversation – as if by joining in, Lady Mayurah had given all the other mages permission to give their opinion.

'Are you the Mad Sehwol?' someone shouted. A couple of apprentices asked who this lightborn was supposed to be anyway, mad or not, and Tatters made out someone who sounded suspiciously like Kilian saying, 'That's just Tatters.'

Maybe curling into a ball isn't such a bad idea, Lal admitted. The noise was getting worse, and now there was shuffling, pushing, pulling, shoving, and it would only be a matter of time before magic was added to the chorus.

The mindlink that put an end to their chatter was like lightning: everything was briefly still, as if petrified in silver light.

You will be silent. Lord Daegan hadn't held his punch. The weaker apprentices winced. *This is not up for discussion.*

He pointedly looked around the hall, where mages were still waiting, half fearful, half thrilled, to see what the outcome would be.

'Sir Leofric, Sir Passerine,' the supreme mage said, singling them out. 'Let us retire to more private quarters. We shall discuss your proposal.'

There would be nothing to discuss, Tatters knew.

The triumvirate would become a reality.

* * *

When the fight was broken up between the high mages, when at last Passerine's plan to rule the Nest was put in motion, Isha managed to talk to Tatters in private.

Their training had been interrupted. Nothing could be done until Passerine returned. It was noon, and the only sensible thing to do was to eat lunch. Isha took a seat beside Tatters in the Nest's mess. She needed time alone with him, to know if he would find words to say what had happened to him, if she would be able to ask about Yua, if she dared.

'That was an eventful training session.' She winced at her own words. She had no idea what else to say. 'How are you?'

He shrugged. She was still shocked by how emaciated he had become. He had also shaved his beard, which was maybe why the lines of his face seemed so alien to her. He looked worse than this morning: wan, pale. Sick.

'Better than I was in prison.' He rubbed his eyes and his forehead, scrunching his nose, as if only just waking up. Maybe he was still waking up from the nightmare the cells had been. 'And you?'

'Fine.'

She wondered what Kilian would say, how he would turn this awkwardness into something familiar, something friendly. Nothing sprang to mind. They ate. She stared at her plate. Tatters scratched the wooden knots on the table's surface with his thumb.

'Could you do me a favour?' he asked.

She was relieved. They could act, rather than speak – they could try to find that old familiarity again, somewhere else.

'Of course,' she said.

'I need to visit the Pit. If you have a few hours to spare…'

She was already on her feet. 'I have all the time you need.'

On their way out, people kept staring at Tatters. They didn't brush over him as before. Apprentices gawked when they recognised him. Mages studied his face, his clothing, his neck, trying to determine whether he was a threat. The contrast between his robes and his collar attracted a different kind of interest from his rags and dishevelled appearance – people weren't wondering what he was doing here, but who he was.

In town, the reverse happened. People turned their gaze away from a high mage and his apprentice. Before, Tatters had blended into the crowd, his collar giving him a sort of disarming charm, the proof that he was harmless. Alongside him, Isha had enjoyed the ripples of that aura, the feeling that she wasn't one of the mages, but one of the people.

She was the underdog now.

They reached the makeshift palisades that cut the Pit off from the rest of the city. The two sentinels who always lounged at the gates stood up well before the two mages reached them. They didn't quite block the entrance, but stood close enough that it would require squeezing between them to pass – and no-one, Isha believed, would want to squeeze between the two muscly figures.

Tatters and Isha stopped and touched their foreheads, greeting the guards in iwdan. The unfriendly postures mellowed as the guards recognised them.

'I've got a message for Arushi about her sister,' said Tatters. Isha's heart caught in her throat. She wasn't sure whether to laugh or weep. Tatters' face was grim. 'This is important, and personal.'

One guard had used ochre to draw criss-cross lines down his horns, like the pattern on a viper's back. Isha wondered if that meant something, if only that he was tough enough to be venomous.

'What news?' he asked.

Tatters unknotted a pouch around his belt. He opened it, presenting it to the khers in the flat of his hand. It contained a piece of charcoal. The kher sentinel looked long and hard into Tatters' eyes. Tatters said nothing. He closed his hand around the shard of black ash, and both guards, in mute agreement, moved aside.

They resumed their walk in silence – theirs, and the silence they brought with them. If mages had stared and humans averted their eyes, khers stopped when they passed. There had been a time when Tatters was such a known figure that the khers didn't skip a beat at the sight of the ragtag collarbound. But two well-dressed mages intruded on the life of the slums. Housekeepers beating rugs free of dust interrupted their chores, children playing with sticks dispersed like flocks of birds. Groups of idle women sitting in circles on the ground, smoking earthenware pipes, paused their raucous arguing, froze halfway through pushing wooden game pieces across their goatskin mats.

After a gruelling walk, they reached Arushi's house.

They stopped before the entrance. 'This is where I need your help,' said Tatters. 'Could you please go in and introduce me? Say I've come to see her, I've got a message about Yua, and that...' He hesitated. 'There's some sentence in iwdan. Something about asking for permission before stepping into the house.'

'What makes you think you're not welcome?'

Tatters knew this house better than she did; he'd slept here, on the thick woolly cloths they threw on the ground in place of bedding. She'd found him sitting on the slab of stone that served as a front step. She could hardly pretend she was closer to Arushi than him.

'Rituals,' answered Tatters. 'You've got to respect the proceedings. Plus, she won't be as chuffed to see me as you think.'

'She'll be happy to see you,' said Isha. 'We all are.'

'Thanks.' He smiled his first sincere smile since she'd seen him with Passerine – but it was a fleeting, like a cloud chased by the wind. It disappeared as soon as it touched his lips.

'It's something about crossing into the land beyond and crossing into the hearth,' he said. 'Skies, I can't remember. Do you think you'd be able to repeat a sentence in iwdan, if someone told you?'

Isha nodded. 'I've been trying to learn iwdan.'

Tatters called out to one of the women busy sweeping her side of the street with a broom. Once he'd explained what he needed, her expression softened in understanding. She recited a sentence for Isha to repeat, in quickfire iwdan, which seemed to rhyme. *Tiyayat tta adefi, amettin csi.* Isha struggled to make sense of it, but she would be able to repeat it.

Tatters waited outside as Isha pushed through the bead curtain.

'Tid-idir,' she announced in a loud voice, to make herself known.

Inside she found Uaza, squatting in a corner of the living-room, resting against the wall. She was plucking a goose, and there was white fluff all around her. She had stuffed most of the feathers into a wooden bucket, but the smaller ones had floated out of it and covered her like snow. The bird's neck drooped next to her foot, its dead eye pointed towards the ceiling, its beak half-open, showing a serrated rim like tiny, pointed teeth.

'Heh, it's the soulworm,' she cackled. As Isha stood in the entrance, unsure whether she was invited in, the old matriarch waved her forward. 'Come, come, I've missed your soulworming.' Although her skin was smooth and her face as perfect as a plump twenty-year-old's, her horns had curved even more deeply. The skin was swollen where the annulated horns pushed inside her skull. Her eyes were bloodshot.

'Where have you been? I thought I'd be dead by the time you came for another visit.'

She touched Isha's face as if she couldn't quite see, despite the sun flooding in through the curtain.

'I have brought a friend.' Isha wondered how to say it. It didn't feel like an announcement to make lightly. 'It's Tatters.' Uaza made a sound of surprise with the back of her throat. 'He's got news about Yua.'

'Heh!' the kher exclaimed. 'Why doesn't he come in?'

'He wanted me to introduce him.' She recited the ritual phrase, as best she could. 'Tiyayat tta adefi, amettin csi.'

Uaza lowered her face. 'Ah.' She let out a deep sigh, then rubbed her eyes, wincing as her arm brushed against her ingrown horns. 'He knows about us. It is good.' But she didn't seem happy, and yellow tears seeped from the corner of her eyes. Isha wasn't sure if it was simply pain from the horns, or age, or something she had said. Fear, deep, primal, rose inside her. Something terrible had happened. She could taste it in the air.

The old kher patted her shoulder. 'Learn from what he does. One day, who knows, an iwdan blessing might mean something to you.' Then she lifted her head and called out in her own language: '*Tawa! We have a guest.*'

Arushi's head poked through the trapdoor in the ceiling. Her hair was ruffled, caught at odd angles around her horns. 'What now?' she grumbled. She recognised Isha. 'I'm coming down.'

They hadn't talked since the last time Isha had come to their house. She didn't even know Tatters was alive. Isha shouldn't be the one to announce it: they should be able to see each other without this ceremony wedged between them. She fretted while Arushi unrolled the rope ladder from the trapdoor and climbed down from the upper floor. Every breath Isha took tasted of ash.

'What is it?' Arushi asked, eyeing her mother, who hadn't taken up the goose again, but was sitting with the bird across her lap, wiping her cheeks.

'Tatters is alive, and he knows what happened to Yua. Tiyayat tta adefi, amettin csi,' said her mother.

Isha saw Arushi pale, a complex mix of emotions crossing her features. Out loud, all she said was: 'We need everyone to be here.'

Arushi sent one of Yua's sons to fetch the other members of the tidewran who were playing board games outside. Although

37

Tatters must have been standing by the entrance all this time, watching khers he knew piling into the house, he didn't follow them inside, and they didn't mention him as they gathered around Arushi. It was daytime, so there were mostly women and children, the odd idle male. Ganez was nowhere to be seen. Only when the extended family had unrolled carpets and placed themselves in a semi-circle facing the door did Arushi turn to Isha.

'He can cross the threshold.'

Thoroughly uneasy, Isha held back the beaded curtain for Tatters. Her hands were shaking. She could feel the emotion of the household pressing down on her shoulders like a physical force.

He stepped inside, keeping his eyes cast on the ground. She had never seen him like this – he didn't cross anyone's gaze, didn't speak. He placed himself in the centre of the room, before Arushi, and kept his face downcast. Arushi stayed standing. They didn't bridge the gap between them. They didn't speak words of relief or love.

'Say what you have to say,' said Arushi. Her voice was rough with emotion.

She already knows what he's about to say. The weight crushing Isha grew stronger, compressing her lungs, gripping her throat.

Tatters didn't look up. Isha could see him clutching his piece of charcoal. 'I was in the prisons beneath the Nest. Below the official cells. That's where I saw Yua.'

No-one moved. Isha realised the only people standing were her, Arushi and Tatters. It was too late to sit down, move away, as it would only attract attention. But she was conscious of being there, facing the circle of relatives, and it felt disrespectful, nearly indecent, to be standing tall as this was unfolding.

'She died there,' finished Tatters. 'I'm sorry.'

Uaza let out a sound like a moan, which morphed into a sob. Arushi took in a ragged breath. Isha wasn't sure she would be able to breathe again.

'How did it happen?' Arushi asked.

Tatters held onto the charcoal harder. His hand was stained black. 'It was a painless end.'

'Was it quick?'

He kept staring at the floor. Isha saw him plant his feet more firmly in the ground, bite down on his lower lip. 'No,' he croaked. 'But it was painless.'

The children were staring with large black eyes, their pupils dilated, their mouths half-open. The shock of the news had hit, but not the grief. Uaza picked up the goose and, absurdly, started plucking it again. She didn't put the feathers in the bucket. She tugged at the cold flesh and put handfuls of feathers on her lap, wiping her eyes with her wrists. Tears crawled down her face, slowly, the way water drips from stalactites in a cave, as if forever.

Isha felt light-headed now, from lack of air. If she didn't inhale, she would faint, but her throat was locked, her lungs were crushed as if under a giant fist.

'Is there anything else we need to know?' Arushi asked.

'No.'

Isha forced herself to swallow a thin trail of air. There were black patches at the edge of her vision, which cleared as she exhaled.

Arushi opened her mouth to say something, but she was interrupted by a soft thud. Her mother got up, resting one hand against the wall. It was a long process, and everyone waited respectfully as she pushed on her joints, her heavy horns threatening to topple her as she rose. She kept one hand around the goose's neck. It hung limply beside her.

'The mages gave you those clothes?' she asked. It didn't seem possible, but Tatters bent over even more. He seemed to recoil at the question. He nodded.

'I can't hear you.' Her voice had hardened, although it was hoarse.

'Yes,' said Tatters.

'What did you do to get them?'

The attention of the household settled on Tatters. Isha became overly conscious of the confined space, the cramped living-room with rammed earth walls looming from every side, the bodies crammed close.

'I am a mage's collarbound,' said Tatters, although that didn't answer the question.

'Weren't you always?'

'Yes.'

Uaza nodded. 'That's all I wanted to know.' She tried to sit down. Despite her young face, she slipped, because of her trembling hands and fragile bones. She dropped the half-plucked bird. Arushi rushed to help her, and half the household rose to their feet, but the old woman slapped her daughter away, falling heavily on the ground. Isha felt pain in her teeth as the horns scratched against the wall, leaving a soft welling of blood underneath the right temple, where they bore most deeply into her skull.

'Is that all?' Arushi asked the assembled khers. When no-one answered, she turned to Tatters.

'Yes,' he said.

He didn't lift his head, but signalled with his hand for Isha to follow him. The bead curtain chimed behind them.

Once outside, he knelt in the dust before the entrance. He paused, charcoal in hand, resting it against the front step. Isha remembered, then, the only other kher funeral she had witnessed. She remembered Yua kneeling as Tatters was now kneeling, before Ka's house, drawing a complex symbol in front of the grieving household. She pictured Yua, the knitted wool around her horns, her fingers stained black, stooping, drawing. And now, it was their turn to trace the symbol of death, for her.

Tatters didn't seem to know what to do. 'We need to tell the others this household is grieving,' he mumbled. 'If you're not from the household, you're not supposed to look a grieving iwdan in the eye, so they can weep without shame.'

Before he could ask, Isha searched for the kher who had helped them before. Once Isha had explained the situation in her patchy iwdan, the woman came to crouch beside Tatters. She took his hand in hers, guiding him. Together, they drew a horizontal line, then small vertical lines growing out of it like branches, then thorns, thistle growing from the earth and, at the end of the line, two curves, two horns, half-buried.

Once they were done, the woman squatted backwards, leaning her weight into her feet. She rubbed Tatters' shoulder, briefly nodded at Isha, and left them.

It was only then, when Tatters got up at last, when he stretched, that Isha realised he was crying. His tears were leaving two lines down his cheeks.

Isha followed the iwdan tradition and looked away.

* * *

Tatters followed Isha through the Pit, trying not to think, trying not to breathe. It was hard to know when he would be welcome in Arushi's house again. It might be days, weeks, of waiting, of grieving alone, of thinking of her, of Yua.

But as they reached the gates, Arushi's voice – the warmth, the familiarity of that voice! – called him back.

'Tatters,' she said, out of breath, maybe from the run, or maybe from grief. 'Wait.'

He couldn't hold her eye. He couldn't look at her face. In his mind, he could hear Yua's laughter. Arushi's hand circled his wrist, squeezed. She pulled him closer. He let himself be drawn in.

As he nuzzled against her horns, he took in the smells that clung around her – spices from the broth, smoke from the fire, leather from her shield. He couldn't pull away. The solidity of her, the softness, was something he had craved without knowing it, in the loneliness of the prison.

'Join us,' she said.

He tried to whisper something about family and belonging and the fact that he had no right to be there, but she shushed him.

'You are family.'

She took a step back and, at last, he could look her in the eye. With her features blurred through his tears, she could have been Yua. But when he wiped his eyes, he saw the slight variations, the sharper cheekbones, the heaviness around the brow, the fuller mouth.

'The bearer of grief needs to ask for permission before laying down his load – it's good that you followed the ritual.' She spoke without bitterness, only pain. 'Now you can be with us.'

Behind her, looking confused and frightened, stood Isha.

When Tatters turned to her, she managed an uncomfortable smile. 'Thank you for coming with me,' he said.

She shook her head. Her tattoo seemed to flicker across her face, as if the black lines were shifting along her cheek. 'It's nothing. I wish I could do more.'

Arushi didn't invite Isha inside, but when both women exchanged a glance, Tatters spotted an understanding there, some unsaid agreement. They had learnt about each other, then, while he wasn't there.

Winter happened without us, Lal thought.

Isha took her leave.

Gently, Arushi guided Tatters back to her hearth. She seated him beside her, amongst children mourning the loss of their mother, a mother mourning the loss of her daughter, cousins and nieces and people Tatters only vaguely knew, mourning the death of someone they had loved. Everyone cried with unabashed, free tears. He felt choked, dammed – unable to be as openly heartbroken.

'Tell us what happened.' Arushi was speaking with difficulty, as if through a fog. When she turned to Tatters, she smiled – brave, afraid, the smile of her sister.

She held his hands lightly. He had been shackled with kher horn for so long, he had forgotten her touch could come without fear, that Lal could fade away but he would still feel safe. Arushi brushed her thumb along the scars imprinted across his wrist.

'I need to know,' she said.

So Tatters told her. Once he started speaking, he found more words inside him, words he hadn't known he'd been hoarding, words to summon the things that had been unformed and unnamed: the darkness, the glint of Sir Leofric's eyes, the cold, the other khers dying beside him, the loneliness, the lacunants in the courtyard whom he could still see when he closed his eyes, the snow, the woman who had asked to be hanged, the scent of blood, the slickness of the stones, Yua, her laughter, sharing water as sharp and cold as the river, as clear as life outside the cells.

The iwdan listened. Arushi held onto his arm as if she could pull him out of the memory, tear him away from the lawmages, and, when he felt her beside him, he sometimes believed she would.

Children came to sit on her lap, pressing against Tatters in the process, warm and alive, like the fire flickering behind him. He had never talked to anyone so openly. He looked at the sores in Uaza's forehead, the slow death she welcomed without fuss, the thick horns dulled with use. He looked at the children with their large pupils, with stubs on their foreheads that marked the start of their lives. And as he talked, something, at last, came loose.

Humans hid their mouths behind their hands, closed their eyes, turned their faces away. They paid professional mourners. There was such comfort, sobbing with iwdan, with broken hiccups and ragged breaths, letting the tears drip off his cheeks.

Adults came and went, hugging, weeping, kissing each other, stroking each other's arms, squeezing each other's fingers.

Tatters could feel the grief, as if it would never leave, as if it was a cut bleeding salted water.

The men returned from the fields. They showed as much abandon as the women. Everyone shared what they loved about Yua, what ached now they had lost her. 'What will they do with the body?' Uaza asked. 'Will they throw it over the Edge, like the thankless, thoughtless humans do?'

'It's your fault,' Ganez told Arushi, and Tatters would have got up and fought for her, if she hadn't got up and fought for herself. She slammed both hands against her brother's chest, pushing him several step backwards, and screamed that she had loved Yua. Ganez shoved back. They shouted at each other in iwdan until, suddenly, Arushi let herself drop in Ganez's arms, and he hugged her against his chest, and the anger thawed like ice into what it really was: more water, more tears.

After the sun had set, the family turned to ceremony.

The neighbours had left food and charcoal on the doorstep,

which the men brought inside. They also carried in wood, to carve a likeness of Yua's horns. The children would make trinkets to bury in her place – wooden beads, small painted figures, which usually kept a kher company in the grave, but which would have to help anchor Yua, let her return where she belonged. Some groups mixed paints; Ganez sanded down a branch. The smells of half-eaten food, of sawdust, of ochre being crushed, filled the room. The family wouldn't rest, only sleeping in small bursts, until the rites were completed.

The charcoal was for Uaza to use. She drew symbols across Arushi's hands, fingers and nails. Most of the children and cousins had a circle around one ankle, each decorated differently, with elaborate leaves or flames or waves, which Tatters could just about make out within the curves and arabesques. The markings of grief.

Uaza also used chalk. She drew the same symbol on everyone, white against the black horns, something with sharp lines like bones. Tatters gathered the traces of chalk would serve to guide Yua's spirit until her funeral. Uaza spent care and time on these, and without needing to be told, Tatters understood that Yua was twice lost: without a body to bury, far from her kin. She would need clear symbols, bright like stars on the polished horns, to find her way home.

When Uaza waved Tatters closer, he wasn't sure what to expect. He had assumed he wouldn't be included. But she asked him to put out his hands, and drew black lines and circles across them.

'What do they mean?' he asked.

'They are shackles. Some broken, some not.' She pointed to where the delicate circles broke off into interlocked triangles. 'The shackles of pain are broken. The shackles binding you to Yua's murderers are not.' He didn't know what to answer. She traced the matching spirals around his thumbs. 'Here is the sharing of water. Yua was aman, you know. Water means a lot to a longlived.' She drew a circle which ran, unbroken, from knuckle to knuckle, linking his fingers like rings. 'And the mark of death, here, unbreakable. Spreading like fire. Fire will devour us all, in the end.'

He felt the soft, youthful hands against his skin, and he tried to imagine what it was like, to be old, to have outlived your youngest child.

Untroubled by the lack of horns, she drew lines in chalk across his forehead, starting from his temples. He closed his eyes, sore from crying. He was exhausted. Emotion had thundered through him like the waters rushing over the Edge, leaving him dry and empty. He let the delicate hands touch his brow, focusing on the feeling of the cold chalk sticking to his skin. He felt the change of texture when the old iwdan picked up the charcoal and added something in black. He breathed in the metallic smell of coal.

'Black because it is something to be proud of,' she said, before he could ask. 'What you did for my tidewran, how you protected her in her time of need … That does not take away those robes you are wearing. It does not forgive. But it matters.'

Tatters nodded. His throat was knotted, as if he had swallowed muddled rope. By carrying stories of their life against their skin, maybe the khers had learnt to live with everything at the same time, pride and shame not cancelling each other out, but coexisting.

He went back to the fire, letting Uaza continue her rites. She marked herself last, in slow circular movements, drawing over her horns with her eyes half-closed, the lines neat despite the absence of mirror.

While he crossed the room, Tatters wasn't touching anyone, and Lal resurfaced.

It's night outside, she said. *You need to go home.*

She was softer than usual, mellowed by his sadness.

This was necessary. It was good you were here. But they are not our people.

Tatters reached Arushi. She was seated beside a group of children, helping them mix ochre with water and egg, to make a paste to paint with. Her skin glowed in the heat of the fire; her hands were red stained with gold.

'I think I need to go back,' he said.

He thought she would ask him to stay, but she agreed with Lal. 'Yes. You won't be able to help prepare the funeral.'

She got up, calling over another woman to tend to the children.

'I'll come with you.'

Outside, the cold caught them by surprise. It stung their raw eyes and numbed their lips. They held hands. Tatters found he couldn't let go. He remembered Yua's hands, so slim, so small, the nails rough and torn where they caught against his thumb.

In the Pit, the snow packed along the tents was melting. In the city, it had turned to muddy sludge, brown and grey, puddles spreading around the receding ice. By day, people would have challenged a mage and a kher together. But at night, their silhouettes smudged by shadows, nobody bothered them. It would be spring soon. In the moorlands around the Nest, the first sprouts of green coloured the tips of branches, uncurling into the night.

They walked towards the Nest as they would walk towards an executioner, trying not to stare at the tall silhouette, trying to ignore the shadow it cast, large enough to engulf them. When they reached the bridge, Arushi took away her hands, long enough to rub the knuckles together, blowing on her fingertips to warm them. Her breath was milky white.

He wasn't sure what pushed him to speak. 'Twice in my life, I faced someone I thought would kill me, and I told them to do it,' Tatters said. His words filled the night with their weight.

He thought of gazing into Passerine's black eyes, into Leofric's green gaze, and not doubting for one moment that they would cut his throat, and waiting, hopeful, for them to lift their knife. 'Who does that twice and lives?'

'Someone who is not an iwdan,' she said.

The only reason I survived the prison is because I am a mage.

'I should be dead,' said Tatters. 'Not Yua.'

'That's not it,' said Arushi. 'No-one should be dead.'

She squeezed his hand, avoiding the temporary tattoos. 'Do you have brothers or sisters? Or did you?'

Tatters pictured a silhouette beside a hanged man, the mush of brothers shoving for space at dinnertime, his youngest sister, always by his side. 'Yes.'

When they moved past the lacunants, Tatters was aware of the black marks on the path behind them, muddy footsteps in their wake. She let go of his hand.

'My siblings all live in Sunriser country,' he said. 'I don't know what happened to them'

Most of them, said Lal.

'My youngest sister lived with me,' he added, on impulse. 'Lal. She …' He didn't know how to continue. 'She died.' And then, because it was a lie, he amended: 'No. She didn't. She would have died. She lives in my mind. It's a mindlink thing.'

She won't get it, Lal said.

Arushi didn't answer at first. They went past the sentries, a kher who recognised the head of guards and a lawmage who spotted the black cloak. Both knew better than to stop them.

'Your sister lives inside your mind?' Arushi repeated.

'Part of her can live there,' Tatters tried to explain. 'The part of her that was her mind.'

You're wasting your time, said Lal.

Be nice. Say hello.

Lal's sarcasm could cut through skin. *Tidir, woman who will never see me.*

'She says "tidir, woman who will never see me",' Tatters repeated out loud. 'Sorry. She's a bit difficult.'

Lal huffed in annoyance; Arushi didn't answer.

His heart sank. 'You think I'm mad.'

Arushi shook her head. The white chalk on her horns glimmered like kindling in the moonlight. 'I think that if I'd had a chance to hold on to Yua, even if I had to pay for this with my mind, with my privacy, even if that meant people would call me mad, then I would have held her close, with everything I have.'

The courtyard was quiet. It was a few hours before morning, too early for the servants to be up, too late for the apprentices to be returning from their drinking. It was poised between people rising and sinking into sleep, a rare moment when everyone dreamt together. Even the horses in the stables, the dogs stretched out in the warmth of their hay, the seagulls huddled in their nests of stone, slept.

Arushi and Tatters embraced tenderly, as if scared they would break.

Chapter 3

Tatters woke up to Passerine nudging his shoulder from a distance, as one might poke a sleeping dog, as if it might bite if startled. When he opened his eyes, Passerine took a step back.

'Get dressed,' said Passerine. 'We're needed outside.'

Tatters scrambled to his feet. On the rumpled sheets, he spotted black traces where the temporary tattoos across his fingers had rubbed off. He fumbled to get dressed.

'Speed up,' grumbled Passerine. 'And wash your face. Rub off any traces of iwdan culture – we'll be speaking to believers.'

Don't give us orders, Lal thought.

Tatters smoothed out the robe, patting it with the flat of his hand. In a bowl of water beside the hearth, he rinsed the markings off his hands and his face. The charcoal stained the water like ink.

He followed Passerine out of the room, then down the corridor. He was forced to trot after the high mage, who walked with such long strides he was nearly running. They were headed for the main staircase. Even from afar, it was clear there was a commotion: Sir Leofric was talking with a nervous servant at the top of the landing, studying the scene below with a detached expression.

At the arches, merchants were dismantling their stalls, taking refuge inside the Nest, pushing wares to the side, while a flutter of harried servants were moving decorations out of the way, clearly torn between their duty to prepare for the Homecoming and getting all important goods out of the courtyard as quickly as possible. Tatters could see a woman putting up a green-and-gold garland, which another servant was trying to take down at the same time from the opposite side of the arch.

'There is, um, trouble. At the gates. A group of…' The ungifted before Sir Leofric stammered his way through the sentence. 'I don't think the guards can do anything about it. The kher guards themselves are, well, it is probably best if you come to see…'

Sir Leofric let out a sigh between his teeth. 'May you grow tall, Sir Passerine,' he said, spotting them. 'Duty calls, I'm afraid.' His eyes glided over Tatters, not quite landing.

No greeting for us, said Lal. *I guess collarbounds don't require decency.*

I prefer it if he ignores us, said Tatters.

'It seems the kher guards have decided to show their true colours,' Sir Leofric clarified, still addressing Passerine. 'I have to say, you're awfully quick. I've only just heard the news myself.'

Passerine was frowning. 'I heard the priests who had come to help with the Homecoming festival were asking to meet the new lightborn. I thought it'd be best to see what they wanted.'

Sir Leofric let out a brief chuckle. 'Ah well. This might be interesting, then.'

'We might have to negotiate with the priests,' Passerine warned. Where Leofric was all mockery and laughter, Passerine was all serious expressions, sparse words. How two men so different had decided to ally, Tatters didn't know.

And Passerine is a better man than Leofric, Lal said. *Whatever else he is, he isn't a sadist.*

Yet he's decided to support him against Lord Daegan.

Maybe he's a poor judge of character, Lal suggested. *He allied with Hawk, after all.*

Passerine was still speaking, although Tatters had missed the beginning. Leofric was listening with an unamused, fading smile. 'We could even invite the Doorkeeper to counsel the triumvirate,' Passerine said, obviously ending a train of thought. 'Involving her would help us better understand how the ungifted are perceiving this war.'

Leofric didn't seem convinced. Tatters took this as his cue to say, 'If you are forming a council, you should invite the khers. If they join, you'll get another angle on the situation.'

Silence fell. At first, the high mages didn't speak, unwilling to pick up the conversation, as if it were a piece of soiled cloth. The warning look Passerine shot Tatters was clearer than any mindlink, but Tatters held it. They had made a deal, too. He wasn't fighting for the Nest, not if the khers couldn't be a part of it.

'Did you fail to notice we were talking?' Leofric asked, as if addressing a child.

'Hear me out,' said Tatters. 'You'll need them against the Renegades anyway, and you don't want the guards you've taught how to fight to turn against you. Khers making decisions with mages is long overdue.'

He won't listen – none of them will, said Lal. *The more fools them.*

Passerine knows I'm right, thought Tatters.

'You have a very voluble slave, I must say,' said Leofric, turning his attention to Passerine. 'Does he often speak without your permission?'

Passerine didn't answer, jaws clenched, although he threw Tatters a withering glare and, with it, an exasperated message.

Look what you've done, he hissed. *As if Leofric isn't hard enough to deal with.*

Tatters didn't answer. His mindlink wasn't as quiet as Passerine's, and he risked being overheard.

'I can't blame you. I don't think you can tame him.' Sir Leofric didn't speak louder than a whisper, but there was a threat coiled in his voice, a contained tension. He gave Tatters his most mundane, most pleasant smile. 'Do you know, you are my only failure?' He marked a pause, letting his words linger. The softness never left his voice. 'I hate failure. I think I hate you.'

'I have good news,' said Tatters, struggling to keep his voice level. 'The feeling is mutual.'

'I am glad we agree.' Sir Leofric leant forward, one arm on the stair's balustrade.

Don't let him close, warned Lal. *Physically or mentally.*

'Hate is a fickle thing, though, isn't it?' Sir Leofric mused. 'So obsessive. So consuming. And thrilling, too.'

'Maybe the feeling isn't mutual, then,' said Tatters.

It was an effort to stay still. His hands, bunched into fists, were trembling.

Sir Leofric's eyes flicked sideways as something caught his attention downstairs. He glanced across the hall, losing interest, just as Passerine caught Tatters by the elbow, pulling him down the staircase after him, away from the lawmage.

'If we could return to the matter at hand,' said Passerine.

People were milling anxiously in the main hall, checking the courtyard regularly, whispering amongst themselves. Tatters spotted what had intrigued Leofric: a couple of kher guards, waving people backwards, indicating they should clear the area. Even the apprentices, even the mages, were being herded aside.

Passerine strode down the steps while Leofric followed, a beat slower. With a bit of distance between them, and the thoughts of the merchants, servants, and apprentices, all serving as a screen to hide behind, Passerine mindlinked to Tatters.

What were you thinking, provoking him?

What else am I supposed to do? Tatters asked. *Take it?*

Now it's going to be harder to convince him to listen to the priests, grumbled Passerine, his mind thrumming with annoyance. *He'll think it's a conspiracy to steal his power.*

Tatters followed sullenly down the staircase, across the main hall – now decorated with its blue carpet, like a slice of sky on stone – through the arches.

His heart caught in his throat as he took in the scene outside; even Sir Leofric's step faltered somewhat. In the courtyard, the khers were forming a blockade. Not the male khers, who were banned from the Nest and who couldn't carry weapons – this was an army of women. And their leader was familiar.

Arushi was making sure the blockade was solid, each kher interlocking shields. The traders had been backed into the arches or to the sides, clearing the central space from the stables to the guard tower. No-one was bearing swords. The khers weren't facing outwards, but inwards. This wasn't to keep enemies out, but to trap mages in. Priests, who had come over from the Temple to help with the Homecoming festivities, huddled at the foot of the tower, not a part of the kher barricade but also trapped by it. They wore the undyed, threadbare cloth of believers.

A lawmage who had been close to the tower hurried up to Sir Leofric.

'That kher Renegade got to their heads,' she said. She was obviously worried.

Arushi placed herself at the front of the group of khers, facing the crowd of onlookers. Her padded leather armour, the fold of her shirt, everything made her demeanour more severe, military. Still, the sheath hanging from her belt was empty; she had consciously discarded her sword. She seemed to stand straighter, pain like flint at the bottom of her eyes. Her hands still bore the temporary tattoos of grief.

She was having trouble completing her blockade, however. A group of ungifted was unwilling to budge: the priests. They had been working on a banner, which was spread out on the ground, in the process of being fastened to wooden poles. Only one side had been tied so far, on a post as high as a spear. A priest had lifted it, maybe to keep it out of reach of the khers. In his hands, it became eerily similar to a flag, woven from gold and red thread. The fabrics were poor, the dye cheap, but the meaning unmistakeable: Gelhwos and Raudaz, intertwined.

Two key lightborns: the leader and the warrior. One golden, one red. Just like Starling and Tatters' colours, when they alighted. It was clear this was no coincidence.

It's a statement, said Lal. *The priests want to remind the mages that they're celebrating lightborns for the Homecoming, the very same lightborns the mages are exploiting.*

So, they're upset too, concluded Tatters. *Great.*

The priest holding this symbol seemed to be a middle-aged man, a lean figure, whom Tatters finally recognised as Osmund. He was a preeminent priest who had stood beside the Doorkeeper before.

Arushi spotted the high mages at the arches. Ignoring the priests, giving up on completing her blockade for now, she called out:

'Sir Leofric. We were waiting for you.'

Servants clustered under the arches, or stuck their heads out of the stables, wringing their handkerchiefs, patting their aprons, watching over their shoulders. A couple of stablehands crossed the courtyard purposefully to stand around the priests – to protect them. This only added to the pressure Tatters could feel building up.

'As a gesture of goodwill, you will notice none of us are armed. This is a peaceful protest.' Arushi's voice boomed across the packed space. It had always been wide, but today it felt too narrow for the tensions simmering within. 'You have taken our lives for long enough,' she continued. 'Now it is time you return our dead. We know you have bodies of our people in your dungeons. If you hand them to us, we will peacefully disperse.'

She wants to bury her sister, Lal said.

Tatters could recall kneeling beside his brother, adding Lal's name to the family shrine. It hurt his heart. The ache went up to his teeth. He wasn't sure how he could help.

Would it cost much to give them what they ask? Passerine asked Leofric through mindlink. *Maybe it is worth simply giving it to them, to solve this quickly.*

Leofric made a show of yawning. Like a cat, he pretended he couldn't care less, however dire the situation. *Never yield to the animal you wish to tame*, he replied. Out loud, he said, 'We do not hold your dead. As always, we only collect baina.' It wasn't a very convincing lie.

Passerine turned to the head lawmage and they entered an argument, half in mindlink, half out loud. It was clear Leofric did not intend to solve anything yet. He was waiting, watching, like a hunter poised for the prey's misstep. The two mages formed a chorus of mismatched instruments – the deep ring of Passerine's voice, the light flute of Leofric.

As the mages were debating what to do, the priests started yelling. Tatters heard Osmund's bellow above the confusion: 'Is nothing sacred to you?!'

Arushi's troops had surged forward to seal off the courtyard entirely. She must have decided she wouldn't be heard unless she could impede the mages efficiently.

'Get out of the way,' she ordered.

'Get out of the way yourselves!' someone shrieked.

Priests believed being touched by khers unhallowed them. They would be furious if khers dared manhandle them. If one of the guards so much as brushed against a lightborn – Tatters or Starling – the crowd might turn into a lynching mob.

It would be even worse than collaring a lightborn, in their opinion, said Lal.

Osmund was shaking his post, flag forward, towards the iwdan guards. The believers around him rallied, shoving back against the wooden shields, holding their ground. The rising fear was like bile in Tatters' throat.

Uncertainty had crept onto Passerine's face. Everyone could now perceive it, this fight-or-flight energy coiled like the spring in a crossbow. Beside him, Leofric's smile didn't fade but his mind expanded, not unlike a spider casting its web, reaching out to the weapons he had at hand – the servants, believers and animals within range.

The bell rang. Who had decided this was enough trouble to warrant summoning all the mages, it was hard to know. But the unmistakable boom of a bell too big for humans, a sound that was only heard in times of great upheaval and emergencies, tore through the air, loud enough to drum at the back of Tatters' skull.

Lovely. Now everyone is going to flock to the hall, said Lal.

The summons would only add to the chaos. A press of bodies already blocked this side of the arches, but what would happen when people filled the hall as well, effectively trapping Passerine and Leofric between the apprentices and the courtyard? Leofric wouldn't take kindly to being surrounded. His mind continued to spread, more slowly now, and Tatters realised this was because of Passerine: he was trying to hold back the head lawmage.

If you push or pull bodies through this crowd, you'll cause a panic,
Passerine cautioned.

Who says I don't want to scare them? Leofric answered, struggling to throw off Passerine's influence.

At last, mercifully, the bell stopped.

'Move aside!' Arushi had a strong voice that carried above the chorus of people, above the frightened neighing coming from the stables.

Tatters wanted to join her, but unless he was willing to split the crowd of ungifted – merchants, traders, servants – caught between the mages and the blockade, he would be ground into the flagstones. Passerine was right that trying to control people within a big group would only cause a stampede, currents of people trampling each other.

'You are nothing but the mages' tools, and *they are criminals!*' roared Osmund towards the blockade, repressed rage surging. 'They use khers to do their dirty work, they bind lightborns to debase them! Not content with binding one, they have now tied down another! Does Lord Daegan want to empty the skies?' It was unclear if this was addressed to the guards or the mages, but it did give Arushi pause. 'And have them work beside creatures without souls, who will suck the light out of them?' By creatures, Tatters supposed he meant the khers.

The believers started shouting, in rhythm: 'Your war, our light! Your war, our light!' Some of the ungifted, those along the arches, also picked up the chant, so it not only hummed in front of the mages, but behind them, in the hall, all around. *Your war, our light!*

Osmund harangued Arushi with words sharp with hunger and faith. She was answering him, trying to argue something about death and duty and the downtrodden, but the believers were loud enough to drown out even her.

'You are not fit to set eyes on the lightborns!' spat a woman beside Osmund.

Even from afar, Tatters could imagine Arushi's expression. It would be a small frown to those who didn't know her. A line of tension in her jaw. No-one but khers would notice how she lowered her head, as if bowing, so her horns pointed at the humans in front of her.

Unfortunately, the iwdan beside Arushi didn't have her control. She punched the believer in the face.

A movement of panic. Ungifted who weren't involved scattered – or tried to. They fled towards the arches, but Leofric didn't want to be rushed at. He froze them in their tracks with mindlink, throwing them to the ground if need be, baring his teeth. People stumbled, fell, swore.

A believer knelt, picked up a stone, and threw it towards the pointed black horns – aiming at the blockade in general rather than any particular kher, as far as Tatters could make out. A few high-spirited souls copied her. The kher guards lifted their shields. Soon there was the racket of pebbles bouncing off wood. Cries of 'heretics, bloodcows!' filled the air. Arushi shouted at her guards to calm down, but it was too late. The loyal believers stood their ground, pelting stones.

The hall was filling with the people the bell had summoned, apprentices and mages assembling. And Leofric's mind was twitching, despite Passerine's increased efforts. It was a well-attended chaos: the khers at the gates, sealing the exit towards the moors; the priests and ungifted and stablehands in the courtyard, amongst the half-abandoned stalls; stones flying; the lawmages – Leofric and Passerine included – below the arches, at the border between courtyard and castle; more mages and apprentices on the other side of the arches, inside the Nest.

Still no sign of Lord Daegan or Starling. They must be lost somewhere amongst the mages filling the hall.

Tatters realised that he had braced his legs, changed his posture, but couldn't complete this movement on his own. He tried to force himself, in vain.

Give me permission to alight, Tatters asked.

Passerine answered, *Do what you must. Alight if it helps.*

Tatters breathed in and, as he breathed out, turned into light. He lifted above the crowd, drawing gasps, then landed in the slim slit of space between the priests and the kher blockade. As he returned to human shape, a few stray stones caught his hands and face. He felt one dig into his eyebrow and another bounce off the top of his skull.

Ouch, said Lal. *That one hurt.*

As he was rubbing his face, relieved that he could only feel a bruise, not a cut, Tatters was aware of Osmund giving orders: 'Don't hurt Raudaz!'

The stones stopped, at least. Arushi took a step closer to Tatters.

'Don't touch me.' It didn't come out as he meant it.

Her face hardened. 'Whatever you say.'

They stood a foot apart. Arushi was wearing her leather armour and was thankfully unharmed, although she kept her shield in front of her body. He noticed she took half a step further, to be in front, so she could shield him if the believers threw anything else.

The vision of a lightborn, a creature of myths and dreams, close enough to reach for, had stunned the people into awed silence. Osmund, still gripping his makeshift banner, hailed Tatters.

'I am sorry your master is forcing you to degrade yourself and protect these monsters,' he announced in his theatrical voice.

A rumble of approval from his followers.

'Protecting the khers is my decision,' said Tatters. 'We need to be united, if we want to survive the Renegades.' It was the truth; he hoped it showed. 'But I agree with you that lightborns shouldn't be enslaved. If the mages remove Star... Gelhwos's collar, we might be able to come to an agreement. I will stay to help.'

Osmund stared at him doubtfully.

'Why don't we discuss this?' Tatters offered. 'The priests, the mages, the khers, all together.'

A council representing everyone, said Lal. She was mocking, a bit, yet wistful. *Like something from a fairy tale.*

Osmund's expression didn't change. 'Why would the khers be invited to decide on a lightborn's fate?'

Tatters saw Arushi tense. The crowd muttered low calls that could be insults, or prayers, or wards against evil. Osmund's banner crackled like fire in the wind.

Raudaz is the lightborn of war, after all, not reconciliation, said Lal. Now that the hope of a peaceful resolution was receding, she was all business. *These people worship you. Don't talk to them like peers. Order them to stand down.*

Because that will make things so much better.

Lal didn't sense his sarcasm or, if she did, she chose to ignore it. *It will.*

I don't want to talk to anyone as if they weren't my equals. I don't want to give orders.

Think of it like mindlink, encouraged Lal. *You're crafting something that doesn't need to be real.*

It'll be real for them.

Tatters snapped out of his mindrambling as Arushi pushed past him. He didn't know what had prompted her to move, nor had he seen Osmund's believers step forward, arms interlinked, catcalling as the khers advanced. Men were placed in front, heads low, faces stern. Women were behind, armed with one for the heart – prayers – and one for the hands – stones. Osmund was at the centre of their human cordon, wielding the gold and red flag depicting Raudaz and Gelhwos.

The khers overlapped their shields and marched forward.

Tatters knew what would happen. When flesh and wood met, both sides would push, wood shattering shins, people grabbing at horns, cutting their palms in their attempt to wrench them off. Stones would patter down like rain. It was easy to guess how it would end. The khers would shove forward but the believers wouldn't yield. There might be a death – there would be several wounded.

The khers would win.

And tonight, far from the Nest, far from the mages' impunity, folk would drink and talk about how the khers murdered people; good, light-fearing folk who did their prayers and gave to the poor. Just before the festival of Homecoming and rebirth, as well. Who poured blood before the day of forgiveness? They would dip their torches in oil. They would remember kher cloth burnt.

Lal was right. If he could stop this, he had to try.

He briefly closed his eyes; the noise became even more deafening. He imagined Raudaz as he was portrayed in temples – a dash of red pouring from a tear in the sky, sometimes with fiery irises and scales of iron along his body.

Maybe force is the only path. It was hard to see a way forward without it.

When he opened his eyes, he tried not to see what was there, but to craft a mental image of what he wanted to be happening. He ignored the high, hysterical calls, the sight of stones, of ripped cloth, of blue shields, of faces twisted in rage. He was tall, he was fierce. He summoned fury inside his chest as if he were pulling heavy water from a well, from the depths of his core. If he couldn't craft an emotion that didn't exist, he wasn't a mage.

Before the khers and ungifted could clash, Tatters strode between them. He matched his posture to the one Hawk took when addressing her troops – legs parted, one hand on her hilt, a fist held before her, as if about to punch her audience. He turned his back to the khers as Arushi forced them to grind to a halt, confident she wouldn't trample him.

He roared: 'You call the mages criminals for disrespecting me, yet the first thing you do is disregard my word!'

His shout shocked him as much as it did the protestors. He hadn't raised his voice in anger, not even fake anger, since Hawk had knocked that habit out of him.

They're listening, said Lal.

A precious silence fell, easily broken, like an eggshell holding together the more mercurial parts of the protest. But they were listening for the wrong reasons.

'How dare you doubt my words and deeds? What is faith for, if not shedding the doubt and darkness inside of you, and bowing at the sight of true light?'

Osmund was sickly pale. Arushi stared as if she didn't know him. She looked at him like people, before, would look at the collar – when all they knew about him was that they didn't want to be him.

The priests gathered before the gates watched this figure who wasn't him, listened to a speech that wasn't his.

'You want the auroras' help? You will start by obeying their general's orders!'

With those words, Tatters alighted.

He aimed at the ungifted and flashed through them. He was careful not to be brutal, not to rip out their souls, but simply to brush against them – he held himself back, in the same way he

64

might have held back his hand to turn a punch into a pat. It was an uncomfortable sensation as he touched a mush of minds who, briefly, were marked by his thoughts. To him, it was like passing his fingers through someone else's hair, without knowing who he was stroking. It was intimate and strange. But he clenched his teeth and shot vivid red through them. Most fell into a supplicant position on the ground, to accept the blessing.

Even Osmund couldn't help but bend the knee. Any other act would be faithless.

Once he was done, Tatters landed beside Osmund in human shape. The priest had fallen into a low bow, laying his hands flat on the ground before him, fingers splayed. He'd dropped his banner.

'Do you still think that I am a human's plaything?' Tatters growled. 'Stand up and say it, if you dare. See how light burns blasphemy out of your tongue!'

He imagined he was wreathed in red. He imagined he was staring down Hawk, having the showdown they never had the chance to complete, and that his anger was justified. When he glared at the believers, they lowered their heads, knees and foreheads and hands flat on the ground. Tatters was still holding his 'Hawk posture', but it was the most blatant of lies. He remembered a time when he had been the one forced to kneel.

An imploring prayer went through the crowd like a shiver. Tatters realised it was a plea for forgiveness.

He glanced over the believers' dirty, sunburnt faces, with calloused hands and missing teeth. Without righteousness on their side, they looked old, tired, broken by relentless work. Their hearts were worn, patchwork cloths, which they had sewn together with faith.

'Will you forgive me, Raudaz, for speaking out of turn?' Osmund asked.

He's a man used to solitude and the wind in the Temple, Tatters thought. *It took all his courage to do this.*

He's a petty clerk, corrected Lal. *The last person to shout at him was his mother.*

Tatters leant over to offer Osmund his hand.

'You can make it up to me,' he said. 'By listening to what the iwdan have to say.'

He helped Osmund to his feet. With an ease he had forgotten after years bound to the ground, he alighted, swerved, and landed by the arches, beside the high mages. Satisfyingly, Leofric and Passerine both stepped aside for him. Lord Daegan had arrived, Starling in tow. She cast her eerie, unchanging gaze on him, but said nothing.

Without choosing to, Tatters caught Passerine's glance. His eyes were two mirrors that reflected this scene for what it was – an insult, a joke. Only Passerine could hear the punchline.

Starling must have received a mental order from Daegan, because she announced in her limpid, water-cold tone, 'What Raudaz orders, Gelhwos has willed.'

Everyone repeated this. Osmund touched the ground before pressing his fingers to his forehead, muttering the sacred words. His banner lay in the dust at his side.

* * *

When Isha had first heard the ringing of the bell, she'd rushed, like everyone, to the main hall, only to find the balcony deserted and the courtyard heaving with bodies. She'd spotted Passerine's unmistakable silhouette from afar. When she'd tried to join him, people had parted for her – his followers recognised her, made way for her.

She reached the thick of the crowd at the centre of the arches by virtue of being a well-known face. She didn't know when the Nest had learnt to account for her, but she was grateful for it. Still, she arrived after Lord Daegan, in time only to hear the supreme mage, shocked and furious, as he spat:

'How dare you tell the khers we will listen to their demands? Who do you think you are?'

As Isha came closer, heart pounding, she realised this was addressed to Passerine. His smile was strained, and he had one hand placed warningly on Tatters' shoulder, maybe to hold him back.

'I am the supreme mage,' Lord Daegan all but growled, 'and such promises will not be made on my behalf!'

Tatters opened his mouth, but then winced and shut up. From the glare he cast Passerine, it was clear Passerine's grip on his shoulder was unfriendly. He seemed in half a mind to drop the pretence of being servile and shake himself free, although he kept quiet, for now.

'And telling the priests you are ready to negotiate about the collars is absurd,' added Sir Leofric. It was clear, from everyone's tone, that tempers were running high. 'What next? We'll promise never to use mindlink again? For a smart man, you can make startingly stupid decisions.'

Isha slotted herself behind Passerine and Tatters, unsure how to help. All she knew was that she needed to be present. Under the arches, she had a better view of the courtyard, and she noticed for the first time that a shield-wall had been drawn in front of the gates.

While everyone was talking, Arushi had finished her blockade. Ungifted hung around the edges, and in front of, her barrier. Still, the wall of women stood strong, sealing off the Nest's courtyard, completely blocking access to the gates. A group of priests with nowhere to go, cut off by mages on one side and iwdan on the other, loitered to one side.

Isha, Passerine mindlinked. She hadn't known he'd seen her come closer. *Please explain to Tatters that if he persists, he'll cause a civil war. I'm not getting through to him.*

Tatters? she tried hesitantly.

It was Lal who answered. *Can't you see we're busy right now?*

Maybe don't convince Lord Daegan he's better off with you and Passerine in prison, is all I'm saying, said Isha. She didn't add: We just got you out of it. And at what price?

'Allying with khers? That's a Renegade, mark my words.' A woman's voice within earshot snapped. 'I knew it! He *is* the Mad Sehwol.'

A small group of half a dozen Sunriser mages closed in. Isha knew some of them from the council, or from talking with the Sunriser apprentices and getting to know their customs. As was the Sunriser tradition, they were all using nicknames, some still in Wingshade – Lady Mayurah hadn't translated her name to Lady Peacock, for example, nor had Sir Cintay into Sir Fleeting Thought – but others used Duskdweller titles, like the maiden mage Wren. Lady Mayurah had always been vocal in her displeasure.

One tall, broad, overwhelmingly friendly man was her biggest ally, named Sir Dust. When Isha had asked other apprentices about this, she had been told mages from the Pearls followed a tradition of humility, and thus hosted many a Lady Soil, Sir Stray, or disciple Ashes. Once this had been explained to her, belatedly, Isha had realised that Tatters must be from the Pearls. His nickname must have been given or chosen to avoid arrogance.

'I am not proposing to ally with the khers, but to avoid strife and conflict within the Nest when there is enough without,' Passerine said.

'Who can it be but the Mad Sehwol?' Sir Dust beamed a smile, a sharp curiosity sheathed behind his friendliness. 'Red lightborns trained to fight aren't that common.'

'He no longer belongs to Hawk,' Passerine said curtly. 'As must be obvious by now.'

The irony wasn't lost on Sir Dust. 'A renegade Renegade.'

'Can we be certain of that?' asked Lord Daegan. 'Even so, Sir Passerine, why do I find you talking of banding with khers to overthrow our authority?'

'You are either mad or a traitor,' hissed Sir Leofric.

Passerine kept his cool. His mind never showed fear, never gave an inch. 'I am doing what it takes to win this war. You have trained these guards to hold your castle. It would be absurd to antagonise them now, before Hawk arrives. We never talked about mages losing authority – only about taking into account the khers' current demands. What are a few dead bodies to the Nest? Let them bury them, if they want to.'

Arushi must have heard this because she called out from the centre of her fully-formed blockade:

'We will keep the peace. If you give us what we ask for, we will disperse. If this ends in violence, it will be by your own hand.'

'A small price to pay, surely,' said Passerine, 'if it ensures their loyalty.'

For a moment, it seemed like the incident might be resolved. The crowd went from threats to arguments, from violence to talks – albeit high-spirited, divisive talks.

Maybe, had Sir Leofric not been present, not been in a position of power, things might have ended differently. Maybe, had he had less time to cast his mindlink over the ungifted in the courtyard, he would not have been able to act.

But he was there, and he was not in the mood to chat.

'This is ridiculous,' he snapped. 'The bloodcows will back down. There is no need to take their opinion into consideration.'

'We don't bow to your gods,' Arushi answered. Even from afar, Isha could hear the effort it was to keep her tone civil. 'You cannot scare us with tricks of the light. We want our dead, to bury. We want the truth about what you do to the iwdan you capture. We will not back down.'

Sir Leofric didn't move, but Isha felt his mind expand, a fire caught in a gust of wind. The ungifted stood to attention in unison. The priests got up, faces suddenly blank. Sir Leofric was a strong mage. He took the pliant minds in hand as one would the reins of a horse, and everyone turned away from the khers, whilst all the servants close enough pulled open the stable doors, empty-eyed, with more efficiency than any group should be able to muster.

Tatters moved. It was barely a shiver, not even the start of mindlink, but Passerine's mind slammed down on him so hard that even Isha felt it. It was like watching someone clamp their hand down on a mouse. She perceived a short, quickly-ended struggle between them, no doubt as Passerine convinced him that he couldn't act against Leofric without forever forfeiting their place at the Nest.

Sensing that magic was being used, Arushi raised her voice.

'We will not yield!' she warned. Her tone had lost some of its confidence, but none of its determination.

The lacunants moaned as mindlink brushed through the courtyard, and Isha heard them scrambling on the other side of the gates. From where she was, she could only see the blockade and guess at some of the ripples behind it. She heard the screams gathering momentum, without knowing what was happening.

The thunder of hooves caught her by surprise. As soon as the stable doors were wrenched open by the ungifted, the horses rushed out. Her stomach churned as she realised what Sir Leofric was doing: he wasn't only mindlinking the humans. He was controlling the animals too.

The horses broke into a gallop straight from the stables, picking up speed in the small stretch of the courtyard. They charged into the sea of ungifted, which included the priests. The various pressures put on the crowd – the mages at one end of the procession shielding themselves, the horses trampling through them – meant that some people were being jostled, some were fleeing and some, the unlucky ones, were being crushed.

The animals charged, unnaturally fast, without hesitation, without snorting or lifting their heads, without swishing their tails, with nothing of the behaviour of normal horses – who were known to be nervous, skittish, as concerned as humans about staying alive.

They were much bigger than the khers.

Isha thought the guards would break formation, but the iwdan only tightened their ranks and gripped their shields. The lacunants wailed. The heavy-shoed hooves got closer in seconds, before anyone could intervene. Sir Leofric's mind, from afar, tasted of steel.

Isha saw the warhorses charge, heard the roar of metal on stone. She realised they wouldn't change course, wouldn't jump – they would trample the khers. Arushi was still at the front of the group.

Her mind reached out before Isha could think of the consequences, because she couldn't stand aside and watch people she loved being ground into a bloody mess. She pushed on the lead horse's mind, as hard as she could, and it jumped.

The first horse leapt above Arushi and the khers gathered behind, its stomach brushing against the top of their horns. The delay gave Arushi enough time to duck before the next mount crashed into her, flinging her aside. Isha heard a sickening sound, like bones snapping, but it could have been the wooden shields, or the horse itself, landing heavily on the other side, snorting in terror as Sir Leofric released his hold on it.

The confusion worsened. Sir Leofric stood below the arches, focused on his task. The first three horses were pierced by horns and had legs broken by shields. They screamed in a way Isha thought only humans could. As best she could, Isha split the flow of horses like a fork in a river, forcing them right and left of the gathering, shoving their minds aside so they would swerve. Too late, a couple of other mages joined in, taken off-guard by the speed of Leofric's reaction. Their mindlink was slower, less confident, than the lawmage's. To make matters worse, the courtyard was full of people: priests lined the khers on one side, with servants on the other side, mages below the arches – there was nowhere to go. One of the horses, failing to turn fast enough, fell sideways across the threshold of the Nest, legs flailing wildly, kicking at everyone and everything.

After that, there wasn't much of the blockade left. Or much of anything else.

The khers were on the ground, whimpering, as the rest of the herd galloped over them. The horses didn't even blink at the stench of blood. The ungifted were calm like ghosts, like ghouls, as they carefully gathered stones and sticks to finish the work laid out for them. They gathered in a menacing circle around the fallen khers, rocks and weapons in hand. Everyone, animal and human alike, had empty, depthless eyes.

'Know your place,' Sir Leofric said.

It was easy to tell when Sir Leofric freed the ungifted, even without mindlink. They dropped their makeshift weapons. One stable boy screamed. Osmund went to lean against the wall to retch. The lacunants crept forward from their side of the gate. They knelt in the blood, trying to scrape it into their bowls.

'Disperse,' Lord Daegan ordered sharply. 'Do not cause more of a scene on a day that should be devoted to festivities and forgiveness.' He addressed this to the khers, but his eyes landed on Sir Leofric. The head lawmage only sneered. He had been kept in check before, under Lady Siobhan's rule, but his power and influence had grown in the past few weeks. He was not so quick to bow to the supreme mage as he had been.

The khers who could walk helped those who couldn't. The incident had only lasted a couple of minutes. The gates were wet with blood; some had splashed on the iron doors the giants had built. A couple of khers hadn't got up and lay on the ground, their necks at unnatural angles.

A couple of humans didn't get up, either. The message was clear: nobody who stood in Leofric's way would be spared.

One of the horses, not yet dead, was struggling to get back to its feet with a broken leg. It kept crashing to the ground again. Isha thought she could see bone. In the end it stopped struggling, breathing heavily, gasping as its eyes rolled in its head, searching for an escape.

Isha found herself stepping closer, pulled by some morbid will to see if she recognised anyone. Her foot knocked against something. She leant over to retrieve it – the tip of someone's horn. It was neatly broken off. Isha wiped off the blood and pocketed it. If she left it, it would be recycled as baina.

Although she searched, she didn't find Arushi amongst the bodies. It was a small relief.

She looked into the eyes of the horse lying its full length on the ground, foam and blood mixing between its lips and running down its nostrils. Tatters had nearly managed to broker peace. He'd nearly had mages, priests, ungifted and khers around the same council table, making decisions together. He'd been able to seed the idea, at least.

But it would never grow in earth soaked in blood.

* * *

So much for talking, Lal said. *This is what comes from allying with unhinged, cruel people. Unhinged, cruel ends.*

Tatters stood beside Passerine, trying hard not to throw up. He barely heard the conversation between Daegan and Leofric, their quiet deliberation about what was best to do now. Daegan had a leader's polished tone, which never missed a syllable or dipped as he spoke. Beside him, Leofric stood out as ill-suited for power, too green, too fierce, where the older man bore a quiet strength, like that of a lake or a mountain.

Passerine's hand weighed heavy on Tatters' shoulder, not quite supporting him, not quite leaving him alone, either. It wasn't grounding, not exactly. They weren't friends. But it was something.

Why didn't you let me do something? Tatters asked.

You'd done enough, Passerine said. *Look where it got us.*

Sir Leofric dusted his hands and told the lawmages in a clear voice: 'Round up the horses. Clear up this mess.' He wandered off to check on the damage he'd caused.

Tatters' eyes stayed on the courtyard. He couldn't believe nobody was going to acknowledge what had happened. A few servants were cautiously leaving the arches, hesitantly heading for the prone bodies, to help and heal. The high mages and their close followers stayed put. Unmoved.

As soon as Leofric was out of earshot, Passerine took a step away from Tatters. For the first time since the beginning of this debacle, he turned to Daegan.

'Sir Leofric's skills are not only wasted in the Nest, they are... cumbersome,' Passerine said, in a low rumble.

Lord Daegan lifted a grey, bushy eyebrow. 'What do you suggest?'

'Send him to war,' Passerine said. 'As the Nest's general.'

Tatters wasn't sure if this was the best or worst idea Passerine had ever had.

Send a brutal fighter against Hawk, said Lal. *Let them find out which one is the most ruthless.*

Lord Daegan rubbed his chin. He kept his voice a whisper, his attention on Leofric giving orders. 'How would you convince him to go?'

'By sending your lightborn with him, and granting him temporary control.'

Passerine spoke with his usual confidence, but the words sank into Tatters like stones.

'We shall see,' said Lord Daegan. 'Maybe it is time each high mage gave something of themselves to the war.'

Tatters turned to Starling, but although she was listening to the conversation, she didn't intervene. His heart ached with fear: for her, for him, for both of them. He hadn't been able to protect Yua. He hadn't been able to help Arushi. He wondered if he was fated to watch, powerless, as people suffered.

* * *

Clutching the small piece of horn in her hand, Isha headed for the Pit. The usual khers guarded the Pit's entrance, but after having seen what Sir Leofric could do to a group of determined women-at-arms, Isha wasn't sure how much protection two men without shields could offer. She hadn't even taken the time to change out of her robes, but they let her in. Inside, she found the women in the central square.

They were seated or slumped against the painted wall, adding red to the ochre, brown and gold of the fresco. Children and men without work were heating pots of water on open firepits, rushing with strips of cloth, grinding herbs and seeds together, spitting on the powders to make a healing paste.

It was easy to spot Arushi, wincing as a friend picked a shard of wood out of her arm – remnants from where the shield had been crushed into her flesh. As she drew closer, Isha recognised the helper: it was the guardswoman Tara, muttering under her breath as she tugged the splinters loose.

The most striking, however, was Arushi's horns. The right horn had the tip snapped off.

Isha assisted the iwdan in silence. She cleaned cloth in boiling water, she crushed herbs as instructed. Not everyone was pleased to see her, despite the tattoo, despite having met her before. The robes were hard to dismiss. Still, this was a situation where no-one could afford to refuse a helping hand. As she worked, she used mindlink to soothe the dogs, who were growling and baring their teeth at the smell of violence.

She was kneeling beside a pot of simmering water, mixing cloth inside it, waiting for it to be soaked through, when Ka joined her. His hair was mussed, his chest heaving as if he'd been running.

He let himself drop to the floor. 'What happened?' he asked.

Isha told him while she hefted the dripping cloth out of the pot with a long ladle normally used to stir soup. She put the bandages aside, on a rack, to drip and cool before others could use them. Ka listened, his frown deepening with every word. She wasn't sure where he had come from, but he was wearing human clothes: a shirt, trousers, no traces of an arrud or sandals. The only iwdan touch was a leather band tied around the base of his horns, a more martial version of Yua's knitted decorations.

When Isha had finished, he said, 'We need to talk to Arushi.'

Tara barely glanced their way as they approached, but she shuffled sideways to give them space. She was now binding Arushi's arm. Except for a bruise blossoming across the side of her face, and a swollen, blackened right eye, Tara seemed unharmed.

'The first horse, the one that jumped,' Tara said, in way of explanation, waving at the purple mark. 'Its hoof nearly knocked me out.'

'You did well to stay standing,' said Ka. He ran his thumb over her temple, beside the bruise. It wasn't a sexual touch, Isha understood, but a show of support, maybe the equivalent of a friendly hug.

'I hoped we'd be able to avoid a fight,' Arushi said, gritting her teeth as Tara finished knotting her bandage. 'So much for that. We'll be lucky if they return the bodies of those who fell today.' *Let alone the body of Yua*, was what she didn't say, but what Isha heard.

Tara sat back on her heels, her work done. 'They'll take the horns first, that's certain.'

The four of them fell into gloomy silence. Isha imagined the courtyard, the servants throwing buckets of water at the gates to rinse them, the butcher doing his gruesome work in the shade of the arches, grunting as he hefted the horns out of kher skulls.

'We won't be able to avoid a fight,' Ka said. 'Your ucma knew this.'

Isha knew ucma meant a woman from the same hearth, a child of the same matriarch. Humans would translate this as 'sister', although most probably Yua and Arushi had been half sisters, from different fathers.

'Why do you keep us from fighting back, if you have that fire in you?' Ka's voice was quiet, but hard. He went on in iwdan: *It's time we took up arms against the Nest. We have the weapons hidden here. We should attack while they're weak, distracted by the Renegades.*

'They aren't weak,' Arushi answered sharply. 'And I didn't want to fight today. I don't want to fight tomorrow. That hasn't changed. *If we bring blood to them, they'll bring blood to us.*' She lapsed into her mother tongue for the last part. From the way she said it, the rhythm of the sentence, Isha guessed it was an idiom.

Ka huffed. He slapped his hand against the ground and the gesture couldn't hide that he would have rather slapped Arushi. Isha wondered how Ganez felt about this. If most khers wanted to fight the Nest, using the weapons they had gathered at the price of Yua's life, she wasn't sure how long Arushi would be able – or willing – to hold them back.

'Is grovelling before the mages that important?' asked Ka. His frown seemed carved into his face. The leather at the base of his horns reminded Isha of the leather around the hilt of a sword.

'The guards are the only link we have with the Nest.' Arushi didn't raise her voice. Maybe she was too exhausted to be angry. 'If they decide they are better off without us, then we won't know what they're scheming, who's in charge, who they are throwing in prison, what dissenting mages believe. We need to know our enemies. We need to find allies.'

'*Their weakness is us*,' said Tara. 'Or at least, it could be.'

Isha was glad for her lessons in iwdan, without which she wouldn't have been able to follow this bilingual conversation.

Arushi's eyes were sunken with grief and sleeplessness. She rubbed them, but that didn't bring a spark back to them. 'We haven't got much choice.'

Ka shook his head. 'You always have a choice. But you are choosing your masters over your people, again and again.'

He got up. His frown had twisted now, marring his features with anger. When his eyes rested on Isha, she wondered if he only saw a mage, not a friend. His lips curled, showing his teeth, as he studied the chaos of the central square.

He took his leave. Neither of the women commented on his departure.

'I think I might have something of yours,' Isha said. It wasn't the right moment to do this, but the right moment would never come.

She unfolded her hand to show the chip of horn. Arushi leant forward to take it, wincing as she moved her good arm. It matched. It was the tip that had been broken in the scuffle.

Arushi laughed. It was the dry laugh of a person in pain.

'I'm not allowed to own this,' she said. 'If it's not on my head, it's baina. And if it's baina, it belongs to the mages. My horn, yet it's not mine.' She scoffed and let it fall into her lap.

They sat listening to the whines of wounded women, to the patter of small feet, to the fires spitting as they burnt the damp spring wood. There was the smell of smoke, of comfrey and oil, of blood.

'The more I fight back, the more people I lose,' Arushi whispered.

Her gaze was lost in the distance, seeing nothing, or maybe seeing what Isha could still picture vividly: horns cutting through a horse's flank; the bright red and surprising blacks and purples found inside a live animal; the lifeless, empty eyes; the metal shoes breaking bone, the iron nails catching skin. The screams, both from the iwdan and the beasts.

Isha knew that, however great a storyteller recounted what had happened, in the tavern or around the firepit for others to bear witness, it would never create the same images, it would never burn the same pictures into their minds. She would hear the sound a horse makes when it dies in her nightmares, even years after, she was sure.

Repairing the horn was a gruelling process. First Tara had to drive a nail into the unbroken part of the horn, Arushi pressing her head against the wall, trying not to flinch when the hammer hit close to her face. Once the nail was half-planted, its head needed to be trimmed and sharpened. Scraps of iron fell across Arushi's shoulders as Tara and Isha took turns filing it down. Finally, they placed the broken tip above the nail and hammered it in place.

Isha's palms were sticky with sweat when she stepped back. Arushi ran a finger across the line where the two pieces of horn had been knocked back together. Where she'd touched them, a smear of charcoal stayed behind.

'The visible scars are always smaller,' Tara said.

Arushi shook her head. When she pulled her sleeve over her arm, when one didn't stare too closely at her horns, it was possible to believe she had escaped unscathed.

'There is being scarred,' she said, 'and then there is having to hide your scars from the people who made them.'

Chapter 4

Isha had woken up early that morning and, unable to go back to sleep, she'd decided to attend the festival preparations. The Homecoming was different in tone from the winter celebration. Groniz had been freed from the underworlds, so it was time for rejoicing, forgiving, and bridging gaps.

When she crossed the courtyard, it was bustling with a temporary market, where baskets of worn cloth were piled for townsfolk to take away, the people at the Nest handing out old tools, cutlery, leatherwork. It was hard to reconciliate this mundane scene with the brutality the place had witnessed. Gates that had been splashed with blood were flung open. Stalls were drawn where, the day before, hooves were throwing sparks on the cobbles. Isha wondered how many places across the city were like this: innocuous at first sight, hiding their violence.

At the start of this difficult year, more Sunriser refugees were begging for their livelihood than ever before. The Nest, for once, gave freely. The mages even built hovels for the lacunants to huddle under, repairing anything that had been damaged by the snow and gale. Or, more recently, by galloping horses. The mages buried the lacunants who had died and fed the survivors with more than stale bread and rainwater. Working on the hovels together was an important task, as well as planting seeds, dyeing cloth blue for the ordainments and, of course, crafting presents for one's enemies. The idea was that, after surviving the winter, it was a shame to carry old griefs over into the new year. Foes exchanged presents to indicate the end of their feud. *Unburdening happens in more than one way*, the priests at home used to say. *You can unburden yourself from hate.*

Outside, Isha settled below the gates. On the north side, the ground was less marshy, with more trees. In a clearing a few acres across, before the forest that separated the Nest from the Temple, servants were building a temporary platform for Lord Daegan, strewing sand and straw on the ground. They set up cauldrons and firepits along the walls, in which the cooks fried the traditional yewos pastries with any leftovers from the winter stocks, including dried fruit and sugar, if there was any to spare. Soon, Isha's spot was filled with smoke that stung her eyes, and she breathed in the smell of sizzling oil.

Spring was always a hungry season. The winter supplies were eaten, the crops hadn't grown yet. This year was particularly lean, as the Nest was putting food aside, preparing for an eventual siege. Even the high mages ate less, and contended with bread that tasted of wet, rotting flour. Yewos were, sometimes, the only food available.

The cooks mixed the batter and put a dollop inside the cauldrons, where the boiling oil cooked it in a few seconds, then they took out the deep-fried yewos, draining them with a slotted spoon. The Sunrisers were included, eating with their fingers, ripping off chunks for their children, talking to the pale Duskdwellers sharing food with them, if only briefly. The festival was a time for reconciliation, after all.

When morning was well on its way, the festival began in earnest. Isha wandered closer to watch. The horses paraded first, trotting up and down, lawmages in full ceremonial uniforms

on the saddles – they bore little armour, only the minimum
to protect from arrows, with lots of bright cloth and billowing plumes. The horses lifted their hooves high, their gait
elegant, foaming at their bits, impressive in their blue-and-
gold caparisons. They looked nothing like the beasts that had
trampled the khers.

After the horses, a few high mages demonstrated their control
over armies of ungifted. The ungifted stood to attention incoher-
ently at first, fidgeting, holding their spears askew, readjusting
their helmets. As soon as the mage took control, they became a
well-coordinated army performing figures meant to be pleasing
to the eye.

When they were released, the soldiers dispersed to eat some
yewos, joking with the servants, stuffing the hot cakes whole
into their mouths. Isha wondered if she was the only one to
notice the edge to their laughter, or how glassy their eyes remained.

There was no dancing. Every mage was aware that the skills
they were displaying weren't just for show, but for killing. Every
apprentice was aware that, where their ordainment had meant
freedom before, it now meant being sent to war.

Passerine joined her as she was waiting in line for food,
breaking her out of these glum thoughts. They each grabbed a
glass of wine diluted in fresh water and some sour apples that
had kept over winter, nibbling as they threaded their way across
the festival grounds. They found a spot in the shade, beside the
sweaty horses with the grooms brushing them down. It wasn't
quiet, not exactly, but no-one paid them any attention, and no
mages lingered.

They ate in silence until Passerine announced:

'I need you to leave my service.' He was still focused on his

food. 'And affiliate with another high mage. I would recommend
Lady Mayurah.'

Stumped, Isha forgot to chew. It took her a moment to process what he had said, for her jaws to work again. Her arms were
sore where she had lifted shields and swords during training; she
had bruises down her sides which hurt when she stretched. She
had been fighting, and learning, and fighting some more, and
practising mindlink with the other apprentices during the breaks
from physical brawling. She had been ready for anything, ready
to hear they had to push themselves, wake up earlier, gather
more followers. But this came as a surprise.

'This is a secret you have to keep to yourself,' Passerine said.

'I don't even know what you're asking me to keep secret,' she
answered.

Passerine hesitated. 'Give me your word that you won't tell
anyone.'

This was growing more and more confusing. 'You have my
word. Did I ever spill your secrets before?'

She couldn't eat any more; she watched him, waited. When he
spoke at last, his deep voice was barely a whisper. 'Lord Daegan
has required all my followers fight against the Renegades after
the Homecoming festival. Tatters and I will be staying behind,
to prepare the city's defences.'

It was as if the air had been punched out of her lungs. She
knew, without Passerine needing to tell her, that they were not
ready – not now, not any time soon. She'd hoped they'd get
more time.

'If you change master just before his announcement, you will
not be sent to the front,' Passerine explained.

So that was why he had insisted on her silence. If she told
Kilian, or Ninian, or anyone, his followers would desert him,
and his deal with Lord Daegan, whatever its nature, would be

off the table. Her muscles ached. Her pulse rang in her temples. The implications were sinking in – he wanted to protect her, again, always.

But Isha had never planned to hide in the Nest.

'I'm going,' she said. 'To war.'

Passerine shook his head. 'It's not safe.'

'Not for anyone,' she said. 'It doesn't matter. I'm going.'

'It's even more dangerous for you,' he insisted. 'You have to stay.'

He had saved her, he had shielded her, but he could be so stubborn. Even now, he treated her like a child. Like someone who needed to be protected, but not understood.

'I'm ready to face Hawk,' was all she said. 'I knew I would have to, one day.' And without him, his followers would need someone, a friendly face, to guide them. To follow. What was the point in promising them protection in return for loyalty, if he then abandoned them?

'Do you have any idea what Hawk might do to you?' he whispered. 'I don't know what her plans for you are, but she will not give you a choice.'

'She won't,' Isha agreed. 'But you will.'

Passerine went quiet. He seemed torn, but she knew he wouldn't force her hand. Slowly, he resumed eating. They both drank the tepid, tasteless wine.

A glint of blue caught her eye. A mule was pulling a cart piled high with bright cloth – the capes for the ordained mages, prepared for the apprentices about to become fully-fledged members of the Nest.

'Do you know,' Passerine said softly, 'I was there when you were born. I heard your first scream. The first time you crossed the Shadowpass, you were slung across my back.'

It caught at her heart, cut off her breath. She knew – she

remembered – Passerine's visits to the farm, when Hawk wouldn't attend. He was the one who would do the trip, every year, cloaked in red, to pay her foster parents, to check she was healthy and happy. She had always assumed he was her guardian. But he hadn't, until now, admitted to being a father.

Not her flesh-and-blood father, but a father, nonetheless.

'Yet you left me at the farm, with my foster parents,' she said. It wasn't a reproach, not really. She was reminding him of a fact: of the reason she had grown to be independent.

'Yes.' Passerine sighed. 'Now I find myself wondering... I wanted to care for someone else, return to her. But maybe I did you wrong, not caring for the person who was in front of me.'

Lord Daegan walked up to the platform that had been erected for him. He settled on the wooden throne, overseeing the celebrations. A cloth had been pulled taut above the platform, protecting him from the drizzle. Soon, the ordainments would begin. The war announcement would be next, no doubt.

'It doesn't matter now,' said Isha.

Passerine swapped to mindlink, maybe for the intimacy of it. *What can I say to persuade you not to go?*

You can't, she said.

He let her sense some of his thoughts: a tug at the pit of his chest, like a heartache, a painfully physical sense of loss. A pang squeezed her, but she didn't yield.

This is what you can do, she said. *Trust me. Trust me to do this.*

She couldn't hold his eye. If she looked at him, her bravery would melt.

Once he was ready, Lord Daegan didn't need to clap or call out. When he rose from his throne, the crowd fell silent as groups spotted him, as mages forced the ungifted soldiers and servants to stop talking. On cue, Passerine got up to join him, standing to his left while Leofric stood to his right. Squaring her shoulders, hardening her heart, Isha took her place amongst the listeners. To all appearances, she was a young apprentice eager to hear the supreme mage's announcement.

Lord Daegan used mindlink, leaning his weight into a distinctive malachite cane.

Good people of the Nest, he said, *I know you fear we have a harsh year ahead of us, facing down the rebels from the Sunriser convents.*

His voice in mindlink was calm and fearless.

We overcame the trials of winter. We will overcome the Renegades.

And Isha could nearly believe it, with him standing straight, young still – at least compared to Lady Siobhan – with Sir Leofric and his toothy smile by his side, the undyed belt proclaiming the lawmages' support. Others would join the fight: Sir Passerine who, according to town gossip, always had a new trick up his sleeve and would catch the Renegades off-guard as he had caught everyone else. The two lightborns. The Nest could take on anyone.

Yet she wondered how much of that confidence was due to daylight and a day of rejoicing. It might fade with nightfall.

However, said Lord Daegan, and her anxious heart sped up, *to anticipate the war's demands, we will be ordaining more mages than usual. We have strong, able apprentices who deserve to be a part of what is to come, to claim their share of the glory, without being constrained by their rank.* In short, apprentices were safe, mages were not. The ordainment wasn't so much an honour as an enlistment.

He gave out names. At first it wasn't anyone she recognised but, as his list lengthened and he showed no sign of stopping, she picked out people she knew. Caitlin. Of course, she was a senior disciple. Then it came to followers she had recently trained with. Kilian. *Are they going to ordain everyone, for the sake of sending everyone to war?* No examination had been put in place to check the power of each disciple, yet the names continued to pour out.

Isha was among them. She was the only person chosen who had been studying for less than a full year at the Nest. Other apprentices breathed out in relief when the list ended with her.

Those who had been called forward gathered into the area reserved for the parade. The space was big, yet they choked it. *There's so many of us.* Their number betrayed something of the fragility of the Nest's position. Why did they need so many people if everything was under control?

She shuffled into a corner, uncertain, the hay crunching under her feet. The spring day was cold, wet. Unwelcoming. Kilian found her in the crowd and stood beside her. He smiled, but his eyes echoed some of her fears.

'Look at that,' he said, nudging her. 'You're being ordained the same day as me. Doesn't seem worth working so hard, if even puffins are getting fast-tracked.'

'You never work hard,' she said.

'I wish.' Kilian pulled a face. 'I still have bruises down my arms. I can hardly move them.' He clenched and unclenched his fists to illustrate his point, grimacing.

Isha nodded in sympathy – she still had yellowing bruises the size of fists around her knees and elbows.

Groups of servants combed through the crowd, respectfully handing over the blue capes to the apprentices. The mass of grey shapes turned blue, like the sky changing colour at sunrise. Isha watched as Kilian, unenthusiastically, took the robe he was handed and wrapped it around his shoulders to show his new rank. She did the same.

Her face must had given away some of her discomfort because Kilian said, 'Maybe now that we're mages we'll be able to make

88

a difference.' He sounded doubtful, but she imagined he was trying to reassure her. 'Like you always wanted.'

She thought of the kher blockade, of Tara's blackened eye, of Arushi saying she had hoped to end this without violence. 'Maybe,' she replied.

Once everyone was swathed in blue – heavy woollen cloth upon heavy woollen cloth, under layers upon layers of clouds, in the damp, cool breeze – Lord Daegan addressed them once more. This time he spoke out loud.

'The Nest has been sending soldiers to deal with the Renegades, weakening them at every turn. It is now time we deal the killing blow. To do so, I have decided that one supreme mage is not enough to rule such a beautiful Nest.'

Isha heard gasps, muttered whispers and the odd prayer, but more from the ungifted than the mages. A change in power had been brewing inside the Nest for long enough. *Our leadership is unstable.* Which was another sign that they weren't ready for this war.

Lord Daegan announced the birthing of the triumvirate, which would include Lord Leofric and Lord Passerine. When the crowd of ordained mages clapped, Isha dutifully copied them. It was a dull sound.

'As part of the war effort,' Lord Daegan announced, 'each member of the triumvirate has gifted a part of themselves.'

Sir – Lord – Leofric stepped forward. 'I will gift what I have that is most precious: myself. I will go in person and lead our armies to victory!'

More obedient clapping. Isha watched the proud silhouette he cut, green and blond, the colours of Gelhwos and Groniz. Leofric was in charge of the lawmages, so although he technically had followers, he couldn't bring them along with him. It would be draining the Nest of its guards. Isha suspected he would take a couple of lawmages anyway, to have some allies at hand. He would no doubt leave someone in charge in his stead at the Nest, to pursue his interests in his absence.

'Poor sods who have to follow his orders,' Kilian murmured next to her.

He might sacrifice his soldiers like he did the horses, without caring for their lives, Isha mused. She couldn't put it into words – the blood, the howls of khers, the sneer on Leofric's lips. She stayed silent. She knew who the poor souls to follow his command would be.

Passerine was next, his belt the blue of Byluk, the colour of death and mourning. 'I will gift my followers, to protect Lord Leofric and to serve as his blade.'

As armies went, the fifty or so followers Passerine had painstakingly gathered wasn't a huge amount of people, but it was highly symbolic. She glanced at Kilian, who had grown sickly pale, beads of sweat across his forehead as if from a fever. He didn't have time to recover from the shock; Lord Daegan spoke last.

'I will gift my lightborn, to be Lord Leofric's guiding light.'

This time, the ungifted hooted and cheered. A high mage, a lightborn and a battalion of mages was a force to be reckoned with. To the people, it must have seemed a blessing to have leaders who would, at last, put their own lives on the line.

Isha could feel the damp on her skull, like an invisible weight.

'I will also gift Caitlin, one of my precious followers,' Lord Daegan went on, 'whom I trust to help Lord Leofric to the best of her abilities.'

Kilian laughed, without joy, because it was that or crying. 'At least Caitlin gets dragged into this with us, I guess.'

'A present and a spy,' said Isha.

Lord Daegan retreated beneath the protection of his platform, while lawmages got all the new mages to swear an oath of loyalty to the Nest. They did so standing in the mud, the mist catching on their skin, the two heavy layers of wool drinking the water and weighing them down further. The air was still, as thick as oil.

At last, it was done.

* * *

Tatters found Isha behind the firepits where servants were cooking pans of yewos. Far from the flames, in the shade of the keep's walls, in the path of the hissing wind, it was cold. She was the only person there, aside from a couple of lacunants who, after having been attracted by the noise, were lurking at a safe distance.

He brought her a yewos, which burnt his fingers, and gave it to her where she was sitting cross-legged on the grass.

'Congratulations,' he said. 'You're an ordained mage now. The pupil outgrows the master and all that.'

She accepted the pastry, wincing when he gave it to her, passing it from one hand to the other, blowing on the tips of her fingers to cool them. In the end she ate it, maybe just to be rid of it.

'Thank you,' she said through her mouthful. 'But you're in a high mage's robe, so I'm not sure I've outranked you.'

He shrugged. 'I always wore black robes. They just weren't that clean before.'

She laughed at that. 'I should have known.'

He stood beside her, watching the crowds chatting around the firepits as the dough sizzled. Beyond the fires, it was possible to make out the mages ambling across the grounds, the stretch of earth where the horses were resting after the parade, the bright flags limp in the windless air, Lord Daegan's wooden throne.

He sat on his raised boards, beneath his makeshift canvas roof, Starling, Passerine and Leofric beside him.

'Are you sure you shouldn't be with them?' Isha asked, following Tatters' gaze.

'I was told to meet them at noon.' The sun was nearing its summit, but he only shrugged. 'Passerine can wait.'

Let him fret, Lal agreed.

Isha stretched out her legs in front of her. 'Would you tell me the truth if I asked?'

'You can ask and see,' he answered.

'Why doesn't Passerine use the collar?'

Careful, Lal warned.

It's broken, he said, swapping to mindlink. It didn't prevent mages from eavesdropping, but at least it limited what the ungifted could hear. *Or damaged, you might say.*

When Isha answered, her mindlink was subdued. *What happened?*

He hadn't talked about this to another soul except Lal. He wasn't sure where to start. How could he admit that he had been foolish enough to cross the Shadowpass by night? How could he explain that he'd survived?

Legend had it that one could cross the Shadowpass if one remembered to count every step along the way. When he thought about it, the memory rose in black, oily waves. The mouth of the cave like a gaping, toothless monster with gums of stone. The glint of moonlight on Mezyan's white horns. The brief touch of his friend's hand on his shoulder. His voice as he said goodbye.

'I'm sorry it came to this. I hope you make it.'

Those were the last words Tatters heard on the Sunriser side of the pass.

The shadows shifted with the gracefulness of water. When he placed his foot inside the tunnel, they lapped at his feet; ripples broke around his toes with a sound like shattered glass. After two steps, there was no shore, no sense of depth or direction, only darkness. And cold.

It was the cold of high up in the mountains, where the air is rare, where breathing cuts through the mouth. It was the cold of deep waters, where their weight crushes the lungs, where each gasp brings more seaweed and salt than breath. It was the cold of places not meant for people.

Placing one hand on the rough wall, Tatters strode forwards. The irregular surface served as his anchor; something that wasn't ever-changing or drawing shapes in the corner of his vision; something that didn't sometimes ring, sometimes screech; as if the shadows were both supple and brittle, both liquid in their beauty, yet breakable as crystal.

At his seventh step, the one when he stopped counting, Tatters felt the sharp edges of the waves. Instead of foam, the Shadowpass had blades, screaming as they chafed. They didn't cut through flesh. They cut through the mind.

He should have died in those tunnels, groping for a way out as his sense of self ebbed away to be replaced by the flowing shadows. A sane person would have crossed during the light-tide. But Tatters couldn't wait for the tides. As soon as the collar compelled him to return, he would, whatever obstacles stood in his way. His only hope was that the Shadowpass was too thick a barrier for the collar's binds to reach through.

Nothing could keep the shadows at bay but light. So Tatters used the only light he had.

His skin glowed. His hair, his eyes, his mouth radiated light. He would have alighted, but he couldn't, not in so dense a pool of shadows. He was a bird trying to fly with wings caked in mud. Instead, he cradled his light around him, wearing it as a mantle, burning the only wick at hand: himself. He fed the fire with the collar, with every bind he could dredge up, gifting the gold and the magic to the darkness. And he walked.

He never stopped, even when his hand was worn to blisters from trailing it along the wall. He slipped, bruising his knees, his shins, his ankles. He forced his eyes to stay open, seeing nothing, tripping again and again as the passage wound and wove, as the ground rose and dipped. Nothing stayed the same but the darkness, which never abated.

He didn't want Lal to be eaten by the waves. He could feel her, as he never had since he'd lost her, as he would never after, a weight that he was hugging to his chest, as if carrying her against him like a child. At times, he imagined he could even feel her breath, warm against the crook of his neck.

When the waves had feasted on the collar, on whatever magic they could suck out of it, like sucking marrow out of bone, they turned to other foods. He let them devour what he couldn't hold tightly enough; he let fragments slip away, parts of himself he would never find again, couldn't even name now. Maybe he'd known his father's face. Maybe he'd loved someone at the Renegades' camp. Maybe he'd hated someone, too. That was the curse of the Shadowpass – had it taken Lal, he would never have known there was a piece of him missing.

Whatever price was paid, it was worth it. Had to be worth it. He hoped, desperately, that it had been worth it. Because he ploughed through the Shadowpass and rose on the other side with the dull, grey glow of dawn.

Two things became obvious. He couldn't alight anymore. The collar was broken.

And we were alive, said Lal. *We were free.*

When he turned to Isha, she was holding up the hem of her robes, spreading them evenly across her knees. The sun was high. The shadows were far.

How could he tell her any of this?

He settled for: *The truth is more difficult to believe than a good lie. I crossed the Shadowpass at night.*

And that was it? she asked.

He still remembered the shrill sound of the shadows when he stepped away from them, like the hiss of something letting go against its will.

Yes, he said. *That was it.*

The silence was an easy one. They listened to the festive noises, the whine of a lonely fiddle, the snorts of horses, the giggling of children. People were swapping presents: pins and brooches, colourful ribbons, an extra feather for their cap that an old foe turned friend had given them.

'You know, I never did thank you,' said Isha. 'For bringing me to the khers. The iwdan, I should say. For opening my eyes. For being kind.'

'People are only cruel when they think they're right.' The fiddle caught a wrong note and pushed into it, making the strings wail. Tatters ignored it. 'That's important to remember when things turn sordid. That the Renegades think they're being fair. That the mages think they're worthy leaders. That the iwdan believe they are finding balance.'

Isha hummed in agreement. Two figures were pushing past the fires to join them. Tatters recognised Kilian, carrying a wineskin under one arm, with Caitlin trailing behind.

'Hey, puffin,' Caitlin grumbled in lieu of greeting. 'May you grow tall, Tatters.'

From Kilian's apologetic smile, Tatters could tell he'd tried to shake her off and failed. Her mind was brittle, defensive. She knew she was unwelcome.

'What do you want?' Isha asked. She extended a hand towards Kilian as she spoke, and he gave her the wineskin. She drank in long, greedy gulps, eyeing Caitlin all the while. Tatters noticed the way the two girls looked at each other: attentively, as if fiercely conscious of each other's gestures, ready to react to the smallest tilt of head or hand.

'I won't be able to call you that anymore,' said Caitlin. 'Puffin. I guess today still counts.'

She was babbling to fill in the blanks. The shape of her thoughts indicated she had come for a reason, and she was frightened of facing Isha and Tatters together.

'You've never been shy, Cat. Spit it out or leave us,' Isha said, handing Tatters the wine. When he took a swig, the icy liquid hurt his teeth. It had been diluted with water – he hadn't expected it to be this cold.

'All right.' Caitlin breathed deeply. 'Tatters.' He raised an eyebrow as he passed on the wineskin to Kilian.

Caitlin surprised him. She dipped into a low bow, then knelt. He had never seen her rest her leg in the mud. He had never seen her with her head so low he couldn't see her eyes, only her auburn hair. A sickly feeling curled inside his heart as he realised what was happening. She took some soil from the ground and touched it to her forehead. Then she cupped both her hands together, as if to collect water, and lifted them in front of her.

'I hereby hand my soul to Byluk,' she said. He wondered how often she had pronounced those words. She wasn't a practising believer, not to his knowledge. It was rare for mages to admit they had wronged their enemies, to admit that they needed Byluk to take this weight away from them. 'To be judged as I deserve, for the stones my soul has carried.'

What is she on about? Lal wondered. *She isn't holding a present, for starters.*

Tatters was just as perplexed. 'Before I accept or decline,' he said, 'care to tell me *why* you're my enemy, exactly?'

Kilian and Isha were gaping. Caitlin didn't lift her chin, didn't hold his eye. She kept her head bowed, her hands raised. No wonder she hadn't wanted an audience. Her voice was clear, albeit a bit shaky.

'I am the person who called the lawmages on you,' she confessed. 'If you were looking for who to blame, it's me.'

Tatters hadn't thought to hunt down the person who had denounced him. He studied Caitlin. Watching her, he could only think of Yua, the way she had also pressed her hands together, the stones in her horns not unlike the pearls in Caitlin's ears. It was hard to look at her and not imagine the same skull sticky with blood, that same voice cracked by something that was not a cold.

When Tatters didn't answer immediately, leaving a gap, Isha filled it.

'So, are you disappointed?' Isha asked, biting. 'Tatters is alive, despite your efforts.'

Caitlin's voice was strained when she said, 'Don't be cruel, puffin. It doesn't suit you.'

That answer only seemed to annoy Isha more. '*I'm* the one who's cruel? Because I tell the truth?'

Caitlin made a sound not unlike a hiss. She lifted her head this time, hands still cusped together. She threw Isha a defiant glare. 'For what it's worth, I thought he was a Renegade. I thought he wanted to get us all killed.' Her mind was wary, not unlike fine threads pulled taut, before their breaking point.

'I wanted to get you a present,' she continued, addressing Tatters. 'But I couldn't find anything that you would need. And it all seemed ... small.'

She had beautiful, undamaged features. She had grown to be

taller than him, he knew, when she stood her full height. No-one had ever grabbed her hair to drag her into a cell. No-one had ever made her bleed. She had never hugged her knees as she listened to people dying.

What could he say? An apology didn't erase what had happened. Inside him, Lal was twisted inside his chest, or maybe it was anger, a knotted, spiked thing that clotted his lungs. Time, no doubt, would do what the Shadowpass achieved so swiftly: dull the memories, remove the rawness. Hide everything in deep, reassuring shadows.

He sighed.

Oh no you don't, Lal snarled. *She's not getting away with this.* Without his permission, she spoke to Caitlin directly through mindlink. *You have nothing to give us? You can take, then. Take the burden of what happened. See how you like it.*

Before Tatters could think of stopping her, Lal threw memories at Caitlin, crowding her with visions that didn't need to be invented to be gruelling. The first kher he had heard die, the rustle of his breath as it faded. The woman who wanted to be hanged, screaming, screaming, screaming. How familiar the smell of blood became when it wreathed him for days. Pain, nearly as an afterthought, aches and bruises and something worse, the sort of animal pain to which death is preferable. Snow. Yua's fingers between his hands, calloused, warm, wet.

Caitlin let out a small sound, like a whimper, and nearly fell forward. She grabbed his hand. He held her, preventing her from collapsing, and it was the jolt he needed to stop Lal.

That's enough, he said.

I'm done, anyway. Lal was cold as steel.

He hoisted Caitlin up. The mindlink had been brutal, but brief. It was already fading; she found her footing without his help. A vision wasn't a memory. A few seconds of sharing weren't a lived experience.

But it is something, Lal said. *At least now she knows.*

Tatters glanced at Kilian, who was sipping at the wineskin, pretending not to be listening; then at Isha, who was glaring holes into Caitlin's back. They thrummed with disapprobation, Isha especially, a sourness he could practically taste on his tongue.

'I accept your gift,' he said, even though there hadn't been one. What were the ritual words? 'May Byluk lift the weight from your soul as I lift this weight from your hands.'

Caitlin took her hand away, regained her composure. She was shaken, he could tell.

'I . . . I am glad you've accepted,' she mumbled.

'Well.' He looked around for something to do, somewhere to escape to. 'I'd better join Passerine. It's past noon.'

He left the apprentices – the recently ordained mages – together. He found he couldn't muster more anger against Caitlin, only weariness, that it had come to this.

He had made mistakes too. He had wanted to be forgiven, as well.

* * *

Caitlin didn't leave once Tatters was out of sight. Instead, she fumbled to retrieve a parcel tucked into her belt. It was bulky, as long as her forearm, a few fingers thick. Isha was about to tell her to get lost, that Tatters might have accepted her apology but Isha certainly hadn't, but Caitlin spoke before she could.

'Before you say anything, puffin, I'm not doing this for you.'

'Great start,' Isha sneered.

Caitlin readjusted her belt, tugging her robe back into place.

'Don't act all high and mighty. You're not Tatters. I've never wronged you.'

It was an effort not to raise her voice. 'I beg to disagree.'

'But we're going to war,' Caitlin interrupted. 'Being petty will get us killed.' She checked the wrapping around her bundle, tightening the knot of green cloth. 'Mark my words: I'm not losing to the Renegades. Not because of you, not because of anyone.' She took a deep breath, visibly steeling herself. 'So, if this is what it takes...'

She huffed. Squeezing her eyes shut, she dropped to one knee again. Somehow Isha had expected her to skip on the ritual, to cut corners. But Caitlin took soil, rubbed it against her forehead, and proffered the present in her open palms, head low. Isha glanced at Kilian, who shrugged helplessly.

'I hereby hand my soul to Byluk, to be judged as I deserve, for the stones my soul has carried,' Caitlin recited.

Until now, Isha had never received a present during the Homecoming festival. Tentatively, she took the parcel, not yet accepting nor declining the apology. She unbound the square of silk, which could have been a present in itself, revealing the elongated shapes beneath. Kilian eagerly leaned over her shoulder.

It was a piece of armour. Not unlike an inverted bracer for archery, protecting the back of the arm rather than the inside of it. Leather and wood, with straps to tie on the inside of the arm. A matching pair.

'Vambraces,' Caitlin said. Somehow, even with her head bowed, she'd guessed that Isha wasn't sure what these were.

The handiwork was exquisite, patterns carved into the leather, drawings of birds, animals and plants – including, Isha noticed, one kher, its horns growing upwards like antlers. She ran a finger over the faces and hooves, over the ivy leaves shaped along the rims. The dye had been applied in such a way as to make the vambraces a deep brown colour, and the drawings a lighter, nearly orange shade. Caitlin had put some thought into it, at least.

'That's good leatherwork,' said Kilian.

'It's lovely,' Isha agreed, still guarded. She wasn't sure what Caitlin wanted to achieve. Mages didn't give without hoping to take. 'You're being very meek today, Cat.'

Isha was waiting for Caitlin to get up, to give up on the grovelling. But she didn't. She kept her position, head low, although it was clear from her voice that she was grinding her teeth.

'For someone who said we should band together to fight the Renegades, you're being very obtuse, puffin,' Caitlin said.

Isha shrugged. She pulled on the vambraces. They were her size. A snug, elegant fit. Wearing them brought the reality of the war closer. It was clear these were to prevent someone from hacking off her hand while she was holding a lance. She wondered if a piece of wood held together by leather could truly achieve that.

'I'm surprised that you care, that's all,' Isha said. She closed and opened her fists. She would need someone to help tighten the leather laces and tie them, were she to wear these on the battlefield. Were she to forgive Caitlin.

'You don't know anything about me,' Caitlin said. 'Or who I care or don't care for.' There was a tightness in her voice, an indication, for once, that Isha's words were getting through to her. It was a small victory to know that Isha could irritate her.

'You don't know anything about me,' Isha snapped. 'It never stopped you from assuming.'

Caitlin's laugh was shrill like the call of a seagull. Not quite friendly, but the one of an opponent conceding a point. She kept kneeling. It started to drizzle.

'Thoughts?' Isha asked Kilian.

He seemed uncomfortable, trapped, as often, between them.

'It's better if everyone gets along,' he said, a bit too hastily.

Isha nodded. She turned to Caitlin. 'May Byluk lift the weight from your soul as I lift this weight from your hands.'

With a sigh, maybe of relief, maybe of contained annoyance, Caitlin got to her feet. She brushed her robes where the mud stuck to her knee.

'Ah, well, this is good, right?' Kilian babbled, rushing over the words in his eagerness to get the situation smoothed over. 'Just like Passerine and Tatters making out, I mean making up, although I guess both are true, but you don't have to make out to make up if you don't want to ...'

'Wait,' said Isha. 'What are you talking about?'

Caitlin's gaze was unamused. 'You must have heard about this. Passerine and Tatters are lovers, aren't they? I heard they share the same bed.' Her voice indicated she didn't much care either way. Kilian, however, perked up at the sound of gossip, or maybe simply at a subject that wasn't war, forgiveness, or dying.

'Yes, they have this intense master-slave fetish thing going on,' he announced, with the absolute certainty only achieved when someone has no clue what they are talking about.

'I don't think so,' Isha said. 'I think they share a bed because there's a refugee crisis at the Nest.' What with all the Sunriser mages struggling to get enough beds and dorms, let alone private rooms. What with established mages sleeping on the floor in the corridors since they'd been forced to flee their homes. Instead of stating all of this, she asked, 'Where did this rumour even start?'

'It was Ninian,' said Kilian. 'He said something about Passerine not sleeping since Tatters was back, and it snowballed from there.'

'Well, don't speak about it in front of either of them,' Isha said sternly. 'They won't like it.'

They lapsed back into silence. Caitlin stood beside them, as if waiting for the conversation to continue, although they had nothing to say to each other. After a while, she clicked her tongue and strode back down the slope.

Isha watched her go – despite her proud posture, she looked slim and breakable, thin wrists and ankles made for bracelets and bangles, not gauntlets and greaves.

* * *

The wind buffeted his black robes; the sun glinted on his red hair, which had grown longer in prison. Red and black. Tatters belonged to Hawk, even now.

People were gathering for the religious part of the festival. The servants pulled the stocky pans off the fires, staining their fingers black. When Tatters reached the platform where the triumvirate was assembled, he leapt on it, using one hand to push himself up, ignoring the steps down the side. The three lords of the Nest gave him a sour look.

Passerine mindlinked before the dust from his jump had settled. *You took your time.*

Did you have a solution if I left you in the lurch? Tatters was genuinely curious. It wasn't like Passerine *not* to have a backup plan. Without answering, Passerine withdrew from his thoughts, leaving a trail of annoyance behind him. Maybe not. Maybe he'd been relying on his docility. Tatters relished the moment.

'Now that you have graced us with your collarbound,' said Lord Daegan, his eyes riveted on Passerine and venom in his voice, 'maybe we can begin.'

Passerine nodded. His face was closed, but Tatters could sense how furious he was at having been stood up. Tatters ignored them all, especially Lord Leofric, who had a smile that could cut. Instead, he turned to Starling, extending his arm with a flourish. She didn't smile, but she touched wrists with him in quiet acknowledgement.

Lord Daegan had adorned his black robes with a thick gold necklace that hung across his chest, eerily echoing the collars. The pale brown dress Starling wore could have been cheap to make, if not for the embroidery of flowers down the sleeves and the complicated motifs around the neckline. The cloth was cut to show her shoulders, but Lord Daegan hadn't provided her with a shawl. Tatters doubted the dress would have been her first pick, had she been allowed to choose.

Beside them, Leofric was draped in his usual emerald green. He looked like wheat and lush grass, a male Groniz reborn. Even the bone cane tucked under his arm could pass for something benign. It was as white as the pelt of a newborn lamb. Tatters wondered how many prisoners he had visited in his underground cells today.

'Do you have a present for me?' Leofric asked.

Tatters pulled a face at the implications. As if he would kneel and beg for forgiveness from the head lawmage. He was glad Leofric didn't have a present either – he wasn't sure he would have been able to bear it.

'No,' he said.

'You don't want to make peace, then?' Leofric said slyly.

'You're not that special,' Tatters answered, determined not to let the lawmage get the better of him. Leofric's smile froze into place, never leaving his lips, but sitting there like a cramp.

Now you've pissed off Lord Passerine and Lord Leofric, said Lal. *Only Lord Daegan to go.*

Lord Daegan gazed over the people who depended on him,

the children jumping excitedly at the front; servants and soldiers and townsfolk wiping their sweaty brows and craning their necks to admire their leaders; mages and apprentices at a distance, to show that they weren't part of that superstitious bunch, but still close enough to enjoy the show; and the lacunants even further back, made bold by the lenient treatment of the past few days, unaware the favours would fade with spring.

'You will bless the people, at my signal,' Lord Daegan ordered.

Starling nodded and Tatters, not wanting more trouble than he had already caused, copied her.

Her hair was undone; her face was slack. Tatters felt a pang, worrying, not for the first time, about her fate. Behind them, Lord Leofric lurked like the shadow of things to come: a worse master than Lord Daegan, and the battlefield a worse place than the Nest.

Lord Daegan cleared his throat. His voice was that of a born leader, booming like the bells of the Nest. 'We have harnessed the power of the skies.' Knowing what was about to happen, the crowd cheered. 'Dance for us,' he bellowed with a large sweep of his arm, 'and bless this day!'

Alighting would always be strange for Tatters. On the one hand, it gave him an intoxicating sense of freedom, of space, of sky. On the other hand, it would always be linked to the collar. He couldn't alight without it. Without an order resonating inside the giants' gold, he couldn't fly.

You should be able to alight without the collar, Passerine said. His mindlink, as always, was as quiet as the drop of a feather. *But the collar is a deeply traumatic magic, and you've never alighted without. It's not impossible its broken binds are shackling you to your human shape.*

Passerine indicated the crowd with a thrust of his chin, nothing more. *Still, the light is within you, as you'll now prove.*

Even as vague a command as that was enough. It surged in Tatters' blood, like a strong liquor that didn't dull when it reached his stomach, but continued burning within. He glanced at Starling, who was already shimmering, loosening into threads of gold. He closed his eyes to steady himself, to hold this precious, radiant feeling a bit longer. Then he let go.

They rushed together towards the sky. Flying upwards was the most exhilarating part of alighting. It was the vastness of it all, the absence of boundaries and lines, of frontiers and thresholds, only blue, blue, blue, nothing to obstruct his sight, his soul. The power struggles below were about drawing lines and barring people's way across. Up here, it was as if he could breathe unimpeded for the first time.

It was an effort to slow down, to swerve above the festival grounds. Nothing below called him back. Only the Nest was high enough to tempt him. He longed to explore its towers, to skip under its arches, to curl up on its rooftops. The stained-glass windows caught his attention as surely as silver attracts a magpie, or a mirror-trap draws skylarks to the ground.

No wonder Starling fell into the lightlure, said Lal. *The Nest is a huge lightlure by itself.*

Starling flew alongside him, stretched out like a banner. Tatters drew himself out as much as he could, thinning his light to compete with her, although she remained much larger, nearly twice his size.

She flitted up and down as she flew, sending ripples down her body. He copied her as best he could, graceless beside her. She dipped suddenly – or maybe there had been an indication, which he hadn't understood – slipping below him and lifting again, as if to plait their two lights together. Again he followed her lead, enjoying the fact that the sky was theirs, that time was theirs, that everything below was narrow and cramped and none of their concern.

After a few spins and curves, she veered downwards, but he didn't see why he had to return yet. He was enjoying himself. On the contrary, he rose higher, toying with the idea of ascending, leaving everything behind, climbing up to the next worlds which, no doubt, awaited above the skyline.

She realised he hadn't tagged along, cut a line above the high mages' platform, and caught up. She twirled around him, guiding their dance like a human partner would, with the wind in place of music. Delicately – Tatters appreciated that she did this with subtlety – she guided them downwards.

It was too tempting. He played along for a while before evading her, arching his light further afield, closer to the Edge. Would it be as fun to dip downwards, like an eagle, as it was to aim for the sun?

She closed the gap. The way her lights threaded themselves around him became more insistent. He understood the truth of what she had told him, the fact that this elegant body-language, these patterns, had meaning. He must be missing most of what she was trying to convey. Still, he sensed she had lost hope. She was weighed down. She kept drooping back towards the mages, not because she didn't want to fly, but because her wings had been clipped.

He tried to tease her, changing course each time she got near, keeping her at a distance. He wanted to pull her away from her resignation. What had been a dance shifted into a race.

She dashed towards him in a straight line, gaining speed. *Time to see if my theory holds.* He let himself drop like a stone as she reached him, aiming far below the Edge, into the mist that humans had never explored.

It was as thrilling as he'd hoped. The world flashed by, every detail growing bigger, each pebble, each blade of grass, each root seemingly swelling in size until the cliff ended and abruptly everything was cut off, and he was in whiteness so thick he couldn't make out his own light. For a moment he continued, scared and unwilling to be scared, before he thought of worrying about being lost, and reluctantly slowed.

Starling wasn't lost. This time, when she herded him back, he followed.

She circled the platform to the claps and cries of the crowd. She shifted back into human shape when they were only a foot from the ground, landing in a cloud of billowing dust and hay. Beside her, Tatters hit the ground without poise, nearly tripping.

Around them, the applause drowned out all other sounds. Starling stepped closer.

'I am not pleased.' She spoke softly, so the mages wouldn't hear her in the din.

Your dancing skills must be worse than we thought, said Lal.

That wasn't what Starling meant. 'You promised you would be back,' she said. 'I waited all winter for your return.'

Her sadness bit into his heart. He thought of her in the spires of the Nest, and him in its entrails, both as broken.

'I would have returned, if I could,' he said.

He cocked his chin backwards to take in the sky. It wasn't the same as alighting. Starling followed his gaze. They had shared a dance – a language without lies – and they both knew what the other felt.

The celebrations were finished.

Chapter 5

The army marched from dawn to dusk every day. They had to make haste, to catch the Renegades before they had invaded too much of the Nest's land. They were the elite team who would change the tide of the war, although Isha worried that no-one had spent enough time wondering *how* they would change it.

They took the Sunpath, a road that went from the Nest to the Ridge and was paved for the most part; it followed the course of the sun in the sky, hence its name. At first, the countryside was tame, with a settlement every couple of hours. It was mostly fields, long brown lines arching over the hills, green sprouts only just poking their heads out of the soil. Some Sunriser refugees had stopped along the road rather than drift to the Nest, and Isha spotted families with hungry eyes from winter, helping their Duskdweller neighbours cut down woodland to clear space for crops, repairing half-built houses, grim hope in their eyes.

Isha remembered the same landscape in autumn, when she had been running from the Shadowpass and the Renegades, following Passerine. Everything had been bursting with colour: red, gold and orange leaves, black and purple berries ripe on the hedges, hay from the harvest piled high, the smell of cut grass sharp in the air. Now, rather than the shades of autumn, the woodland was speckled with white and yellow flowers, and everything was green – achingly green, as trees only are at the very start of spring. The scent of thick, heady pollen filled the air.

And she was travelling the other way, back towards what she had fled.

It could have been worse, she decided after the first day. Although they suffered small bouts of rain, they were never under a downpour. The Sunpath was easy to follow. It was the road the refugees, the Renegades, and everyone else used when travelling to or from the Nest.

Her blue robes, cut for an average figure, without precise measurements, were tight on Isha. They had been designed for someone much slimmer. Her only consolation was that they were also small on Kilian, not because he shared her curves, but because he was taller than most mages – so they both looked uncomfortable, with too-short sleeves and a tight neck collar.

'So, do I look like a proper ordained mage to you?' he asked, trying to turn the discomfort into a joke.

His clothes jarred with her – they were the deep blue of law and order, ill-fitted to his smile. The dyed fabric made his hair seem even lighter, and his eyes were less blue, greyer, like a younger version of Lord Daegan.

'You'll never look official to me.' She meant it as a compliment, but Kilian pretended to take offence.

'How dare you!' he gasped. 'Show some respect, puffin.'

Aside from the robes, they had been given one lance, one long knife, and one shield. Arushi had checked the equipment handed to Isha carefully. It was a mixed blessing to have the head of guards trying the elasticity of the wood, checking there were no creases in the leather lining the shield. It had made Isha more conscious of the fragility of it all.

A few of the senior followers had horses, such as Ninian and, surprisingly, Caitlin. But Isha and Kilian were each reduced to holding their lance in one hand, their shield strapped to the other arm, a bag with personal possessions and sleeping gear on their back, the knife in their belts hitting their thighs. They walked, treading through the urine, manure and flies the horses left behind.

'How many horses do we have, anyway?' grumbled Kilian. He gestured to the mess on the road. 'It can't be *that* many.'

'You'd be surprised how much animals, like humans, can be full of shit,' Isha answered.

At least that made him laugh.

'Don't you think we should save our breath for complaining when things are actually dire?' Isha teased, to distract herself.

'When things get really bad,' Kilian said, 'I'm not sure we'll have the strength to complain.'

She couldn't offer an upbeat answer.

The villagers were glad to see them. When they approached, gates were flung open, guards stood to attention, people came out of their houses or fields to cheer, handing out a piece of bread, a pouch of water, a trinket for luck, the red of Raudaz often woven somewhere on the charm. No-one wanted to miss seeing the lightborn. Ungifted believed Starling's presence was a good omen. Folk sang her name, *Gelhwos*, and threw plucked petals at the soldiers.

Lord Leofric opened the way, on a stallion with rolling eyes, the whites showing as it jerked its head against its bit. He was also wearing armour, including a chainmail of gold, which struck Isha as a good choice for parading, but a foolish one to go to battle with. Surely gold was soft and bright, making for both an easy target and a weak protection? Of course, Lord Leofric should never get close to any actual fighting. That's what Isha – and a small posse of fifty mages – were there for.

Aside from Passerine's followers, the army also included

conscripted mages and ungifted, reaching, to Isha's estimate, half a thousand soldiers. This was fewer than the Renegades, but the mages could call upon the fortified cities across the Sunpath, where a lot of the Nest's forces were diverted. If a battle were to take place, they would rely on the nearby towns for support.

When the army crossed those well-defended towns, Lord Leofric held the ungifted under his control, mostly for show, forcing them to march in tight rows, their footsteps rhythmically hitting the road. The high mages were also giving instructions to the mages on foot, the equivalent of counting 'one, two' out loud, or beating a drum – it wasn't invasive mindlink, but it helped everyone walk together, so the army was more impressive. Except for the dull thud of their steps, they were silent. That was probably the scariest part, Isha considered, this army coordinating without a word.

Lord Leofric would release his hold on the ungifted once they were back in the fields. Although the soldiers still kept an even pace, shared through mindlink – *one two, one two* – the solemnity slackened somewhat.

'My shoes aren't going to survive this, are they?' said Kilian, after the first few days on the road.

His shoes, after being dyed green then losing their colour, were now worse for wear, the leather flaking. But it was the only pair he had.

'When we get back, dye them green again, for victory,' said Isha.

'If we get back, I'll buy a new pair,' Kilian answered.

It was just banter, but she noted the 'if'.

As time went by, it became obvious how unsuited they were to this task. Her feet hurt. Her hand had sores where she held her lance, the rough wood scraping at her palms. Her left arm throbbed from lifting the shield. She swapped from carrying it to strapping it across her back, which didn't help as much as she'd hoped, as it bashed against the back of her calves, leaving bruises. Kilian's feet had blisters that were painful just to look at, and he winced when he walked, dragging behind.

It was a small consolation to see that the ones on horseback were also suffering. Except for the lawmages, mages weren't used to long trips. Although the pace set was slow, Isha spotted more than one high mage walking stiffly, legs apart, from the ache down their thighs. At the end of a long day, Caitlin didn't so much dismount as drop from her horse, like a sailor whose legs were now unsuited to solid ground.

Isha had been able to do this, less than a year ago. Had she grown weak during her stay at the Nest? *I have grown spoilt*, she decided. She had forgotten that most people worked with their body, not their mind.

'Maybe you were right,' she begrudgingly admitted to Kilian, 'about drinking less beer.'

'Don't even mention beer,' he moaned. He looked utterly miserable. 'I'd drown in a barrel right now, rather than take another step.'

We haven't even started fighting yet. It wasn't a comforting thought.

Every evening, Lord Leofric picked a village in which to stay. High mages slept in the villagers' spare beds, sometimes in barns and sheds when they ran out of space – foot mages had to use their tents, albeit on a flat surface protected by high walls. Ungifted drew the short straw, and slept in tents in fallow fields, outside the city gates. The local mages often prepared a meal for Lord Leofric and shared recent news with him. Except for the glint of weaponry, this could have been a friendly visit from the Nest to its vassals.

Every morning, they left churned earth and grass flattened to mud behind them. The places where the army had camped stood out like sores in the countryside. As they set off, Lord Leofric sent Starling to scout ahead of them. It was a pleasure to see her flying, brightening up the sky above them, knowing she was watching for threats and following the Renegades' progress.

However, she also returned with dire news: the Renegades had strayed from the Sunpath. They had divided into smaller battalions, probably to escape notice, and set off in a variety of alternative routes. The biggest group was heading through the Splits.

Cursing, Lord Leofric changed their course, hoping to cut Hawk off.

The Splits were much rougher terrain. North of the Sunpath, the land was mostly stone. It was still flat, but as rocky as a cliff-face, and dotted with chasms: some only thin cracks like spiderwebs, some gaps that a person could hop over, some a horse could jump, and some impossible to traverse. They criss-crossed the land, shifting with time, which meant that any map quickly became outdated, as fissures that could once be crossed grew too large.

'Apparently, if you go far enough, the canyons are so wide you can see the sky beneath,' said Kilian. 'Like the Edge, only ragged rather than smooth.'

'Don't,' said Isha. She could imagine it, long slices of stone and long slices of sky, like interlaced fingers. 'It makes my head spin just to think of it.'

On wet days, the mist rose from the Splits like smoke from a cracked cauldron. They slowed to a crawl, eyes glued to their feet, and Starling was earthbound.

It was on one such day, after a morning of staring at the ground, listening anxiously when someone stumbled or a pebble dropped down a crack – sometimes bouncing a few times and jamming, sometimes rolling, it seemed, all the way to the bottom of the world – that they had their first clash with the Renegades.

First, they heard them: a horn was blown, calling a group to muster. The mages relied on mindlink, not noise, to summon their troops. It could only be the Renegades. Leofric changed direction, following a long chasm that twisted east, towards the sound. After an hour of marching, they saw them: shapes in the mist, their feet stamping on the ground, the banners like floating flecks of red in the clouds.

The enemy army was on the other side of a gorge as wide as two horses and as deep as the underworlds. The Nest followed the Renegades, stalking them through the mist. The Renegades must have seen them as well – the mages were quiet, but not invisible.

Starling was sent to check on the size of the group. As soon as she crossed the gorge, arrows rained upwards. She returned unhurt, but Leofric was too cautious to send her again. Arrows shouldn't touch her, as they would only fly through her light harmlessly, but he nevertheless kept her by his side. He also moved the army further away from the edge.

I don't want it to become a competition between our archers, he explained to his mages. *A melee is preferable.*

Isha and Kilian were sent for with a couple of Passerine's followers. Their group would stay close to Lord Leofric, using a combination of mindlink and physical fighting to protect him from the Renegades – but only if they got close enough. There was little chance of that happening. Isha tried to convince herself by repeating it. *They'll never push through our army and get to him. I probably won't even have to fight.*

Starling was sent ahead to see where they might be able to cut off the Renegades. When she returned, she landed beside Lord Leofric's stallion, which sidestepped nervously, despite his tight hold on the reins. On the stony ground, horses weren't as sure-footed as humans and slipped easily. Isha tried to ignore the leap of her heart as the stallion stumbled, then regained its footing.

'The gap narrows and ends further to the northeast,' Starling said. 'Until then, it's too wide for humans to cross.'

'Would a horse clear the jump?' Leofric asked.

Not on this ground, it wouldn't, Isha thought.

Starling's face was blank. 'I don't know.'

'Let's hurry,' Leofric decided.

The ungifted moved with automated, precise gestures. Isha realised Lord Leofric and his mages were directing them as they pulled out their weapons, straightened their shields, set a quicker pace towards the end of the ravine. Whilst much noisier, the Renegades caught on and also moved faster. They shouted orders, waved flags, rang trumpets. They were booming and boisterous, but it was obvious screaming instructions wasn't as efficient as mindlinking directly to each soldier.

As everyone made haste, hearing but not seeing their enemies, the Renegades ululated. It was a blood-curdling sound, like a wolf's howl. Isha jumped. It didn't stop, but intensified as they marched faster – high-pitched screaming like banshees, *uli-uli-uli-uli*, echoing menacingly. It was impossible to ignore and, Isha found, as distracting as mindlink. It muddled her thoughts, dried her mouth, increased her pace – and her fear. The mist faded as they approached noon, the sun clearing it somewhat. It still hung in low wisps, but they could make out the enemy.

Despite herself, despite the knot in her throat, Isha tried to find Hawk. She wasn't sure what she would do if she saw her mother. What she would feel. But she needed to see her.

Amongst the Renegades, Isha made out the red silhouettes of khers, but she couldn't pinpoint where the mages and ungifted were, as everyone was wearing the same clothes: ragtag bits of armour, pieces of leather and mail and helmets. No-one with a complete uniform, no-one completely without. Except for a few foot soldiers with horns in their belts, who seemed to be shouting orders, she couldn't pick out the leaders.

The group seems... small, she worried.

What was that? Lord Leofric asked, although she hadn't been trying to talk to him.

This looks like a small battalion, Isha said. They were supposed to be following one of the biggest groups, but she could tell they vastly outnumbered the Renegades. *Where are the horses?* Or the leaders she might recognise, she thought, keeping this to herself. No Mezyan. No Hawk. If they were there, they were hidden. She wondered what was worse: seeing a face she recognised, or not knowing where they were.

The gorge narrowed. It was a deep drop, flared: much larger at the top, then thinning into two walls of stone. It was still a fall of fifteen feet, at least. Isha tried not to look downwards.

Their destination was in sight. Orders rippled out of Lord Leofric, who reached out to all the high mages of his army – even he couldn't control every soldier directly. The high mages, in turn, communicated with other mages, who controlled the ungifted as instructed. Their silent army moved forward, no-one breaking or loosening ranks.

He sent a group ahead to face the Renegades, who were reaching the end of the gorge at the same time as the mages. He stayed at the back, on his stallion, focused. Isha stood beside him, aware of the mindlink thrumming around them, of the heat coming off his horse, of the weight of her lance in her hand. She tried to ignore the mindlink itself, intent on keeping a sure footing, on holding her shield up, on scanning the mist for threats.

She had to guard Leofric. That was all. See any danger before it reached him, take it down before his mindlink was disrupted. Passerine and Tatters had both repeated it to her – Hawk would try to take down Leofric first.

Once he's gone, the army will fall apart, Passerine had warned.

Hawk likes to chop off the heads at the top, not those at the bottom, was Tatters' way of phrasing it.

The soldiers from the Nest approached in formation, clashing with the Renegades in a roar of metal and wood smashing together.

At the same time as the physical battle began, the mental fighting started. *Spitting out broken teeth. Burning spires. Kneeling on stone.* If some mages were busy coordinating the ungifted, others were on the offensive, trying to wrestle control out of the Renegades' hands and take over their soldiers. *Flags being ground into mud, and the picture on the flag is your own face.* Orders and images, as sharp as whip-cracks, broke over the soldiers. The Renegades had mages of their own; stark, hard, mindbrawl emotions thundered across the line. *The sound the chains holding the Edge will make when they break.* It was invisible, soundless lightning, a storm only mages could perceive.

Lord Leofric gestured to Starling. It was her turn to act. She jumped into the air, sliding from human shape into a ray of gold. She flew upwards, lighting up the sullen, bloodied faces of the fighters. To their credit, the Renegades didn't baulk at her approach, but only took up their bows. She lifted above them and, like a bird of prey, swooped down into the fray before rising in the air again. Swarms of arrows followed her each time she lunged. An elegant vulture, she circled before dipping again. Isha knew she struck people's minds directly, ripping their souls from their body, before flying out of reach.

Unfortunately for the Nest, a majority of the enemy battalion were khers, which made it impossible to command them. Isha heard snippets of mindlink being returned to Leofric. *Khers. Ungifted might have kher horn. A few mages. No-one undefended.* Mental locks were in place to prevent the Nest from forcing the enemy soldiers into submission or to let themselves be slaughtered, which was how the Nest had won its last war, over a century ago, when taking control of the Duskdweller Edge.

Starling was also struggling. She spent more time circling, hesitating. Isha saw her dive, change her mind, and veer suddenly. She returned to Lord Leofric, emerging from the mist like sunlight, dispersing it as she landed. It billowed around them, hiding the detail of the fight from sight.

'The arrows have baina tips,' she announced. She didn't state the obvious: if she was hit, or a mage was, she would be forced into human shape, and they would be unable to mindlink.

Lord Leofric frowned. Even Isha had to admire the feat he was performing; he was mindlinking to the high mages, overseeing the whole battle from a distance, while receiving new information, processing it, and making quick decisions.

Lord Leofric – and his retinue, Isha included – were well away from the fray. It was easy for Isha to analyse the situation, to stay calm, to ignore the screams, the clanging of metal, the tang of iron in the air. To think of this as a game, pawns being moved across the board, rather than a struggle of flesh and blood and bile and spit. The Nest had better coordination, especially when they had good visibility, but the mist made it hard to see. Still, they had bigger numbers and were gaining ground, curling around the end of the gorge and skirting the Renegades' line to double back on them.

It was clear the group was too small as the mist rose: only fifty or so soldiers and, out of them, only ten archers, saving their arrows for Starling. No horses, as Isha had guessed. No Hawk. She couldn't decide whether she was relieved or not.

'Keep harassing them,' Lord Leofric told Starling. 'Feint. Make them waste those arrows.'

She flew off. It turned out the Nest didn't need the extra help, however, as they had the advantage in a line battle. If someone fell in the line, the gap was blocked before the Renegades could push their advantage. The arrows couldn't reach the mages, safely out of the fray on the other side of the gorge. The Nest's soldiers were untroubled by the drop on the side of their line, unafraid of stepping over narrow gaps, unbothered by pain. The mages didn't let them feel any of it.

Isha tried not to imagine it: standing above the void, without control over her own body, carelessly manipulated to step over irregular holes. She shoved the feeling away. *Focus*, she told herself. It was harder, now, because she could tell no-one would be able to threaten Lord Leofric, and her mind had space to wander. *Focus, focus. This might be a trap. Look. Stay alert.*

Slowly but surely, they pushed the Renegades back, until someone let out a shout, a horn was blown, and suddenly the Renegades were dispersing. They all headed south, back from where they had come. The Nest's army followed them, but they were slowed by the rocky terrain. They took down a few fleeing soldiers, but mostly they let them run. The risk of galloping on slippery stone wasn't worth the few deaths gained.

Leofric led his retinue to the now-deserted battlefield, where the only remaining Renegades were the dead ones. A woman, a long-healed scar tugging at the corner of her mouth, a crooked sort of smile, with a lance still sticking out of her head, after it had smashed her eye socket into a bloody pulp. A man with a round, childish face, lips parted as if he were sleeping, his stomach split by a blade, bowels torn, the smell of excrement wreathing his corpse. It was hard to put together the distant, clinical fighting Isha had witnessed and the reality of its consequences: people with damaged or peaceful faces; with soft or calloused fingers; with families, lovers, friends, lying strewn on the stone.

'Push the dead into the gorge,' Lord Leofric said. 'It'll be a fitting flight.'

Ungifted soldiers dragged the bodies away, leaving scarlet lines on the stone. Starling landed as this bleak task was being completed. The mist had lifted now. It revealed the barren stone, the ravines scarring the countryside as far as the eye could see, deep wounds of rock.

'This part of the Splits is cut off from the rest of the land entirely,' Starling reported. 'It's a dead end.'

Isha sensed the dull, pulsating anger of Lord Leofric's thoughts.

'And where is Hawk? Where is the main army?' Lord Leofric asked.

The answer was bad news, as expected.

'They went south as we went north,' Starling said. 'They must have turned around as soon as the mist rose.'

Fuming, Lord Leofric forced everyone to backtrack. Although they had won the skirmish, it didn't feel like a victory.

***

The next few days were gloomy. Hawk had crossed the Sunpath, according to Starling, and headed into the woods on the southern side, where her army was hidden by the foliage and harder for Starling to survey. In this zigzagging way, she was drawing closer to the Nest, avoiding altercations, saving her strength for the city. Three or four other groups of Renegades, maybe more, were now speckled across the land, all headed for the Nest in various roundabout ways. The aim was obviously to exhaust the mages, leading them after one battalion, leaving the others unfettered.

Isha didn't believe her mood could drop further, until one afternoon, Caitlin brought her horse to walk alongside her. Kilian was further behind, still limping on blistered feet.

It was difficult to hold Caitlin's eye as she bobbed up and down on the saddle. But Isha couldn't help but notice how regal she looked – the straps of leather around her waist showed off the arch of her back; the glint of a blade answered the glint in her irises. Isha wondered how she pulled this off at times of war, when everyone else was worn and covered in dirt. Caitlin looked like she'd *bathed*.

'So, do the vambraces help?' she asked.

'Sure. They make my feet lighter and now my lance always hits true,' Isha answered, focusing on the path. 'They make me the soldier I could never have aspired to be without them.'

'I don't see any improvement in your mindlink,' Caitlin said.

'And I don't see any improvement in your temper,' said Isha. She wasn't in the mood to hide her sarcasm. 'Maybe I should gift you a rug to scratch your claws on, Cat.'

Maybe it had been too bold. She didn't hear an answer, so she was forced to look up. Caitlin was smirking.

'Well, well, look who's got some bite in her after all,' Caitlin said. 'Here I was thinking you were like Passerine, giving everyone the silent treatment.'

It was all they said that day. But despite the terseness of their conversation, Caitlin came to ride beside Isha once or twice in the following days. It struck Isha that maybe she was lonely – her friends were back at the Nest, most of the mages were Passerine's followers, and no doubt a frustrated Lord Leofric was poor company. She must be isolated. With that in mind, Isha made the effort to engage, even though everyone's patience was fraying as the long hike dragged on.

The Nest's army still had to trudge through the Splits – rocks, rocks, and more rocks, on tender feet; deep drops; echoing falls where stones sometimes tumbled down; wet, sticky mist – and then the farms – nicer land, moss on the rocks, which turned to soil, then grass, then wheat, then hamlets with friendly but scared faces – before reaching the Sunpath.

'Goodbye, home sweet home,' Caitlin said mockingly, waving in the direction of the Splits as they crossed the Sunpath.

'You're from the Splits?'

'You didn't know? I'm from the Barrens.'

The Barrens. It was an ironically named place, as that was where mages – women – who had fallen pregnant could go to give birth, if they wished. It was an orphanage, as Isha understood it. A place built by Lady Siobhan, so that female mages could be rid of unwanted children.

'I didn't realise,' said Isha. 'That must have been ... hard.'

Caitlin made a disparaging sound. 'It was fine. I grew up with ungifted spinsters as guardians. Sometimes young apprentices are sent to serve in the Barrens for a couple of months, to teach the children the basics of mindlink and to stop us from over-running the ungifted. Honestly, it was like the Nest, but with kids: who's friends with whom, who's got the best bed, who's got no friends, the older ones bullying everyone else ...' She laughed mirthlessly. 'A good preparation for what was to come.'

The Nest, but with the immaturity of children and teenagers and no supreme mage to hold them to account, only hassled ungifted? It sounded like a nightmare to Isha.

'They looked after me so my mother would be able to climb the ranks of the Nest,' Caitlin said. Before Isha could ask,

Caitlin continued, 'I don't know if it worked out for her. We aren't allowed to know our mother's name, unless she gives us the right to access the register. Which mine didn't.'

Both our mothers left us behind, in the care of others, to pursue their own goals. Isha wasn't sure what to say. Their conversations often fizzled when they ran out of things to discuss, or kind things to say to each other.

Their army crossed the Sunpath and pursued Hawk into the southern woods. At first, the woodland was what Isha had expected: thick trees blotting out the sun; the eerie quiet of forests; leaves, acorns and chestnuts strewn on the ground; the mud holes of wild boars and their messy tracks. As they made progress, however, there were fewer animal tracks and larger trees, roots reaching out across the path.

As they continued, the trees grew bigger, towering above them, trunks as thick as houses, roots big enough for people to walk along them in single file. Between the giant trees, smaller bushes and plants grew thickly; moss on bark, saplings on moss, vines on saplings. What little humus there was gathered in clumps between the bigger roots. In places, they were walking on, not in, woods.

One windy morning, Isha realised the breeze wasn't only coming from the sides. It whistled up from between her legs. The network of roots was like a latticed floor, but with air beneath and between them. Where the roots weren't thickly entangled, slits of blue sky were visible. She felt sick, tried to ignore it, then was forced to sit down for a bit, on shaky legs. Now that she was looking, she realised that what she had taken for patches of light filtering through the trees were gaps between the roots, with the sky beneath.

At least the Edge drew a neat line between the fall and solid ground.

'It's the Overgrowth,' Kilian explained, once he'd caught up with her. 'There are gorges everywhere, like in the Splits, only the trees tend to bridge the holes.'

She pictured vines linking trees together, trees growing on sheer cliffs. She wondered how large the gaps were, how jagged the land. Were the bigger trees, the ones that seemed to have been planted by giants, rooted in the underworlds, supporting the rest of the forest? How solid was the Overgrowth – and how prone to collapsing?

She walked beside Kilian, trying not to stare at her feet. Above, the knotted branches with the sky piercing between them reflected the ground beneath her feet. The only difference was the road markings, carved in the bark at regular intervals, to help travellers make their way back to the Sunpath if needed.

'Why would anyone travel here?' Isha asked.

Kilian shrugged. 'People rarely go this far. There's nothing here, except for feral khers and wood.'

And Renegades.

'Why don't we avoid the holes?' she insisted.

'We do, mostly,' Kilian said. 'But, you know.' He tapped a foot experimentally on the roots; her stomach lurched. 'If it's solid, why not walk on it?'

As the days went on, it was clear this would be a hard terrain to battle on, maybe even harder than the Splits: the Overgrowth was thick with bushes, all growing out of or on the bigger trees, creating an underbrush that was steadily harder to plough through. When crossing a crevasse, they spread out the army in long, thin lines, to avoid putting too much weight onto the roots. They walked in files of three to four soldiers abreast. In places, it was impossible to progress at all, unless the soldiers were willing to clear the branches.

They had slowed to a crawl, laboriously struggling through thickets, when the Renegades ambushed them.

A shout – one word in a foreign language. On cue, arrows pelted down from the trees above. Mindlink coursed through the army nearly as fast as the arrows shot down, and Isha found her arm lifting her shield above her head before she'd even realised why she needed to protect herself. Heavy knocks, like someone kicking her shield, thundered from above. Screams, horses thrashing. People had been hit. Startled, Kilian stumbled then slipped. He let out a shout of surprise as his foot went through a thin network of roots and hit the damp soil beneath.

Swearing, he tried to pull himself up. She grabbed the rim of his shield, shoving it upwards, as the second volley of arrows landed, this time mostly thudding on the wooden shields in a chorus of thunks.

People were shouting at Kilian to get up. Isha helped him hoist himself to his feet. The third volley punched at the wooden ceiling above them. Kilian swayed, pale, gripping her for support.

Thank the skies that the Renegades had been forced to give a vocal order, granting the Nest those precious few seconds to react. Mindlink buzzed between the mages, assessing the damage. *Starling nicked with a baina-tipped arrow in the neck, above the shoulder. Wincing on the ground, groping to get to her feet. A shiver of fear at the blood pooling in her collarbone – a splash of relief that the arrow had only grazed her.* Being a mage in the Nest's army was like being a nail in a wheel. The magic rolled on her, and Isha had little control over the visions being shared. *Leofric with broken arrow-tips in his armour, brushing them out of his chainmail. Unhurt. High mages collapsed from their mounts, lying unconscious on the forest floor.*

Isha tried to focus on her shield, on her feet, on not tripping in the hole beside Kilian. The Renegades had stopped shooting.

A horse whinnying desperately, two legs kicking under the treeline. In its panic, it was breaking the smaller roots and branches. If it kept at it long enough, it might rip enough of the Overgrowth to fall, screaming, down into the underworlds.

Out of the muddled messages, she untangled the useful information. *A dozen archers. In the trees, shooting from above. No sign of Hawk. High mages have dismounted to get under the shield-wall. The majority of the army is fine – the arrows only hit the frontline.* Isha's heart was pounding; her arm ached from holding the shield upward. But the sensations were welcome, because they allowed her to put some distance between herself and the army's mindlink.

The small number of archers indicates they're trying to kill Starling and run. They've failed so far. Although they'd aimed for her neck and hit their mark. Had Starling not moved, the arrow would have gone through her throat. *Stay calm.*

She received an instruction in mindlink. It must have come from Lord Leofric originally, but it was being relayed by other mages. Ninian was the person who contacted Isha. His familiar voice – serene, despite the arrows, despite the screaming and swearing – reassured her.

Walk away from the group, in a straight line. Northwest. Keep your shield high.

It wasn't a question. Isha realised she was at the edge of the shield-wall, which was no doubt why she had been deemed safe to leave it. The army had ground to a standstill, shields above their heads. The archers in the trees would have trouble killing many soldiers and the Nest's army could outwait them if need be. For now, the archers weren't bolting. They probably hoped the Nest would have to break formation, enabling them to take down a few more high mages before making their escape. Maybe forcing Lord Leofric to wait was also part of Hawk's plan, granting her an even bigger lead in her race to the Nest.

Can you stand? Isha asked Kilian.

I think I've twisted my ankle. He held it higher, balancing on his good leg. *I'm fine. Be careful.* His mindlink thrummed with fear. *Don't let Leofric waste your life.*

Squeezing his arm briefly, Isha left the shield-wall.

As soon as she moved, arrows came down like hail. She gritted her teeth, praying the shield would hold. She was acutely conscious of the vambrace around her arm, of the fact that leather could slow, but not stop, arrows. She pushed through bushes that came up to her thighs, and she stepped on them cautiously, brambles catching at her clothes. She prayed the bushes were growing *on* something and that she wouldn't sink through them; she tried not to imagine being swallowed by branches like quicksand, bowing under her weight. She flinched as two particularly vicious shots broke through the wood of her shield. They stuck out like teeth in front of her face, as if her shield had grown two pointed canines.

She tucked her head under her forearm, breathing in the smell of leather. Before a shot touched her head, it would have to go through the armour and her arm. She was smaller than her shield, so as long as she held it at the right angle, it would be impossible to aim for her legs or chest. She would be fine, as long as she kept her cool.

She stared at her feet, making sure to put them down flat, squeezed between the thicker thorn bushes, and tried to ignore the thuds above her head, knocking her shield against her skull.

You're far enough. Isha became aware, as Ninian mindlinked with her, of what was happening. Several soldiers, all mages, had been sent away from the core of the army at the same time, spreading out like tendrils. They were Lord Leofric's eyes. *Look up. Tell us where the archers are.*

Isha took a deep breath. There was no refusing. A perfectly coordinated army only worked if its members obeyed the head mage. It was all very well for Kilian to advise her not to squander her life, but if she didn't comply, her mind would be taken over and she would be puppeted instead. Better to be in control; better to be able to decide on the safest way to serve.

What would be the least risky approach? Slowly, she lowered the shield in front of her, still protecting her arms and chest, and peeked the top of her head above the shield to look around her. She caught glimpses of armour, red armbands, a glint of sunlight off a helmet. She only just had time to lift her shield again as an arrow whistled past her, missing its mark.

She shared what she had seen. *Again*, Ninian answered. *We need more.*

Isha ducked above her shield then hid again. She did so three times. Each time, her heart sped up and she wondered if this was how she would die, without a chance to defend herself, without glory, with an arrow through the mouth or neck. One bounced off her shield and skidded upwards, only narrowly missing her eye.

At last, the high mages had seen enough. Ninian shared everyone's visions, creating a global view of the trees around the army and where the Renegades were placed. It was like floating out and away from her body: Isha became part of something bigger, a creature that could perceive its surroundings through many eyes, in which her physical self was but a small limb amongst many. The army was spread out in coils like a snake. The archers were perched in trees, at regular intervals, and had been patient enough to wait for the Nest to be in their midst before shooting. Based on the scouts' mindlink, Ninian pinpointed them.

Instructions washed down the army; the snake shivered. The archers had stopped shooting; they were waiting, poised, for an opening.

Two things happened at the same time.

Without any giveaway, without a word being spoken, the shield-wall broke. All the Nest's archers rose above the shields, took aim, and released. At exactly the same time, ungifted foot soldiers rushed towards the Renegades' trees, three to four to an enemy, and climbed them to take them down. The Renegades were left with a few split seconds to decide whether to aim for the other archers or for the foot soldiers – or whether to run.

Blood on the branches. Bodies dropping, breaking smaller branches, not always reaching the ground, sometimes hanging from above. Arrows in leaves, in branches, hitting living wood or shield planks, or sometimes, crucially, hitting flesh, scratching bone, breaking teeth, tearing holes.

It was brief, bloody, efficient. It was hard not to be impressed by how deadly the Nest could be. Mindlink allowed the army to move like a monster, not a group of people. Death to individual soldiers were mere wounds to the beast.

Isha became aware of straps biting in her arms and sweat and salt on her tongue. A kher archer slipped from a branch and landed not far from her, crashing through the underbrush. Isha rushed towards her, heart in her mouth, but when she arrived the kher was in no shape to fight. Her arm was bent at an angle, the wrist clearly broken, a bruise already spreading across the hand. The arrow stuck out of her other arm, having neatly gone through the biceps.

Take prisoners, if possible. Leofric's voice, relayed by Ninian. It was, as always, cold and clear.

The kher groaned in pain as Isha disarmed her, hands fumbling for the knife still in her belt, aware of how close she was, close enough to feel the kher's breath on the top of her head. The kher let herself be helped to her feet, walked three steps, and threw up. Only then did Isha notice the blood staining the kher's ear, running down the nape of her neck.

The kher finished spitting bile on the ground and looked up at Isha. Smiling wryly, she said something in Wingshade and pointed at her head. Frowning, Isha lifted her hand to her hair. An arrow had got caught in her curls. She felt the wooden shaft, stuck as neatly as a hair pin. The metal point had cut a few strands of hair, but her curls were thick enough to hold it. The incongruity of the situation made her want to laugh.

It was absurd, but here she was, smiling to the enemy. The kher's grin widened.

'*You nearly got me,*' Isha admitted, removing the arrow from her hair. Whether the kher understood Duskdweller iwdan or not, she chuckled.

Isha held the kher by the arm that wasn't broken, gripping her elbow. She was careful to keep her prisoner in front of her and to avoid touching any skin or horns. The Renegade leant heavily into Isha for support, limping as they headed back to the army; she was too battered to offer much resistance. It was bizarrely intimate – a warm body by Isha's side, rough armour brushing against her arm. She threaded her way through the crowd of mages and ungifted up to Lord Leofric, who had cleared a small area at the foot of a tree, on a cascade of roots not unlike a staircase.

Only two archers had been captured alive. Isha helped her kher kneel on the wooden floor before taking a step back. The other prisoner was an ungifted man. The two Renegades glanced at each other, nodding in recognition, the same relief in their eyes – *you're alive, as well. I'm not alone.*

Glancing over his prisoners, Leofric ordered the kher killed.

It was a beat too fast for Isha to process. Maybe she had been naïve, but she hadn't anticipated Leofric would bother taking prisoners just to butcher them. An obedient ungifted sank his blade into the kher's throat, before Isha could think to move, before the kher could think to defend herself. It was a quick death. A garbled sound. Blood hissing instead of breath. A slumped body. Isha felt a tingle beneath her chin, where the ungifted's blade had cut; the cold, nearly soft, touch of steel under her jaw.

She had been a few feet away. She could have – she couldn't have. There hadn't been time.

Lord Leofric picked the human for what he needed. The archer had been battered by his fall, two teeth knocked out of his mouth. Sir Leofric's fingers sank into the man's face, thumb digging under his cheekbone, two fingers pressing next to his eye, hard enough to bruise. It was impossible not to tense, not to want to slap Leofric's hands away, or to avert her gaze. Isha was rooted to the spot, like one of the trees of the Overgrowth – immobile, frozen, yet growing on nothing, hollow, with only emptiness below.

The man tried to shake himself free at first, but as soon as Leofric's mindlink hit him, he went limp, as if he were a puppet with cut strings. His eyelids drooped. For a while no-one moved: the Lord of the Nest, in his golden armour, let his nails sink into the man's flesh, holding up his head, ignoring the slight drool at the corner of his victim's mouth. What Isha felt was like vertigo, like falling through the underworlds, if that feeling could curl in the pit of her stomach.

Even from a distance, it was clear the mindlink was brutal. Leofric pillaged the man's thoughts thoroughly, taking his time.

With his free hand, Leofric lifted his pendant. He normally kept it safely tucked against his skin, beneath his chainmail.

When he pulled it out from beneath his clothes, the mercury within shimmered. With mindlink, he tore out a shred of the archer, a slice of self, as thin as a sliver of skin flayed off a face, and placed it within the quicksilver, blending the memories with the metal. It was a particular kind of abuse, one only mages could perceive, the theft of thoughts.

When Leofric let go, the man's head lolled, unable to sustain its own weight. He let out a long, drawn-out moan, not as if he were in pain, but as if he couldn't hear the sound of his own voice and was trying to find it again. He ignored the corpse of his friend beside him.

'I know Hawk's trajectory,' Lord Leofric announced. He slid his pendant away, out of sight. 'We'll cut off the Renegades at Byluk's Hoofprint.'

He didn't spare a glance for the lacunant he'd made as he returned to his horse. His high mages followed. An ungifted soldier hesitated, checking the mages and the Renegade, adjusting his hold on his dagger. He was the man who had slit the kher's throat. He hadn't much cared for her, but he cared now, for this man. Maybe he didn't relate to khers, but he did relate to a soldier who, like him, had no magic to defend himself. His thoughts were obvious even without mindlink. What to do with the lacunant? Leave him, and hope the Renegades might find him, or that he might be able to survive on his own? Grant him a quick death? Keep him with the army and pray Leofric didn't notice?

The ungifted spotted Isha watching him, jumped, then backed away with a bow, hastily shuffling back to his comrades. Isha unknotted her water pouch and placed it beside the lacunant, who was staring at his hands, flat against a root, sing-songing something. She was light-headed, floating. Nothing struck her as real.

She rejoined the army. They were tending to their wounded: a doctor was fussing around Starling, while Kilian was strapping his ankle by himself. It wasn't sprained; the pain had surprised him, but it would recede quickly.

All that was left was wood stained crimson. Blood dripping without a sound into the underworlds. And a man running his fingers along the bark, engrossed in the sense of touch.

* * *

While Lord Daegan focused on fortifying the Nest, Tatters and Passerine concentrated on defending the city. The river curved in the shape of an S, flowing from the south, cutting in front of the city's main gate – the Sunpath Gate and its drawbridge – then following the city walls on the northern side. When it reached the other side of the city, it curved the other way, north to south. The shallow waters also became deeper, creating a chasm that finally ended over the Edge. This meant that the northern side of the city was well-defended: any army would have to wade through when trying to attack, leaving them vulnerable to the city's archers.

The problem was the southern side, around the Farmers' Gate. The ungifted were given the thankless task of digging ditches, cutting down trees, building fortifications. The siege weapons were placed on the other side of the makeshift walls, protected by the ditch, to launch stones at incoming soldiers.

With Leofric out of the way, the first thing Passerine had done was negotiate a deal with Lord Daegan. Despite his reluctance, even Daegan had to admit the Nest was not winning this war without its guards. The supreme mages agreed to offer the khers who were ready to fight for the Nest a 'blood right' – a form of citizenship. To all intents and purposes, they, and up to five members of their family, would become honorary ungifted. They could have normal jobs. They could own property outside the Pit. Male members of the family could carry arms. Finally, they would not be harvested for baina. Their bodies, in death, would be as sacred as a human's.

The blood right only came into practice once blood had been spilled: the rights would only be granted after the war. Still, it was the best offer the mages had ever extended to the iwdan.

With Daegan's permission, Tatters now had to coordinate a mixed group: ungifted, mages and khers, who would all be fighting together.

Even from afar, as they crossed the Farmers' Gate, Tatters could see his groups weren't mingling. He spotted Arushi and a few other khers, an all-female cast of guards. They had brought stacks of shields and wooden weapons, bundled together with rope, as asked. Tatters caught Arushi's gaze. He smiled, but her expression stayed wary. Across her hands and wrists, she still had the temporary tattoos of grief for her sister, smudged where the rope had scraped her skin.

The apprentices and young mages were off to one side, form-ing a semi-circle, rubbing their arms in the cold, kicking dew off clumps of grass. They were chatting, but through mindlink, so the khers couldn't hear them. Beside them, standing aloof, were the Sunriser mages. They were also talking, both in mindlink and out loud, but only in Wingshade, excluding the Duskdwellers.

The ungifted were divided into two groups: professional guards and enlisted folk. The guards clearly felt they were elite, or at least more elite than the other ungifted, and they were joking loudly, bumping shoulders and bashing fists in a show of strength to hide their nervousness. The enlisted, aware they were neither mages nor adept at weapons, were shyly standing at the edges, hardly daring to look up.

The air was sharp and clear. The white sky was patched with grey. As Tatters and Passerine drew closer, all eyes landed on them – the browns and blues and blacks of humans, the deep dark irises of khers.

Passerine took the lead and addressed the crowd: 'Thank you to the iwdan for helping us today.' The contrast between his respectful address to the khers and the tell-tale black of his robes struck Tatters.

Maybe that's what I sound like now, he thought. *Powerful and condescending.*

Passerine continued, 'First of all, I would like to tell you about the blood right.' He explained it in broad strokes – Tatters studied the khers' faces closely, trying to gauge how they were taking the news. It was an eclectic mix: surprise, disbelief, anger, hope. Arushi's face was studiously neutral.

The blood right was materialised by an iron ring. Any kher who agreed to it could carry it, to show their affiliation to the Nest. When Passerine explained the blood right would only come into effect after the war, Arushi asked, 'And if we die during the fight?'

Passerine inclined his head. 'Then up to five members of your family will benefit from the blood right. They need only show us the ring.'

Once he had detailed the conditions of the blood right, Passerine moved on to more practical considerations. 'We will combine mindlink and sparring. I am confident the iwdan and guards can help everyone learn the basics. Once everyone is comfortable with their weapons, we will form two groups. We will fake an attack on the gates, so we can train in more realistic conditions.'

Excited whispers rose, but Tatters felt his stomach drop. The mages couldn't even fight yet. They couldn't learn at the pace the war required.

What choice do we have? Lal shared his misgivings, but she had a harder heart. *These kids will fight the Renegades, with or without training.*

He recognised most of the younger mages: the ones with a serious mien; the ones distracted by something being said or done beside them; the ones who dismissed speeches as faff and didn't listen; people he had taught once, or seen in the corridors, or given a piece of advice while sharing a beer. They were all so young. Had he ever been that young? Apprentices, only a few days ago. Adults, now. If Hawk made it to the city, she would treat them as such.

What is the collective noun for a group of mages? he mused. *A flight? A gaggle? A charm, maybe. A charm of mages.*

It's a prattle if it's apprentices, said Lal, drawn into the game.

An unkindness if it's high mages, Tatters added.

A murder of lawmages, said Lal. *Like a murder of crows.*

Passerine was still speaking. He introduced Tatters as their teacher for today, from whom they'd all be taking instructions. When Passerine was done, Sir Dust grinned widely.

'Ah, a fellow Pearl! The Mad Sehwol was supposed to be a compatriot, although I always doubted it.'

'How did you survive the Scarlet Siege?' Lady Mayurah asked abruptly.

'Would you believe me if I told you I don't remember?' asked Tatters. 'Now, please grab a weapon.'

The humans flocked around the weapons as the khers unpacked them. The younger mages laughed excitedly, hitting the wooden swords together, with no skill, for the pleasure of the hollow sound they made. The older mages were less inclined to fool around as they armed themselves. It was easy to tell who had military experience: if they had, they took a shield. If not, they resented carrying the heavy slabs of wood, about four feet high, which had to be strapped onto the left arm.

Tatters had never fought with shields when he lived with the Renegades – they were too heavy to alight with. At a stretch, he could carry his knife and a two-handed spear in lightborn shape, transforming those into light with him. That was the most he could manage. But aside from lightborns, everyone else should love their shield. It would probably save their life.

At some point, he would need half the people to use two-handed weapons and the other half to use a shield-and-sword combination, so they could be organised into a half-decent formation. But for now, this mess would do.

Once everyone had a wooden sword, khers included, Tatters called out: 'Place the tip of your weapons together.'

Khers and mages formed a circle, their swords touching at the centre. Only Passerine and Tatters stood aside.

'You are going to rattle your weapons together,' said Tatters. 'And when I tell you to, you'll break apart. This is a training circle. Once you've broken away from the centre, everyone is fair game. You can fight anyone in sight. If you get a hit that would have killed you if it had been sharp metal, you put a knee on the ground to indicate you're out. We're going for the last one standing.'

It had been a long time since he'd done the same exercise, under a harsher sun, on the other side of the world.

'Rattle!' he shouted.

A flock of seagulls took flight, startled at the thunder of practice weapons bashing together.

'Break!'

The khers and ungifted guards knew this exercise – they were quicker off the mark. As soon as they heard the cue, they jumped backwards, shields high, keeping themselves out of reach. The mages found themselves with their backs to the khers, becoming easy prey. Lady Mayurah, Tatters noticed, wasn't fooled. She was amongst the first mages to hasten away from the centre, spinning to block blows from the sides, slipping in the mud in her effort to protect her back.

After that, the fight proceeded swiftly. The khers were at an advantage as the sticks were lighter than metal, and thus easier to use than their normal weapons. They had better training than the ungifted guards. They slapped their swords against the mages' backs and elbows, no doubt with a bit of vicious satisfaction at being allowed to hit back, for once. The mages and untrained ungifted fumbled and dropped what they were holding, or swung their shields wildly left and right to parry, not realising this meant they were leaving openings on the other side. Some of them landed a couple of hits, mostly on other humans.

Soon, as expected, only khers were left standing. Arushi crouched behind her shield, barely moving her feet and her wooden blade, never giving her colleagues an opening. When she twisted sideways, the shield covered all her body. Only her toes and her horns poked out. After some running and swearing, only Arushi and another iwdan were left standing – Tatters gathered she was called Tara. She had a black eye, which no-one dared point out, probably a remnant from the blockade. Most khers had bruises and scratches that were best ignored.

The two women circled each other with the attentiveness of soldiers who were used to fighting together. Everyone was watching them from the ground, where bruised humans and khers were kneeling. Tara pounced forward, slashing her sword towards Arushi's neck. Rather than dodging, Arushi straightened, parrying the blade with her horns. The stick slammed against the horns, snapping in half. Ignoring the fragments of wood flying around her eyes, Arushi landed a hit on Tara's wrist, letting her sword run up the arm until it lodged in her friend's armpit.

'If this was metal…' started Arushi.

'Then you'd have a big chip cut out of your horns,' interrupted Tara.

Arushi was unruffled. 'You wouldn't have a right arm anymore.'

My, my, aren't khers competitive? said Lal. *Who could've guessed?*

'All right, let's end it there,' said Tatters, gesturing for everyone to get up again.

They did a few other circles, with similar results. The mages became more reactive. The fun wore off – their muscles were unused to the tough work, they were covered in bruises, and they wanted to avoid more hits to the joints. Their faces were flushed with effort, their knees wet with dew. No-one complained. They were saving breath to fight.

On the contrary, the khers were starting to enjoy themselves. They catcalled and encouraged one another, picking favourites and rivals they wanted to beat. For the moment, his disparate group wasn't blending, but Tatters hoped it would happen, given time.

After the third circle, as Tatters was considering whether it was time to change things up, Lady Mayurah dropped her wooden sword to rub at her arm.

'This is ridiculous,' she grumbled. 'Why aren't we using mind-link to control the softminds?' She meant the ungifted; softmind was a common Wingshade term for them. 'That would be the most efficient way to deal with feral khers.'

The thin, angular man called Sir Cintay tried to lessen the harshness of her question. 'There is no need to be rude,' he muttered. 'But I do feel we are not using our natural talents and are at a disadvantage.'

'We'll get to that,' said Tatters. 'For now, focus on the physical fight.'

Lady Mayurah's gaze was fixed on Tatters. 'Easy for the Mad Sehwol to say. We aren't all natural killers.'

This Mad Sehwol business was starting to grate on his nerves. He'd had many unflattering names in his life, but he hadn't wanted that one to stick.

At this point, Milky would be better, said Lal.

'I'd appreciate it if you called me Tatters,' he answered.

'Would you prefer another one of your titles?' Lady Mayurah's voice dripped venom. 'The Bloodslave, maybe? The Red Scourge?'

'Call me anything but the name I chose for myself, Lady Mayurah, and I will call you Lady Long-tailed Tit.'

Sir Dust exploded into such boisterous laughter that Lady Mayurah winced. He laughed like dogs bark, so loudly that it was unclear whether it was supposed to be friendly or not.

'I can be the Coal Tit, and our dear Lord Passerine can be the Blue Tit,' Sir Dust said. 'We'll make quite the convent. I suppose, sehwol, you will have to be the Great Tit.'

Despite himself, Tatters relaxed. Maybe it was only the familiar Pearls accent, or maybe it was Sir Dust's honest amusement. Consciously or not, Sir Dust had managed to break the tension. Passerine yielded a tiny smile, more out of politeness than anything else; Lady Mayurah grumbled a half-felt apology.

They resumed their training. They had precious little time and an army of youths who weren't ready to wield steel.

We're nearly done with the circles, Tatters decided. *Then we do lines, then we try defending the gates.*

Let them use mindlink for the lines, said Passerine, *so they'll be more coordinated.*

Make sure you have iwdan and mages in the same lines, so they're forced to talk to each other, Lal piped up.

As they were drawing together for another circle, Arushi, cheeks ruddy with cold and effort, turned to Tatters.

'It's all very good telling us what to do,' she said. 'Aren't you going to join in?'

A provocative glint lurked in her eye. Before Tatters could answer, Lady Mayurah said, 'Yes, I'd like to see you try.'

She still sounded grouchy; maybe she was sick of being beaten. A few other mages agreed with her, either out loud or through mindlink.

Care to join us? Lal asked Passerine.

I suppose I must. Even when he was using mindlink, something of his voice, the depth of it, remained.

Reluctantly, Passerine armed himself with a two-handed spear, slinging a shield across his back. Tatters thought of Hawk, how she brought people around her, how she never stood apart from her army but was always the first in the fray. He went to pick up a sword. People cheered: some of the younger mages, but also some of the khers and ungifted, obviously enjoying the idea of having a go at their leaders. Tatters lifted a shield – skies those things were heavy – and joined the centre of the circle.

They'll all be after you, warned Lal.

And I'm as rusty as the giants' gates.

'Rattle!' he announced. He liked the sound of wood bashing against wood, the feeling of his blade meeting resistance, aching to fight. He let the moment linger, while everyone was working themselves up to the right state of mind, warming their arms and their hearts. 'Break!'

He darted away from the centre, ducking behind his shield, trying not to slip on the wet grass.

To your right! said Lal.

Tatters swerved to catch the hit, keeping his shield arm folded across his chest so he wouldn't be tempted to move it away from his body. He put up a decent fight, overall, although Tara landed a strike in his ribs that winded him, and he went down well before the end.

Once he'd put a knee to the ground, he got a chance to observe Passerine. It was clear he hadn't been away from Hawk for long and wasn't as out of shape. He moved gracefully, keeping his enemies at a distance, slicing or stabbing with his spear at anyone who tried to close the gap. The iwdan realised too late he posed a real threat: he won the round.

They gathered for another attempt.

'Do you know that people at the Nest are saying you're our only chance against the Renegades?' asked Arushi. 'So much for that theory.'

'Give me a chance,' Tatters said. 'I'm warming up.'

He didn't fare much better during the next circle. A group of khers, without concerting each other – or maybe they had chatted between the exercises – decided to gang up on Passerine. Tatters only noticed them as he put a knee to the ground after a particularly sneaky blow to the small of his back.

Passerine was taller than most khers, unintimidated by them banding together. As they drew closer, he dropped his spear's backhand, tucking it under his elbow so it wouldn't droop downwards, and grabbed for the closest horn. It was clear the kher wasn't expecting it. She shouted in surprise as he tugged to destabilise her before throwing her to the ground. Tatters watched, shocked, as Passerine demonstrated what fighting dirty could achieve: using every advantage of height and strength and a ranged weapon, hitting people with the backhand of the spear when needed, or with his elbow, he took out most of the iwdan opposing him.

All the others are too proper, too technical, Lal pointed out. *He isn't too precious for punches or kicks. He's not unskilled, just unscrupulous.*

Yes, said Tatters. *Like he expects to die if he loses.*

The last one remaining was Tara. She closed the distance with Passerine before he could place his spear between them – good reflexes – but when she lifted her sword he gripped her hand, pommel and all, and twisted. With a cry, she loosened her hold on her weapon. He was pulling her blade out of her grasp when, fuelled by the same heightened adrenaline that obviously burnt through Passerine, Tara headbutted him.

He staggered back. A silence descended, sudden after the clash of blades. Tatters could hear some of the mages' intakes of breath. Passerine was clutching one hand to his face; he lifted the other in a sign of surrender, dropping to one knee. Tara stared after him, trying – and failing – to hide how horrified she was. When Passerine moved his hand, it revealed blood pouring down his nose.

Now a kher has hurt a high mage, Lal said. *Great. So much for peace.*

After the blockade had been treated so poorly, Tatters didn't want to imagine what punishment the Nest would put together for an iwdan successfully bruising a mage. A few training bumps were acceptable, as long as the khers gave the impression of holding back, of playing nice – but an attack to the face felt different. Tentatively, he announced the end of the circle. People got to their feet, staring at Passerine expectantly.

Passerine wiped his nose, which thankfully didn't appear broken, and extended his arm for Tara. It took her a second to understand the gesture and to touch wrists with him.

'Good work,' he said, unfazed. 'But let's not go overboard, shall we?'

And with that, the incident was dealt with. Maybe he had

trained with the Renegades for long enough that this didn't feel like anything but routine; maybe he was pretending he'd forgotten how a high mage would usually treat a kher who won, even fairly, against them. He acted unfussed, like nothing out of the ordinary had happened.

Bless the underworlds, thought Tatters.

'Maybe it's time to switch to line battles,' was all he said out loud.

Tatters organised them into two lines, shields and swords in front, spears and poleaxes at the back. He led one group, Passerine the other. With their longer range, the spears could try to slip past enemy shields, either to the sides or above, and the axes could wrench them open, all the while hiding behind their allies' shields. The people holding shields, with their shorter, one-handed weapons, could block the enemy's strikes, or bash at their spears to force them downwards. Often, a line broke when a couple of shield-wielders fell, leaving a gap, which made it easy to kill the people on either side of the hole.

Mages were better at this, because they immediately knew where there was a gap and could quickly communicate through mindlink if they saw a blow menacing an ally. If push came to shove, they could take control of ungifted to fight using their limbs. It evened out their lack of training. The ungifted guards could, thanks to the mages' mindlink, share knowledge and battle-awareness with the other humans, information travelling as fast as thought through the line.

Tatters had lost most of his old reflexes but some of them came back after a couple of bouts. It was an intoxicating sensation, both being himself and elsewhere, battling while being aware of every one of his allies' limbs and weapons and failures and victories, mind spread out thin across the line, like an animal with too many arms and legs learning to master them all. It was a visceral, shared form of combat.

Still, their form was far from ideal. The mages were confused by the way the khers acted independently. They tended to focus too much on mindlink, then got disarmed and hit because they weren't parrying anymore. When the inevitable shoves down the line bumped human and iwdan together, the mages lost their magic, and often panicked. Ungifted were stuttered in and out of mindlink, depending on who they were touching, which was jarring.

Rather than calling out vocal orders, mages blamed the khers for their lack of discipline. The khers, in return, blamed the mages for being clumsy soldiers. The ungifted stayed quiet, but it was clear they blamed everyone else for interfering, mentally and physically.

They're not listening to each other, Tatters realised.

Surprise, surprise, said Lal.

Somehow, he had to encourage them to mingle. He put an end to the line-battling exercises.

'That was a good start,' he lied. 'Now we'll work in pairs.'

He paired off khers with humans and, when there weren't enough khers to tutor everyone who needed it, he paired the ungifted guards with mages.

'See what you can teach each other,' he said. Hopefully that would help. At least they'd be forced to learn each other's names.

He glanced over the ragtag band they formed, as rundown as the Renegades had once been, spread across the grass, messily trading blows. The gates of the city loomed behind them, but they weren't caught in its shadow. The sun had cleared patches of blue in the grey quilt of the sky. He strolled between the pairs, trying to instruct them on how to improve. It was more difficult than teaching mindlink. He knew less; he knew only that this was something they needed to learn. Passerine also observed and advised, like an old crow hopping between groups, cocking his head sideways as he surveyed the fights, eager, it seemed, for carrion to feed on.

Tatters pushed back against the images that threatened to flood him, the memories of training with blunted weapons, the first time Hawk had strapped a shield to his arm. Passerine standing between the trees, the glint of his spear against the red foliage. The smell of damp wood. The taste of crushed berries and clear water.

When he reached Arushi, she was duelling Sir Cintay. They were both polite and professional. It was clear Sir Cintay was losing, if only from the mud smeared over one of his sleeves up to the elbow. That must have been a nasty fall. Grateful for a break, he took Tatters' arrival as an excuse to stop the exercise. Arushi also lowered her weapon. One of her horns looked crooked – it was barely visible, but to the expert eye, to someone who knew her well, it was possible to tell it had been damaged recently.

'What advice are you going to give me, then?' There was an edge to her smile, another emotion behind the playfulness.

She is angry, said Lal.

Do you think so? He hoped not. Her smile bared her teeth. *Mildly annoyed, maybe?* He wondered if it was the blood right that had angered her, for being too little, too late.

'I wouldn't dream of giving you advice,' he said, to appease her. 'I was checking on Sir Cintay.'

Sir Cintay nodded, then dropped his wooden sword, so he could rub his bruising wrist. He had a drawn expression as he said, 'I'm afraid I'm not a natural.'

'No, no, please tell me, I'm all ears,' Arushi interrupted. 'Impart your lightborn wisdom to me.'

Ah.

Her smile didn't waver, but it became closer to a sneer.

You should have seen this coming, said Lal.

Arushi lifted her sword. It was only because he had been training that he saw the arc of her arm and guessed she was going in for a swing. It was a half-teasing, half-you've-pissed-me-off sort of tap. Old habits kicked in. He skipped out of the way, stooping so he could grab Sir Cintay's sword. Now he had raised the stakes – she hadn't expected to miss. The second blow was faster. When he parried it, the shock ran up his arm.

Lal was unsympathetic. *This is what comes from flirting with soldiers.*

Sir Cintay gaped. A few other sparring groups paused. Arushi had made herself known as the best soldier around and Tatters was their teacher, so a spat between them was bound to attract notice.

'Maybe we should do this later?' he said, taking a defensive stance just in case. He didn't have a shield, and she did.

Arushi shrugged. She had the upper hand, after all. She pushed forward, leaving him with no choice but to step backwards.

'Were you going to tell me one day?' she asked. 'Say, introduce me to your family and call lightning down from the sky?'

Before he could answer, she lunged. He threw himself sideways and only just managed to deviate her sword with his, pushing it away from his stomach. This brought him too close to her shield, which she slammed into him, making him stumble back. She could have pushed her advantage, but she was toying with him. She let him recover his balance.

Now everyone had noticed what was happening.

'Is there anything else I should know, for that matter?' Their audience didn't seem to bother her. Maybe she was doing this the iwdan way, sharing it with the tribe. 'Anything important that you really should have told me straight away, like the fact that you can fleshbind, that you are a lightborn, that you are Passerine's collarbound?'

Tell her Hawk was your first love, said Lal. *That'll go down well.*

Not helping, answered Tatters.

The next blow was strong enough that he felt it in his teeth, even though he blocked it. The leather of his shoes was flat and worn, and he skidded on the damp grass. From the corner of his eye, Tatters spotted Passerine stepping closer.

'Or maybe you will let me discover it when everyone else does,' Arushi said. 'I learnt the fleshbinding through Ka. The lightborn stuff when you deigned to alight in front of me, and half the Nest for that matter, to talk to some priests. What's the next big thing? Isha will knock at my door, maybe, and kindly let me know, as obviously you can't be bothered.'

They had drawn a crowd: everyone was staring rather than sparring. Hopefully they understood this as leaders butting heads, not as a romantic spat. Horn-humping was still illegal.

Are lightborns exempt? Lal mused. *You should ask a priest.*

The priests believed touching a kher was bad enough. *Let's not*, said Tatters.

'Catch,' said Passerine.

Tatters reacted to his voice before he could quite process what he had said. He saw the long piece of wood coming his way and only just had time to grab it, letting go of his sword in the process, forced to use both hands to hold the hefty stick.

It was a two-handed spear.

That is a very unhelpful way of being helpful, Tatters mindlinked towards Passerine. *Can't you use your authority to put an end to this?*

Oh, I wouldn't dare interrupt, Passerine answered.

Tatters turned the spear upside-down, so the metal tip pointed behind him, and he was aiming at Arushi with blunt wood. The two-handed weapon was taller than him, and although it wasn't as good at protecting its wielder as a shield, it had enough range to keep the enemy at a distance.

Arushi let him find his bearings, but she wasn't smiling now. 'Care to answer?' she asked.

'I wish I had a good answer,' he said. 'But to be honest, no, I don't think I would have told you. It didn't feel safe.' *Nothing feels safe.* 'The more I tell you, the more at risk you are.'

This wasn't the right thing to say. Arushi's face closed.

'Can you use that?' she asked, indicating the spear with her chin.

'Once upon a time I could, yes, but I would rather...'

She attacked. She was faster than him: she pushed past the end of the spear, slammed it sideways with the shield, and charged while he was struggling to regain control of his weapon.

Alight out of the way! advised Lal.

There was a split second when Tatters could have done something, but he hesitated. Alighting seemed like an overreaction. Then the moment was gone, and Arushi was upon him, a compact ball of wood and horns. His balance disrupted by his heavy spear, he fell on his back on the slippery grass, keeping his weapon in front of his face to protect it, holding it horizontally above him.

Arushi put her foot on the spear, pinning it to his chest, and him to the ground. She leant her weight into it – not enough to hurt him, but enough to stop him from squirming. Stray locks of hair fell down her cheeks when she bent towards him.

'I don't tell anyone anything,' he said. 'It's nothing personal.'

He tried to smile, to defuse the situation, but her frown didn't loosen. She pushed closer to him, resting her wooden sword on the soft, muddy soil.

'You can fight better than that,' she said. 'Where's all the flashy lightborn flying you can do? Or the fleshbinding, for that matter? Do you know why you're not using it?'

He didn't answer. He wasn't sure what she was getting at.

'You trust me not to hurt you,' she said. 'I wish I could trust you not to hurt me.'

Her words punched much harder than her fists. He wanted to answer something, but anything he could say died on his lips. She had dark irises, as black as her hair, as black as the mud beneath the bright green grass. Everything glinted with wet and rain. A line showed across her horns where Tara had smashed her sword.

'It's not true that you don't tell anyone anything. You would tell your sister the truth.'

Not always by choice, though, said Lal.

Arushi took a step back. Somehow, he didn't think the ache in his chest was a bruise. While he picked himself off the ground, shaking his cape to get the clumps of grass off the fabric, she turned to the gawkers.

'What are you lot looking at?' she snapped.

Everyone dutifully pretended to be absorbed in their training.

* * *

After a couple of hours, they paused for a break. The khers and ungifted carried buckets to the river and returned with ice-cold water – Tatters forced some of the apprentices to contribute. The factions were starting to interact, if only to gossip about Arushi's outburst. They had been thrown together long enough to get to know each other, without quite meaning to. Tatters spotted Sir Dust holding out his hand to Tara, to help her carry her bucket. Where they had been training, the grass had been trampled into mud, so they had to move further away to find a spot where they weren't treading in sludge.

He also noticed a few khers chatting with Passerine, distrustful frowns not quite hiding their yearning for the hope the blood right gave. Passerine was explaining to them how to procure themselves the iron rings, from one of the Nest's smiths in charge of the distribution. It was unclear, from their postures, whether they were convinced or not. It was clear, however, from the wary glances of the other khers, that this would be a divisive subject at the Pit.

Once he was done, Passerine joined Tatters. They both kept away from the heart of the group, giving them space to talk and quench their thirst without their leaders breathing down their necks.

'You've lost your fighting skills,' said Passerine.

'I thought I was getting them back.'

'You're decent at dodging,' Passerine admitted with a shrug. His voice was still a surprise to Tatters, even after all these years, so deep it seemed to echo from caves within his chest. 'You fight to evade. But when Hawk gets here, avoiding her isn't going to be an option.'

Passerine's profile was whipped by the strong wind, his cropped hair pushed backwards as if plastered to his skull, as he watched over their miscellaneous band. Lady Mayurah and Sir Cintay were sharing a cup, dunking it into a bucket. Sir Dust playfully splashed some water towards a younger mage, earning himself glares from the ungifted who had carried it.

Passerine spoke matter-of-factly. 'You're going to have to teach them how to kill.'

Tatters decided that the shiver that went through him was only due to the breeze. 'I don't think it's something you learn. It's something you do.'

That was where Lady Mayurah was wrong: nobody was a natural killer. It was something one became. And it was another lie, to believe they could win this war. A side could win, maybe, but people only lost.

It was uncomfortable to stand together, to listen to the wind rustling through Passerine's cloak, to his soles squelching against the damp earth. It should have been the comfortable silence of old friends, but it wasn't. It was filled with questions, as if neither of them was quite sure the other wasn't a threat.

'There is another solution,' Passerine said. 'I may be able to unlock the giants' magic hidden within the Nest.' He paused. 'But I would need your help,' he admitted. 'It is lightborn magic.'

'What can it do?' Tatters asked.

'That will depend on our ability to use it,' Passerine answered. 'It may be an escape route, it may be a weapon. It may help or hinder.'

Talking with Passerine was like wrestling an eel: he always escaped. As soon as you thought you had a grip, he slid away.

'Well, it cannot hurt to try, I suppose,' Tatters said.

What could go wrong, after all? Lal asked.

Chapter 6

By the time Tatters had finished the drills at the city gates, it was evening. He met up with Arushi in the Pit, after her last patrol at the Nest.

'We need to talk,' he said, after greeting her and her family.

She was unimpressed. 'Do we? I guess that depends on if you'll tell me the truth, for a change.' However she mellowed enough to add, 'Wait here. I need to change.'

When she returned, she had put on a blue and green arrud, which hung loosely around her shoulders. It was the colours of the sea, water and algae and sun and darker depths, blue and green and flecks of silver. Underneath, she wore a human shirt, bleached, with puffy sleeves, and looser trousers than her uniform normally allowed. She looked relaxed, unguarded. Beautiful.

'You look lovely,' Tatters said.

'I wish I could say the same about your robes,' she answered, 'but truth be told, I preferred the old one.'

'You like me unkempt?' he asked, mischievous, hoping to draw a smile out of her.

She was unamused. 'I prefer you out of uniform.'

Unfortunately, that's what Passerine's oversized black garments were, in the end: a statement.

They headed out. The Pit was full of bustle. A festival would soon be taking place – the Sar festival, if Tatters remembered correctly, which, like the human Homecoming, was about rebirth and spring. Visitors from nearby cities and villages had gathered for the occasion: Tatters spotted many unfamiliar faces. Even more surprising, he saw khers who had sanded down the outside of their horns and bleached them, like Mezyan did, which Tatters had always thought was a Sunriser iwdan tradition. The white horns stood out amongst the black ones, stark and naked. There were also a couple of mixblood folk with stunted horns, human features recognisable despite the red skin, who mostly kept to themselves in smaller groups. Horn-humping was illegal, but when halfblood children were born despite the laws, they were reluctantly tolerated by the mages. Their parents were another matter.

Tatters couldn't help but look at people's hands. He spotted a few iron rings, but not as many as he would have liked.

As they crossed the Pit, before he lost courage, Tatters said, 'I want to apologise.' He sucked in a deep breath. Even the smells were different today: pots of scented oil were being opened, religious items with heady aromas. The smoke from the pipes left a new tang on the tongue – maybe they burnt a different blend of herbs for the festival. 'And tell you the truth. Anything you ask.'

Beware what you promise, Lal said. *I'm not helping you out if she asks about Hawk.*

Arushi's gaze swept over the crowd. 'It's too busy in here,' she said at last. 'Let's head out.'

In the city, they didn't hold hands, so as to not attract attention. Even with their hands chastely apart, a human and a kher together was rare enough to draw glances. The black robes helped: ungifted didn't dare challenge a high mage on the law. They stared, but they didn't curse or point fingers.

'Everyone is talking about your new blood right,' Arushi said, as they ambled towards Siobhan's statue. 'I have to say, I didn't think it possible, but you've managed to mess with us even more. You've got everyone bickering like children. No-one agrees on what to do about the offer.'

'Take it,' he said immediately. 'Force the mages to recognise you as citizens.'

Arushi didn't answer at first. When she did, she wouldn't hold his eye. 'I don't want to argue about the war.'

'Let's not talk about it, then,' Tatters said. 'As if it isn't happening.'

For one night, I guess you can pretend, said Lal.

After crossing the main square, Tatters guided Arushi into a side-street where a Sunriser family, eager to make some coin out of the Duskdwellers, had set up a makeshift grill. He'd spotted them a couple of weeks ago, having been attracted by the smell of grilled fish. They had built a fire, and were stuffing fish with wild garlic, battering everything with crumbs, before cooking it. They were Samudra, from the shore of the Inner Sea, who had changed their fishing grounds to the treacherous waters of the river that crossed the Edge. They still wore driftwood trinkets, polished shells and pieces of glass and colourful pebbles, hanging from their belts in complicated patterns that revealed their tribe and trade.

A couple of people were waiting for their turn, so Tatters and Arushi joined the queue. The centrepiece was a stocky metal grill suspended by two hooks: one dangling from a shopkeeper's sign, the other from a hastily-assembled pillar of wood and rope. The refugees fished by day, as far as Tatters could make out, and cooked by night, selling whatever excess they had. Poaching was illegal, but the Nest obviously didn't care enough to remove them.

When they reached the front, the young man who was cooking the fish flashed them a smile.

'An iwdan!' he said. He spoke the Duskdweller language with a typical Sunriser lilt. 'We sometimes fished with your kind, before we left the water tribes behind.'

He quickly turned over the fish which were sizzling above the fire.

'The water tribes?' Arushi repeated.

'Haven't heard of them?' he asked, his brow sweaty, his eyes on his work. 'The iwdan who have rafts. Nomads on sea, rather than on land.'

'Apparently they have huge drifting cities all roped together, big enough to form islands,' said Tatters. 'According to the stories.'

The boy shot him a startled look, belatedly realising they were together. His posture grew tenser.

Humans befriending iwdan must remind him of the Renegades, Lal said. *Not good memories, apparently.*

Tatters glanced at the silhouettes behind the young man. A few adults – other family members, he imagined – were seated along the wall running behind the grill. A couple were watching the clients, the food, sometimes throwing the branches they'd scavenged from the forest onto the flames. But not all had bright, lively eyes. One young girl – older than the boy, maybe nineteen or so – was drooling over her chin. One adult man, broad-boned, but thin with hunger and hardships, was tapping his nails against his teeth, repetitively, obsessively.

Victims of the shadows. Like he might have been.

'It's good to know our people still have places where they can be free,' Arushi said.

'The world is yours, tamya, the world is yours,' the boy mumbled. He took two slim sticks, which had been sharpened at one end, and stuck them through a couple of fish. 'Here you are,' he said, handing them over.

They took the fish, thanking him, and Tatters paid the young Sunriser.

'I know just where to eat these,' he said.

'Lead the way,' Arushi said, tentatively licking at some of the hot breadcrumbs.

He guided her to the Raudaz shrine.

Ironic, when you decided not to speak of war, Lal sneered.

How about you let me enjoy this, he answered, *and find some way to amuse yourself other than ruining the mood?*

The Raudaz shrine was in a small square off from the centre of town. Because the city was devoted to Groniz and Byluk, with the Temple just nearby, Raudaz lay half-forgotten in a narrower, grimier area. Mostly Tatters avoided reminders of Raudaz, but he had to admit this shrine was rather nice. It was a round wooden structure, not unlike the Temple in its architecture: a dome, pillars to uphold it but no walls, a ditch carved in stone running around it in which to discard the objects that heavied the soul. It had the added advantage of being isolated enough that they'd probably be the only people there.

But the features Tatters liked most were the threaded prayers. Along the rim of the roof, believers hung red items for Raudaz. The gifts went from frayed, faded pieces of thread to precious scarlet; from hand-knitted red wool to rope hastily rubbed with ochre. Usually, the shrine never had more than that, innocent pieces of trivia hanging from its beams.

But, of course, war was on everyone's minds.

This evening, the most common offering was a knife. It was traditional to knot a piece of red thread around the handle and tie the knife upside-down, the blades touching and clinking in the wind, an eerie echo to the windchimes.

'That's grim,' said Arushi. 'But I'm starving.'

Without any more ceremony, she sat on one of the stone benches that circled the shrine. Tatters settled beside her.

'Raudaz isn't just the lightborn of fighting.' He felt forced to justify himself. 'He can be the lightborn of love. Of passion, in general, be it anger or desire.'

Arushi took a bite of fish. 'Don't worry,' she said, still munching. 'I don't mind your outdoor tavern. The food is excellent, for one thing.'

Tatters ate his own portion. The garlic, cooked inside the fish, was like a crunchy core to the tender flesh. It tasted of distant shores, of standing with his toes in the sand, cold waves washing over his feet. Nostalgia squeezed his heart. Duskdweller food would never match this flavour of childhood.

Eating close together, Arushi's arm sometimes brushed against his, and Lal flickered in and out of his consciousness, like a hand brushing above a candle, light appearing and disappearing in turn. The sun, as it dipped beneath the Edge, set the red threads of Raudaz aflame.

'What an idea,' Arushi said after her meal, licking her fingers clean, 'to give garlic to someone you're hoping to kiss.'

Tatters laughed. He was relieved to hear her mention intimacy. 'Well, we've both eaten it now.'

Arushi leant her weight against him; he was grateful for it, for her, for the way she grounded him. Lal disappeared.

'I don't mind,' he said. The stone bench was cold and narrow, but he truly didn't mind. All that mattered was the warmth of her against him.

She smiled. When she nestled against him, her horns pressed two half circles against his neck. It wasn't altogether unpleasant. 'You're right,' she said. 'Who cares?'

She drew him to her until they were snuggled close, folded

together. He passed an arm across her shoulders, under her arrud. The rough wool scratched the back of his hand. It smelt of dye, and of her.

'But I have one condition.' Although they were cuddling, her tone was firm. 'No more lying and hiding. No more secrets. I'm sick of your secrets.'

The truth. It terrified him, but maybe that was why he needed Arushi, why her scent turned his head, why her body against his sped up his pulse.

'Yes,' he said. 'No more secrets.'

They stayed in that position, breathing in each other's presence, as if they would never get enough of each other's touch. The sun had all but set now, and the air was cooling. Still, like many young lovers, they had nowhere they could be alone, so they stayed outside.

'Before we go any further,' Arushi said, 'is there something I need to know you haven't yet told me?'

Hawk. The Renegades. The collar. Fleshbinding. Alighting. 'I can tell you a bit more, if you wish.'

So he did. As a story, it was a strange one. Growing up in the village with his mother and half-siblings and Lal. The boisterous sehwol children. How, when they grew too impious, the village talked of sending them to a mage convent. Or, that failing, of building a pyre, so the fire would turn their souls into lightborns. Their mother pushing them out the front door for their own safety, telling them not to return. Getting into trouble for illegal mindlink. Fleeing the lawmages. Alighting, Lal leaving her body, catching the eye of the Renegades, and everything that came afterwards. Tatters tried to keep it short, yet it was a long story.

'There. You have it all.'

Arushi made a thoughtful sound with the back of her throat. 'Why didn't you tell me any of this?' she asked.

'I didn't cross the Shadowpass to remember. I crossed it to forget.'

They watched the sky, the stars rising overhead as the mild spring night settled around them. He dipped down to kiss her; when their lips touched, a shiver arched down his back, tingling from the nape of his neck to his hips. The chimes of the shrine tinkled and tolled.

She pushed him away gently. 'We need to talk about this.'

He took her hand in his. He leant in as if to kiss her fingers, but when he felt her tense, he only placed his forehead against them, breathing in her smell.

'I'm not sure what you want us to be,' she said. 'Last time we had sex, you were so upset... And afterwards, we never got to talk. You were arrested, and you just disappeared.' She sighed. 'You are always disappearing, in a way. Every day, it feels, I learn something that changes everything I know about you. You keep shapeshifting.'

He kissed her hands then, as softly as he could, only brushing his lips against her knuckles, before straightening.

'I want... I would like us to be together. Lovers, or partners, would be the human words for it, I suppose.' He brushed a strand of hair back from her eyes, letting his fingers linger against her brow. She was beautiful, if anxious, in her thick blue arrud, which bulked and hid her body, but couldn't hide the graceful line of her neck, the strong, honest grip of her fingers. The arc of her arm, before it disappeared beneath the clothing, where patterned tattoos forever lined her skin.

'But maybe we should lay out some ground rules,' he admitted. He was glad to have chosen the secluded shrine: they were alone in the square to discuss this, with no-one to watch over them except, perhaps, the lightborns above.

'So, what was the problem last time?' she asked, resting her cheek against his shoulder. 'What can we do so you don't walk out on me after we sleep together?' Her tone was cheerful, but there was real hurt behind the words.

He wondered how to phrase this. A nightbird, quiet as a ghost, flew overhead, a pale shape swiftly come and gone. The knives' blades swung like sinister shards of silver, reflecting the rare light around the shrine.

'When we make love, I'd like us not to fleshbind with other people.'

She had started nuzzling against his neck, but she stopped and pulled a face. 'Never?'

He amended to: 'At least not without me knowing before-hand. Long enough beforehand that we can discuss it properly.'

'All right.' When she rested against him again, he kissed her hair. He could get used to this, he realised, sitting close, holding her in his arms, without Lal, without anyone but them and the stars.

'Another rule: I can have as many lovers as I want,' said Arushi.

So much for us two and the stars. This was a kher tradition he was familiar with, and it wasn't something he could ask her to leave behind. He nodded. 'As long as you don't bed them at the same time as me, fine.' He nudged her ribs. 'I didn't know you were one for having lots of lovers.'

She laughed and playfully shoved him back, not truly wanting him away, not letting go of his arm. 'Well, if you're not going to fleshbind, I'll need *someone* to stop sex from getting too dreary.'

'Ouch!' He found himself laughing too. 'So, you think it's going to be dreary, nothing less…'

Her face became solemn. She cupped his chin in her hand, and he reclined into her touch, resting against her calloused skin – the skin of a working woman, of a soldier.

'Listen,' she said, 'if I wanted another iwdan, if I wanted this to be easy, I could. But I want you. I want to make this work. But there is a huge difference between intimacy and sex. Between love and lovers.' She shook her head. 'The human tongue is too limited. There is the person you lie in bed with, and the person you share your life with. Those are different.'

She had wide, deep black eyes; a serious gaze.

'We share decisions. We share children. We share truth. We share the hearth. We needn't share sex, unless you want to. Lovers come and go. Loves, who stay, who see us through hard times, they are rarer. And precious.'

'I want this to work too,' he said. He wasn't sure how to answer the rest. His heart felt fill to burst.

When their lips met, they were slow, careful. His fingers were cold, and his legs ached from sitting on stone, yet warmth blossomed.

'There is the Sar festival soon,' Arushi said, breaking away first. 'The iwdan equivalent of your Homecoming.' Then, very cautiously, obviously conscious she was treading uncertain ground: 'It's a fertility festival.'

It was Tatters' turn to grimace. Thankfully, Lal was still cut off.

'Hear me out.' Arushi was undeterred. 'Young people who come of age usually have their first lovemaking night on the Sar festival. They choose a partner, and they bed only that one person. They share the fleshbinding with a small part of the community. It is, ah, how to put it, a softer way to be introduced to fleshbinding in groups, for pleasure.'

She gave him time to consider it, so he did. He tried to unknot the complicated tangle of emotions and desires.

'This...might be possible. Last time was nice. I mean...' The sex was good, but everything else was horrifying. How did you say that to someone you loved?

She was trying to be reassuring. 'It could be a small group, hand-picked. Say five or six of us, maybe? We could choose people you know, such as Ka.'

Tatters winced. 'No, no,' he said. 'Definitely not people I know.' *Imagine talking to Ka afterwards, knowing what it felt like for him. Worse, for him to know what it felt like for me.*

She cocked her head to the side, her horns touching his jaw-line. He kissed them, letting his lips rest against their rugged surface.

'Let me get this straight,' she said. 'You'd rather share with people you don't know?'

'By far,' he agreed. 'What about nice strangers, whom I've never seen before?' A thought struck him, and he hastily added, 'And no-one blood-related.' He cringed just at the thought.

She snorted. 'I don't get it. You'd rather *avoid* friends and family?'

'Skies, yes. A thousand times yes.' He wondered if she was going to ask him to justify this and, if so, how he would explain the visceral feeling that twisted his gut each time she mentioned it. It would be difficult to clarify why he was upset without insulting her, her family, her traditions.

But Arushi let it go, chuckling to herself, maybe at the strangeness of human ways. 'Don't decide now. But you do realise that we share blood to fleshbind so, technically, everyone is blood-related?'

'You know what I mean,' Tatters said. 'I'm not so hornless that I can't tell the difference between a hearth and a neighbourhood.'

They laughed. If someone had asked, Tatters would have said he was happy. Yet as he melted into Arushi's embrace, her arms stiffened.

He disentangled enough to see what had caught her eye. It was a Sunriser priestess. She had come to the shrine, he assumed to tend to it, with a bucket of cold water to wash its floorboards and pillars. She wore only coarse wool, undyed, with no shoes. She was staring. When he straightened, rather than turn away, she crossed the square towards them. Self-consciously, Tatters pulled away from Arushi's hug.

The priestess stopped in front of them. She put her bucket down. She had huge black catlike eyes that eclipsed all other features, and she had spotted the collar. And the nature of their relationship, as well. Tatters wasn't sure how much trouble the Temple could cause with an accusation of horn-humping – probably not much, with Passerine to shield them – but it could make for an unpleasant scandal. He braced himself for cries of blasphemy.

But the priestess's voice was quiet. 'I don't understand.'

'Think on it, then, rather than bothering us,' Arushi snapped.

The priestess ignored her. She was middle-aged, leaning towards old. She was small, with long, silky black hair, bronze skin. She wore a bracelet of red thread, which she'd knitted in patterns and interwoven with driftwood and ochre. It recalled a Samudra trinket, although no other charms adorned her. Dropped, no doubt, to lighten her soul.

'Why do you love and protect the khers?' she asked. She had eyes only for Tatters. Clearly she knew he was one of the fabled lightborns the mages had captured.

'I …' He fumbled for words. *I am not a god.* 'I want to love and protect everyone,' he said instead.

To his horror, she started weeping.

He got up hastily, throwing Arushi an apologetic glance. He led the priestess a few steps away, rubbing comforting circles into her shoulders. She clung to him like a woman drowning, mumbling incoherent words about two daughters being drafted for the war, not her own children but a poor widow's only future;

and having to explain to the widow that it was for the best; how it had broken her heart to wipe those tears, and how she had asked Osmund why the lightborns had sided with khers and slavery and the mages and war and cruelty, and not understanding his answer, and how she had been told to unburden herself to be lighter, but the more she let go, the heavier she felt, the more it hurt...

He wasn't sure what he could do but whisper inane consolations. Over her head, he glanced at Arushi, who was resting against the shrine's supporting pillar. Her face was blank. Idly, she was wiping her fingers on her trousers.

At last, the priestess rubbed her nose, sniffing. Her breathing, still choked, was levelling.

'Why? Why do you abandon us? Why do you leave us to suffer? We die when we run. We die when we fight. We die when we try to be heard.' She hiccupped into her hands. 'All the light's blessing goes to the khers. They take you away from us. They take all our light.'

'No,' he said, before he'd quite decided what else to add. She lifted those wide-blown pupils to him. He wondered how to explain it: kindness wasn't a resource that ran dry once it had been spent. A kindness given expanded, grew. And one suffering didn't cancel out another. Saying the khers and ungifted had to push each other down to survive was a convenient lie the mages told.

No blessing is so stingy that it doesn't include us all, Lal said. *Be generous, woman.*

Tatters decided to rephrase that somewhat. 'When the sun rises, it shines for the bugs, for the earth, for the stone, for the trees...' He wondered if he should add the khers to this list, but decided against it. 'For the beasts, for the humans. The sun that doesn't shine on you isn't lost or taken from you.'

The priestess listened intently, as if he were a fount of wisdom. He wished he hadn't forgotten most of his religious upbringing.

'There is enough light for everyone,' he concluded. Her focus was unsettling him.

She finished wiping her face on her wrists, pulling up her bracelet to spare it from tears and snot. He managed to persuade her she was tired, from fasting and holding vigils, and should return to the Temple. Nodding, she retrieved her bucket. He gently sent her on her way.

'Sorry,' he said, returning to Arushi's side.

He sat beside her, but they failed to retrieve the lost intimacy. Arushi seemed pensive. Her eyes followed the priestess until she'd left the square.

'If you had to choose,' Arushi said, and her tone sent his heart racing, even before he heard her question, 'between the Renegades and the Nest, what would you decide?'

Tatters closed his eyes briefly. 'I thought we wouldn't talk about the war.'

'Yes,' Arushi admitted. 'But this is important.'

He opened his eyes. The dancing knives winked, small flickering stars.

'Before you answer,' she said, speaking too quickly. 'I need to show you something. Someone.'

They had to walk back to the Nest first. They spoke little, but held hands when there was no-one else in sight.

When they crossed the bridge, the giants' gates loomed ahead of them, gaping, rusting. The lacunants slept beside the entrance, in temporary structures of packed sticks and mud, a weak defence against the night chill. Rather than crossing the gates, Arushi and Tatters skirted around them, following the outside walls. The lacunants were sleeping for the most part – a restless, fitful sleep – but a couple woke up as they passed.

Arushi had trouble finding who she was searching for: lacunants slept together for warmth, like hounds snuggled together in a kennel. Finally, she pointed towards a man bundled in dyed cloth, huddled at the threshold of one of the shelters. He was resting his head against the low entrance, only big enough to crawl through, with his face turned towards the warmth inside. He was sleeping deeply. At first, Tatters thought there was hay stuck around his ears, until he realised it was his hair's natural colour.

He couldn't see the man's face, but he took in his bulk, the colour of his curls and, when the clouds parted and the moon granted them some light, the marks of smallpox down his neck. He must have lived by the gates a while now, but covered in dirt, robes torn, diminished, hiding in the makeshift shelters, Tatters hadn't recognised him.

Or maybe finding a familiar face in this crowd of empty gazes was hard, especially as mages were so used to looking away, not wanting to see.

'Varun,' said Arushi.

'I used to call him Goldie to tease him,' said Tatters. He felt empty. He should feel victorious, maybe, viciously satisfied, but he was only dazed. 'What happened?'

Arushi hesitated. When she spoke, she whispered, maybe to avoid disturbing the sleeping lacunants. 'His memory was damaged by mindlink. Too damaged.' She explained that she had stumbled upon Varun in the prisons, while they had been hunting for Tatters. She'd asked Isha to cut off parts of his memories, so he wouldn't remember seeing them. Obviously, Isha had taken it too far. 'This is our doing.'

Tatters stared at Varun. A stain, maybe mud, maybe something else, had spread down the back of his robes and along his legs.

169

'Doesn't he have family?' Tatters asked. But family could be far. None of his own siblings would be able to tend to him, should he one day need to live beside the gates. 'Friends? People who care enough?' He pictured Sir Leofric working for months, maybe years, with Varun. Entrusting work and prisoners to him. Yet the head lawmage wouldn't spend coin to give his colleague decent care.

'I would have thought so,' said Arushi. 'Obviously not.'

They watched the once-lawmage in silence. His teeth chattered slightly, even through his sleep. It gave his snores a shaky, rattling rhythm. His dreams would be like his mind, broken, confusing; nonsensical and terrifying things that would haunt him until his body fell apart.

'I am showing you this, because, in the end, that is the only choice,' Arushi said. 'I didn't want it to end this way. But either we destroy them, or they destroy us. Blood or soil. I don't know if you've heard the story.'

'I have,' Tatters said. Although he hadn't thought about Itri's tale in a long time. 'I suppose I'm soil.'

Vengeance was a simple cycle. You hurt me, I hurt you. You hurt my friends, my friends hurt you. Yua was still dead. What comfort did it bring, to know a man with no memory of the wrongs he had done suffered and soiled himself and shivered?

'I will never side with the Renegades,' Tatters said at last. *Never again.*

'Even after what the Nest did to Yua?' Her voice was still soft, but sad.

'You don't know what the Renegades have done, to people just like Yua,' he answered.

'If I am forced to choose...' Arushi started.

Maybe it was her tone, or the regret in her eyes. But Tatters couldn't bear it; he interrupted her, blurting out, 'It won't come to that. I'm sure we can bring the iwdan and mages together, without the Renegades. The blood right is only the first step. You'll be able, in time, to make the mages recognise you as their equals.'

She hesitated. 'It's never been done before.'

'No. But that doesn't mean it's impossible.' If Hawk could change the world, shape it to her will, why couldn't they, as well? He desperately wanted to believe it.

'I guess you're right.'

She was agreeing, but her words still dropped stones inside his soul. He wondered if this was what the Temple meant, when it preached that love could burden someone, prevent them from flying.

They held each other close as if, should they clench their arms hard enough, should they grip with enough love, a rift wouldn't come between them.

* * *

The day they arrived at Byluk's Hoofprint, Isha's stomach was so knotted the ache was louder than her thoughts. The Hoofprint was a clearing in the Overgrowth where a huge tree was grow-ing sideways, in a half-circle reminiscent of a horse's shoe. The clearing itself was solid earth, underworlds be praised, but the top of it was lined by the wide trunk – or maybe it was a huge root, Isha mused – providing a natural wall. The clearing itself wasn't so much grass as moss, with small pine saplings poking out here and there.

From the Hoofprint westwards, the Overgrowth gave way to normal woodland. This meant it was a good meeting point where the Renegades could regroup before marching on to the

Nest. Hawk apparently planned to meet up with a couple of her independent battalions at the Hoofprint.

With this knowledge, rather than trekking through the Overgrowth, Lord Leofric had led his army back to the Sunpath. On the Sunpath, they moved faster than Hawk, as they weren't reduced to struggling through brambles but could benefit from a nice, flat, paved road. They had sped down the Sunpath, only turning when they'd come level with the Hoofprint. It seemed they had succeeded: the Renegades hadn't yet arrived. The Nest could ambush them here, cut them off at last.

They picked the higher ground, protected by the giant tree, strewing soil and sand where they built their firepits so as to not set fire to the moss. It was only early afternoon, but everyone wanted food and warmth and rest. The pace on the Sunpath had been just short of a run; they were exhausted. As they waited, their army lost its severe hierarchy. Everyone clustered by clan – mages, ungifted, followers who knew each other from the Nest.

Isha was too nervous to eat. Kilian, however, laughed more than before, as if trying to cram in all the happiness he could before the dreaded battle. He hadn't been so merry since they'd left the Nest. He was currently chatting animatedly with a young woman who was teaching him how to juggle. Although she knew it was only his way of coping, Isha found him difficult to bear. She couldn't muster even the smallest smile.

'I'll go stretch my legs,' she said.

'After what we walked today?' Kilian scoffed. 'The only thing I'm stretching now is my luck with these apples.' He winked, pleased with his wit, as he tried to juggle two apples in one hand. The one he dropped rolled down the wooden trunk, narrowly avoiding the firepit.

'See you soon,' Isha said.

She waved the people around her firepit goodbye. Ambling

across the army's camp, she tried to think of nothing, letting the background noises soothe her – talks, shouts, the roll of dice, the sound of armoured soldiers slumping backwards, the clang of weapons being set aside. Forests were silent, she'd noticed. When the birds weren't singing, the Overgrowth didn't sigh, didn't whisper. The human bustle reassured her.

At the top of the slope stood a series of tents. Most high mages had retired to nap, leaving guard duties to the foot soldiers. Yet as Isha walked past, she perceived the hiss of mindlink.

You will bow to my will.

She paused. The faint mindlink went unnoticed from the folk gathered around the firepits. The other high mages were either sleeping or consciously ignoring it.

It was coming from Lord Leofric's tent.

Despite her better judgement, Isha inched closer. The tent's flap was closed, so she couldn't see inside. She hesitated. It would be easy to pretend she hadn't heard anything, to continue her circuit back towards the main campfires. But unease tugged at her heart. She lingered.

He hasn't spotted you yet. The mindlink, addressed to Isha this time, had Caitlin's distinct lilt. It was also emanating from within the tent. Aside from magic, the space was silent. *You'd better get away before he does notice.*

Do you need help? Isha asked.

No answer. No mindlink, not a whisper. Her heart was hammering in her mouth.

There was no-one else. Clearing her throat, she pulled back the tent's flap and entered.

'Sir,' she said, wondering what excuse she might spin, 'I was looking for Caitlin and...' She trailed off mid-lie.

The tent was dim, with only the sunlight filtering through the fabric to see by. Leofric was seated on a wooden chair, which had been assembled by ungifted, which they had to dismantle every evening and carry on the horses' backs. Starling was cross-legged beside him, on the floor, close enough that he could pet her. He was running his fingers through her hair. As Isha's eyesight adjusted, she noticed how stiff the lightborn was, jaws clenched. She had a bandage around her neck, clean, well-maintained. It was hard to tell whether she was in pain or not – her stillness was unnatural, her features taut.

Caitlin was standing, as unsettled as Starling, if not more. Defensive mindlink swathed her.

'May you grow tall,' Lord Leofric said. The smile which lit up his face sent a shot of fear down Isha's spine.

'May you grow tall,' she repeated.

'Now I have all three concubines,' he said, indicating the three women with one sweep of his sleeve. He kept one hand in Starling's hair, not quite stroking anymore, not quite grabbing, yet. 'Lord Daegan and Lord Passerine are lucky men.'

She didn't answer, glancing askance at Caitlin. Caitlin was frozen, fists clenched down her sides. Slowly, Isha realised Leofric was trying to take control of her mind, trying to take control of her. He wasn't doing it in a brutal, open way: it was more like watching someone uncurling another person's fist, slowly pulling at the fingers. The strength he was putting into it wasn't all he could summon, if need be, but it was clearly unwanted.

'You are both meddlers,' Leofric said calmly, not releasing the force he was putting on Caitlin. 'But Isha, I know you are the better person. How about you take Caitlin with you? You could both entertain each other.'

He didn't want to keep Caitlin in, Isha understood belatedly, but to kick her out. To puppet her, as he would an ungifted, and march her away.

'I'll leave with Starling,' Caitlin hissed, 'or not at all.'

Leofric's hand knotted in Starling's hair, briefly, then let go. He still touched her, however, keeping his hand on her shoulder. Starling was hard to read, but it was clear her breathing was shallow. Isha had never seen anyone successfully frighten the lightborn, until now.

'Isha?' Leofric repeated. His tone stayed soft, as if he were hushing a wild animal. He was increasing pressure on Caitlin as he spoke. It was like watching an adult wrestle a child to the ground, not brutally, but with intent, sitting on their back and holding their wrists. It was clear she wouldn't be able to shield herself from his mindlink forever.

Now the fear was taking hold of Isha, as well. She tried to ignore her pounding heart. 'I'll take both of them off your hands, sir.'

If anything, Leofric seemed amused. 'I don't think you will, no,' he said. His hand slid from Starling's shoulder to the nape of her neck, thumb resting on her throat, fingers curled around the collar. The gold shone brighter at his contact, light streaming through his fingers. He forced Starling to turn her head towards him; although she posed little resistance, it was clear he was gripping her hard.

'You haven't seen this,' he said. 'You will leave Starling and I alone.' Starling winced at the way he was holding her but she didn't try to pull away. Maybe she couldn't. 'If need be, I can make you leave. And make you forget.'

Could he beat both Caitlin and Isha thoroughly enough to remove the memory of this moment from their minds? Isha feared that he might be able to.

She felt paralysed, incapable of pushing Leofric off Starling, incapable of making decisions, of finding the best way out of this. She wasn't brave. The truth was she felt weak: she had been jittery all day, and now the anxiety had solidified, caught her limbs, wetted her back with sweat, pumped her with useless panic and clouded her thoughts with white noise. She hadn't expected to have to stand up to Leofric; she wasn't prepared for it.

'Or, if you insist,' he whispered, 'you could stay and watch.'

Leofric pulled Starling close to him, dipping down to meet her, and if not for the way his fingers clenched, showing she was struggling against him, they could have been two lovers drawing closer for a kiss. The lightborn's irises had turned red. She cringed at his breath on her face.

'Escape from him, Starling,' said Caitlin. 'That's an order.'

The collar reacted, to everyone's surprise – save for Caitlin's. Starling slitted through Leofric's fingers like sunlight. She reformed close to the tent's door, out of reach. His hand closed uselessly, without being able to grasp her. His features twisted, at that moment, from enjoyment to rage.

'Lord Daegan has given me some loose control over her binds, in case you overstepped,' Caitlin said. Starling slipped out of the tent, letting some afternoon sunlight in, and fled. Hopefully to find help – although who could she call upon, to stop the Nest's general? Who had the authority to prevent him from harming two followers?

'I've decided this is overstepping,' Caitlin concluded.

His mindlink slammed into her like a battering ram. Caitlin recoiled with a sound like a whimper. Without thinking, Isha got into the way, lessening Leofric's hold.

He changed target with practised ease. *The battle had started. She was on the frontlines, with the ungifted, on the uneven terrain of the Splits, and she stumbled as she lunged with her lance. The kher archer she had seen before, who should be dead, had the same smile as when they'd met, the half-amused smirk. She plunged her sword into Isha's chest, the blade biting through her lungs, gore filling her mouth, the pain overwhelming, throwing her to her knees as she coughed out blood.*

Isha was blinking, getting her bearings. He was strong, much stronger than either of them, as was made clear by the fact that Caitlin, too, was still recovering from his blow.

Lord Leofric's mindlink was violent, intrusive. But his voice was sweet, gentle. 'I wonder how I'm going to entertain myself, without the lightborn.' He got up lazily, as if to remind them that there was no rush, that he could reach them in his own time. 'Maybe you have an idea, Cat?'

'I don't much care for men, sir,' Caitlin answered, her tone as sour as it was polite.

'That's a shame,' Leofric said, as he ambled closer to her. 'You won't be able to enjoy it.'

He grabbed Caitlin's wrist. She gasped, but her movement to pull away was aborted as he struck in mindlink. Isha had to do something. She had mere seconds to act, and Caitlin was going to be knocked unconscious, and *she had to do something*.

Before Isha could, however, a message was spreading like wildfire, all the mages sharing the same few words, the knowledge flitting from mind to mind, soldier to soldier. For a few seconds, Isha thought this was another nightmare crafted by Leofric. But it wasn't: this time, it was real. *The Renegades are in sight. Prepare to fight!*

Suddenly everyone was running. Lord Leofric dropped Caitlin, leaving her crumpled on the floor, struggling to regain her breath. He strode towards his armour rack to throw on his gold chainmail. Instructions and images flooded Isha's mind, but they brushed through her without context. The sloped trunk framed by the trees; men and women in armour she didn't recognise, with nails and metal plates glinting under the leather, and

177

mail running along the helmets like a widow's veils; ungifted starting to fan out in well-ordered rows; two apples rolling forgotten, trampled underfoot.

She knelt beside Caitlin to help her to her feet. 'Don't worry about me,' said Caitlin. 'Get your weapons!'

Isha ran out to find her shield. In the confusion, she nearly skewered three people in her attempt to ready her lance. She couldn't make sense of the madness, didn't even know which way round the army was facing – or wanted to face. A horse shoved into her as its rider turned it around. She caught up with Kilian as he ran into position, slipping on the smooth bark, using the tip of his shield like a cane for balance.

Kilian opened the way, towards the bay stallion Lord Leofric mounted, the pale shape of Starling standing beside him. Leofric was putting his foot in the stirrups as they reached him. The messy army separated into layers, ungifted in front, then mages, then high mages, Leofric at the backlines, protected by Passerine's special squadron – her, Isha thought with dread, and a couple of others.

The fate of the Nest hung on the outcome of this battle.

Chapter 7

From the top of the clearing, Isha had a clear view of the Hoofprint, and the two armies bracing for battle. However chaotic the Nest's muster had felt, it was obviously faster than their opponents'. The Renegades were still preparing, ululating as they rode wildly, emerging from the Overgrowth on horseback or on foot. Soldiers were reciting the Renegades' call to arms: *Through pain, to victory.* Others didn't bother with words, and simply howled. *Uli-uli-uli-uli.* The scream went through Isha's heart. She recognised it, as if she'd heard it in nightmares before, or as a child. A long-buried memory, the smell of blood, the shouts of *uli-uli.*

Her mother would be somewhere amongst the soldiers.

The ungifted formed two rows, shields lifted, lances poking out from between their ranks. The high mages on horseback spread out behind the line to carry out Lord Leofric's orders. Because a couple of high mages were out of action, ordained mages replaced them. Caitlin and Ninian were amongst the frontline mages. Isha watched Caitlin's silhouette as she galloped towards the front of the group, her hair tightly knotted beneath her helmet, her tell-tale blue robe bright and obvious, strewn over her horse's rump.

Atop his stallion, Lord Leofric was safely behind the army,

where he could see what was happening and direct the soldiers accordingly. Isha, Kilian, and Passerine's 'elite' followers gathered around their leader. Their task was to make sure Lord Leofric could control the army uninterrupted, by killing anyone who came too close.

Starling stood nearby. Her composure had been shattered. She kept glancing at Leofric, then the Renegades, then the sky. Isha saw her close her eyes, head tilted upwards, and the longing on her face was so obvious – *please, let me be elsewhere, let me open my eyes and not be here* – that it broke Isha's heart. Starling opened her eyes. They were all still here.

Let's block them before they can leave the Overgrowth, Lord Leofric ordered.

Isha could taste leather in her mouth. The horses smelt of sweat. *Uli-uli-uli-uli.* The Nest's army marched in orderly rows down the clearing, towards the area where the Renegades were still mustering. *Uli-uli-uli-uli.* Towards the high-pitched animal calls; the slimmer, taller, armoured horses; the disorderly mess of bodies trying to clear away from the underbrush before they were attacked.

Isha scanned the soldiers. For the moment, she didn't recognise anyone. As Leofric rode forward, out of the shadow of the giant trunk, Isha checked the Overgrowth surrounding them on either side. Anyone could be in the trees. But they would have a long stretch of clearing to cross before reaching Leofric, and they couldn't arrive from behind. As long as Isha saw them as soon as they broke out of the Overgrowth, she would be fine. She would have time to react.

The front rows of the Renegades, the ones who had managed to leave the forest, put a knee to the ground. Behind them, their archers started shooting.

Lord Leofric reacted swiftly. Everyone in the army, as one,

stopped to form a shield-wall. The mages stayed at a distance, out of reach of the arrows. The ungifted huddled behind their shields, heads protected behind the wooden barrier, tightly packed, without a space between them to allow an arrow to pass. On the other side, the Renegades kept shooting. Lord Leofric waited it out; his army, obedient, paused as he desired.

When the arrows stopped – either the Renegades had realised this wasn't working, or they had run out of ammunition – the ungifted rose at once.

Isha spotted a kher on horseback with white horns. Mezyan? Her heart was thumping harder now. Someone she knew, if only by sight – the image of the kher archer smiling at her rose, unbidden, to the forefront of her mind – someone she'd seen at the Nest, holding up a red banner, dreaming of a better world, hushing the whole Nest with his enthusiasm. On horseback. With the intent to kill. Within reach.

And her mother would be here. Her mother *was* here. There were a couple of sturdy battle steeds whose riders were more heavily armoured, wearing blood-coloured capes. One of these red-clad riders was Hawk.

Isha steeled herself, but she felt something physical, like a clench in her gut, at the realisation her mother was now the closest she had been since Isha's flight from her foster home. That she could grab her.

That I can fight her, Isha corrected.

The Renegades on horseback cantered alongside their troops, attempting to flank the Nest's army. The Nest's hive mind was immediately visible. Lord Leofric could guess where the Renegades were headed by the direction their horses were facing, and he shifted his soldiers accordingly, spreading out to one side to cut off the horses and herd them towards the centre of the battlefield. He had the higher ground, at the top of the slope, and thus a perfect view. Beside him, Isha could see their troops' movements just as clearly. The Renegades didn't have enough horses to put pressure on both sides, so Leofric simply curved his army where they tested his defences, like someone cupping his hands to hold in water.

I hate him, Isha thought. *He's a hateful man. And without him, we'll lose this fight.*

One thing at a time, she decided. Win this battle. Then see to the next. She wasn't giving up on fighting Leofric, she was postponing it.

When the two sides met, Isha gritted her teeth. The silence on the Nest's side broke as weapons clashed, lances hitting lances and scratching shields, wood breaking, people screaming in pain as a hit landed. The arrows started again. This time, the Renegades' arrows were flying far beyond their front line, not even trying to reach the ungifted soldiers. They were aiming for the mages. Although they had better mobility with their horses, the mages were focused on controlling the army or mindbrawling, which made them slower to react. Most of them galloped out of the way, but Isha heard shouts and sensed panicked messages shared through mindlink, some suddenly cutting off.

Why isn't Ninian doing his job? asked Leofric. A mage – Caitlin, Isha realised – shared her vision with their leader: a glimpse of Ninian, still on horseback, clutching the reins in one arm, the other tucked against his chest, pale but determined. Shouting rather than mindlinking orders. His left arm had an arrow shaft deeply embedded in the muscle. Baina arrows.

Their communication suffered. It was easy to spot when orders weren't being transmitted anymore. The ungifted without instructions were disorganised, scared, messy. Isha saw pockets break along their line, before suddenly reforming as Leofric ordered the mages to strain themselves more, to control more people beside their usual squadron. He was also stretching himself, to stay in contact with his seconds-in-command along the line as the chaos increased. He stitched his army back together, although Isha knew it had to be with looser control.

Still, the ungifted were losing ground. The frontline was backing into the high mages, who in turn were closing in on Leofric – and his guards. The sounds were louder now. The battle was coming to them.

'It's absurd to waste talent here,' muttered Lord Leofric. With mindlink, he picked out most of the people around him. *Go fill our ranks*, he ordered.

Isha and Kilian hadn't been chosen. They exchanged a glance before huddling closer to Leofric. Members of their group broke ranks and headed towards the battlefield, running to where they were needed most. Their protection unit was reduced to ten people.

She didn't know which was louder: the roar of soldiers, the pulses of mindlink, or the beating of her heart.

The line was a mess now. Where the arrows hadn't hit their mark, the ungifted were ploughing through the Renegades – their coordination was inhuman, greater than anything a regular army could achieve. They didn't stagger when wounded, but continued fighting through pain, through fear, with the same level of skill. But where the Nest's army had weak links, it had taken time to regain mindlink discipline. The neatly traced line was now a zigzag, with parts where the Renegades' army had pushed forward and parts where the Nest's army had. It was difficult to tell who, if anyone, was winning. Their numbers seemed about equal, which meant that not all the Renegades were here yet. Isha tried not to panic at that realisation.

She had to keep watch, not get distracted by the battle. Isha checked her surroundings again, painfully aware of how little she could see in front her, beyond the bulky shoulders and shields and horses of the frontline. She focused on the sides instead, straining her eyes at the lush woods for glints of metal.

'Starling.' Leofric didn't drop his mindlink control as he spoke. 'The mages on horseback won't have baina. Take them out, but be careful. Your life is paramount.'

Starling shimmered as she alighted. Isha couldn't help but gaze after her as she arched over the battlefield, circling, biding her time. When the shower of arrows abated, she plunged, slamming sideways into one of the riders. It should have worked. She should have ripped out their soul and moved on to the next, plucking fighters like flowers, crushing them one by one without resistance.

It didn't go as planned. As Starling hit the first rider, she bounced back, flying into the other direction. Her light went out abruptly. She must have hit the ground. *Mirrors*, Isha understood, too late.

Starling didn't rise again. They might have lost their lightborn. A shock, a tremor, like an earthquake but within their minds: a ripple that started from Leofric and spread across the whole army, jolting everyone. He'd been shaken. They couldn't afford for him to be. Glancing up, Isha could see the side of his horse, the stallion kicking the earth, Leofric in the saddle, hair sweaty and mussed. A muscle was jumping on his jaw, a nervous tic.

He'd regained control – but he had slipped.

I don't have any visibility!

Caitlin's message was frightened, but firm. She should have only shared the mindlink with Leofric, but in her panic she was sending it too widely, to Isha and the other mages standing beside their general. With the words flashed a vision of the battle close-up: a mess of people, mud, the crash of blades, the stench of blood, more mud, the moss churned into clumps. Arrows fell around her; one smashed into her helmet, hard enough to make her stumble. Her horse was kicking beside her, lying on its side, arrows poking out of its chest.

I can't give orders from here, I can't see what's happening, said Caitlin.

Leofric was unfazed. *Just do as I say.*

Caitlin slipped on something or someone, nearly fell. She didn't have a shield. Her horse was thrashing, two more riders were behind threatening to trample her, and in front, in the gap in the line, a Renegade was lunging, his lance narrowly missing her, hitting the horse's leg. Blood danced in an arc from the metal tip, and Caitlin followed it with her gaze, down the wooden lance, the leather-clad grip, up into the eyes of the Renegade. They were not bloodshot, not wild, but calculating. Calm. He was ready to strike again.

You're polluting us with nonsense, Leofric said. Without warning, he cut Caitlin off.

Isha could imagine the second lunge, the way the arm would move forward. She could picture, in those few seconds, the lance's metal point piercing Caitlin, breaking skin, entering the lung, going through the light blue wool, staining it red as it emerged, brutally, on the other side.

And she wouldn't allow it.

Isha mindlinked to Caitlin. As the lance was thrust forward, Isha tried to throw Caitlin sideways, taking control as she would with an ungifted. Taken by surprise, or maybe aware Isha was an ally, Caitlin obeyed. She ducked to the side, grabbing the lance from the fallen ungifted to her left, as instructed. She – Isha – they struck the lance coming their way, forcing it sideways. Isha tried not to look at the line as she would people. It wasn't a woman's corpse on the ground, chest cleft open, the shield strap cleanly cut in two. It was a spare shield. It wasn't an ungifted by her side, sweating, grunting, his lips moving silently as something trapped inside him screamed to be let out, even as his blade tore through the enemy. It was an ally.

Caitlin let Isha take charge while she returned to her primary concern – coordinating her line. The ungifted on either side, whose focus had wobbled, tightened their ranks.

Don't get me killed, she said, all but leaving her body, projecting herself into the surrounding minds.

Isha was suddenly on the frontline, standing beside a soldier, a gap to her right. The third time the Renegade tried to stab her – Caitlin – the person Isha was currently in charge of protecting – Isha knocked their lance aside. The Renegade's eyes were just visible through the helmet, glinting between two veils of chainmail. She let her own weapon follow the line of their wrist, arm, shoulder, up, up, until the face, the underside of the chin which was left unprotected. She pushed through the sudden resistance, the flesh and tongue and the roof of the mouth. The mouth split open into a scream, teeth stained red, blood gushing.

Keep it up, Caitlin said. *I think if we—*

The rest was lost to Isha, as Kilian screamed, 'We're under attack!'

Torn away from mindlink, she was abruptly back in her own body. Her head whipped up, in time to see a group of Renegades on horseback – a small group, only six people or so, plainly dressed in leather armour – dashing towards them. She didn't have time to wonder what had happened to Caitlin.

The riders had cleared half the distance between the forest and Leofric. She hadn't seen them break away from the Overgrowth, too focused on the battle. She was between them and Leofric's stallion.

Isha mindlinked, pulling the lead horse sideways, forcing it to change its stride and crash into the one next to it. The two riders tumbled to the ground, horses yelling, their legs caught together, the people going down under their mounts. But when Isha aimed for the next one, who was rapidly gaining ground, she hit a mental shield. A mage. The horse's mind was protected by the determination to push forward, hatred for the Nest and what it represented, the bright red of a banner.

Through pain,

To victory.

Shit. She heard Kilian's mindlink as he caught up to what she was doing and, like her, noticed the mages. Out of the four remaining riders, two were iwdan, two were human. She didn't have time to mindbrawl the mages before the squad reached them.

She braced herself for the impact, lifting her shield and her lance.

She tried to thrust her lance into the horse as it reached her, but the shock of it bashing into her shield sent her tumbling, the wood shattering under the blow. For a moment, everything was black and red; she tasted mud and blood inside her mouth, saw the sky, the trees, and rolled on the slippery moss, lying dazed.

The Renegades' squadron went through them like a warm knife through butter. The horses hit the people on foot in full force, the Renegades lifting their spears above the Nest's shields and planting them into the mages on the other side, or using their weapons to swat the mages' lances out of the way of their charge. Mindlink crashed over the group in a wave, forcing everyone's minds on the defensive. Lord Leofric spurred his horse away; the frightened animal barely needed the instruction, already galloping before Leofric dropped his mindlink to take the reins.

One of the humans, Isha assumed a mage, strung his bow. He was at the back of the group and hadn't taken part in the full-blown charge. *The arrow tips are made of baina.* He took his time aiming at Leofric's retreating back.

As she scrambled to her knees, Isha noticed she'd dropped her lance. Her left arm screamed in pain; there was still the leather buckle of the shield around her forearm, with a few large splinters attached to it. It felt as if someone had tried to wrench her elbow out of its socket. She pulled out her knife, but before she could step forward, the bow was loosened with a twang.

It was a good shot. Lord Leofric slumped on his stallion, but he stayed on the saddle, grabbing the mane. Three of the four remaining Renegades sped up after him.

Kilian was getting up, with less than half of their elite team, all looking as stunned as Isha. Five. They were only five. The archer on horseback glanced at them, scowling. Backing his horse, using only his legs to instruct his mount, he put away his bow and pulled a sword out of its scabbard.

Mentally, Isha reached out for his horse, but he was already there, his mind bristling. He sensed her presence and attacked immediately. *What do you think you're doing?* he asked. *Was that your trick?* He projected an image of the two riders falling with their horses, bones crunching as they went under, as heavy limbs were slammed against their own. But he placed Isha as the main protagonist, as the person who was on the ground, grass in her mouth, nose smashed against a stone, feeling her ankles snap in the stirrups as the horses writhed.

It shouldn't have been enough – the trick of swapping out victims in a crafted mindscape was a cheap one, after all – but it had just happened, before her eyes, and the image was imbued with the power of truth. At the same time, he tightened his legs around his horse, which sprang forward. As she disentangled herself from his mindlink, Isha realised she had nothing but a naked blade she didn't know how to use without a shield, and that she was going to die here.

The mages from the Nest pounced, their minds like claws grabbing at him, and the Renegade faltered in his charge, arm lowering as their mindbrawl overtook him. When the horse didn't slow down, Isha lifted her knife. Two heartbeats afterwards, the Renegade was upon her.

She swung wildly, throwing herself sideways. Stupidly, she closed her eyes. Tatters would have berated her for it. Still, she struck flesh, maybe the man's leg, maybe the horse's flank. He was slow to retrieve the reins, to make his mount spin to face her. But she sensed her support was also waning – a kher was crawling out from under the two fallen horses, spitting as she rose, wiping her bloodied mouth on her sleeve as she drew her weapon. Isha wouldn't be able to rely on Kilian and the others' help much longer.

She parried the rider's next blow, but only barely, and she had to use both arms to steady her weapon. Her left arm throbbed in protest when she lifted it. The horse nearly trampled her, and she struggled to dodge, too busy defending the blows to be able to attack. The Renegade was becoming faster, no longer impeded by mindlink. From the corner of her eye, she was vaguely conscious of the others taking a defensive stance to fight off the kher. She saw nothing but confidence in both Renegades. *They have no doubt they can take us, even two against five.*

To her surprise, she felt Kilian mindlink to her. *Mindbrawl him*, he urged. *Keep him busy.*

She wanted to argue that it was hard enough not getting killed, but as the horse swerved, bringing the Renegade in line for the next blow, she attacked. She threw herself to the ground, trying to aim between the horse's legs. At the same time, she mindlinked the image of herself gutting the horse from underneath the Renegade, emerging on the other side covered in gore while his animal collapsed beneath him. She knew she wouldn't be able to pull that off, but she did try to get under the horse's belly, got kicked in the knee and – trying to ignore the flash of pain, or to build it into something else, into the horse's pain, into her mindlink – she limped to the other side, still forcing her images onto the mage.

He was confused, if not defeated. She could sense his concern for his mare – she knew from his mindlink that it was a mare – but of course that hadn't been personal enough to harm him. But she had managed to make it vivid enough to breach his defences, at least.

That was all Kilian needed. The rider was too slow to prevent Kilian's interference: suddenly the mare bent her front legs, as if preparing to lie down. Isha saw her chance as the rider was thrown off, toppling as the horse leant forward, trying to recover his equilibrium by spreading his arms, using his sword for balance. She lifted her blade, rushed him, and planted it into his back, between his shoulder blades.

She pushed, dragging him off his saddle as the horse regained its independence and reared out of her way. The rider slammed onto the ground, Isha atop him, still desperately pressing her knife into his spine, not sure what would be enough to kill.

When he didn't roll around and fight back, she pulled out her knife, backing away from the blood. Her sleeves were soaked. Her hands were filthy.

Kilian was still standing, eyes round with horror. The kher had been killed by the others, but not before she took down two of them.

Three. Of their small defence squadron, there were only three mages left.

Her gaze travelled across the bloody scene: one of the horses who had crashed at the start had got up, while the other whined on the grass, one of its legs broken, the bone jutting at an angle that hurt just to look at it. Beneath it, she could make out the shape of a Renegade. The kher woman, who with her armour bore an uncanny resemblance to Arushi, lay face-down. Isha's hands were glistening with hot, red liquid.

Beyond their small group, the Nest's army was in pieces. The chain of command had collapsed. The ungifted, now conscious in the midst of a battle they hadn't started, dispersed like a flock of startled birds, offering little resistance. The Renegades had broken through their line in four, no, five places.

They planned to do this from the start. They sent a small group to take down Lord Leofric, and they knew that would be enough. They must have circled around the battlefield when the fighting began, doing a large detour in the woods, undetected, for this surprise attack. *The battle hinged on that team. On us.*

And we failed.

'What do we do?' Kilian asked. Beside him was another apprentice, only recently ordained as a mage, with blood up her blade and her elbows. They both had fearful eyes. They both hoped she had answers.

At that moment, the strangest feeling manifested itself. Isha felt taller. She felt bigger, thicker. Her thighs and calves were hot, from the chafing of the saddle, from the warmth of the horse between her legs. She knew she was standing – Isha could *see* she was standing – but she felt seated. Leather rubbed at the inside of her hand, where the reins bit into the skin, even though her palm was empty. In the other arm, her long knife was lighter, easier to carry, an extension of her will. Her lungs expanded, and it was as if she were breathing with different lungs, that were larger than hers.

For a confusing moment, it was as if Isha had stepped into a giant. As if someone else's body was her own.

'Isha? What do you want us to do?'

And then she realised.

'Shall we go after Leofric?'

It was fleshbinding.

'They're coming closer, we need to decide *now*!'

But only the Renegades could fleshbind. No-one in the Nest's army had that gift. And to fleshbind, one had to share blood – that was one thing Isha had learnt from spending so much time with Ka. Furthermore, fleshbinding could be used to find people, in the same way the khers had used it to pinpoint where Tatters was in the prisons. So someone, somewhere relatively close by, wanted to find her.

Only one woman in this army shared her blood.

Her mother. Hawk.

'Isha, are you even there?' Kilian said. 'Oh, skies ... I ... I think s-she's a lacunant.' He sounded on the verge of tears.

Hardly aware of her decision even as she made it, Isha grabbed the closest horse's reins, the mare. It was distracting to feel someone else's hand grabbing something different, but she did her best to ignore it. To ignore the sensation of being enveloped, smothered, eaten by her mother.

In my dreams. On my face. In my flesh. Will she ever leave me alone?

'Kilian, stay calm,' Isha said. 'I'm not a lacunant.' She searched for a second horse for him. The one who had fallen and survived, after rising, was looking warily at them from a distance. She pointed him out to Kilian. 'Get that one.'

As he ran to do so, she grabbed one of the unbroken spears off the ground. She pulled the blue robe off one of the bodies on the floor. Afterwards, she was amazed at how level-headed she'd been, how cold. But she was giddy with adrenaline, so she wiped her hands on her legs, leaving red smears there, and tugged the blue cloak off the corpse without giving herself time to think about it.

She speared the weapon through the cloth before putting her foot in the stirrup. The mare sidestepped away from her as she tried to hoist herself up. She tightened her hold on the reins, cursing under her breath, and tried again. This time, despite the horse shying away from her, she managed to throw her leg over. She pushed herself into the saddle.

Soldiers were rushing up the mossy slope, slowed down by bodies and blood.

Kilian was helping the other mage – what was her name already? Was she the one who was teaching him to juggle? – onto the other horse's croup.

'Run,' Isha ordered. 'Westwards.' *Towards home.*

She turned the mare, who was reluctant to follow her orders, and nudged her into a canter.

It was a struggle to control the horse with one hand whilst hefting up the banner in the other. The mare was unhappy about having to head towards the rumble of people fighting, and unhappier still when Isha spurred her forwards, hoping she would speed up. It was only when they got closer to the fighting, when the mare sensed blood and death, that at last she broke into a gallop.

The sounds and smells and sights of the battlefield were overwhelming; yelling, neighing, the clang of weaponry, the thuds of bones and wood and flesh bashing against each other.

'Run!' Isha shouted, as loudly as she could. The mare's ears pricked up, but Isha could barely make herself heard above the screaming. *Run,* she mindlinked, as broadly as she could. The mare had found her stride now, legs thrown far in front, each step longer, until it felt as if she were about to alight across the clearing.

The field was a brown smudge of upturned moss, saplings and roots ripped out of the ground, and it was a miracle that her mare didn't slip, but she bounded forward, gracefully jumping over the fallen bodies, extending her neck as she picked up more speed. People flashed on either side of Isha, but they were only shapes and colours, brown leather, red capes, the glint of metal, the burn of light reflected by a mirror. She clutched the banner against her, letting the wood dig into her sides, hoping the bright blue cloth streaming behind her was enough of a statement.

'Retreat!' she repeated. *Lord Leofric is down, we need to retreat!*

She heard the whistle of arrows and crouched low on her saddle, low enough that her head was buried in the mare's mane, the banner held horizontally above her. The cloth was hit by arrows, nearly knocked out of her hands.

We've lost, we're leaving, run!

'Get out of here!' she screamed, muffled by the mane, breathing in and spitting out stray hairs.

She willed herself to keep her eyes open, to keep control on the reins. Before she had time to change course, she emerged in an empty area, where the Renegades had collapsed the Nest's line. On her right, she glimpsed the archers and the mages in their red cloaks. On her left, she saw the khers and foot soldiers, turning back towards her, having finished their grim work.

Swearing, Isha dropped her spear, letting the bright blue cloth tumble into the gore. Ahead of her was a swarm of soldiers. She wasn't even a quarter of the way through the line, she had spread the message to only a hundred or so soldiers – but she would never reach the other end alive. The mages would have to relay her words. *Run away! We're going west, back to the Nest. Lord Leofric is down. Share the message!*

She turned the horse around in an arc, intent on going the other way. East. She would be followed, she knew, and she hoped she could bring enough people after her to spare some of the Nest's soldiers. Or at least give them a head start. Unfortunately, her mare slackened the pace, maybe thinking she was amongst friends. She probably recognised the Renegades' horses, having lived with them. Isha slapped her legs against her flanks, clicking her tongue, desperate to get her to gain speed again.

Hooves thundered as a rider headed for her. A rider with a red cape. Tall. Confident. Sword in hand. Isha didn't need to see her face. The way her heart clenched was enough.

Hawk.

'Come on, they're your friends but not mine,' Isha said, smacking the mare's rump with the flat of her hand.

She squatted as low as she could while staying in the saddle, pressing the mare on. It was a long-legged, slender Sunriser steed. However, so was Hawk's mount. It was only a matter of time before she caught up.

Isha bit down hard enough to hurt her jaw, and instilled some fear into her mare through mindlink – just an inch, just enough for her to put that extra effort into the run. They were bolting away from the battlefield; the cover of the trees was in sight, but still out of reach. Although each stride felt longer than the one that came before, still Hawk's horse caught up, galloping alongside her, until they were sprinting forward at the same speed, side-by-side but several feet apart.

Isha only needed a few seconds more, a few strides, to reach the Overgrowth.

Hawk mindlinked.

Abruptly, Isha was a child again. She was standing in front of her farm, holding her foster mother's hand, bouncing excitedly on her heels, pointing down the path to where Hawk was coming up to her. She let go of her foster mother's hand, nervous now, and wiped her palms on her thighs. But Hawk was grinning. Without further formalities, she picked her up, lifting Isha into a bear hug.

Hawk's arms closed around her. Maybe it was meant to be an embrace, but it caught her like a lock.

In her flesh. In her mind. In her dreams. And now, even in memory, her mother, holding her tightly. Holding her so that, even if she squirmed, she wouldn't escape. For a second, Isha feared she would panic, drop her concentration, fall off her horse. But she managed to stay grounded. She was a mage. She could deal with mindlink – even this soft, insistent mindlink, which wanted to be kind, but refused to let go.

She had won enough mindbrawls to know how to disengage herself from a foe. Isha split herself in two.

Her tattoo expanded, the ink swelling into wings, her birdself, her eyas, growing to its full size, transforming into a bird of prey curled into Hawk's arms. And while her double cosied up to Hawk, Isha became like the ink, lost solidity, dripped away from the firm embrace. She was liquid, she was impossible to grip. She slid away, and reformed at a safe distance in mindlink. Away. Apart.

Hawk looked down at what she had caught. It was a huge black bird with talons and a sharp beak and a beady eye. But it wasn't her daughter.

What are you . . . ? Hawk stuttered.

The eyas isn't your daughter. It never was, Isha said. She felt strong, solid. She had escaped her mother. In mindlink, she was herself, complete, untattooed. She held her mother's gaze. *That's just the lie you wanted me to become.*

Isha shoved Hawk away. It was like breaking the water's surface. Her mind tore itself free.

The mare burst into the forest, and a branch crashed against Isha, nearly knocking her off and laying all her efforts to waste. She lost a stirrup, clutched a mix of mane and reins, pulled herself back on the saddle as her mare jumped over a fallen log, throwing her off-balance again. It was sheer luck rather than skill that prevented her from being tossed to the ground.

She clung to her horse like a drowning woman to a piece of flotsam. She didn't even care where they went, as long as it was away. She didn't waste time trying to remember where the Overgrowth was solid ground and where it was foliage growing over the void. She urged the mare forward with mindlink, *run, run, run*, and she held on with all her might, struggling to get her stirrup on again, to ignore the sounds of pursuit behind her, the crunch of hooves on twigs, the shout Hawk let out when she lost sight of her.

Run, run, run, she begged.

* * *

When her mare slowed, Isha untightened her fingers from the reins for the first time. Her hands hurt from being clenched too long. It wasn't so much that they were safe, but the mare was soaked through with sweat, panting as if she might collapse.

'Sorry,' Isha whispered. With mindlink, she had pushed her mount further than she wanted to go. The poor thing sounded as if she were choking.

Isha strained her ears as her horse stopped, head hanging low, still struggling to catch her breath. Isha petted her; her hands came back foamy white. She couldn't hear the Renegades behind her, although she knew for sure they had followed her into the forest. She wasn't sure they had been running for long enough to throw them off, but at least they weren't close anymore.

Breathing heavily, in time with her mare, Isha extended her mind around her. She couldn't sense a human presence. She let out a sigh of relief.

Unfortunately, she had run in the opposite direction she had told people to go: she had fled to the east.

Her body ached, as if she were a slab of meat tenderised under a mallet, bruised all over. Her left arm, especially, throbbed with every heartbeat.

'Come on, be good,' she said, pushing her mare forward, letting her walk as slowly as she wanted, as long as they were moving.

They kept the same limp pace until the afternoon faded into dusk. As night fell, Isha forced herself to consider the situation. *Away* wasn't going to be enough; soon she would have to decide what she was going *towards*. She didn't have anything with her. She needed a river. A map. An idea of whether she'd been going in circles or not.

Sore from her long ride, she dismounted. She loosened the mare's girth and guided her by hand. She had no idea how to find what she needed.

They walked through the thicket, pushing down on branches, breaking twigs out of their way. It was dark by the time Isha heard the trickle of water. The dense branches prevented moonlight from filtering through, so she kept bumping into obstacles and tripping over roots. She only found the brook when she splashed into the water, wetting her shoes up to her ankles. Her only comfort was to know that she must be far from trade routes and villages, hopefully out of reach.

The mare drank in long gulps, immersing her mouth in the water until it touched her nostrils. Isha joined in, drinking, rinsing her face, wiping some of the grime off her hands. The blood had dried in brown stains down her wrists; she rubbed it off, leaving a copper-coloured trace in the river.

'All right, we need to find a place to sleep,' she told the mare. The horse blew through her nose, which Isha decided to understand as an assent.

Isha wasn't confident sleeping in the forest. There were only brambles, pine needles and nettles on the ground, with nowhere flat to lie down. She might have been able to sleep in a tree, but she was worried about falling off. Although they were both exhausted, she persevered, this time following the brook's course, the mare in tow.

She hoped the water would lead her out of the Overgrowth. Instead, after a few dozen yards, it dropped between two roots and into the underworlds, disappearing into white mist. She shuddered at the thought that, by scrambling blindly, she might have been unlucky enough to find a gorge rather than a source of water. She continued straight ahead.

It couldn't have been very late – only a couple of hours after sundown – when she sensed it. It was faint, shimmering at the edge of her senses. Someone's mind. She froze, fearful; her mare copied her, ears turning to catch the creaks and whispers of the forest at night. The person wasn't moving. Cautiously, Isha extended her mindlink towards them. It wasn't a human being, but something less complete. The echo of an emotion, a trace which a mind had left, which still remained. It was to a real mind what a painting was to a real person.

Curious despite herself, Isha headed towards it. The presence guided her like a beacon. She slowed down, straining her eyes, but she couldn't make out a shape, only the clear-cut thoughts. It was when she was nearly upon it that she caught sight of gold on the forest floor.

Leaning over, Isha retrieved a flat semi-circle of metal. It was as big as a fingernail. Because gold, like quicksilver, could absorb emotions, it had soaked up feverish, unfocused thoughts, which now radiated out of it. As she turned it between finger and thumb, she realised what it was: it was a ring from someone's chainmail. And she knew only one person who wore gold armour.

Rubbing her arms for warmth, rubbing her mare for comfort, Isha searched the forest, scanning it with mindlink, as far as she could reach. There it was – a tinkle, a wink. A mind too complex to be an animal's. She squeezed the ring in her hand as she hunted.

She found the next one. And the next.

Lord Leofric's chainmail must have suffered a blow, for its rings were coming undone, spilling from his armour. Most of the time they had got caught on low branches and thorns, or against jagged bark. Each gold ring still vibrated with the thoughts that had flashed through his mind as he fled, although they were so incoherent Isha wasn't sure how he was still conscious.

As she grew closer, she saw the tracks. These were harder to find, without a hunter's eye, with nothing but mindlink to search by. Footprints pressed into the pine needles. Blood smeared against a trunk. A wider trail of squashed ferns, as if someone had dragged themselves across. In the end, a light.

At first she thought she'd imagined it, but then she perceived a mind – a fully-fleshed, complete mind, awake, glowing with anxious thoughts – and when she turned towards it, there was a flicker burning between the trees. With every step closer, the fire grew more obvious, the shadows it cast lengthier.

Who are you?

The person beside the fire must have heard Isha's mare tramping through the underbrush. They lashed out, the message more threatening than friendly, their mindlink familiar.

Caitlin? Isha couldn't hide her surprise any better than Caitlin herself, whose relief was clear, even though she quenched it.

Isha pulled her mare into the circle of light. Caitlin was seated on the floor, beside a small firepit, between an oak's two large roots. She looked terrible. Her hair was knotted with dirt and leaves, locks stuck together by sweat and blood. Bruises marred her forearms, her swollen hands, her face. Beside her, sleeping under her blue cloak, was Lord Leofric. On the other side of the fire, Starling was curled into a ball, her face turned away from the flames.

'What are you doing here?' Isha asked. Once close to the fire, she noticed for the first time how cold she was. It felt as if her bones were shivering.

'I should ask you that,' was Caitlin's answer.

With a grimace, Caitlin pushed herself to her feet and stepped around her smoky fire. Isha braced herself, ready for a reprimand about how she'd dealt with the battle, but Caitlin pulled her into a hug. Overjoyed at having found someone else to talk to, Isha hugged her back. They squeezed hard, and didn't speak, and when Caitlin let go, she didn't catch Isha's eye.

As Caitlin went to sit on one of the oak's sturdy roots, Isha tied her mare to a low branch, petting her, using mindlink to communicate that she could now relax and fall asleep, should she want to. She took off the saddle, too exhausted to properly rub her down. Isha sensed the animal's tiredness but, like her, the mare was pleased to be by the fire. She recognised this from her years of travelling. This was a human's safe place.

Isha settled beside Caitlin, extending her hands towards the flames, close enough to scorch herself.

'Underworlds be praised,' she whispered. She dropped the golden rings to the ground. 'I found you with these,' she went on. 'It was an easy trail to follow.'

Caitlin grunted, leaning over to pick up one of the rings. She studied it, then threw it into the fire with a sigh. It wasn't clear to Isha if the noise she made was one of pain or not; she didn't seem severely wounded, but her movements were stiff.

'Well, the Renegades will find us soon enough,' said Caitlin, 'if we leave them signs like that.'

'I picked up the ones I could find.' Isha crouched closer to the fire, rocking on her heels. 'Why did you run away in the wrong direction?'

'I didn't have a choice. Starling…' Caitlin pointed to where the lightborn was hugging herself on the ground. '…has an order which forces her to save Lord Leofric's life. That's not something she can fight against. And I won't go back without Starling. Lord Daegan will have my guts for garters, for one thing. So we both hunted him down, found him alive, and did our best.'

'What about his stallion?' Isha asked.

Caitlin shrugged. 'Stupid thing was long gone when we got to him. And you?'

Isha recounted what had happened, leaving aside the more compromising details. Caitlin nodded along, her face a mirror of Isha's own feelings – a wince when she readjusted her position, a glazing over her eyes when death was mentioned, a mind closed and brittle, which kept watch despite the fact that there was little they could do if someone found them.

'You told people to break ranks and run?' Caitlin said.

'What would you have told them?'

Caitlin didn't answer. The fire was sputtering, more smoke than flames, but it was warm. Caitlin threw dried pine cones on it when it seemed to weaken; they blazed as they took.

'One of us should sleep,' said Caitlin. 'Or we won't be able to make it tomorrow.'

'Why aren't you sleeping?' Isha asked.

'I can't.'

Caitlin's gaze was boring into the fire, eyes red with smoke, as if it were one of her silly contests and the first one to turn away would lose. But Isha understood the haunted, drawn expression. Neither of them wanted to dream tonight.

'I'll keep you company,' said Isha. 'I'm not that tired.'

They both stared blankly at the Overgrowth. Trees, trees, trees. A black canopy made darker by the starless night. The silence was restless, filled with unstated fears.

'You didn't grow up on a farm, did you?' Caitlin asked.

Isha rubbed her forehead. 'Why would you even ask?'

'Because of your tattoo. You're not just some farmer's daughter.'

Her heart stopped, or so it felt. Everything was still. Not a blade of grass trembled, not a grey cloud moved.

'What do you mean?' she asked.

'You must know,' said Caitlin. She was still looking into the fire, fixedly. When she spoke, the smoke she unwittingly breathed in gathered around her mouth and nose. 'I've seen the Renegades' flag often enough now. I don't know how I missed it before.'

Isha wasn't sure what to say. All this work, trying to keep the mages together, to save everyone, to hide her links to the Renegades, only to be found out now, when she had picked a side, when the story written on her cheek wasn't the one she had chosen to follow.

'What are you going to do?' Isha asked. 'Tell Lord Leofric when he wakes up?'

'As if I'd tell that asshole anything,' Caitlin scoffed. Then her amusement faded, her expression returned to its previous bleakness. She shook her head. 'If you were a traitor, you would've shown your true colours by now. I'm just curious.'

What do I have to lose? Isha found herself telling Caitlin about her tattoo. How Hawk had branded her when she was so small she couldn't ever remember a time without the black lines of ink smudging her features. How she had grown with it, sometimes ignoring it, sometimes self-conscious about it, as she worked on the farm, as her foster parents watched her grow and learnt to love her. They had taken her in so they would receive some extra income; they kept her, she hoped, because they grew attached to her.

The tattoo had followed her everywhere, long before the Renegades' name was known on this side of the Shadowpass.

It had never been a sign of love. It had always been a flag.

As she spoke, a weight lifted off her chest. A breeze rustled the trees. The night shook like the sea, branches rising and falling with a slow sigh. When she stopped, the silence, after the rhythm of her sentences, seemed to be wider than before.

'And I thought my mother was bad,' Caitlin said, with a self-deprecating smile.

Despite herself, Isha smiled in return. Caitlin leant across to rub her shoulder, in a half-caress, half-hug. She was human, she was warm, she was the only friendly face for miles. Maybe that was why Isha let her weight rest against Caitlin. Maybe that was why her heart slowed at the contact, appeased, as Caitlin drew an arm around her.

They listened to the night and the spitting of the fire. As dawn washed over them, they fell asleep uneasily, leaning against each other for support, without quite having decided to.

Chapter 8

Tatters was slightly out of breath, forced to take longer strides to keep up with Passerine, who was pacing the arena, studying the tall stained-glass windows, comparing them to a rough sketch he'd done of them. As far as Tatters understood it, Passerine wanted to translate the symbols drawn there, but he was struggling as to whether it was important to follow the iron-wrought lines between the panes of glass or, on the contrary, ignore those and read the coloured glass, considering the iron like spaces between the words.

'I can't help but feel that if ancient words of power were inscribed in the stone, something would have happened by now,' Tatters said.

'The language is archaic,' Passerine said. 'I am having trouble translating it.'

Passerine stopped in his tracks, frowned, and turned his picture the other way around. Tatters was growing tired of his antics.

'This one,' Passerine said, handing over a sheet of paper. The picture was another confusing symbol, a muddle of lines and spirals.

They had been doing the same thing for hours: Passerine drew symbols, and Tatters alighted, drawing the lightborn letters in the air. It was akin to speaking words out loud after seeing them written down, Tatters supposed. The exercise was doubly difficult – it required regular alighting and decoding Passerine's scribbles.

'You know, this would be a lot easier if you explained what you're looking for,' Tatters said, studying the picture. It was like trying to understand a dance pattern from someone's sketch.

Passerine, lacking patience, was not the best teacher. 'You will do as you're told.'

Passerine was good at hiding what he thought, but Tatters had lived on the fringes of his life long enough now. The stance, the strained shoulders, the unformed snarl at the corner of his mouth – this was Passerine being particularly obtuse. He was raring for a fight.

What's his problem? he wondered.

He's been like that all day, said Lal. *Clearly reading lightborn doesn't do anything for his temper.*

Passerine crossed his arms, drawing himself to his full height, which was always impressive, as he was much taller and broader than Tatters.

'Get on with it.'

Sighing, Tatters yielded. He wasn't much use to the war, anyway, not when Hawk might be able to reclaim him and use him against his own camp. He examined the drawing one last time before handing it back. As he focused, light spread from his fingertips to his toes, drawing a red halo around him. He flew towards the ceiling, savouring the rush of it, trying to repeat the twists and turns he'd seen on the page.

He let himself drop beside Passerine. So far, they had nothing to show for their efforts.

'You must have translated some of this, right?' said Tatters. 'We're not working blind?'

'Most of it is useless,' Passerine said. He had stepped up to the giants' panels and placed one hand on the glass. Green, glossy light filtered through his fingers. 'Information about who built the Nest, how to grow wheat, how to exploit the river's strength to make flour.'

'I mean, that sounds useful,' said Tatters.

'I am searching for a weapon against Hawk. Not farming advice. This one.' Passerine tapped the drawing Tatters had just copied. 'This roughly translates as 'the fire within the stone'.' He corrected the sigil, lengthening parts of the circle, untightening the coils. 'Try it again.'

Tatters complied. Again and again, he tried to spell the light-born letters; again and again, nothing happened. The repetition was wearing him. Once, he cheated: he followed the original lettering, the stained-glass windows, copying their curves, hoping he'd picked the same ones Passerine had been observing.

Unfortunately, Passerine caught him messing around. 'Do you think this is a game?' he asked, as Tatters landed.

'I'm showing some initiative,' Tatters answered. 'You should be pleased.'

It's not like you're making any progress, Lal joined in, sending the message in mindlink to Passerine. She couldn't often jump into conversations with people; she was enjoying the opportunity to do so.

As often happened, though, Lal pushed Passerine to the end of his tether.

'You have no idea, no understanding,' Passerine all but snarled. 'I am an old man, and I have spent my life trying to help Hawk make the world a better place, and in the end we only made it a bloodier one. I saved Isha because there was something to be saved, even if nothing could be salvaged for me. And then I found the Nest's secret. Do you know how hard it was to gain access to the council room? Do you know how sick I am of everyone taking up my time with petty squabbles when there is real work to be done?'

Passerine didn't even pause for breath, each word following the other like a quick exchange of blows.

'I fought to gain access to the lightborns' writing, and now I can read it, at last, but Hawk is heading straight for us. If she gets here before I'm done, I'll never get to the end of this, I'll never *know*.'

The longing in his voice might have been real, but so was Tatters' frustration. 'Know what?'

Passerine's short burst of emotion was already under control. His expression was cleansed of feelings. 'That is none of your concern.' He walked away, keeping his gaze set on the windows, picking a quill from his belt for his next notes.

'You can't do this without me,' Tatters warned. He didn't like the tone Passerine was using. He wasn't there to be shouted at, then ignored. 'Give me a reason to not help, and I won't.'

'You can't do this without me,' Passerine answered, with such confidence that Tatters found himself bristling.

He was behind Passerine. The high mage was staring straight ahead, through the coloured glass, but Tatters could tell he was conscious of the presence behind him, his whole body poised like a cat about to pounce.

'Show me the stupid sigil again,' Tatters demanded.

He stared at it until his eyes watered, but he couldn't make any more sense of it than before. Maybe different parts of the symbol should be done at different speeds, the way a quill could slow or quicken as it covered the page, thickening or thinning the ink. It was worth a try, at least.

He shoved the paper into Passerine's hands before alighting. Their relationship felt even more fraught than usual, on the verge of breaking. Work was needed to focus them away from each other. This time, Tatters consciously varied his rhythm as he twisted and turned, accelerating and stalling in turn.

Something shimmered. When Tatters shifted back to human shape, the air was thick as if with fog. The stones exhaled. A heat, not as burning as vapour but just as tangible, rose from the walls and floor. The cold, impersonal arena mellowed; the air, when Tatters breathed in, was lukewarm.

Passerine didn't seem pleased. He touched the floor, briefly, with the tip of his fingers. His face fell.

We've found the Nest's heating, said Lal.

Tatters couldn't help but laugh. This was useless against Hawk, of course. He pressed the flat of his hand against the flagstones. The rough sandstone was comfortably warm. Hours of labour, for this. Had they succeeded in heating up every stone of the Nest? It would be a wondrous thing, the whole building comfortably tepid, without any need for fires during the long winter nights. It was a miracle, albeit not the one they had wanted.

'The fire within the stone,' he mused. 'Literally.'

'Shut up, collarbound.'

Something within Tatters snapped. Before he could quite decide to, he punched Passerine.

A lot happened at once. Passerine either felt the blow coming or was faster than Tatters remembered. He spun sideways, moving to grab Tatters' wrist before it could touch him, cape unfurling as a flag would, or like a diving bird, with a sound like a whip cracking. Simultaneously, Passerine pounced inside his mind. Tatters hadn't planned this part. Luckily Lal was there. She blocked Passerine's access, before crafting an image of Passerine beside Hawk, then beside Lord Daegan.

Is this what you wanted to be? she asked. *When you were young and you looked up at the stars and you dreamt, did you dream you would follow other, better people?*

Tatters helped, adding an image of Passerine gazing up at the night sky with longing, with hope.

Passerine's hand closed around Tatters' wrist; an iron grab that pulled him closer, using his momentum to topple him forward. Passerine brought his knee up as he tugged Tatters into range, and there wasn't much Tatters could do to block the kick before it smashed into his stomach. But he managed to catch Passerine's leg with his free arm and pull away, gasping for breath, biting against the pain in his chest, trying to throw the high mage to the ground.

Passerine stumbled backwards, recovered his balance before he experienced a humiliating fall, and immediately had to deflect another punch from Tatters, bringing his arms close to his face to protect his nose. The bastard was lucky he was so tall. In mindlink, Tatters sensed he had touched upon something – there was a weakness there, something about watching the clouds drifting through the sky and wanting to be with them, floating alongside their graceless, bumpy bulks.

But rather than pressing his advantage in mindlink, Tatters retreated from Passerine's mind. They shouldn't be doing this. He was stupid to have started it.

You didn't start it, Lal said.

Where Tatters had planned to take a step back, he was forced to take a stride, as Passerine's elbow came flying towards his face. Passerine followed up with a kick, which should have hit Tatters' knee but only got his leg when Tatters moved. Still, the crunch of shoe against shin made Tatters wince.

We aren't finished. Passerine's mind was full of contained anger. *I want to settle the score.*

Settle what? Despite himself, Tatters felt his hands curling into fists. *I've been tolerant so far, for the war's sake, for Isha, but push me any further and I swear I will—*

You have no idea what was lost because of you. Passerine's fury shocked Tatters, not for the first time. It was an old anger, which rather than withering had festered, had rotted while they were apart, and now seemed to taint all of his soul. *I had to start from scratch because of you, and now you're mocking me for failing?* Again the smell of burnt paper. Hawk's face in profile, lit up by the flames. Unmoving and unyielding, as she so often was. Someone screaming as she took away their scrolls, their notes.

Passerine's mindlink was full of words being eaten by the flames, of pieces of stray paper floating towards the sky, like small, self-consuming lightborns, curling on themselves and growing black as the embers went out. *It was taken from me twice.*

Before Tatters could wonder – could ask – what had been taken, Passerine attacked. He didn't craft an image: he projected a memory towards Tatters. In some ways, it was worse.

Tatters could see himself from the outside, as Passerine did, which was uncanny: small and slight, certainly, but fit too, as he had been then, with a mobile face, even when he was sullen. What Tatters remembered mingled with what Passerine had witnessed, Hawk standing before her tent, frowning in that absent way she had, as if she didn't realise how hard her face could be. Warm dawns, scorching days. The red leaves of the Rohit Pattra. The first spat they had over the collar. The way Hawk had imprinted into the binds, into Tatters, that she would control his life from now on.

Dodge! shouted Lal.

Tatters was ripped from the mindrambling, brought back by his sister's call. He didn't have time to duck, despite Lal's warning. Passerine hit him. The fist caught him on the side of the head, scrambling his thoughts.

Passerine closed the gap between them, but Tatters struck with mindlink while his body was still trying to straighten, before he had fully recovered. They traded a few blows, in the empty arena, with no-one to witness their unfettered combat. The patterned light coloured their fingers blue, their hands green, their teeth purple. It painted masks across their features, made the white of their eyes glow red. Their minds, evenly matched, scratched at each other without successfully sinking in their claws.

They broke apart, panting heavily.

'What did I ever do to you?' Tatters managed to ask, between gulps for air as hard as sobs. 'You don't have the right to hate me! *I* have the right to hate *you*!'

Passerine was just as breathless, yet somehow he managed to drip venom into each word. 'I hate how little you care, Tatters. How little you do. How apathetic you are.'

Tatters wasn't sure what he'd been expecting, but it hadn't been that.

'The lightborns have an excuse, maybe,' Passerine hissed, still struggling to breathe. 'They fly high above the human world, too high up to engage with it. But what about you? You're down here. You live with people. You see what they go through. You can alight, mindlink, fleshbind. You are the most powerful being on this side of the Shadowpass.'

It might have been a compliment, had it not been spoken with such vitriol.

'Yet you choose to do nothing,'

Tatters was stumped. He lowered his fists; despite himself, his fighting stance loosened. Passerine spoke with such fire, as if something was still smouldering inside his soul, as if the flames could still be seen, flickering behind his pupils.

'What can I do?' Tatters asked. 'Have you forgotten the collar?'

'The collar is one of your excuses,' Passerine spat. 'Like Lal.'

Me?

'What's Lal got to do with this?'

Passerine had also abandoned his combat posture, but lines like iron still ran down his neck, his arms, his fingers, pushing out his veins. He'd dropped his quill, but he didn't seem to notice. The parchment on the floor soaked up the ink from the broken nib.

'I heard you interact with Lal for years,' he said, his voice as hard as his body, words sticking out like blood vessels. 'You created a double that's self-centred and only cares about survival. And you made it into a vulnerable little sister who you had to protect, and, how convenient, she lives inside you, so your most important concern is to protect her – in other words, to protect yourself. A lovely lie that you're selflessly saving her when only selfishly saving yourself. Face it, Tatters, Lal is a convenient escape. She's not your sister. She is a thing you made, to serve you.'

Tatters couldn't breathe. It wasn't that he believed what Passerine said – it was that it was so clear that Passerine believed it.

He lived with us so long, thought Lal, *yet he never understood us.* But even she was rattled, Tatters could tell.

'And you could break the collar now,' Passerine went on viciously, 'if you truly wanted to. You could always break it, but you never will. It's more comfortable this way. It takes away your agency. It means it's always someone else's fault – mine, Hawk's.'

No. No, that wasn't right.

'But I fled.' Tatters found his voice, and he discovered it wasn't half as fierce as Passerine's. He sounded frail, hesitant. He sounded like someone losing an argument. 'I left the Renegades.

I crossed the Shadowpass.' Saying it out loud gave the words truth, weighted them with more power. Tatters ploughed on, 'If I didn't want to be free from the collar, I wouldn't have achieved that.'

Isn't that what you're so upset about in the first place? Lal asked Passerine. *That we left?* She was also regaining confidence.

'But what did you cross for?' Passerine threw his arms into the air. Tatters had never seen the composed mage so obviously out of control, so much under the hold of his emotions. Maybe that was why he repressed them – because they were too strong to deal with. 'To hole yourself up in a tavern, playing dumb, pretending you are like the khers, that you partake in their suffering, when you are nothing like them, like us, like any of us. That is despicable.'

Passerine barely paused in his accusations.

'Do you know what you could have changed, if you had tried? In all those years during which Hawk wasn't yet here?'

Something doesn't quite fit, Lal pointed out. *There is something he isn't telling us. Why does it matter, what we do? Not everyone is a hero, but he doesn't hate everyone. He's hiding something from us.*

'We are different, Passerine.' At last Tatters' lungs weren't screaming for air; at last his heartbeat was calmer. 'You're like Hawk. You want to be special. You want to rewrite history. Well I *don't*, all right? I don't want to be a sehwol and save the world. I want to live in my tavern with my loved ones and find peace.' And it was such a precious dream that it hurt to imagine it, hurt to try to hold it, even, especially, now. 'Did that ever cross your mind?' Tatters asked softly. 'That we are different people, with different goals?' Lal was right. He should be allowed mediocre dreams. What he yearned for shouldn't matter this much to Passerine.

'You never had ambition.' Again, Passerine wielded the sentence like an insult.

'Yes.' Tatters held his eyes, bitter, black, so much deeper than his, eyes like night spreading at dusk, the kind of darkness that could swallow the horizon. 'That's the secret. I called myself Tatters so I wouldn't have ambition. I didn't want it.'

They stood apart, two silhouettes of different sizes, ages, skin tones, gaits, lives. Despite their differences, however, Tatters felt a strange kinship with Passerine. For a moment, it felt as if they might find a way out of the maze.

But then Passerine said, 'With your powers, you weren't insignificant. You just chose to be. And you chose it because you didn't suffer enough.'

How dare you tell us we didn't suffer, growled Lal. *What would you know?*

'If you were a kher, if you were an ungifted, you'd thirst for change,' Passerine insisted, maybe answering Lal, maybe simply finishing his trail of thought. 'The only reason you don't is because you're a sehwol, a mage. Everything comes easily to you.'

The colours shifted between them, the lines of the arena turning with the sun. Evening was catching up with them, lengthening the shadows that cut the arena into sections.

'Look what power does to you,' said Tatters. 'Look at the ways in which it breaks you. I knew power would go to my head, corrupt me. It did Hawk.'

'She made a difference, when you did nothing.' The lights across Passerine's face were ochre. When he spoke, his teeth were red, as if dipped in blood. 'You are such a waste.'

Tatters felt each of Passerine's reproaches like a cut, as if the mage had carved lumps out of his chest, had pulled out his organs and stamped on them and now expected him to put everything back and pretend this fight hadn't taken place. *Maybe*

Passerine is right. Once he'd crossed the Shadowpass, once he'd arrived in the city, he'd wanted nothing more than to rest at the Coop, to drink and be merry and be left alone. *Maybe we could afford to be happy.*

Still, it didn't explain why a bonfire crowded his thoughts, nor what had been lost.

Tatters was willing to discuss this – had it been up to him, he would have invited Passerine to sit down, to talk more, to find out what it was, exactly, that cut so deep, what shard of glass had trapped itself inside their hearts, slicing through one of them when the other spoke, to remove the broken shards of their past lives, to agree on *something*, anything.

But Passerine stepped forward first. His teeth went from red to blue, unhuman, strange. 'I need you to do one thing for me,' he said. 'And you will do it. One way or another.'

His arm was flying towards Tatters' neck, his intentions clear. Tatters was too slow; Passerine's fingers curled around the gold, gripping it like a master grips a yoke. At the same time, he mindbrawled, using the memories of Hawk first placing the collar on Tatters, taking advantage of every inch of their past he could lay his hands on.

How dare you! snarled Tatters. He kicked Passerine, once, twice, then, that failing, feeling the collar warming, he slammed his fist in the crook of Passerine's elbow. He hit downwards, forcing the arm to let go. At last he managed to break free, but it was clear Passerine would not allow this to end peacefully – he wanted to take control.

Passerine was trying to exploit a double weakness: the collar, in a way no-one else could; and Tatters' tendency to get lost in the past.

Two can play that game, said Lal.

In the real world, Tatters managed to spin out of Passerine's way, although his vision was blurred by memories and mind-link. He was vaguely aware of the tiled floor, of the outline of Passerine's body. He clenched his jaw when he blocked Passerine's next swing with his forearms. At the same time, Passerine was trying to recall the past, to raise it like a revenant, bring it back to haunt them. But Tatters wrestled against him, placing his own recollections first. Hawk saying, 'Tell me, are you still jealous?' Every compliment the Renegades had ever given Tatters in front of Passerine, such as 'The new recruit has beaten you to it!' or 'Isn't Tatters doing well?'

That was what the scrolls were. He could remember now. The bound books that Passerine had filled with precise, cramped writing. His research. Passerine was studying lightborns. He'd wanted to see if humans could alight. He wanted to teach humans to transcend their flesh.

And he studied, and studied, and sacrificed his life to this goal, and then Tatters was the one who could fly.

Lightborns in legends often had the names of birds. A passerine is any perching bird, a category that includes most songbirds. *That's it.* Sometimes winning a mindbrawl was simply knowing your opponent. *I know why you hate me.* Passerine had the will, but Tatters had the gift. The realisation gave Tatters a rush of power, of control, such as he hadn't felt since the prisons.

Tell me, Passerine. Are you still jealous?

Tatters knew about envy. He projected the feeling towards Passerine, the longing, the regret, the fierce wish to have what someone else had, to be who someone else was.

And he was right. Passerine was still jealous.

It was like finding a crack inside a wall that he hadn't known was there, and bringing the whole edifice down. Something within Passerine's mind broke, some certainty, some strength, and his fears burst forth. Great wafts, pieces of mind coloured with emotion, poured out of him. As often with soulsplintering, before Passerine's mind sealed itself off, it swallowed anything that came too close: a thick fog, as impenetrable as the Edge's mists, spiralled around Tatters. It circled him like a whirlwind, cutting off the outside world. Soon it had solidified, and Tatters stood in the eerie quiet of the eye of the storm. There was no escaping a splintering mind, so he didn't try.

And then they were elsewhere. The mist faded into the deep blue of the night sky. It was an old memory, Tatters could tell, older than their relationship, older maybe than Passerine's time with the Renegades.

In his mindscape, Passerine was standing beside the Edge – not the Duskdweller Edge, which was wet and grassy, but the Sunriser Edge, where the Inner Sea and the end of the world met. A narrow sandbar separated the shore from the void. The waves whispered as the high tide ground shells into dust. It was a dangerous place to be, yet Passerine didn't seem frightened. He stood at the very end of the Edge, where the cliff abruptly fell into the underworlds, where it was easy to confuse a piece of packed sand for solid ground and tumble down to your death.

Lightborns were flying overhead. More than Tatters had ever seen gathered in one place: ten, maybe fifteen of them, dancing together, their blues and greens and golds mingling, patterns shifting against the night sky. For a time, there was only the rumble of the tide. Tatters realised Passerine was kneeling, naked feet deep in the sand, his knees tender where shells and driftwood and seaweed caught against his skin.

'You can't do this to me.' Passerine's voice sounded raw, like a voice used for the first time.

The lightborns drew a complex symbol in the sky, and Tatters understood it, because Passerine did. They were writing a sigil too intricate for Tatters to grasp its full meaning – but the gist of it was something to do with banishment. A punishment. Being forced into human shape, forbidden to alight.

Passerine let out his breath slowly. The sea sucked in its waters and sighed. Further down the shore, the sand turned to sharp shingle, orange and white, the bright colours dulled by the night.

'No,' Passerine whispered – begged. 'No. It's humiliating. I don't...' He trailed off.

As the lightborns drew a new symbol across the horizon, Tatters realised this was a scene he had seen before. It had haunted Passerine's dreams.

The writing was fast, flashing before Passerine as the lightborns spun, but he followed it with ease. It was about the taboo against governing humans, even when they indulged in worship. To not encourage them to obey lightborns, to let them grow. To be humble. Passerine laughed, but it was a laugh that was only bitterness, as rocky and deep as the chuckle of the waves.

'Humble? Why should we, of all people, need to be humble?'

Tatters tried to untangle himself from the memory, to break Passerine out of it. He wasn't sure he wanted to know what had happened. He wasn't sure he wanted to know why this man was stranded in this desolate place, why he could read the words of gods, why he was kneeling against the ground, grabbing fistfuls of sand to dam the emotion rising inside him, why he felt such grief, such despair. But despite Tatters' efforts to regain control, Passerine's mind was stronger, like a maddened horse galloping in one direction, whatever order the rider gave it through the bit.

Passerine pressed his forehead against the sand. For a moment he couldn't see the dancing lights above him, although he could see the glow they cast across his hands. He breathed in the smell of salt. He felt the grit as it pressed against the lines of his brow.

He was young. As young as Tatters had been, maybe, when

he first wore the collar. At that age when the mistakes one made could affect one's whole life.

'There,' said Passerine. 'You've got your humble.'

When he lifted his head again, the lightborns already seemed further away, as far out of reach as the stars. The waves were hypnotic as they rolled, spitting silver-white spray.

'Please, I'm asking you to reconsider.' Fear crept into Passerine's words. Tatters wondered if that was why his voice was so deep – because it had been marred by this place, caught between the unfathomable sea and the endless skies. Black and grey. Foam and stars. 'I didn't do anything wrong. If it was wrong, I did it for the right reasons. It's ... I didn't want any of this. All I wanted was a new aurora.'

But the lightborns were receding like the tide, and that stretch of earth was growing larger, damp sand speckled with driftwood, long black strands of seaweed, pink round shells – and Passerine, who was also being left behind.

One lightborn lingered, a pale blue, a surprising dash of daytime sky in the night. She – somehow Tatters knew she was a woman – danced. No, not a woman. A child. Passerine knew her, but his feelings were so tangled that Tatters couldn't quite grasp what his relationship to her was. As she wrote against the sky, the letters were nothing Tatters could decipher, but when sadness welled inside Passerine, he understood what the arabesques meant.

Goodbye.

'I will return,' Passerine whispered. 'This is not the last time I see you.'

He spoke too low to be heard. The blue lightborn flew away, but her light didn't seem to fade, only to grow brighter as it grew smaller, until it was lost between the stars. Then there was only the unmoving moon and the continuous chant of the sea. Passerine's regret, as deep and circular and grey as the slow motion of the waves.

Tatters managed, at last, to free both Passerine and himself from the spill of his mind. Panting, he returned to reality, shocked at how vivid the recollection had been, how fresh.

To his credit, Passerine had stayed conscious. He was swaying on his feet, but he hadn't fallen.

Passerine was a lightborn, said Lal. *A lightborn who was banned from the skies.* Tatters could sense her horror at the thought. His heart hammered inside his chest, and he felt ready to bolt, as if he needed to run.

Look on the bright side, said Lal. *It's not as if Passerine would ever forgive you for being a sehwol anyway.*

Tatters couldn't leave Passerine here, in the arena, in public, vulnerable enough that a green apprentice could plunder his secrets. Reluctantly, he hoisted Passerine's arm over his shoulders and accompanied him to his rooms. When he leaned too heavily, Tatters gritted his teeth, trying to ignore the fact that his load was taller and heavier than him, that it was a struggle to support him.

He wouldn't have done this for you, had places been reversed, Lal unhelpfully pointed out.

As they walked towards his chambers, however, Passerine's mind seemed to clear. The weight he was transferring lightened, until he was only resting a hand against Tatters' shoulder, as if for balance.

'How are you?' Tatters asked. He kept his voice neutral.

Passerine sighed. He brushed his free hand across his forehead. 'That was my own fault.'

'I can't say I disagree,' said Tatters.

'No. You wouldn't.' Passerine's voice was weary as he pulled his keys from his belt and unlocked his door. They entered the room together, and Passerine let himself slump in the armchair. Tatters could have fussed over him, handed him a blanket, a glass of water – but why would he? Lal was right. He had already done more than expected. He didn't owe Passerine more.

He would have left, but Passerine spoke first.

'Do you know why it happened? What crime I committed, to be on that beach, that night?'

His eyes were like the pits in the Ridge, black holes that led down to the Shadowpass, wells from which one could only pull dark, twisting shapes. It was impossible to read his expression.

'I interacted with humans. I wanted to guide people. To be, like Hawk, a force of change for a better world.'

The aftermath of the soulsplintering still hung around Passerine – the shore, the sea. The shingle cutting his skin. The sigil drawn in fiery lights on the horizon, the last goodbye.

'You have the power I sacrificed to this world, which I was forced to give away because I cared, and yet you don't care. You keep taking things from me, again and again,' Passerine said. 'And then you forget what you've taken, when I'm left to remember and grieve.'

Passerine was still in a state of shock, Tatters realised. He was only speaking because he was stunned, a foot in the past, unsure of the reality around him. Tatters had seen enough people mind-rambling, or skimming that line, losing control, if not completely, enough so for their barriers to be down. He recognised it.

If there are any secrets you want from him, it's now or never, Lal said.

'Tell me,' said Tatters. Part of him cringed; he was preying on Passerine at his most vulnerable. But he needed to know. 'Tell me what happened.' *What I gave to the Shadowpass, to avoid carrying it across.*

His legs were weak beneath him; his head was spinning.

He went to sit on the chair across from Passerine. It was less comfortable than the leather armchair, but the world stabilised somewhat. They were both old. They had weathered too many storms. Although Tatters' hair wasn't streaked with white, like Passerine's, he knew his features were as exhausted, his eyes as hollow.

Passerine said, 'Hawk made me promise you would never, ever leave. That if I had control, I would ensure your loyalty.'

Without the hearth, the light in the room was low. The walls, the floor, the bedposts, the windows had as many shades as the ash.

'And then I left,' Tatters said.

'And then you left.' Passerine nodded. His mind was still raw enough that thoughts crossing it rose to the surface. The scent of burning vellum, like something roasting. The brittle, sharp sound of paper being eaten by flames. 'She was furious, as you can imagine. She burnt everything I owned.'

Scrolls being fed to the flames. A voice screaming. Tatters imagined arms like shackles clamped around him to hold him down. Passerine was a tall man: it would have been no mean feat to restrain him. He mindlinked a vision of Hawk. Her severe face. Her resolute frown. The armfuls of words that she threw, without looking at them, into the fire. The sizzling, crackling, spitting, popping sounds.

All his notes on alighting, to break the ban placed on him, Lal thought. *She destroyed them.*

It must have been the most precious thing he had, Tatters realised. *His life's work.*

And worse still, he couldn't use the lightborn magic without a sehwol, Lal said. *Without us, he couldn't even attempt to free himself.*

'Was that when you left the Renegades?' Tatters asked. For the first time, he believed it was possible, that Passerine had indeed deserted.

Passerine shook his head. 'I had nothing left. I would never return to the skies. I would never be free. I only had Hawk. Until…' He trailed off. For a moment, his features settled, nearly gentle. 'Until I saw what she wanted to do to Isha.'

Passerine's mind was steadying; fewer ripples shivered through him, like water slowly growing still.

'I didn't want to send Isha to war,' Passerine whispered. 'I have lost one daughter already.'

Briefly, Tatters glimpsed her – a streak of blue crossing the night sky, the silhouette of a child lightborn.

Tatters looked at the charred remains of the wooden logs in the chimney. He imagined what it would be like, to be banned from the skies as a young man, to strive to return to your people, how much hope would be invested into your writing, into your research, into that slim, nearly impossible chance of flying again. And how difficult it would be to have to admit, one day, that you wouldn't be able to see your child again, that the short, agonising parting on the shore had been the last time you'd set eyes on her.

If only to give himself time to gather his thoughts, Tatters rang the bell for a servant to bring some hot water so they could brew tea. Passerine didn't keep wine in his chambers, but he did have a wall where he hung little linen pouches, their spicy fragrance catching Tatters' nose when he opened them. They smelt of the past, of home.

Passerine got up to clear his desk, while Tatters prepared the jug for the brew by spreading the leaves at the bottom. When Passerine let his hand rest against the writing desk, his long fingers stood like a strange, long-legged animal with a paler underbelly. The maid returned with the hot water, and they watched in silence as the young girl poured it, as the scents of herbs filled the room. She curtsied and took her leave.

'What was your original name?' Tatters asked.

He half-expected Passerine to dance, as Starling had. But instead, Passerine leant over his writing desk, taking out his quill and dipping it in ink. He pulled a sheaf of vellum closer. After a pause, he drew the sigil in one movement, his hand never hesitating, the nib flying across the paper with some of the grace of Starling curving in the sky. A convoluted spiral covered the page, not unlike a maze. At the very end, ink spilled out of the quill, leaving a small round stain at the bottom of the sign.

'*Birds who sing, who sigh, who croak, who cry,*' Passerine read out loud. 'Although that's a loose translation. Another one would be: *the small feathered creatures which can make sounds.*'

Tatters found himself reaching out for the paper, imagining a blue lightborn drawing the sigil into the night sky, how the beginning of the symbol would already be faded as the lightborn danced the end.

What would it be like, to never be able to dance his own name again?

'Hawk told me "Passerine" included all songbirds, even those, like the crow, who don't so much sing as make a racket. It felt like an appropriate name.'

Tatters gazed at the ink drying on the vellum. Passerine poured them two steaming cups from the jug. The aromas of their past lives filled the room. Tatters watched the line of Passerine's wrist while he served the tea, revealed as his sleeve slid up his elbow, the black cloth pulled taut, and wondered how deeply it would cut to be exiled twice – from the skies, from the Sunriser lands.

'There is a world where we were friends,' Tatters said.

Passerine shook his head. 'At best, there is a world where we were not enemies.'

Chapter 9

Isha was dreaming. She cursed herself for dozing off.

She was sitting beside a fireplace, but it wasn't the one she had fallen asleep by. It wasn't in the woods but in the mountains, a circle of stone on the top of a rocky slope. She must be on the Eastern side of the Ridge, as she could see the sun rising on the horizon, gold daylight slowly washing over the world. Two horses were grazing on the moss nearby. She was wearing armour, unstained, untorn.

Hawk was on the other side of the fireplace, whetting her sword with a stone. She had removed her leather jacket, revealing a dirty, sweat-stained undershirt. Small mountain flowers, yellow, pink, were growing in messy bunches on the slope behind her.

For a while, neither of them said a word. Isha wondered what the easiest way to wake up would be.

'Mezyan told me a story once,' Hawk said, not lifting her eyes from her work, still sharpening her blade. 'Blood, or soil. Would you like to hear it, my eyas?'

When Isha didn't answer, Hawk took it as agreement. She put her blade down on the grass beside her and knotted her hands. She gazed into the fire, gathering her thoughts, before she spoke.

'Once upon a time, there was a male kher called Itri. Itri was in love with a kher matriarch and belonged to her hearth. She had had many children with him and other lovers. The matriarch had had difficult births and was pregnant again. The healers were worried this birth might kill her. She had a bad fever.'

Hawk told the story in the iwdan fashion, with short, matter-of-fact sentences, few names. It reminded Isha of another fire, of another story, of the touch of Uaza's fingers on her cheek, tracing her tattoo.

'Itri feared his love would die. He went to hunt. On his hunt, he met Timessi, the god of fire. Timessi told Itri that if he killed his eldest son, his family would live eternally healthy and youthful, forever renewed, like the flames.' Khers never tattooed flames on their body. From her time at the Pit, Isha remembered Timessi was considered an evil force, whom the other gods kept in check. 'So Itri called his eldest son and told him to come with him to hunt. He took his axe. When he was deep into the woods, he chopped off his son's head, his arms, and his legs. He made five piles and built five pyres. He burnt his son. Timessi was pleased.'

Hawk's voice was deep, entrancing. Despite herself, Isha found herself listening.

'When Itri returned, his youngest son came bounding out of the hearth. "Father, father," he said, "I see there is smoke on the hillside. Call my elder brother, together we will carry water to quench the fire."

Then his middle son came out of the hearth. "Father, father," he said, "I see you have been hunting. Call my elder brother, together we will clean your axe and hands."

Then his love came out of the hearth. "Itri," she said, "call my eldest son, that he might meet his youngest sibling. I am alive and well, and this is his baby sister."'

Hawk paused. She lifted her gaze from the firepit between them. She had eyes like hooks, which caught at Isha's heart and tugged.

'Then his family looked up. They saw Itri's face, his eyes. They had no words. Itri explained what had happened, why he would do such a thing.'

Isha felt like Itri's family, watching Hawk's face, her eyes, having no words. She traced a scar with her gaze, wondering who Hawk had killed to stop that blade.

'His love gave her baby to one of her children to hold. She stepped closer. She said, "Maybe, had you not given to Timessi, I would have died. Maybe you would have dug two graves, for me and for your daughter, and maybe you would have buried us. Your hands would have been covered in soil."

She took his hands and showed him what they were coated in.

"Wouldn't soil be better?" she asked.'

With a slow exhale, which might have been a sigh, Hawk leant over to pick up her sword. She placed it across her lap, retrieved her whetting stone, but didn't start her work again. After a while, it became clear the tale was at an end. She seemed to be waiting for Isha to respond. Behind them, far beyond the mountain's drop, across the valley, the sun was rising.

When she was met with silence, Hawk said, 'That's all there is to it. It's blood or soil. I chose blood.'

Hawk put one hand flat against her sword. Maybe the cold steel against her palm served as a reminder of what choosing blood meant. Isha thought of Lord Leofric in gold armour, leading the Nest's army, in full glory, his stallion champing at the bit. And she pictured him grabbing Starling by the neck, running his fingers through her hair, sneering at her scared expression, at any attempts to stop him.

'I didn't want to dig any more graves,' Hawk concluded.

The sun hadn't yet reached the valley, which was still plunged in shadows, plains and fields and forests a dark green. But daylight streamed across the top of the mountain where they were seated, casting a gold aura around the flowers, creating a reflection in Hawk's sword, making the glow of their fire seem small.

Isha could feel daylight against her eyelids. She would be waking up soon.

'You should think about that question,' Hawk said. 'Blood, or soil?'

* * *

Isha woke up nauseous. She was lying on the ground. Caitlin was already awake, dripping some water from her waterskin into Leofric's mouth. He was still unconscious, lying as still as the dead between two roots. Starling had rinsed her hands and face, leaving finger-shaped traces down her neck. A few eggs were in a pile by the firepit. Their fire had long since died.

'I sent Starling to find a river and some breakfast,' Caitlin said once she noticed Isha was up. 'You look awful.'

'Thanks,' said Isha. 'You're looking spruce as well.'

Caitlin snorted a laugh. Her hair was matted with mud and blood. Aside from pushing back the sticky locks, there was little she could do. Giving up on trying to tend to Leofric, she came to sit beside the fire, rolling a raw egg in Isha's direction. Without a fuss, Caitlin cracked an egg on a stone, lifted it above her mouth, and ate it raw. Isha copied her, but the gooey, slimy texture sent a shiver down her spine. She forced herself to swallow.

Starling watched them carefully, studied the eggs, scrunched her nose, and went to sit on the other side of the unlit firepit without touching the food.

The forest was the same as yesterday: trees and trees and more trees. It would be easy to wander in circles, lost, for days on end. Everywhere in the Overgrowth looked alike.

'What do we do now?' Isha asked, once they'd finished their meagre breakfast.

'What is there to do?' said Caitlin. 'We'll never make it back to the Nest before Hawk. Even if we do, three of us won't change the tide of this war.' Her eyes were rimmed with black; she appeared to have slept even less than Isha. 'We have to wait until Lord Leofric either recovers or dies. Until then, Starling is stuck by his side.'

Isha imagined the Nest, underprepared, with Passerine and Tatters scrambling to defend it. She imagined Kilian, somewhere in the woods, ambling aimlessly, trying to follow the setting sun glinting through the canopy.

Starling hadn't eaten. Where she had rubbed at her face, she had missed a trail along her ear. It was dirtied with dried blood.

Isha felt cold and helpless. 'I am so sorry we dragged you into this,' she said.

For a moment Starling said nothing, her face unreadable. Isha went to check on her mare, pouring some water into a dip between two roots, watching the animal gulp it down gratefully.

'You are the second person to say that to me,' Starling said at last. 'It is a rare occurrence, in humans. They are seldom sorry.'

Caitlin started. Even Isha had trouble hiding how shocked she was. Like everyone else, she had grown to view Starling as a silent, subdued figure – magical, certainly; deadly, no doubt, but quiet and godlike – well above human considerations.

'It's hard not to be sorry at the mess we've made,' Isha answered, slowly.

'Yes,' said Starling. 'You kill and enslave and kill more. You should be sorry.'

'We were hoping to prevent the Renegades from enslaving more of us,' said Isha. A thought struck her; she wondered whether Starling would care. If she did, it wouldn't hurt to be on a lightborn's good side. 'Do you know Hawk, the leader of the Renegades?' Isha went on. 'She is the one who bound Tatters.'

Starling didn't frown, didn't smirk, didn't show any sign of having heard. Only Caitlin lifted an eyebrow, surprised Isha had this information – or that she had shared it.

'How do you know?' Starling asked. Her eyes had turned golden; maybe it was only a trick of the light.

'He told me,' Isha answered. It wasn't quite the truth, it wasn't quite a lie. She was a mage, after all.

A wet, whimpering wind hissed around them. The mare snorted through her nose and rubbed her face against her front leg to scratch an itch.

'I wish there was something we could do,' Isha said, absent-mindedly petting the mare. 'I wish we could at least make sure everyone lost out there makes it back.'

'It would take too long to ride out and look for everyone,' said Caitlin.

'Maybe we could build a fire?' said Isha. 'Something people could see and head towards? There's enough wood.'

Caitlin seemed dubious. 'Are you sure they'd head towards something burning? Wouldn't they assume it might be Renegades? Wouldn't the Renegades find us that way, for that matter?'

'Would the Renegades bother backtracking for us?' Isha

asked. Even she wasn't sure Hawk would risk losing time just to get her hands on her daughter. After all, Hawk would know she was close by, after yesterday's encounter and their shared dream.

'I could fly out and find them for you,' said Starling.

Isha's heart leapt. Hope flared inside her chest, as sharp as pain. 'You would help us?'

Starling shrugged. It was a stiff, stilted gesture. Isha wasn't sure Starling completely knew how to use it. Caitlin carefully took another egg, broke it, gulped it down, as if she weren't listening to this conversation. But Isha could tell she was attentive, worried she would break the spell if she spoke.

'If your friend orders me to, I would have to.' Starling indicated Caitlin with a vague dip of her head.

'No need for orders,' Isha said quickly. 'That's a terrible idea. But if you would agree to fly across the forest and find the mages there... and the ungifted, if you could tell them where to find us... You could tell them to head for the smoke. We could build a bonfire.' She tried to control the excitement leaking into her voice. They could do this. They could gather their scattered soldiers.

'If there is anything we can do in return,' Caitlin said, 'an order you would like me to lift, if I have the power to do so, or to enable you to do something you have been forbidden, then I would be happy to.' Her voice was cautious, the tone mages used when playing a political game. She obviously wasn't sure her intervention was welcome.

Starling's gaze went from one mage to the other, then settled on the sky. 'I would agree to a trade.'

'We should start with the battlefield,' Caitlin said. 'It's an easy meeting point, and we can check whether anyone survived.'

233

Isha nodded. 'Let's do that. Return to the battleground and gather everyone there.'

They would need to find a way to transport Lord Leofric, but they had a horse, after all. They wouldn't have to put him on their shoulders.

When they hoisted Leofric onto the mare, Isha had a chance to see his injuries. Caitlin had patched him up as best she could, but it was clear he had been hit by two arrows, one in the stomach, the other in the back. Caitlin had removed the arrows and tightly bandaged his chest with his undershirt to stem the bleeding. Two red patches stained the cloth. If his gut had been pierced, he would die whatever they did. Him still being unconscious didn't bode well. He was feverish, which also didn't bode well. They had no bandages, no alcohol, no poppy milk, no medical expertise.

Overall, Isha didn't fancy his chances.

Still, they slung him over the horse, fastening him in place with the stirrups' straps. All they could do was carry him and hope. Although neither of them mentioned it, Isha could feel the relief they all shared at Leofric being unconscious. None of them would be sorry, she suspected, if he did succumb to his wounds.

As if to answer her thoughts, Caitlin said, 'A shame he's such a talented mage, isn't it?'

'I suppose that's why he is the way he is,' Isha said. 'Being a talented mage means he got away with it.'

Caitlin hummed in agreement. They set off, Starling guiding them, Isha holding the mare by the bridle. They made slow progress, trying to ignore their aches and bruises and scratches.

It was strange to walk the path she had run. Mostly they walked over giant trees, their roots as thick as pathways. In places, however, they thinned, and they crossed areas over thin

234

webs of roots, knotted together like latticed wood, which bowed under their weight. Isha tried to ignore the fact that below them, the void awaited. She hadn't even remembered the woods were suspended, hanging above the Edge, when she was fleeing for her life. It shouldn't matter now.

And the Overgrowth was beautiful, in its own, alien way. Birds chittered; leaves rustled. Light fell in patterns, illuminating the wisps of mist rising from the ground. Bright green leaves, new spring shoots, were so bright they hurt the eye. The air smelt of moss and vegetation, but also of something sweet – blossoms, maybe. In places, the sticky sap of pines gave out its sharp, perfumed scent.

With Starling's guidance, it took them half a day to reach Byluk's Hoofprint. From afar, it was just a gap in the trees, a splitting of the Overgrowth. A ray of light and a patch of blue sky between the trees.

But as they reached the clearing, the woodland smells were replaced with the iron-sharp tang of blood, with the sickly, insidious smell of rot, with other, unnameable smells. They reminded Isha of the man who came to help butcher animals back at the farm. He always carried those scents about him, the smells of bodies that had been cleaved, opened, emptied. Caitlin, Starling and Isha fell silent.

Byluk's Hoofprint wasn't quite flat. This meant what could run, drip, slide, had done so. What could fall had. What couldn't had piled at the bottom of the clearing. From afar, it seemed to be a long brown and red snake, with a few mottled blue scales. It could have been the huge corpse of a felled monster that had started to ripen.

As they drew closer, however, it was clear it wasn't one creature. Caitlin paused to breathe deeply, through her mouth, steeling herself. When she nodded, they crept closer. A shudder went through Isha as she made out silhouettes, as the huge beast divided into multiple bodies. As what she had taken for a torn root became an arm. As what she had understood as a pile became three people, limbs tangled, as if hugging. As what she had thought of as a discarded helmet revealed itself to be filled, still, with the head that had been wearing it.

The abandoned battlefield wasn't quite silent. Soft moans. Soft tearing sounds. The flap of wings as carrion birds took flight. The rustle of big shapes not unlike dogs slinking away into the Overgrowth. The bone-deep creak of wood.

The breaths, whimpers, pants, voices, of survivors.

Caitlin turned away from Isha to throw up. Her retching joined the other sounds. Isha wondered why she wasn't sick. She felt detached, observing herself from the outside. She was aware of each detail with aching clarity, but they didn't quite strike her as real. She moved like an ungifted, as if someone else was controlling her body from afar.

She made her way across the battlefield, seeing but not feeling. A woman with both legs caught under her horse, staring upwards, so blankly it was hard to know whether she was alive or dead. A man who had dragged himself on his elbows quite some distance before dying, the slick line of blood drying on the wood. A hoof split in two. An arm with a kher bracelet, the rings of horn achingly familiar, the arm familiar too, maybe, if she squinted, although she would never be sure – who could guess, from a few hairs, a few freckles, whether an arm belonged to a friend?

With Caitlin, they carried the living who could be carried. They built a bonfire at the top of the slope, where what was left of the Nest's camp still stood. The Renegades had pillaged most of the food and useful goods, but a few things they'd left, maybe because they didn't want to overburden themselves. A few bandages, herbs, animal feed. Even barrels of water – probably because they were too heavy to transport.

Isha fed the fire, careful to circle it with stones. Caitlin boiled water in a cooking cauldron and did her best with the remedies at hand, while Starling scoured the forest for survivors.

At first, it was them, the dead, and the dying.

Hawk had taken care of her own: if there had been any Renegade survivors, they were long gone. Starling found a few ungifted who could walk and talk. A few more came out of their hiding places in the Overgrowth. The people who could help did so, throwing branches on the fire, piling stones around the pit, helping bring the flames high. They threw moss on the fire, wet pieces of bark that smoked heavily, making everyone cough, but drawing a clear, obvious grey line of smoke in the murky sky.

We're building a hearth, thought Isha. They were literally making a tiyayat, a place to gather and be safe.

A couple of mages trickled in, some carrying others. A young ungifted, a woman who'd been in charge of supplying the army's meals, had managed to rein horses together, and had saved the mages she could find, hefting them onto the saddles. She also had some knowledge of which herbs were useful for healing, and her expertise allowed her to take over from Caitlin, giving instructions to the others.

As dusk settled, the light of their camp became more obvious. Folks arrived who had walked all day, hiking through the woods, limping over uneven ground. Isha and a couple of others took the healthier horses to scout the area around the battlefield and to escort stragglers back to safety. They dug out Ninian's lover from under his horse, miraculously unscathed. The Renegades hadn't murdered the wounded or pursued the fleeing. Although the situation was dire, there were more survivors than Isha had allowed herself to hope for.

No Ninian. No Kilian. They found a mage who'd suffered from a blow to the hand, and had kept his fingers in his purse, cradling his half-cut stump. After a couple of trips out to the forest and back, Isha was shattered. The work was emotionally, as well as physically draining. Everyone had a horror story from the battlefield. She had to ride out, her thighs rubbed raw as she was unused to horse riding, then walk back, her feet leaden and aching, as the person on the saddle told her how they'd survived.

All the while, soldiers fed the bonfire as if their lives depended on the brightness of the flames. The shadows of the people loomed larger, longer, than the trees themselves.

Isha worked by dusk as she had by day. This second sleepless night blurred her eyesight, made her steps unsure. The mare was also worn; her hooves knocked against the high roots, and she stumbled twice over fallen branches. Maybe she couldn't see very well.

At last, Kilian returned. Underworlds be praised, he was unharmed. He had a small group with him, four other mages.

'I followed instructions,' he joked weakly. 'I went west. It took us longer to backtrack.' He'd handed over his horse to Lady Mathilda, whom they'd found lying unconscious in the Overgrowth and who'd kept throwing up once she was awake. Her helmet had been bashed into her skull, denting metal and bone.

'Good to have you back,' Isha said, squeezing Kilian into a hug.

'Me too – that is, as long as you have enough water for everyone,' said Kilian. 'We haven't found a river since the battle-field. My teeth are starting to stick together.'

She pointed to the firepit, where they had some resources. Lord Leofric was still feverish, lying on a bed of packed leaves. He had been treated by the ungifted who knew what she was doing, and had slipped in and out of consciousness all day, never staying awake for more than a couple of minutes, and never coherently.

Isha was about to head out again when she spotted a flash of gold before her. Starling slid back into human shape like a snake slinking out of its skin.

'That's it,' she said. 'That was everyone I could find.'

It must have been well past midnight. The queasiness was belatedly sinking into Isha's stomach; her legs were shaky beneath her. If not for the horse, she might have dropped to the ground.

The thunk of hooves echoed behind her. Isha glanced over her shoulder to see Caitlin, her eyes deeply set, tiredness etched into her features. For once in her life, she didn't look bright and beautiful. She looked aged, broken, worn.

'Is that everyone?' she asked Starling.

Starling nodded.

Caitlin slumped in her saddle. 'Good.'

'There might be more,' said Isha.

Caitlin shook her head. 'Look at you. Look at us. Let's try to sleep tonight, at least.'

They made their way back through what was now a camp, albeit a messy one, of eclectic fires and hungry faces. At the centre of their makeshift gathering point, the warmth and glow of the fire meant they were comfortable, but that everything around them was one large shadow, where it was hard to make out friends or threats. Thankfully, it also hid the hulking shape at the bottom of the slope, the thing they could not ignore and could not bury.

Caitlin stopped her horse. It lowered its head, blowing air out of its nose, relaxed and relieved – unlike his rider. She had frozen, alert, senses reaching out around her.

I can feel someone's mind close, Caitlin said. *Not one of us.*

Isha gazed out into the dark, trying to find them, turning her reluctant mare around. It was only as they drew close that she spotted them: a flash of white first, then the red skin beneath the polished horns. As they reached the first fires, it became clear they were a group of khers, a unit of thirty or so Renegades, some wearing armour, some nasivyati, some a bit of both, draped cloth around their hips but leather padding over their shoulders, or naked feet but thick trousers reinforced with nails, or high boots with only a scarf to cover their chest.

At the front of the group was a kher wearing a red scarf around his neck. His face was weathered with age, the lines uncanny on a kher, the short, shorn hair peppered with grey. Down each finger – Isha knew without seeing them – he had tattooed black lines, one around each knuckle, symbolising hanged men.

They were coming from two different directions, she realised, on either side of the elongated tree that gave the Hoofprint its name, and had them hemmed in. And, yes, Caitlin was right, Isha could now perceive a background humming, gifted minds, only just letting go of their iwdan friends to reveal themselves. A couple of mages scattered amongst the khers. Everyone in their camp who could scrambled to their feet, gathering in fearful circles around the firepits. They hadn't been expecting another fight. Most of their soldiers didn't get up, either unconscious or unable.

Mezyan took one look at Isha and, to her dismay, smiled. He motioned for his people to wait.

Don't move yet, Isha warned, sending the message widely to her bedraggled soldiers. They outnumbered the Renegades, but having been taken by surprise, they didn't have a formation, their weapons were scattered. They were exhausted and unprepared, hastily-doctored men and women lying strewn about the ground. Lord Leofric was out of action, and none of them had the mindlink to command the whole army properly, let alone Isha, who had never attempted to control a battleline.

'Isha,' Mezyan said, and what shocked her most was that he knew her name. She had expected him to call her the eyas. His voice was the same as when she had heard him address the crowd from the Nest's balcony; a confident, loud voice. But he softened it for her. He sounded less fierce when he said, 'We would like to make a deal with you.'

Isha was aware of the thing lying at the bottom of the slope. It exhaled smells stronger than smoke. It was filled with snuffling and chewing and sighing.

She could picture the arm again, vividly. The red, swollen wrist. The bracelet of horn. The way the bone jutted out where there should have been an elbow.

'If you lay down your weapons,' Mezyan said, 'then we will not harm you. There is no need for violence.'

Isha glanced over his Renegades, men and women with mismatched clothes, varied skin tones, all shades mingling. Yet they all looked the same. It was the eyes, hardened by war. And the weapons, some of which were already drawn. Even those who hadn't yet taken out their swords had them to hand, fingers resting on the hilts.

They encircled the mages, if not completely, then enough to be threatening. Instinctively, the Nest's few unimpaired soldiers drew closer, around the main firepit, around Isha. She got her mare to back away further, hooves drumming on the roots. She and Caitlin were the only people on horseback.

'Hawk won't harm you, Isha,' Mezyan continued in his reasonable tone. 'I can guarantee that.'

She wondered if Hawk had sent him her way, or whether, while travelling with his own small battalion, he had spotted either their lightborn or their fire. Or maybe he was just late to the Renegade's meeting point.

Your mother wants you back, Caitlin said, keeping her mindlink subdued. Every mind around Isha tasted of the same tangy, sweaty flavour: fear.

'You know what we fight for,' Mezyan said. 'We fight for justice. We fight for peace. We fight against slavers who manipulate others to do battle for them. No-one is here, holding a sword, who does not believe it is for the best.' He had a fatherly smile, the kind Passerine might have when she had succeeded at a particularly difficult mindlink trick.

It was hard to hear his words and not believe them. She wanted to believe them. She thought of horses ripped apart by iwdan horns, of Lord Leofric watching with uncaring eyes as ungifted washed away the blood that marred the gates. Arushi's scars, that she had to hide from those who had made them. The conscripted ungifted, huddled in the front courtyard, asking if there was much danger, if they would see their families again, one day soon. If it would hurt.

'We will take good care of you, all of you,' Mezyan promised. 'If you surrender.'

The politeness couldn't quite hide the firmness behind his tone. There was no need for violence, maybe, but he would use it if she refused.

The wind turned, the breeze carrying a reminder, the scents that were not pine sap, not blossoms, not rotting leaves. She could picture a dead man's face; the unrecognisable features, robbed by Byluk of what made them the smiling, grieving, grateful, hateful person they were in life. They hadn't found Ninian, in the end.

'Do you know how many Hawk killed to get here?' Isha asked. Soil or blood. Graves for those she loved, or swords for those she despised.

'There is always a price.' Mezyan was unruffled.

Isha found the words that had been simmering inside her. Even as she spoke, she heard Caitlin's mindlink, her brief, *Be careful!*, but she ignored it and raised her voice: 'Is this the price of justice?' With a large sweep of her arm, she tried to encapsulate the shadows, the night, the stench.

Mezyan lowered his hands, so they rested close to his weapon. 'Injustice has a higher price,' he said.

'How can you talk about justice if you're pillaging villages, using refugees to cross the Shadowpass, torturing those who don't bend the knee?' Isha asked, aghast. Her horror, she realised, was contagious – the mages around her, even the ungifted, were tightening ranks, unsheathing their own weapons, finding wells of courage from which to draw. Their fear still tainted the air, but it was tinged with other emotions now, with something not unlike anger.

Mezyan kept his voice conciliatory. 'I don't want to start a fight.'

But you will, if you think it's worth it, Isha thought, viciously.

Mezyan pinned her with his piercing gaze. 'Surrender. You know it is the right thing to do.'

She could have believed it, maybe, before. And she still believed the Nest wasn't right. It needed to be altered, needed to be radically changed, every stone had to be undone and built again, yes, that she believed with all her heart – but the Renegades would only swap out the hangmen and the hanged.

They wouldn't destroy the gibbet. Blood or soil. Were those the only choices? To bury, or to have others buried?

She kept her mindlink as invisible as Passerine had taught her, as she told the mages to be ready to fight. 'You can tell Hawk I am unconvinced,' she said.

'That is a shame.' Mezyan sighed.

He lifted his hand, a sort of half-wave, a sign that was hardly a sign.

The Renegades surged forward.

It made for a messy fight. Ungifted hurriedly grappled for their weapons. Mages raised their mental barriers, but their attack front was splintered: some decided to target the rare human Renegades, while others took control of ungifted, sometimes jostling other mages from the Nest for mastery, as that was the only way they had been taught to wage war. Starling shot towards the sky like a comet, a ray of gold that disappeared into the thicket of the Overgrowth. She would be little help against khers, maybe no help at all unless Caitlin gave her orders.

Isha was only able to pull out her sword before the Renegades bridged the distance between them. Her mare snorted as she shied backwards. Isha kicked the soldiers who came too close, regretting the absence of a shield. She hadn't thought she'd need it. She shared images of the battlefield with her allies, a sweeping gaze across the firepit and the Renegades from the height of her mare. Caitlin rode beside her, her mindlink clear and sharp, organising the mages, gathering the ungifted into units, trying to summon order from the chaos.

Despite Isha's efforts, a couple of Renegades closed in, Mezyan included. She pulled the reins harshly, trying to avoid the swinging blades. His second swing she parried; the third forced her back. He wasn't aiming for her face or arms, she noticed, but dipping low, trying to hit her ankles, to get her to lose her balance and fall off her mount. She couldn't back away much more without stepping into the fire: she could feel the heat at her back. The mare was fighting against her bit, with jerks of her head, snorts of pain or frustration or fear.

The other Renegades hung back; everyone was cautious not to hurt her. But Caitlin and a couple of other mages were around her, engrossed in mindlink, and they wouldn't benefit from the same special treatment. Isha wanted to help, but fighting Mezyan took up all her focus. She was faintly aware of screaming, but she had to keep her attention on his eyes, on his hands, covered in thin black lines like ropes, on the flash of silver as his blade cut the air.

A swing of his sword cut the mare and severed the saddle's strap. Isha was thrown sideways, slipping off, feet still caught in the stirrups. She rolled on the ground, gripping her sword, throwing her arms over her head to avoid getting trampled. She only just dodged a hoof, kicking off the stirrups. She made it to her feet in time to block Mezyan's next hit – barely. But now they were level.

He was a better warrior than her. It took all her speed to prevent his blows, to guess when he was feinting. Each hit that bit into her blade, rather than her skin, took away some of her endurance. She was already panting, while he seemed unruffled.

I'm on my way, Caitlin thought. *Hold on.*

Before Isha could tell her not to, that Mezyan was too dangerous, Caitlin dropped her mindlink and closed in on Mezyan from the side, urging her horse forward to attack from a blind spot. Isha shared Mezyan's position exactly, but still, he was swifter than them. As soon as Caitlin lurched towards him, leaning down on her saddle, her knife clumsily waving in his direction, he turned, slammed her blade downwards, and lunged. The tip of his sword went straight for her eye.

Isha shouted out, too late. Caitlin lifted her hand, her knife only just catching the blow, failing to deviate it. Her mindlink abruptly cut off; a spray of blood dirtied Mezyan's fingers. Caitlin fell off her horse, blood matting her hair, face downwards. He would have delivered the killing blow then and there, if not for Isha.

From behind, she kicked his knee with all her strength. He stumbled, unbalanced. As Mezyan tried to regain his footing, Isha brought down her sword. Her blade caught the dome of his skull, ricocheted off his helmet, slid down across his forehead, cut his eyebrow. It was only a shallow blow – he shied away from her before she could blind him.

They were in the middle of the fray now, in the thick of the battle where ungifted and mages alike were struggling. Their lines had no structure; the khers were immune to mindlink; the ungifted were panicking. Kilian was nowhere to be seen. They were losing.

By her feet, Caitlin lay unmoving, blood pooling around her.

Gritting her teeth, Isha mindlinked with the people closest to her as she backed away from Mezyan, too busy wiping the blood from his eyes to follow, for now. She pulled a shield from a fallen soldier, balancing mind and body as Tatters had taught her. *Let's make a circle!* She wove a small group of soldiers around her with mindlink, reassured by the weight of a person on either side of her, the two ungifted fighting relentlessly. She placed her shield between theirs; she struck when they did. *We can do this together!* In front of her, the Renegades were khers with harsh tattoos cutting through their features. Yet they could have belonged to the Pit. One young man with a broken nose could have been Ka.

The man beside her was run through by a Renegade lance – it pierced his stomach, and came out hauling guts. The ungifted crumpled with a howl of pain as a new soldier took his place, closing in the line, keeping it tight. Still, they were caving in.

The mindlink across the line was fractured. The ungifted were lost without leadership and proper training. There was only so much Isha could do whilst dealing with the khers in front of her. A lance ricocheted over the top of her shield, nearly stabbing her face, and she realised that, although they would try not to kill her, even the Renegades couldn't prevent a deadly blow from slipping through.

She thought of Caitlin lying on the ground, her hair flowing off to one side, blood following the locks. She found herself backing down; she was losing concentration. Her arm was tiring.

A mind lifted across the Hoofprint like a gust of wind. It caught everyone in its grip. It was a decisive mind, and it washed away all of Isha's thoughts, cleansing them, leaving her with the knowledge of her place in the line, nothing else. She was a cog. The wheel would turn. She saw nothing but the kher in front of her. She understood nothing but the need to land her sword in his throat. She wasn't an individual anymore, but an arm, a nail, a piece of the entity that was the Nest's army.

Silence fell suddenly. No-one remembered how to scream. They only knew how to kill.

The army clawed, and bit, and spat, and struggled. The Renegades weren't ready for this level of coordination, for this unwavering control. Maybe because of the abrupt change, maybe because Mezyan was wounded, maybe because the eyas was lost in the throng and impossible to retrieve, they retreated. The Nest advanced with the calm certainty of a thrown stone, of a loosened arrow. Weakness had been seared from their line. Isha no longer belonged to herself; her teeth thrummed, her vision swam with other people's memories. She was entirely under the sway of mindlink. She would have walked over the Edge, one step at a time, had the mind invading her willed it.

Until the control loosened. The ungifted were still under the effect of mindlink, but the Renegades were fleeing, and Isha realised she was stepping over someone's body. She looked down; her foot was pressing on a kher's cheek. The idea of walking across someone's face, of planting her foot in a woman's unblinking, open eye, nearly made her regret not surrendering to Mezyan.

She stumbled backwards and, for the first time that day, threw up. Bile filled her mouth, slicked her teeth. She spat and coughed until her throat was raw. Glancing around, she saw other mages shaking themselves free from mindlink. A flash of blond hair – Kilian – was backing away from the frontline, headed towards the fires. Towards Caitlin.

She ran. She didn't marvel at their victory. She threw herself by Caitlin's side, lifted her head onto her lap. She ignored Kilian's voice, his muddled words, him telling her not to move an injured person. She couldn't hear anything but the pounding of her heart. She couldn't see anything but Caitlin's pale features, drawn tight, the jagged line across the side of her skull. She couldn't feel anything but the blood – hot, terrible blood, all over her hands, all over her legs.

Caitlin was breathing. Hands shaking, Isha pushed the locks out of her eyes. She realised she was crying. She could barely make out Caitlin's face through her tears, barely discern the discarded knife that had saved her life.

'She's alive,' Kilian was saying. 'She'll make it. We made it.'

Beyond the carnage, propped up on one elbow, leaves stuck to his clothes and hair, sweaty with fever still, but lucid, his mind sharp, was Lord Leofric. His green eyes surveyed the scene he had caused, the Renegades he had sent running. She could still feel his thoughts, bright things squirming in the background of her mind. He released his hold slowly.

The floor was thick with bodies, friends and foes, like a butcher's home after lambing season.

* * *

Mezyan had narrowly missed Caitlin's eye, but cut deeply enough to reveal bone, down her temple and the side of her head. A doctor roughly sewed back the skin. It made for an ugly, uneven scar. She blinked back to consciousness as the needle was penetrating her flesh – an unmerciful awakening. They got her to bite into a leather strap until they had finished their work.

Dawn was only a couple of hours away. Leofric had organised shifts of guards, but most people had sunk into sleep, if unconsciousness caused by exhaustion and bleeding could be called sleep. People with medical skills were awake. People with wounds minor enough were awake. People with nightmares vivid enough were awake. Yet everyone was subdued – muffled whimpers, muffled crying, muffled whispers. The horses held their heads low, snorting through their noses. They were tired too.

Lord Leofric was sleeping. How he managed such a peaceful, unbroken rest was beyond Isha.

Even when Kilian curled onto his side to catch a few hours of shut-eye, as he called it, she stayed beside Caitlin. Starling kept her silent company, her eyes glowing golden. She didn't look as tired as the humans. Maybe her true shape had revivified her. Maybe lightborns never slept when they flitted across the sky.

With a grunt, Caitlin pushed herself into a sitting position, despite Isha's murmured protestations.

The stitches were swollen, red. The corner of her eye had been caught by the tip of the sword, making it seem more open. The whites spilled, somewhat, as if her eyelids continued grotesquely down the side of her face. The doctor had shorn the hair that was in the way, leaving a gap.

'You should rest,' Isha said, even though she had done nothing but keep watch.

'I want to hold my promise,' Caitlin said, her voice thin after the day of hardships. Wincing, she turned to Starling. 'What can I do for you?'

Starling threw her head backwards to stare at the sky. The clouds hid any stars away from view, although a bit of moon was peeking out, breaking through the fog. 'I would like permission to dance.'

Caitlin's face creased in pain when she tried to nod. Instead she spoke carefully, without opening her mouth too wide. 'Please do. I relieve any ban preventing you from dancing. Actually, I remove any bind I have power over. Do as you please.'

Starling's face caught the light reflected from the clouds. Her eyes had changed again. They were a pale shade of blue now, nearly grey. For a moment, it seemed as if she might say something to them, and Isha waited, expecting a word of wisdom from the embodiment of a god.

The tips of Starling's fingers shimmered silver, as if the moonlight pooling around her was changing her to mercury. As the sparkling grew to encompass all of her body, the light shifted from silver to gold; sun-touched. She flew upwards, curving and twisting, illuminating the night with words no-one but she could read. Then she flew higher, grew fainter, until she was only a glimmer against the clouds, then not even that.

Caitlin sighed. 'It's absurd, but I thought she might dance for us where we could see her.' Maybe she didn't realise her words were filled with longing.

Tentatively, she ran her fingers along the swollen, tender skin, the bumpy stitches. Isha stamped down on the urge to lean across, to promise that everything would be fine, to draw Caitlin into a hug, to place her lips against the hot skin to cool it. She didn't know where the impulse had come from.

Instead, she only said, 'I understand Starling needing to be alone, far from us.'

Caitlin's voice was a rough whisper. 'I thought we might get some beauty at the end of a day of ugliness, that's all.'

Chapter 10

The army could be roughly divided into three categories: those who could fight, those who could walk, those who couldn't even do that.

They left just after noon the next day, with most of the ungifted, a few of the mages. They tucked Lord Leofric onto a padded saddle and carried him with them. Isha took the lead. It was an easy burden to take – contrary to life in the Nest, out here in the wild, no-one else wanted the responsibility. She asked the soldiers to organise themselves into columns: people who could fight on the outside, the wounded on the inside of their rows. Those who couldn't walk they left behind with a couple of healers. Starling was tasked with warning the closest villages and asking them to send help and resources, and to carry the injured folk back.

Once Starling had returned, they sent her to the Nest. She had to warn Lord Daegan and Passerine so they could attempt to slow down Hawk's progress, giving the remains of the army time to reach the city before the Renegades.

Against her expectations, they walked at a good pace. Without the mages holding tightly onto the ungifted, overseeing their every step, everyone made faster progress – the ungifted because they could choose their own footing, the mages because they weren't drained by mindlink. They cut through the Overgrowth, hoping to find a shortcut out of the woods. Isha commanded a hundred or so soldiers, a small battalion of survivors. They'd only retrieved about twenty horses; Hawk must have stolen the rest. They formed columns, the horses in front, no more than three people abreast, drawing lines through the forest. When they could, they followed the wet roads of rivers.

Still, they weren't safe. At night, they spotted fires, lights that couldn't be from villages. Hawk was ploughing through the countryside. Isha tried not to think about whether she might be slowing her progress to the Nest to see if she could get her hands on her eyas. One night, Isha thought she spotted flickers in the Overgrowth, maybe a retinue of warriors who were not friends, and she told the army to stifle all their fires. But it was impossible to know for sure whether it was reason or paranoia driving her.

It was a long, gruelling walk. At first, Lord Leofric was asleep most of the time, his skin hot to the touch. However, as the days stretched on, as they reached the Sunpath, he recovered. If not completely, then enough to guide them.

As soon as he was well enough, Lord Leofric came to ride beside Isha. He was still wan, one hand resting against his side, as if to soothe a stitch. She knew he was pressing against his arrow-wound to dull the pain.

'I heard you did good work in my absence.' She wondered if he was mocking her, but his voice was neutral.

'Thank you. I did my best.' It was a safe enough answer.

Lord Leofric winced as he readjusted his position on the saddle. His teeth were clenched to the point that the veins down his neck showed. Still, he was riding at the front of the army. Isha didn't want to admire the man, but she had to admit, begrudgingly, that he was tough. He wasn't one of the soft-spoken, mild-mannered mages of the Nest. He had battled through fever, dragging himself back to consciousness. He had fought off Mezyan from the stretcher where he had been laid out to die from his injuries.

'If you can fleshbind, now is the time to tell me,' Lord Leofric said.

She kept her gaze in front of her. 'It is a kher tattoo, sir, but I cannot fleshbind.'

He didn't answer. They rode together, side-by-side, in an uncomfortable silence. His jaw was set, his eyes hard. His core was welded with steel, she sensed. He wouldn't go down easily.

'I need you as my right-hand woman,' he said. It was an order. 'None of the other halfwits are worth a damn. Lord Passerine was right in that regard.'

She bowed her head, hiding her thoughts.

The following days, she rode beside Lord Leofric. The soldiers grew used to seeing her, not even a high mage, standing beside him. She kept her mouth shut. She followed orders. But her tattoo made her instantly recognisable, and meant she changed from a figure that mages dismissed to one they sought out when they had questions or worries to put to their leaders. Isha discovered she intimidated people less than Leofric, struck them as less aloof than ordinary high mages. They trusted her to listen which, in a way, was worse. She felt more responsible to do right by them.

At the same time, Lord Leofric wanted her to control ungifted, as that was the skill she most needed to practise. Isha spent hours drilling soldiers down the roads, seeing the path through myriad eyes, gripping steel through myriad hands. At the end of the day, she dreamt of columns of soldiers snaking through the woodland. She woke up feeling she had phantom limbs, arms and elbows and backs and hips that didn't belong to her.

She couldn't achieve Lord Leofric's level of coordination.

This wasn't something she'd ever learnt. This was the only talent neither Passerine nor Tatters had ever honed. She was terrible at ungifted control, but long, boring days of forced marching taught her the basics. She would never be great, but she could become good enough.

To outpace the Renegades, they stuck to the Sunpath. Hawk would have to make her way through rougher terrain as she went around the Sunpath, avoiding its patrols, strongholds, ditches, lawmages and conscripted soldiers. Maybe Mezyan's failed attack had made her skittish, or maybe she didn't want to damage the land she intended to rule. Starling reported that Hawk was circumventing busy towns, only picking useful fights. In each fortified village, Leofric chose fresh mounts, stuck the high mages on them, replaced his exhausted soldiers with new ones – conscripted guards, for the most part – and rode on. Only mages were irreplaceable in this army. In this way, the horses were always peppy, walking at a brisk pace. In this relay race, the goal was to reach the Nest with their army before Hawk got there.

All the while, Lord Leofric followed the main road, forcing a hard pace on everyone.

They walked. They walked for hours, for days. They walked until their feet blistered, bled, healed, hardened.

They walked until they saw the Nest silhouetted against the sky, grey stone on white mist.

* * *

'Are you awake?'

It was Arushi's voice. With great effort, Tatters opened his eyes. Crusts stuck his eyelashes together. The light was too bright. He managed a nod; he didn't trust himself to speak.

The last few days had blurred into hours and hours of strenuous training, of building fortifications around the Farmers' Gate, of meeting Starling briefly, always with a dash of fright in her eyes, as she described the Renegades' advance, the race Lord Leofric and Hawk were each trying to win. They had strived to awaken the Nest's magic with Passerine, attempting everything they could think of. Aside from the Nest's heating, they had found some sort of rain-makers, which poured water inside and outside the building; whole walls that could slide and move open – that particular discovery had nearly destroyed a wooden staircase – and ways to make the stained-glass glow in the night.

It was clear the Nest was a wondrous thing, much more than a castle, something that could unfold into another shape, some sort of complicated machine they didn't have all the keys to unlock. But they found nothing that would be useful against Hawk.

After a particularly frustrating day of nothingness, Tatters had decided to spend the evening with Arushi. There had been a lot of drinking, as he recalled. And he might have agreed to fleshbinding, he realised, as bits of the night coalesced.

'Sorry to bother you,' Arushi whispered. She was already dressed. 'The army has returned.'

Tatters was too hungover to feel afraid.

'I'd better find out what's going on,' he said.

Arushi nodded. 'Sekk iss.'

She leant forward and placed a kiss against his lips. His mouth felt bruised and tender, but her kiss was like cool water. It anchored him into the here and now – this kiss was real, everything else was memory. It was only when she pulled back that he noticed Arushi carried about her a distance, a sort of nostalgia, as if she were already mourning what they'd lost.

'You're still not wearing the ring,' he said.

257

He didn't have to elaborate, to explain that he was referring to the iron ring, that he meant she hadn't yet officially signed up for the blood right. Her face closed.

'I should go,' she said. 'It's going to be a long day ahead.'

But she didn't leave the room. He sat up on the straw-packed bed, rubbed his eyes, and sighed into his hands. He struggled for the words he wanted to say. *I feel like I've tried everything I can to show you that I care.* What did it matter, in the end, that he cared? *The blood right is such a boon. It will make such a change. What more do you want?* But he knew what else she wanted: atonement for past crimes, something stronger than a promise to ensure that iwdan would not be harmed in the future.

'Please,' he said at last. It was the only word that sprung to mind. 'I don't want us to be on opposite sides of this war. I ... I can't even begin to imagine it.'

She knelt beside the bed. She took his hand. She spoke softly. Because of how tender she was, he knew she would not say something he wanted to hear.

'I can't promise you I'll fight for the Nest. I can't.' When she shook her head, he followed the line of her horns as they moved. 'Every time I consider it, I see Yua's face. I hear her voice. You must understand.'

Yet just under half of the kher guards had taken up the blood right. Did Arushi see Yua's face when she talked to her colleagues? He wondered what deep conflicts must be dividing the Pit, as families who had agreed to the blood right opposed the ones who hadn't. Nobody spoke about it outside their hearths, he'd noticed. They unsaw the rings. They wore what they considered pride, what their detractors considered shame, and coexisted.

'Tell me you'll consider it, at least. Tell me ...' He paused. He wasn't sure he could bear to hear it out loud. *Tell me you won't be on the side of the people I'm sent to kill.*

Her expression softened. She kissed the back of his hand. 'I promise.'

Before he could say anything else – and anyway, what else was there to say? – she was out of the room.

He crawled out of bed and reached for the jug of water placed beside it. Lazily, Lal emerged. As he drank from the jug, he realised that he felt heavy, bloated. It was as if the air itself was more leaden than usual. After one swig, the collar tightened; he couldn't swallow anymore. He choked and had to spit out a mouthful.

Hawk is getting closer, said Lal. *The collar must feel it.*

What a reassuring thought.

Tatters left the house. Once outside, his spinning head settled somewhat. His footing was uncertain. He could still feel strangers touching him, although by now he really shouldn't. Did fleshbinding sometimes have an aftermath? He would find out, he supposed, if he survived long enough. The hands were pulling downwards, he fancied, weighing down each step.

Still, walking did him good. It unknotted his sore muscles. It was a wet day, with a light wind and a drizzle. It was the kind of insidious rain that could hardly be felt but soaked him through in minutes. Tatters lifted his head to the sky and let the droplets stroke his face, cool his collar, run down his hands. It washed away some of the khers' fleshbinding.

When he reached the Nest, soldiers were huddled under the arches while servants were carrying weapons inside, piles of shields filling with water despite their efforts. The stablehands were unsaddling and scrubbing down the mounts. The horses shook their heads, drops caught in their manes. A couple of ungifted were queuing in the dampness of the arches for food.

Everyone was wet and miserable, and Tatters fitted right in. His legs hurt. His head hurt.

From the sidelong glances, he must look as rough as he felt. He imagined his eyes rimmed black from the sleepless night, the contrast between a high mage's black robe and a beggar's haggard features.

You're not a beggar, Lal corrected him. *You're a soldier, like them.*

I wish I wasn't. Yet here he was.

Idly, he combed his hair with his fingers. It squelched.

He made his way to Passerine's chambers, where he pushed the door open without knocking. They were his chambers too, now.

'Where were you?' Passerine asked. He was standing in the middle of his room, as if about to head out, but stopped in his tracks when Tatters came in.

Why, good day to you, too, Lal answered.

Tatters was in no mood to explain what he'd been up to. 'That's none of your business.'

He crossed the room and went for the wardrobe, shrugging out of his black cloak. He flung it against the wardrobe door and rummaged inside for something dry to wear. He was in his undertunic, but he was too worn out to be embarrassed.

'May you grow tall,' said Passerine, sarcasm palpable. 'Did you have a nice day? Are you comfortable? Are there any other niceties you'd like me to pretend to care about before you tell me where you'd disappeared to?'

'Why, thank you for asking, I am having a shitty morning,' Tatters answered. 'And I was at the Pit, not that you care. Happy?'

The collar was strange. When Tatters touched his neck, it was hot enough to melt gold, had it been normal gold. But he couldn't feel the scorching heat against his neck, only against his fingers.

Passerine was watching him closely. 'The collar already knows, doesn't it? Hawk is getting closer.'

Incredible, did you guess that all by yourself? asked Lal, biting.

Tatters shrugged. He pulled Passerine's red travelling stana out of the wardrobe and draped it around him.

'Are you an idiot?' Passerine asked when he saw which piece of clothing Tatters had chosen. He glowered at the bright red fabric as if it were a personal insult. 'You're wearing the Renegades' colours the day our army comes back defeated?'

'*Our* army, is it now?' said Tatters. 'And here I was thinking it belonged to Lord Daegan.'

He went to sit on the bed. Blue and white patches marred his vision. A headache was closing in, a band of iron across his forehead, as unyielding as the collar. His bones were made of rusted iron and grated against the strain every time he moved. He wanted to lie down and sleep this day away.

'Hilarious,' said Passerine. 'Let's discuss semantics rather than strategy.'

'Do me a favour, just shut up,' snarled Tatters. 'I can't deal with you right now.'

'I'll go and find Isha,' said Passerine. 'We need more information before we decide anything. Stay there.'

With those words, he strode out the door. Tatters' head was ringing with pain. When he let himself drop backwards on the bed, sleep fell across him like a blanket.

He became conscious of the sound of voices, and realised they must have been talking for a while without rousing him. He was still half-dozing as the words became clearer.

'You have it all planned out, don't you?' Passerine was saying. His tone was only half-mocking, with a hint of admiration.

Tatters kept his eyes closed, his breathing even, hoping he might be left alone if he appeared to be sleeping. Lal agreed, and kept their thoughts subdued.

'I've had long days of riding to think it through,' Isha answered. She sounded confident, assertive. 'And the knowledge of what losing a battle feels like, to make me want to win the next one.'

Tatters could hear steps, pacing, the scrape of wood on stone. They were ambling about the room, pulling chairs across.

'You've grown,' Passerine said.

Isha gave a self-conscious laugh. 'Well. With a mother like Hawk, there isn't much choice but to grow, is there?'

'You had a father too,' Passerine said. Tatters noticed the past tense. He wondered if now was a good time to indicate he was awake. But he didn't want to interrupt them, and he'd admit to some curiosity as to what Passerine might tell Isha if he believed no-one else was listening.

'But he wasn't there,' Isha said. Her thoughts were bright as glow worms in the night. Tatters could tell she nearly asked what Passerine knew about her real father, but refrained from doing so. *The father who was there at my birth, who carried me through shadows, who protected me and feared for me, is already here. I don't need to hunt for another one, uncaring, elsewhere.*

Passerine and Isha seemed ... connected, Tatters supposed. In alignment, like stars that follow each other's course through the sky. Their silence was a shared one. Passerine's mind was filled with tender nostalgia, of cradling a baby in his arms, of cradling blue light as it curved between the clouds.

'You had a daughter, didn't you?' Isha asked.

Passerine's mind became akin to still water, so dark one couldn't see the bottom. 'But I wasn't there,' he said.

This had grown personal. Tatters hadn't intended to spy on them, not truly. He made a show of yawning and stretching before sitting upright. When he'd rubbed the sleep out of his eyes, and opened them, he found Passerine and Isha by the chimney, staring his way.

'Ah, Tatters, we were waiting for you,' said Passerine. 'I hope you're ready for what comes next.'

'It was a mess,' Isha said, without preamble. 'I've been telling Passerine about it. It wasn't a fight, it was a slaughter.' She was all business now. Tatters wondered what was worse: being sore, wanting to throw up, or her expression. 'We're underprepared. We ran back here in a panic.' The Nest's army had survived by fleeing, hiding, praying.

'Hawk's been tactical in her killing,' Passerine added. 'She wants to lay siege to the Nest, that much is clear.'

The two of them kept speaking – about defence strategies, about Starling's inexperience in battle, about Leofric's state. Wearing a torn shirt, with a mage's robe hastily thrown over it, Isha was focused only on war preparations. Passerine brewed some tea while she paced the room, asked whether they had maps, lamented the defeat they'd suffered.

Beside her, listening, offering solutions and alternatives, guiding her, Passerine was like a taller shadow, trailing her every movement and idea.

It's what he's always been, Lal said. *He was Hawk's. Now he is her daughter's.*

'The question is, I suppose, do we think the blood right was enough?' Isha asked, jolting Tatters from his daydream. She turned towards him. 'What will the khers do during the battle?'

He shrugged helplessly. Some khers had sided with the mages, at least officially. Some of them, surely, wouldn't want to put themselves at risk, and would stay in the Pit, maybe barricading it against intrusions. Some of them might be ready to take up arms for the Renegades, but how many? And would they have been able to prepare, to muster, without the khers who had taken the blood right opposing them? It was hard to know with iwdan. Normally, if a rebellion was brewing, everyone would know. They'd speak about it. Wouldn't it have leaked back to the mages by now? Wouldn't one guard, at least, have spilled that sort of secret?

Maybe, said Lal, *but maybe not. Khers are better than humans at disagreeing, yet standing together.*

'I don't know,' Tatters answered truthfully.

'It would be best to invite the families of all of those who agreed to the blood right inside the Nest,' Passerine said. 'If we free them a dorm, it shows goodwill.'

'And it adds a good reason to not betray the mages if they have your family hostage,' Isha said wryly. Before Passerine could argue, she shook her head. 'No, you're right, of course. Let's do that.' Although it would mean emptying a dorm of human refugees, Tatters assumed, exiling them to corridors and corners. It was sure to be poorly received by the people being pushed out.

They continued to discuss contingency plans. Their words washed over Tatters. Hawk was here. She would be able to rekindle the collar's power. They had failed to find magic that could stop her. His headache had returned, tougher than before. His mouth tasted sour. Closing his eyes, he let himself drop back onto the bed.

'Are you listening, Tatters?' Isha asked. 'I have an idea for dealing with Hawk.'

He waved vaguely with one hand, to indicate she had his attention, but didn't open his eyes.

'How would you like to be drunk on the day the Renegades arrive?' Isha asked.

He pushed himself up on one elbow and cracked his eyelids open. 'Now we're talking. What's the plan?'

* * *

By now, Isha should have been at the mess, sitting on something other than the floor or her horse for the first time in days, eating something warm and filling. Instead, she was on the well-trodden path winding through the moors, walking towards the Temple.

She had been about to rest at last when she'd heard that the Doorkeeper and the priests were refusing to leave their sacred grounds, despite the Renegades' approach. They would stay in the Temple, undefended. No doubt they would be decimated. Lord Daegan and Lord Leofric couldn't care less – Lord Daegan had gone as far as saying that he wouldn't mind if the priests and their outdated beliefs jumped off the Edge. Passerine and Tatters were both unbelievers, perplexed as to why the Doorkeeper would want to make a stand. Which left Isha.

She trudged through the moors as the sun started its descent. It wasn't quite a sunset yet, but the sky was already changing colour, long streaks of clouds dotted with pink and white like cherry blossoms.

She heard a rhythmic trot behind her which turned out to be Caitlin, mounted on a small, Nest-bred horse.

'I saw you from the ramparts,' Caitlin said in place of greeting. 'Why aren't you taking a break by now?'

'I could ask the same of you,' Isha answered.

Caitlin shrugged. When she pulled on the reins, the horse obediently stopped, then immediately grazed the heather. On one side, Caitlin seemed untouched by the war. It was only when she turned that the scar was visible: a big, ugly, irregular thing that tore past her eyelid down the side of her head.

'Jump on,' she said. 'It'll be quicker.'

Isha accepted help to hoist herself onto the croup. She drew her arms around Caitlin's waist, as that was the easiest way to secure herself without stirrups or saddle. Both Caitlin and the horse were warm, comforting in a way Isha hadn't expected. She relaxed under the lull of the regular gait. Exhausted by days of trekking, she rested her head against Caitlin's shoulders and closed her eyes. Caitlin smelt of horses, of mail-oil, of the untamed outdoors.

Isha reluctantly woke from her snooze as the shoed hooves clinked on the paved road of the sacred land. Yawning, she let herself slide off as they reached the front of the Temple. Only a couple of priestesses were milling about, along with some devout ungifted.

Isha couldn't help but see the Temple with a soldier's eye: open doors with no locks nor hinges, open windows with no shutters, sapling-thin beech trees of silver bark, a complete absence of barriers. An openness that invited everyone in, including invaders. The mirrors on the domes, the windchimes in the branches, none of it would serve them against the Renegades. The baskets of discarded goods contained shoes, clothes, belts, but nothing of defensive value, even if the priests could be persuaded to use them.

Osmund spotted them from afar and came to greet them. Caitlin dismounted, letting her horse chew on clumps of grass.

'It's good to see you, Osmund,' Isha said.

As always, he seemed tired, thin. Each time she saw him, she had the impression the wind had eroded him a bit further. 'I am glad to see you made it back,' he answered.

They touched wrists. Before Isha could wonder how to ask to see the Doorkeeper, she was stepping out of the Temple's entrance.

The old woman glared at the horse, which was leaving prints in her wild garden and munching on her heather bushes. Despite wearing only a tunic, with no coat and no shoes, she didn't shiver. Her hands were lined with age, covered in small brown spots. The skin on her knuckles was papery where she clenched her stick.

She descended the steps towards them, letting mud dirty the soles of her feet as she drew closer.

'I thought the mages were busy sharpening their claws,' she said.

Her voice, like her eyes, was piercing. She reminded Isha of the gnarled trees that grew despite all odds on the Edge, roots clinging to the stones, stunted yet impossible to dislodge.

'Isha has proved to be an unusual mage,' Osmund said. He introduced Isha to the Doorkeeper, explaining he had met her before, and seen her perform purification rites. 'I vouch for her,' he concluded.

The Doorkeeper glanced at Caitlin, but she stood a step behind Isha, arms crossed, unwilling to speak.

'I have come to ask you to take refuge inside the Nest,' Isha said.

The Doorkeeper shook her head. She didn't even speak. At first Isha waited for an explanation, before realising she would not receive one unless she asked.

'Why?' she said.

When the Doorkeeper answered, her tone stayed even, her voice soft. She was unassuming, yet Isha could sense a core of willpower, impossible to budge. A weed, maybe, which could be culled, its leaves plucked, but which would grow back again and again, just the same.

'I will not burden myself with hatred, with weapons, with death, all for a war that does not concern me, for men who are arrogant enough to bind lightborns, for a woman who is arrogant enough to want to bind countries.'

How to answer someone who expressed herself this clearly and calmly? Isha struggled to find the right words. 'I understand this Temple is devoted to Byluk and letting go.' But it couldn't be all it was, surely. 'But isn't it also devoted to Groniz?' At last, Isha found her words, like a runner finding her stride. 'Groniz gives. She gives us the greatest burden of all, with all the other burdens that go with it: feeding, sleeping, protecting, fighting. She gives us life.'

Isha was conscious of Osmund in front of her, listening intently, of Caitlin just behind, loosely holding her horse's reins, of the priests and priestesses who had paused in their work to see what their leader would decide. The Doorkeeper shook her head again.

'I told the mages I would have nothing to do with them unless they freed their collarbounds. I stand by my word.'

Before Isha could answer, Caitlin took a step forward. 'I understand.' She was harsher, louder, than the Doorkeeper. Isha nearly waved for her to step back, to stay quiet, to not annoy the believers any further. She might have attempted to shush Caitlin, if Caitlin were the sort of person who could be shushed.

'It wouldn't look good, would it, if after making such a fuss, standing up so bravely to the supreme mages, you hid inside the Nest,' Caitlin went on. 'I get it. You've got your pride. We all do.'

She threw her reins around her horse's neck.

'Let me show you what you should do with your vanity.'

Caitlin bunched her hair into her fist, twisting it and lifting it above her head. With her free hand, she took her knife from her belt. She hacked at the beautiful, lush auburn hair, not caring about how smoothly she cut it. The blade bit through the strands until she was holding a long mass of hair in one hand, letting her scar stand out starkly.

Caitlin stepped towards the Edge. The wind was greedily stealing locks from her fingers even before she let go. The sunset devoured what she'd given it. Without the long hair, her features were changed, starker, more angular. She sheathed the knife.

'Hair grows back,' she said. 'Pride grows back. You know what doesn't? The lives of your people.'

Her eyes seemed larger as well, Isha noticed, now that there was nothing to hide their intensity. Her irises were brown, the colour of earth, of land, of trees.

'If you stay in the Temple because of some misplaced obstinacy, you'll die. Your people – the priests, priestesses, believers, who entrusted you with their lives – will die with you.'

The sunset streamed colours around and above Caitlin, framing her like the windpaths around the council room. Something expanded in Isha's chest, something she wouldn't have been able to name, a feeling that widened her, pushed at her ribs, ran down her arms, tingled in her fingers.

It didn't fade when the Doorkeeper and Caitlin talked some more, exchanging arguments first, then, as the Doorkeeper let herself be convinced, information regarding possible lodgings in the Nest. It didn't fade when Caitlin rode ahead to organise freeing space for the priests; when Osmund gathered the goods and people from the Temple; when the sky faded from purple to night; when Isha walked beside the Doorkeeper along the moors, in the growing shadows, not daring to help the old woman find her step, but too worried to leave her alone; when at last everyone was cared for, and only Isha and Caitlin remained.

Once they were done and back in the apprentices' female dormitory, Caitlin sighed. She rubbed her uninjured eye, letting some weariness land. They sat on the same bed, side-by-side.

Isha leant across the bed and ran a hand through the cropped hair, the short, thick pelt that still hung around Caitlin's ears. The tingling in her skin climbed from the tips of her fingers up to her chest, settling there, as insistent as an ache.

Caitlin looked at her, not pulling away from her touch.

'I can't believe you cut it,' Isha said.

Caitlin only smiled. She picked at where her wound met the corner of her eyelid, the skin still pink and raw. Without her hair, it was impossible to ignore the line the sword had dug into her flesh.

'I can't believe you're being sentimental about this,' she said. 'What does it matter?'

It didn't, Isha supposed. She let her hand drop away.

'Do you think we'll win?' she asked. 'I mean, when Hawk arrives.'

Caitlin did a half shrug, half flinch. But she held her chin high when she answered, 'Well, I for one don't plan on losing.'

The dorms were as grey as the sunset had been abounding with light. Yet Isha had absorbed the colours, somehow, and they still thrummed inside her.

Chapter 11

Tatters had been drinking heavily even before he reached the ramparts. When he arrived at the bottom of the city gates, he was already feeling light-headed. He kept sipping from his wineskin as he walked the length of the walls, where men and women in armour were shoving for space, with the high mages trying to impose a semblance of order. Every couple of yards, a staircase was built into the walls, to provide access to patrol the area above.

Don't fall off, Lal warned.

No balustrade nor barrier hemmed the outside of the steps; Tatters stuck close to the wall. Lord Leofric was hard to miss, both because of the brilliant gold of his armour and the unyielding firmness of his mindlink.

Mind fuzzy with drink, Tatters climbed up to where Lord Leofric was overseeing the preparations. In a way, the alcohol was helping – the view from the ramparts didn't shock him as much as it should have. Rather than horror, Tatters felt a dim sense of dread. He drank another gulp of sour wine.

Lord Leofric had picked a spot halfway between the Sunpath Gate and the Farmers' Gate, on the southeast side of the city. The northeast was protected by the river. The third and last entry to the city was the High Gate, which led to the Nest. As it

271

was on the western side, closer to the Edge and the bridge, it should be spared. Or at least, reached last – Passerine was guarding it with Daegan's followers, such as Caitlin, because it was considered the safer job, and Daegan hadn't wanted to risk his support in the frontlines.

The Renegade army was gathered in the fields east of the city; Hawk evidently hadn't wanted to attempt a breakthrough during the night, so the camp was only starting to shake itself now. The numbers were enough to send a spike of fear through Tatters' gut. A couple of thousand, maybe? He worried Hawk had let Lord Leofric win the race back to the Nest, pacing herself so that all her dispersed groups could join her. Even after the losses, the city could muster enough ungifted to match her army, but certainly not as many trained soldiers or mages.

Hawk was always good at getting people to die for her, Lal said glumly.

Eyes narrowed into slits, Lord Leofric was watching the Nest's conscripted army, mostly ungifted, as they gathered on the other side of the hastily dug ditches. Archers were aligning on the walls, interspaced with mages who could direct their attention and arrows to important areas of the battlefield. Their efforts were centred around the Farmers' Gate, as they hoped the river would protect the Sunpath Gate. Everything was still at this messy, just-before-the-battle stage, during which no-one knew when the action would start, and no-one was quite in the right place.

'Ah, our first lightborn is here,' said Lord Leofric in a silky voice.

'Where is Isha?' Tatters asked. He didn't want to deal with Leofric alone.

'On her way, with Lord Daegan's collarbound,' Lord Leofric

answered, turning his pale face back toward the river. Maybe it was only the dawn light, but his skin seemed grey.

With a bit of luck, the wound's infected, said Lal.

He did seem out of sorts, which wasn't entirely reassuring, considering he was the only person competent enough to hold the city. Lord Daegan himself was in the safety of the Nest. Supposedly, he was guarding against any unpleasant surprises, such as Hawk finding a way to circumvent the city and raid the Nest directly.

The unpleasantness is right here in front of us, said Lal. *Only it isn't a surprise.*

You're particularly uplifting today, you know that? Tatters took another gulp of wine. He felt detached from the scene below him. Skies, he felt detached from his own body at this point. The wine tasted better with every swig.

Isha climbed the stairs, Starling in tow. Her armour unsettled him, although it shouldn't have. Something about how worn it was, already. Her padded cap, stained in places, pressed down on her hair, only allowing a few matted curls to poke out around the edges. She held her helmet loosely under one arm. Even Starling had a no-nonsense approach to clothing, wrapped in a bulky gambeson with a small, glinting blade slung around her waist.

'Have you been drinking?' Isha asked.

'Like a man waiting to die,' Tatters answered.

Her plan is like one of Hawk's, he thought. *Absurd, new, could just work.* She wasn't the awkward kid who'd entered the Coop last year, not anymore, that much was clear. She was a strategist, now.

Like mother, like daughter, said Lal. Tatters wasn't sure whether that was good or bad news.

Isha greeted Lord Leofric, before going to stand at the edge of the ramparts, watching the armies below. The drifts in the crowd as it prepared for battle reminded Tatters of a storm brewing, the way everything shivered and moved in the skies and the seas.

'Where are the khers?' he asked.

'The ones with the blood right are serving on the Sunpath Gate,' said Lord Leofric, interrupting Isha before she could say anything. 'The others are hiding in their Pit. The bloodcows are cowards, as expected.'

Tatters didn't answer. In the rush of the morning's call to arms, he hadn't crossed paths with Arushi. He prayed she was on the Sunpath Gate, or huddled at home. He hoped those were the only alternatives.

The Renegades blew their horns. The long, mournful sound sent shivers down Tatters' back.

'Let's check you can fleshbind from this distance,' Isha said.

'Time to shine already?' Tatters said.

'If you can't fleshbind, then we might need you down there, with the foot soldiers,' she said in all seriousness.

Tatters imagined himself amongst the throng crawling beneath the gates, like ants about to be trodden underfoot, or drowned and carried away by the river. A front line was required, but he, like everyone else, didn't want to be part of it.

'Here goes nothing,' he said.

He brought the wineskin to his lips, focusing on the tepid liquid, how it tasted of wine on the verge of becoming vinegar, astringent, bitter, yet reassuring. He homed in on his physical sensations, the rough stones beneath his feet, the hide of the wineskin against the palm of his hand, the breeze touching his cheeks, the dust lifting from the ground and filling his lungs.

Then he fleshbound with Hawk.

He hadn't done so in years. He didn't even know if sharing blood once in a lifetime was enough to maintain a link. He was at a fair distance from the Renegades, too. But fleshbinding could be stretched far, as long as one was above ground, up to a couple of miles or so. The connection struggled with thick obstacles – stones, walls, mountains – hence why Arushi hadn't been able to find her sister in the Nest's underground prisons. Rock smothered the iwdan art, though no-one knew why.

As he sent his sensations away from him, his head cleared. His vision sharpened. An invisible weight, a sort of heaviness and weariness in his muscles, faded. He had succeeded. He had handed his drunkenness over to Hawk.

'It worked,' he said. He drank more wine. It had the clear taste of water, of nothing.

'In that case, don't stop drinking,' Isha said. 'We don't want her to be able to think clearly, let alone ride a horse.'

'Let's hope incapacitating her proves sufficient,' said Lord Leofric.

A part of Tatters wondered whether Hawk could face the Nest, even as drunk as a lord, and still perform in battle. He suckled the wine like a newborn would their mother's milk, hoping to have her out cold.

'Most monsters fall if you cut off their head,' Isha said, cold determination in her voice.

The red-clad army pushed through the river. The Renegade soldiers waded through water up to their waist, weapons held above the current. This was not what the Nest had expected. They had ungifted soldiers on the other side of the river, of course, to impede the Renegades, but the bulk of their forces were much further south, behind the man-made defences.

Leofric didn't need to wave or blow a horn. He mindlinked to the archers, and arrows rained down thickly on the Renegades, forcing them to lift their shields above their heads as they ploughed through the waters. With the smoothness of a swarm, ungifted left the Farmers' Gate to rush to the riverbank. With the advantage of being higher above the waterline, they could form an effective blockade. A smaller part of the Renegade army also attacked the fortifications around the Farmers' Gate, but it was a lacklustre attempt that didn't prevent Leofric from diverting most of his soldiers north. Lord Leofric moved his army like a conductor controlling an orchestra, conscious of each note included in the chord.

Starling alighted, lifting above the scene. 'Take down the mages on horseback,' Isha instructed. When Starling flew, she was a golden comet crossing the battlefield, shining her light above the struggling men and women.

It could have been us, Lal said. *We could have been there.*

We fought as lightborns so often, Tatters said. *It feels strange to stand aside.*

Passerine had given Tatters permission to alight throughout the battle. The collar glowed dimly with his orders. But Tatters didn't want to risk being seen and summoned.

He noticed Hawk didn't call back her troops, despite the arrows, despite the fact that her frontline would die as they arrived on the other side of the river. She still had the element of surprise: the Renegades reached the bank before the bulk of the Nest's forces. With numbers the Nest lacked, they climbed the muddy banks. Still, they slipped in water-soaked clothes, hefting shields mottled with arrows, only to die at the hands of coordinated ungifted on the other side. The waters frothed red.

Starling fought from the sky. Watching her stole Tatters' breath away. She dived from high above, the size of a god, the colour of a star, before hitting a frail human silhouette, often knocking them off their horse. Often, but not always. Sometimes she went bouncing back the other way, and it was painfully beautiful, hard to follow with the naked eye, the swiftness and brightness of her, suddenly changing direction.

It's impossible to fight a lightborn, thought Tatters.

Yet that doesn't stop Hawk from trying, said Lal.

The Renegades continued to push. The bodies clogged the shallow river around the Sunpath Gate, making for easier passage, although the wilder waters further north were still standing fast. Slowly, the Nest's soldiers gave ground.

'Let's see if alcohol clouds Hawk's judgement,' Isha muttered. Tatters sensed her exchanging quick messages with Lord Leofric. She was serving as his right-hand woman, after all.

What an ally to be burdened with, Lal thought. *What a man to be second to.*

The Nest's soldiers pretended to cave in, allowing a passage in their ranks. From above, Tatters could see the trap being laid: both sides of the army were still fighting and controlling the bank, only opening a narrow corridor. Once the Renegades stepped through the gap, they would be hemmed in by ungifted on all sides, and cut down like weeds. But it was impossible to see this without having an aerial view, which Hawk lacked from the flatness of the moors.

As expected, maybe because of the drink, maybe because the risk was worth the reward, the Renegades pushed their advantage, pooling into the chasm. Using mindlink, Lord Leofric closed his ranks as if tightening a fist, spears like nails sinking into the Renegades, cutting off a chunk of their army. For a moment, it seemed, from the way the Farmers' Gate held its ground, from the way the Sunpath Gate had put the Renegades in difficulty, that they could win this after all, that they could beat back Hawk and force her to rethink her strategy.

Then two things happened at once.

A squadron of khers, horns pointing out of their helmets,

charged through the river on horseback, intent on helping the Renegades caught in Lord Leofric's grip. At their head rode a white-horned half-kher. Mezyan. Tatters recognised him with a pang.

Before the Nest could deal with the riders, the army defending the Farmers' Gate collapsed.

Something must have happened. The messages being mind-linked from the southern gate became confused, then completely disjointed. The archers didn't seem to be shooting any more. The discipline the mages had imposed slackened, which meant the ungifted lost their capacity to hold a line. The Renegades pushed forward into the loosening ranks.

Isha spotted the same breakdown of their formation as Tatters, and visibly paled. She called out to Starling. The lightborn joined them, her silhouette briefly blinding Tatters before she landed. As she shifted back into human form, Isha said, 'Go and help the Farmers' Gate. They can't possibly give mirrors to every foot soldier, which means you'll be able to target the human Renegades and take them down.'

Starling nodded. 'Before I go, I've seen Hawk. She's staying in their camp, with a couple of guards. But it seems she has found a way to fight off the fleshbinding.'

Already? said Lal.

She must be sharing it with her soldiers, Tatters realised. As with pain, drunkenness could no doubt be diluted, so that twenty people felt mildly tipsy, rather than one person being blackout drunk.

Starling was already radiating golden light by the time Isha added, 'Be careful.'

I'm dealing with the bloodcows, Lord Leofric mindlinked. He was standing very still, like an animal about to bolt or bite.

'Wait, I'll give you a hand,' said Tatters.

It was a bit of a stretch, but if it had worked with Hawk, it would work with Mezyan. If he was fast enough, Mezyan wouldn't have the time to negate the fleshbinding. Tatters dropped the connection with Hawk, for now. He focused on the rider he could see in the river. The link was old, yet easily rekindled. He shared his drunkenness with Mezyan.

The horse reared, or maybe Mezyan's grip on the reins slipped. The charge continued, iwdan pushing across the Nest's lines, but the head horse stumbled, and the leading figure dropped like a stone in the foamy waters, disappearing from sight.

'Good job,' Lord Leofric said, sounding surprised at his success.

'Yes, I...' Tatters stopped abruptly. A wave of cold closed around him. As soon as it happened, he realised what Mezyan was doing. It was obvious, yet he hadn't seen it coming.

He hadn't expected Mezyan to share something back.

His mouth filled with cold water. Something hit his shoulders, above his head, blows like hooves raining on his back, his neck, his skull. Tatters fell onto his knees, only faintly conscious of Isha beside him, trying to hoist him to his feet. When he inhaled, he breathed in slimy, muddy water, which burnt through his lungs. He was choking, he was drowning, heavy iron-shoed hooves were bruising his arms... And then, suddenly, his head was cold but clear, he was breathing air, and the wet, slick armour hugging his chest was the only thing pulling him down.

Tatters coughed helplessly, choking on water he hadn't swallowed, shivering from a dash in the river he hadn't suffered from.

'Well, Mezyan is alive, I know that much,' he said, rubbing his sore throat as the fleshbinding receded. As soon as he could, he steered the iwdan magic towards Hawk once more. Unless she was also in trouble, undergoing some sort of physical discomfort, she was a safer target: she didn't have anything negative to share in return.

He glanced over the ramparts. The battlefield was a mess, the Nest's soldiers flanking the Renegades, the iwdan trying to break the Nest's hold, bodies and banners mingling so thoroughly it was hard to tell where one army began and the other ended. The iwdan were screaming something at the tops of their lungs, charging in an arrow-shaped formation, horses dripping red-tinted water. It was impossible to make out one swimming kher amongst the people being washed away by the river.

Isha helped him get to his feet. 'Thanks for that,' she said. 'I'm afraid we need you to do an overview of the Farmers' Gate and tell us what's going on.' Their southern army was behaving like a bunch of headless chickens, defending, pushing and backing down with no obvious pattern. 'You're the only one who can travel fast enough.'

'What about Hawk?' he asked.

'If she does cause trouble, I'll mindlink you,' said Isha.

'I can't alight and fleshbind,' he warned.

'I know. Keep it up as much as you can, we'll manage with what we've got,' Isha said.

He focused. The light filled his fingers, his hands, his wrists. He jumped off the ramparts on the city side, alighting as he cut through the air. As a lightborn, the mess of stairs, of soldiers keeping the gates equipped, of streets busy with ungifted and mages, were no obstacles.

He flew south towards the Farmers' Gate, only to find half of their mages and archers gone, and the other half fighting for their lives. But they weren't battling the Renegades, who, although they had crossed the ditches and destroyed the siege weapons, hadn't yet reached the walls.

They were fighting iwdan. Not those from the Renegades – the ones from the Pit.

Shit. Tatters flew in a circle above the ramparts, assessing the damage. Then, because he had to, he headed for the Pit. The Pit was southwest of the city, conveniently placed between the Farmers' Gate – which Leofric had drained of resources, where the army was currently collapsing – and the High Gate, the fallback option for the mages, their escape route back to the Nest.

The khers were rebelling.

How many? Lal asked. She wasn't surprised, only determined to overcome.

More than I would have hoped, he thought. *More than there should be, actually*. He was shocked by their numbers, before he realised some of the iwdan had to be trained Renegades. That was why there had been so many unfamiliar faces, so many khers with the polished horns of the Sunriser tribes. Hawk must have been using the cover of the Sar festival to bring weaponry and soldiers to the Pit. It had all been organised right under his nose. And the Nest, which couldn't tell one kher from another, had let this happen.

Do you think Arushi is amongst them? he asked.

We'll worry about that if and when it's relevant, said Lal. *You should act before it's too late!*

The khers were going to cut through the mages easily, attacking them from an unexpected direction, with minds immune to mindlink. With allies on the inside, Hawk was certain to win.

First, the High Gate. A couple of mages and high mages were standing in loose formation, obviously not expecting to be of much use yet. Tatters landed beside Passerine, sliding into the mud, finding his footing as he hit the ground. His ears were ringing, and for a moment he wasn't sure why, before he remembered the alcohol. When he fleshbound, his head cleared.

'Hey, you know the cushy job you were given?' he asked. A couple of high mages gathered closer; Lord Daegan's people, a woman he vaguely recognised, with long, jet-black hair, and a couple of others – men, for the most part, with square Duskdweller faces. A couple of Sunrisers, including Sir Cintay. Caitlin in the back. 'It's not cushy anymore. The khers are rebelling. Groups are leaving the Pit and coming for you.'

'That's impossible,' the woman snapped. 'We gave them the blood right. What reason could they possibly have for refusing it?'

Pride, said Lal. *Dignity. Revenge. Take your pick.*

A couple of other mages joined in, saying the khers were all either high or shagging – it was well-known they cut off from humans during their Sar festivities. Surely, the sober ones had accepted the blood right ages ago. Passerine ignored them; his mind was alert, already mapping the city, the distance to the Pit, and their possible getaway routes. Even without spying on his thoughts, Tatters could tell he took this seriously. He knew Hawk, after all.

'Armed?' Passerine asked.

'Yes,' said Tatters. His gaze caught Caitlin's. She had shorn her hair; a half-sealed cut that started at the corner of her eye revealed matted scar tissue down the side of her skull. She looked nothing like the bright young girl who had been sent to war; she looked like someone who had already weathered too much. 'And you can count on about twice as many khers as the Pit usually holds.' Which was about a couple of hundred iwdan, the size of one of Hawk's semi-independent battalions. 'The additional khers are probably trained Renegades. I'm going to

282

help the Farmers' Gate before it falls,' Tatters concluded. 'They'll be here in five, maybe ten minutes.'

'What can we do at such short notice?' said Sir Cintay, appalled.

'Five minutes is more than you would have had without me,' Tatters answered.

He was about to alight again, having done his duty, when Passerine said:

'Catch.'

Tatters experienced a sensation of déjà vu as he turned, as the two-handed spear was thrown his way, as the tough wood landed with a smack into the palm of his hand.

How else were you planning to fight? Lal asked.

'Thanks.' He wasn't sure why he said it; he was anything but thankful. The spear felt heavy, even when held with both hands. He thought of Passerine telling him he had lost his touch, that he had forgotten how to kill. He thought of the fact that he would be attacking people he knew – Ka with his fierce, toothy smile; Tara, competitive card player and soldier; iwdan he had grown to know and respect.

Don't break down now. Passerine's mindlink was steadfast. *Fight.*

The collar warmed at the words, in time with Tatters' quickening pulse. He had picked a side. He had to do this now.

When he alighted, the weapon slowed him down. He was surprised at how bulky it felt, even once he had shifted into light. No doubt birds of prey experienced a similar discomfort when carrying game between their talons. It made his flight awkward, unbalanced his smooth turns. He flew over the Sunpath Gate without landing, mindlinking the situation to Isha and Lord Leofric – his explanations a mix of words, memory and visuals – before heading for the Farmers' Gate, which needed him more.

He circled it once, trying to work out which sections were doomed to fall to the khers and which parts he could still protect. The ramparts were narrow, forcing the khers to fight in groups of two or three at a time, diminishing the advantage they'd gained from surprise and greater numbers.

Tatters picked a staircase that hadn't yet been taken. He landed at the top, where iwdan could come from two places: the ramparts themselves, if they'd made it to the top already; or the steps below. A terrified-looking mage was on the landing, giving out confused orders in mindlink, shaking so hard his sword barely stayed straight.

Tatters checked he could hold this spot by himself – he could see a kher climbing up the stairs, and further away, having just thrown an archer over the walls, two were making their way across the ramparts. This would do. Until the Renegades climbed the fortifications, of course. Then he'd have three fronts to defend, which was a feat he couldn't perform.

He didn't give himself time to think. If he stopped to reflect, he would be paralysed. He mindlinked broadly: to the mage beside him, to the archers and mages beyond.

I want the mages to focus on the outside! he said. *Don't let the Renegades climb the walls, whatever you do. Archers, turn towards the city. Shoot at the khers. Got this? Archers on the inside, mages on the outside. Trust your allies to have your back. Don't turn around.*

Order was restored as the mages concentrated on holding their army, as the archers started fighting the khers with some sort of coherence. It was too late, in the thick of battle, for Leofric to bring soldiers back from the river to the Farmers' Gate. But this was the entrance being pressured on both sides – this was the one Hawk intended to fall first. The showy crossing of the river had been a deadly, elaborate feint. Tatters held the spear above his head, hands moist, trying to ignore the thumping of his heart.

Take your knife, Lal said. *Just in case.*

He did so. He held the knife in his back hand, clasping both weapons together, pressing its blade along the shaft of the spear. The knife was a failsafe, which was always useful on a battle-ground. It was his old knife; the bone handle fitted perfectly into his hand. He'd used it to cut cheese, to peel apples. He'd used it for the mundane long enough that he'd forgotten it could also serve to kill.

The first kher closed the distance with him.

Now! said Lal.

It was more natural than he'd imagined. The adrenaline sobered him better than a long sleep. Long-lost movements came back to him, steps, lunges, the clash of blades on bone, the taste of blood in his mouth. Spearwork was all angles and sidesteps. It was all about being slippery, on the offensive even when taking a step back. It was the art of the unexpected.

The khers climbing up the steps had a tougher time of it – they were lower than him, and as soon as they were within his reach, he thrust his spear towards them. The first time, the metal tip hit horns, not bone, but it threw the kher off-balance and off the steps all the same. Tatters didn't want to aim for the face, but that was the easiest shot from this position. A strong blow to the helmet sometimes stunned, most often killed – always forced a kher back.

The khers on the ramparts were harder work. Tatters had to parry one, aim for the other, keep both at an arm's length. They weren't used to a mage who could parry with his spear, who could use the wings on the side of his blade to force shields away from their bodies. These were not soldiers. Hawk must have decided this was an easier job, reserved for untrained iwdan.

As such, they couldn't do much against him, especially in this narrow space, where the fact that they outnumbered him didn't help them.

The stairs, again, said Lal.

The figure climbing up the steps was an armoured kher. A woman. No doubt a guard from the Nest. No doubt someone he knew and had trained. *Don't*, said Lal. *Focus.* She kept her attention on the woman as Tatters fought the men in front of him.

He slipped his spear beside a kher's shield, twisting his wrists to prise it off, turning sideways so the spear could hit flesh, not wood. He put all his strength into the lunge, and the kher was shoved off the side of the ramparts, screaming.

Pain, acute, like the cut of a blade down his sides. Tatters gasped and took a step back, raising his defences, but he couldn't see where the blow had come from.

The guardswoman, Lal warned.

She was close enough for him to strike. Tatters spun towards her, but as he extended his arms, he felt sharp pain again, down his elbow this time, as if someone had bruised it. He nearly dropped his spear in shock.

Fleshbinding, he realised.

She took advantage of his confusion, keeping her shield high above her head, running up the last set of steps. As she reached the top of the staircase, shield still protecting her face, he aimed for her stomach. Her sword came down swiftly, knocking his spear towards the ground, where it scratched the stone.

When she lowered the shield, he saw her face, firm behind the helmet.

'Arushi,' he gasped.

This was bound to happen, said Lal. *Don't let it get to you.*

Arushi didn't seem surprised; she must have braced herself for this moment. Along the rampart, another guard joined them. It might be Tara, although it was hard to tell with the Sunriser chainmail hanging around the sides of her helmet. And a third kher, male, with a billhook. Its curved blade had more reach than the swords.

Despite himself, Tatters took a step back. He thought of them training. Of Arushi telling him that he trusted her not to hurt him. He knew exactly how she would charge; he'd seen her do it once, which was enough. She was a good soldier, but she underestimated him. She would be predictable.

'I am sure you understand,' Arushi said.

She rushed him. Time seemed to slow down as she slammed her shield against the spear, throwing it sideways, opening up, briefly vulnerable, as the shield left her body.

This is what the knife is for. Lal was thrumming with anticipation, dedicated to winning this fight.

Tatters could see it in his mind's eye. It was a spearman's oldest trick. One hand dropped the spear, while he closed the gap and plunged his knife into the opponent's neck. It was a standard move, quick, easy, deadly. Lumbering idiots who ran straight at you had it coming, was the general feeling amongst the Renegades, when they'd taught him this move.

Killing Arushi would be easy.

He alighted. Rather than drawing close before her slower sword could reach him, rather than staining his blade red, he flew out of the way. His spear clattered to the ground. Her sword cut through light, and he felt nothing more than the brush of a feather. He lifted above the messy battlefield, which would be messier soon, no doubt, as discipline broke down again.

He returned to Leofric and Isha, who were still holding the Sunpath Gate, although the khers had managed a breakthrough.

The Renegades were putting pressure on the Nest's army like a pair of pincers.

Lal was fuming. *Is this how we let Hawk win? Is this why we die – because you were feeling weak?*

'I can't hold the Farmers' Gate,' Tatters said. He was nauseous. Maybe it was the wine.

They had lost the city. They would lose more if they couldn't make it to the safety of the Nest.

And it's your fault, Lal said.

Isha, her eyes and mind invested in the battle below, didn't answer.

'We have two lightborns, we are *not* losing,' said Leofric. His jaw was tense with contained anger, as if he could bite down on his power and keep it that way, locked in his teeth, through sheer strength of will. He turned to Tatters and snapped, 'Keep fleshbinding with Hawk, collarbound.'

Maybe he should. While Leofric mindlinked to Starling, summoning her back, Tatters tried to fleshbind. He failed, and found himself throwing up over the side of the gates instead. Swapping between shapes and drinking might not have been the best plan Isha had ever come up with. He was wiping his mouth clean, wincing at the acrid taste in his mouth, when Starling landed beside them on the battlements, an arc of light so elegant it was hard to remember she had been slaughtering soldiers.

Before Leofric even gave his order, Tatters guessed it would be stupid. The desperate took rash decisions.

'Go to the Renegades,' said Lord Leofric, 'and kill Hawk. Do not return until she is dead.'

Starling bowed. The top of her skull, her hair, her neck glowed as she alighted. Tatters was dimly aware of Leofric ordering the foot soldiers to retreat, to disperse inside the city. He didn't seem to care that he had just condemned Starling to death.

Tatters alighted with a lurch that was graceless but threw him into the sky after Starling. He had no idea what he was going to do, how he was going to help.

He hadn't been able to save Yua, but he would not let Starling's life be wasted by the Nest.

You're not discouraging me from doing this? he asked.

There is no point. Lal was as poised as him, as bristling, as frightened. *This was bound to happen. I always knew we would have to face Hawk one day.*

Her mind was filled with bleak conviction. Maybe Lal was right, and fate, not luck, had brought Hawk to the Nest. She had cornered Tatters against the edge of the world, in the end.

When a creature is cornered, it fights.

* * *

Crammed between Leofric and the walls, Isha fought with every ounce of strength she had left. She hardly saw the scene before her eyes, too invested in other people's minds, carrying other people's weapons, guiding other people's hands as they lunged. They had managed, laboriously, to spread their army equally on the two fronts where they were needed, Sunpath Gate to the east, Farmers' Gate to the south.

Lord Leofric looked drained but determined. 'We'll have to retreat towards the Nest,' he admitted through gritted teeth. The lightborns might be able to stop Hawk, but they wouldn't be able to prevent the gates from falling to the Renegades.

The Nest backed down. The only way out was the High Gate, to the west. They had to abandon the river, their natural fence. Isha descended the ramparts, each step unsteady beneath her. Being so close to the supreme mage wasn't helping – she kept being washed away into his mindlink, her vision clouded with images of the battlefield. Trying to stay independent was like struggling to swim upriver.

Beneath the walls, the world tasted of dust. The screaming was deafening. Weapons clashed fiercely as soldiers bled through the gates, gathering in the main street. The Renegades, hemmed in by the doors, couldn't use their numbers to their advantage as much as before.

The mages could have held fast, maybe, had the iwdan from the Pit not made it impossible. A line of soldiers only worked if it could focus in one direction. The walls that should have been pelting the Renegades with arrows were under kher control. Stones, arrows and unsavoury articles were being thrown onto the mages from their own ramparts. It was untenable.

Leofric's plan, which he shared in mindlink, flashed across Isha's thoughts. She could see the army in small bands, each mage acting independently, using guerrilla tactics throughout the city. *Each mage takes twenty ungifted*, Leofric instructed. *We know the city better than them. Disperse in the streets, regroup at the High Gate.* Before anyone could protest, just as the main body of soldiers crossed the gate, Leofric left with his retinue, bringing a group of ungifted with him.

Isha was left to fend for herself, controlling a small team of soldiers. Mind reeling, a step behind her line, she ushered them into a side-alley, away from the gates. The Renegades broke into groups as they entered the city, streaming behind the mages. At first, panic squeezing her chest at suddenly being in charge, trying to find her way while keeping the Renegades on horseback at bay, Isha didn't appreciate Lord Leofric's tactical brilliance.

People screamed. Swords sank into flesh. Helmets went flying, chunks of metal and skull smashed together in a bloody mess. Isha wasn't human – she was a thing of many limbs, an insect wielding twenty weapons at once, scuttling backwards on forty feet, seeing the same scene fractioned through numerous eyes. When one of her arms was severed, when one of her eyes was gouged, she only growled and picked up more iron from the discarded limbs. Pain didn't reach her. The Renegades before her bore no faces. She saw only targets, chinks where the armour was weaker, angles where skin could be torn.

It was all they had against the Renegades, this hive-mind; without it, they were nothing.

The violent buzzing that had taken over her mind dimmed somewhat as she realised they had killed the last of the Renegades following them. They were, briefly, not in the midst of battle. She counted her ungifted. About fifteen men and women remained, eyes blank, terror and pain washed away from their features. As her control lightened, they blinked, returned to the world. One of them glanced down from the shaft of his spear to the gore staining his arm up to his elbow.

High-placed mages were sharing an overhead view of the streets, indicating exactly where other Nest retinues where, where Renegade soldiers were placed. The Renegades couldn't use their numbers to their advantage in tight spaces, and mages could, through mindlink, ensure they helped any squadron that was having trouble. Lord Leofric had been right: this was the best way for the Nest to fight.

Isha forced herself to remain calm. She stayed at the back of her soldiers' minds, a reassuring presence, she hoped, but not an overbearing one.

I'll help us fight, she mindlinked. No point in making a sound and giving away their position.

She bent over one Renegade – a kher, she noticed absently, smaller than most humans, about her size. Despite her armour,

Isha wasn't armed for fighting in a line. She was supposed to stay at the back.

But what was the point of training with Passerine, of learning how to blend mindlink and physical fighting, if not for this? She retrieved a lance from the corpse, tugging the weapon out of the limp fingers. She also pulled off his shield, strapping it to her forearm.

Once ready for battle, she placed herself at the centre of the line. Relying on other mages' mental maps of the city, she avoided the Renegades, sticking to back-alleys and narrow streets, jogging at a soft pace. Her breathing was laboured by the heavy weight she was carrying; her soldiers panted but didn't complain. Everyone was focused on surviving this day.

A stray thought crossed her mind: *Is Hawk still alive?* Would she feel it, would she know, if her mother were dead? It was not the time to agonise about it, Isha decided. That was the lightborns' battle. Leofric was right. It was pollution, it was nonsense. A more useful question was: *Could we retake the city?*

The mages might be able to force the Renegades into costly, drawn-out skirmishes. However, even as she considered it, Isha realised it was impossible. The khers from the Pit knew the city as well as the mages. They were the Renegades' most precious asset in navigating the streets. Furthermore, if the mages didn't get out through the western gate before Hawk reached it, she could control all entryways to the city – and all exits. The mages would be trapped inside for her to dig out at her leisure.

They had to get out.

The moment of quiet they enjoyed – running, breathless, through empty streets with barricaded windows – was short-lived. Closer to the High Gate, the battle raged. Passerine was there somewhere, Isha knew, and so was Caitlin.

She heard the regular thumps of crossbow bolts hitting wood.

Her retinue arrived behind a line of khers, from the Pit as far as Isha could tell, using bows and crossbows against a smaller team of mages. The iwdan were a ragtag band, with a mix of weaponry, and an even more eclectic mix of armour. Most of them were civilians, women heavy from giving birth and tending to their hearths, who were fighting fiercely for a better life. A couple of bright-eyed men were there as well, too young to be adults. Including one who tore Isha's heart: Ka, who stood half-naked in defiance, with his tattoo of a bull and his whip-marks stark against his back.

The mages had been forced into a shield-wall, stuck, unable to leave the street they were barricading. A familiar mind was in charge, but the mindlink was uneven, so the mage trying to establish order was, if anything, adding to the confusion. She would berate him later.

Kilian, I'm coming! Isha called out.

From behind, she charged the iwdan. They wielded mostly long-range weapons, so they dispersed before her – even Ka ran. She didn't think he recognised her in the confusion. Isha couldn't bring herself to give chase. She had never wanted to kill iwdan. She had wanted to stop the Renegades, to stand up to Hawk, but somehow two fights had become one.

How is everyone? she asked the soldiers of the shield-wall as they got up from their crouch. *Kilian, where are you?* she added, realising she couldn't spot him amongst the soldiers. *Weren't you guarding the High Gate?*

Am I with Byluk? Kilian's mindlink was slurred. It froze Isha. Outside of the frenzy of combat, he shouldn't sound this disjointed, as if he were barely clinging to consciousness.

'Our commander has fallen,' a woman blurted out. 'After Lord Passerine sent us to support the troops inside the city.' Her shield was mottled with arrows; a blow had dented her helmet

REBECCA ZAHABI

and left a line of dried blood down the side of her face. She had the wide-blown pupils of an ungifted who had flickered in and out of consciousness in the middle of the battlefield.

Isha dropped the mindlink. 'Where *is* he?'

The woman pointed to a shape lying on the floor. 'Over there.'

With mindlink, Isha organised the soldiers in a half-circle to control this area and keep this bit of pavement as their own. She checked the people who had been hit by an arrow or a bolt, trying to get as many of them up as possible. She found Kilian slumped underneath his shield. With trembling hands, she reached out for him. She couldn't see a fatal wound – no injury to the face or neck. A bolt had gone through his elbow, though, and blood had run down his arm, pooled along his side, and had been soaked up by his blue robes. The cloth was gorged with red.

'Kilian?' His eyes regained focus when she spoke. She could have cried in relief. 'Byluk will have to wait. We're still with Raudaz, for now.'

'Is that better?' he asked weakly.

She shrugged helplessly. Depending on his condition, it might not be.

She helped him to his feet. He couldn't lift his right arm, nor move his hand. Apparently, he couldn't feel it either; he didn't wince once. As soon as he moved, blood dripped down his fingers.

'We need to get out of here,' Isha said. The ungifted woman helped her tie a hastily-made tourniquet around Kilian's arm to staunch the bleeding.

'Let's go,' she said. Kilian was pale from blood loss; there was the glint of terror in his eyes.

I'll protect you, she promised. He wouldn't die here. She

294

wouldn't die here. They would get through the gates, even if they had to pave the streets with skulls to get there.

She closed her eyes. She breathed. When she opened them again, her mind wasn't only hers. She had become a monster once more, a thing of many arms, many legs, many eyes. She had lances, shields, spears, swords. She had mouths that tasted of blood.

She was a beast, and she would live.

* * *

Soaring over the Renegades' camp was like passing through a memory. Tatters recognised some of the tents. He recognised some of the faces. He recognised some of the beasts of burden. He had walked on this lush grass on hotter days, and smelt the roasting game hunted from the forest, and breathed in the smoke from pine wood being placed on the fire. He had listened to the glasses clinking, as if in answer to the chainmail being lifted off its rack. He had shared this violent, simmering energy.

When Hawk had bound him with the collar, he had spent nights dreaming of her demise. He couldn't remember what he had felt. He must have imagined taking her down as a lightborn, what bringing that sort of death might feel like, but he couldn't remember it.

We'll find out soon enough, Lal thought.

Starling brought panic wherever she flew. Horns were blown, the few Renegades who had stayed at camp mustered, gathering their weapons. Those who were vulnerable to lightborns lay down so they offered smaller targets to alight through. They had been drilled for this situation, obviously, as humans hunkered down, leaving the camp in the hands of iwdan.

And Hawk. She wasn't the kind to lie down on the floor and wait.

At first, she was a dot of brown, a patch of frayed leather brigandine. Starling aimed for her with the certainty only the collar brought. Tatters followed, a wake of red to her gold.

Then Starling was flung in the opposite direction, and it was all Tatters could do to place himself behind her to cushion her fall, to keep her above the swarm of khers. Starling was larger than him, more imposing, and despite them both having little weight, she still threw him off-balance. He kept her from crashing into the tents or the ground, where she would have returned to human shape, where she would have been vulnerable.

He waited for Hawk to call upon the collar, as he had been expecting since the battle had started. She didn't.

Maybe she didn't have the time: Starling shook herself, rose in a lance of light, and dived back down. From above, the tents rustled as Starling flew through them, flags clapped, fabrics threatened to tear. The glint of Hawk's strike-mirror caught the sun. The two women whirled around each other, but if their dance had been words in the lightborn tongue, it would have spelled death.

Tatters joined the fray. Despite his speed, by the time he reached Hawk, two khers were beside her, making it harder for him to manoeuvre. He didn't recognise the two Renegades. He lifted above them, circled once, dipped down on Hawk. She rolled out of the way, sword in hand, not bothering with a shield. Skimming past her, he spotted sweat and dirt on her forehead and in her hair; standing up to Starling was taking a toll on her.

Maybe we have a chance of winning, after all, said Lal.

He charged at Hawk again, weaving around the khers, taking sharp turns, trying to catch her unaware. Starling stayed high, swooping towards Hawk's strike-mirror, whereas he kept close

to the ground. It was counterintuitive to a lightborn, but also to
a soldier: the khers flailed wildly, struggling to hit a low target,
as if trying to hunt a rabbit with swords. When he closed the
gap with Hawk, as she lifted her mirror to reflect him away,
bracing herself for the impact, the pull of the collar slowed him,
strangled his leap.

He bounced off her mirror and picked the sky as a retreating
ground. The collar was seeking to assert itself, magic hissing and
spitting like water poured on hot stones.

I can't fight her, Tatters said. *The collar is preventing me from
harming her.*

We can work against those binds, Lal said.

Below him, Hawk spun, crouched, moved with a litheness
that belied her age. Starling dipped, circled, shoved, and yet
always seemed to be thrown back, always seemed to be reflected
by the mirrors.

Wary khers, used to following orders but not to wasting their
lives, gathered around the pair. Tatters circled above, a long, red,
shimmering vulture. He was confronted with the same problem
as the khers: how to help without getting in the way? Tatters
was worried about blocking Starling's path, especially if his flight
was going to be unexpectedly broken by the collar.

For a while, neither woman managed to take the upper hand.
He wondered why Starling insisted on crashing down with
repetitive bullheadedness. Surely she'd realised this wouldn't
work? Was she only trying to appease the collar?

She broke Hawk's strike-mirror.

He heard the crack, the shattering sound, the yelp of surprise.
Tatters hadn't realised that was possible – maybe it wasn't for
him, but Starling was much weightier. The sound of breaking
could have been glass or bone. Hawk's hand snapped back, and
Starling was upon her, and for a split second it seemed she

would alight through Hawk's chest, ripping out her soul by diving through her heart.

Then Starling bounced downwards.

Tatters didn't see the glint of iron, but he guessed what had happened, because he had seen it happen before. Hawk had used her knife to reflect Starling towards the earth.

He had seen it before, because it had been used on him. Passerine had showed them this trick.

This is how you kill a lightborn.

He was plunging towards them before Starling had hit the ground, before her light went out abruptly as she returned to human shape. She lay stunned, pinned under Hawk's knee. The shock would only last a second, but it would be enough.

He was halfway upon them as Hawk lifted her knife, ready to draw it across Starling's throat.

He was on them, shifting back into human form, landing with all his weight on Hawk, as she brought down the knife. The blade bit into his skin, before ricocheting against his shoulder blade. She gasped as he threw her aside, using momentum more than strength. They rolled on the floor, a mess of limbs and bruises. Rather than attempting to disentangle himself, Tatters alighted, slipping between Hawk's fingers like the fabric of clouds, rushing to Starling's side.

He shifted back to human shape beside her; the khers were already closing in.

He was conscious of something slick and wet running down his back, dampening his robes.

'Get up,' he hissed, finding Starling on the floor, dizzy, but thankfully not unconscious. He hauled her up. 'Alight, I'm begging you, come on . . .' She stumbled to her feet. Her nose was filled with blood, dripping on her upper lip.

'Hawk is going to kill us,' she whispered.

'Run back to Lord Daegan,' he urged. 'Tell him to cancel Leofric's order, that you can't do it.'

The iwdan were upon them. Tatters was forced to alight, pulling Starling with him. They both rose skywards as the blades cut uselessly through their light.

Hawk was a warrior who could fend off two lightborns, with or without her strike-mirror. They weren't up to the task, one soldier limited by his collar, the other with no military experience. Hawk wasn't a target they could take down.

That's a lie, said Lal. *If you tried, with Starling's help, you could kill her.*

But what then?

It was the weakness in Lord Leofric's reasoning. Maybe at one point in time, getting rid of Hawk would have dissolved the Renegades. But what she had started was now bigger than her. If she died now, she would become a martyr. The Renegades would take the Nest and, to avenge her, they would punish the mages harshly. With or without Hawk, this war would follow its course.

Leave the battle of egos to the mages, he decided. *I'll be more useful elsewhere.*

Even Lal had to admit the strategy was sound. They had other people to defend – to save, if possible. If he wasn't too late.

* * *

Heading into the High Gate was like wading through the doors of Byluk where, according to the legends, souls battled ceaselessly to be returned to the world above, to crawl out of the mists of the Edge. Like a dead soul clinging to life, Isha fought for every inch of ground gained. Every lunge she made with her spear cut not only the person in front of her, but reverberated along her retinue.

She joined the main army of the Nest, most of which had managed to regroup. Relieved to drop her mindlink, she returned control to Leofric. To Kilian, at the back of the line, she sent a sharp command: *Get yourself to safety!*

Afterwards, she would only remember glimpses: the gates towering above her, their stone roughly hewn into two thick walls, splattered with mud and blood. The sensation each time a weapon thunked against her shield and sent her skidding backwards. The ache in her arm, the trembling muscles in her wrist as she hefted the lance. The stench of guts as human stuffing came undone. Absurdly, a dandelion, amongst the trampled grass, which had somehow been spared.

It wasn't going well, but it could have been worse. Isha was holding her place, her blade felt like an extension of her arm, her mind was strengthened against invasions. If the mages stuck to their formation, they would be able to back themselves into the Nest and regroup. It would be a failure, but not a slaughter. She hung on to that thought.

They stepped away from the High Gate. They stepped away from the bridge. They gave ground until they were in front of the Nest's gates.

Then their line broke.

At first, she didn't understand where the shouts were coming from, why the solid interlinking of their minds had started to crumble. Hysterical voices, hysterical mindlink, no overall vision of what was happening, only blurs of elbows and swords and shields. And the soldier in front of her, the chainmail hanging from his helmet, hiding his eyes, who was pushing his blade forward every time she faltered. Still, she heard a shout of 'behind us!' and, glancing over her shoulder, she saw the doors – the Nest's huge entryway, carved for giants to stride past. Slowly, whining as their aged hinges worked, the doors were swinging shut.

The order must have come from inside the Nest. Maybe it was to keep the Renegades out; maybe it was to prevent the last fighters from entering an already-crowded courtyard. But the result was chaos. Mages abandoned their positions to rush for safety, leaving gaps the Renegades could push through, turning their backs to the ones they should be fighting.

Hold the line! She mindlinked to the people close to her. *We'll make it in time if we don't get killed.*

She ignored the calls for help, the questions in mindlink asking if someone knew what was happening. Instead, she shared an intense feeling of concentration, of being set in their position like river stones, eroded but never broken by the water. She shared an image of the chains set below the bridge, holding the world in place so it didn't fall over the Edge. She breathed. She focused on that, the rusted chains no-one could break, all linked.

A couple of people on either side of her stood fast. They continued backing cautiously, despite the confusion growing around them. Isha ignored the shrieks of people dying, the thunder of horses collapsing, of metal ripping through metal. She lifted her shield high, kept her lance firm although her arm hurt. She wasn't doing much, she knew, to defeat the man in front of her: she was only slapping down his weapon each time it came close, to prevent him from running her through.

The problem with a line was that if an enemy got behind it, it fell apart in seconds. Minds around her shattered or broke away from mindlink in terror; she heard the gallop of hooves beside her, or maybe behind.

She couldn't do this from the frontline. She took a step back and, before the Renegade in front of her could push his advantage, she ordered the people on either side of her to tighten the ranks. She grabbed one of them, a woman with hair as blond as Kilian's, and tugged her into the gap forcefully.

I am not leaving you, she said. *Hold fast.*

She sent her mind as wide as it would go. It was like trying to read five books at once: information, noises, sensations, were coming from every direction. She aimed for the minds that seemed the most coherent and confident. *Show me what's going on. I'll manage our formation.* This should be a high mage's job, but no high mage was there to help. Lord Leofric must already be inside the Nest. Rather than stand beside them, he'd left them to fend for themselves.

A wealth of images, disjointed, imbued with dread, flooded back to her. The smear of blood over someone's cheek. The weight one had to put in their arm for the blade to go through a man's chest. Cutting off three fingers at the knuckles. Wiping something from one's forehead and not being sure if it was sweat or blood.

She tried to sort out the images, not from their point of focus, but from the glimpses of background she could make out. The gates, the doors, the river. Using those clues, she had a vague idea of what their line looked like. It had broken on the right side – it was nearly completely gone – although the left still stood for now.

She sent instructions to the mages. Soon they were moving like a school of fish trying to avoid a shark, the whole group slipping out of reach, curling on itself so as not to expose its back to the fighters. She struggled with this – she didn't have the level of control, or distance, that enabled high mages to manipulate their armies. The people in front kept bumping into her; the back end of a lance smashed against her elbow. The flare of pain made her drop her weapon, reducing her to only using her shield.

Behind them, the Nest's doors were halfway shut. If they didn't get through soon, they would be left outside to be picked apart by the Renegades.

* * *

Tatters flew over the city, trying to determine where he would be able to make a difference. The streets were crawling with soldiers, but the red banners outweighed the desperate, defensive little patches of blue. The main army was retreating from the High Gate. The bridge, however, still held. Tatters glided closer.

Passerine was on the bridge, mindlinking to his soldiers, helping them coordinate. They were a small unit, only thirty or so, Passerine the only mage. They could cover the bridge, but nothing more. Behind them, the Nest's soldiers were hastily trying to reach safety.

From above, it was clear what Passerine was doing: locking the bridge for as long as possible, to give his allies time to flee. It wasn't a perfect strategy, as Renegades were also arriving from the north, having trudged past the undefended Temple, taking the long way round. They were slowed by the moors and the fact that they had to trek around the river before getting to the bridge. Once the Renegades had circled behind him, however, Passerine would be hemmed in on both ends.

Passerine wasn't an idiot; he must be aware of this.

He isn't planning to survive, Lal thought.

Tatters didn't have time to be afraid. Nearing the ground, he willed himself back into human shape. His shoes slapped against the smooth grey stone as he landed. He had only his knife in hand.

'Starling out, Hawk still in,' Tatters announced.

Passerine gritted his teeth. His mindlink, like silver threads, kept the line disciplined. The Renegades were marching in neat rows from the High Gate towards the bridge. It was a choke-point, but they had the numbers to push through. There was no crossing the chasm without it.

'Leofric and Isha out, I hope,' Passerine said. 'On their way to the Nest. I'm still in, as you can see.'

The Renegades were upon them.

They knew each other well. Either Passerine changed stance or Tatters did, or maybe they moved at the same time. But before he could quite decide, Tatters was ducking low, to give Passerine the space he needed to manoeuvre, and he was reducing the distance with the next soldier, aiming for their knee with his knife just as Passerine's spear skimmed above his head, landing squarely into another Renegade's chest, crushing through ribs and lungs. A messy, blood-splattered death.

This wasn't training. This was a fight for their lives. They delivered fast blows, like two feral cats, dodging as much as they attacked, because the first hit was most often the last. Tatters wove around the line, lifting above it as a lightborn, landing where he was most needed, dealing swift, brief strikes, flying away again. Passerine stood in the centre, a pivot around which the other soldiers fought, two heads taller than anyone beside him, his long black silhouette not unlike an axle, the ungifted an extension of his mind. Shields up. Lances forward. Quick blows, no steps back. Pressing up close to the one man whose arm never wavered nor grew slow.

They had lost nearly half the soldiers who had been holding the bridge with them. Their forces were dwindling. They were holding the bridge against Hawk's numbers, but they were losing.

'Go,' Passerine said. He released the ungifted. 'Run.'

Tatters watched them break ranks. Only the two of them left.

The bridge was a wet and sticky red. The river below pumped as hard as his heart. No opportunity to ask whether this was wise.

They circled around each other, never blocking each other's line of sight, covering for each other's back. Tatters slid through the air, touched the ground, took flight, shifting between shapes in a complex, blinding red dance. He covered the short-range enemies with his knife and the long-range archers as a lightborn; the medium-range soldiers fell to Passerine's spear. They broke apart, the soles of their shoes sliding on the bridge. Their breaths steamed white in the cold spring air.

'Not bad,' Passerine admitted, panting. His long arms were holding his spear high, at a defensive angle; sweat trickled down his face. His expression was intent.

'You're decent at dodging,' Tatters said.

The Renegades were regrouping. They hadn't expected such tenacious resistance. They were taking their time to prepare for the last push, lining up a couple of archers. Death would close in like jaws, its teeth made of arms and hands and shields and swords.

'If you know the spell to summon the giants' weapons, it's now or never,' Tatters said.

'I found out the truth,' Passerine said. 'There is no weapon.'

What? Lal gasped.

When Tatters turned, Passerine was recovering his breath. He kept his attention fixed on the Renegades. Blood, and grime, and sweat, marred his face. The sleeves of his robes, soaked, had been rolled up to his elbows.

'The giants were pacifists,' he said. 'There is plenty in the Nest's writings about taking flight or unfolding wings. It's what misled me. But they mean it in a metaphorical sense: working together, thus elevating themselves. Community as a form of ascension. Hence why there's plenty in there about agriculture, and food stocks, and creature comforts. They had a line about ending war, which I hoped would be a weapon.'

His smile was sombre. His eyes were shards of obsidian.

'It was a text about how they would never wage war, nor provide the means to wage it. That's when I knew.'

And you didn't tell us, Lal grumbled, despite Tatters' attempt to shush her.

'I will never alight. We will never defeat Hawk. I will never see my daughter again.' Passerine wore despair without frills. It was in his eyes, nowhere else. 'Is that what you wanted me to say?'

No wonder he had chosen to defend an undefendable space.

On the northern side, the Renegade battalion had finally closed in on the retreating soldiers from the Nest. A group had detached from their allies and was heading their way. The Renegades from the High Gate side were shouting at them. Tatters narrowed his eyes in their direction, understanding from their gestures that they were requesting a surrender.

As if, Lal snorted.

Sighing, Passerine stretched his arms above his head. The wooden spear, splintered in places, yet still whole, lifted and dipped with his arms. He replaced his feet in the proper battle stance. Tatters wiped his sleeve across the handle of his knife and secured his grip.

Arrows, baina-tipped. Tatters swung aside, off the bridge, diving into the chasm as he alighted. He emerged in time to see Passerine, who'd grabbed a shield off a fallen body, rise to his feet. The shield still above his head, he held his spear one-handed, tucked under his elbow to grant him the strength he needed. The world blurred as Tatters dashed towards their enemies, as the chaos became an ever-quickening series of reactions: away from that mirror, away from that arrow, away from that kher;

knife glinting towards that neck, blade sliding into that joint, light breaking through those thoughts.

Passerine was a force of nature, all size and muscle, his range much longer than most Renegade soldiers, his grip solid. Yet his hits were clinically precise. He wasted little of that overflowing strength. He moved as if through a drill, never missing a beat, his mind gleaning information from the soldiers before him, aware of their next blow even as they thought it, before their wrist had lifted. Each time Tatters alighted past, he was awed anew.

Yet Passerine could never succeed. His talent made one believe it might be possible, but it wasn't.

Tatters was above the bridge, ready for his next lunge, when it happened. An enemy spear went past Passerine's block, tips screeching as they touched, sparks flying at contact. Then the Renegade blade continued, unimpeded, into Passerine's gut.

Tatters dived. He all but landed on his knees, not in time to cushion Passerine's fall. Passerine lay stunned, one hand pressed against his abdomen by reflex. The spear had been pulled back, trailing... bits. Too many pieces. The blood was gushing. His lap was red.

His sunken eyes found Tatters, and his mind leapt away from his body. Tatters was stuck moored to the ground. He was aware of the Renegades crowding him, of an already-stained spear taking aim.

Alight, said Passerine. *Let me fly, one last time.*

Tatters heaved it up as the spear came down, nicking the wood, splintering the shield. A huge crack ran down its middle; the two halves barely held together.

It will kill you! Tatters said. He didn't say: I've done this before. The forest had been dark and dense, not the clear sky and wide landscapes the moorlands offered. But he had been this desperate. His sister had been this desperate. He wasn't sure he could forgive himself for ripping Lal away from herself.

I spent my whole life looking for the wrong thing, in the wrong place, Passerine said quietly.

Tatters' mouth was dry. His head was ringing. He was aware of the weight of the body in his arms, still hot, growing heavier. A spear – or was it a sword? A long and sharp and metallic thing – flashed towards his face.

Passerine's mindlink was weakening. *Please.*

Tatters lifted them both into the air, severing Passerine from his body easily, like strong hands holding both ends of a silk sheet to rip it in two.

For a moment, Passerine lived. Tatters was stunned; he sensed Passerine was too. Passerine was a lightborn, after all. His mind could be sustained without his body. He was a dash of blue riding Tatters' red as they bled together through the sky, a wound fit for the giants.

You thought owning me would compensate for being unable to fly yourself, Tatters said. *But it didn't.*

No, said Passerine. Tatters felt Passerine's spirit expand, filled with an unbearable feeling, a longing so strong it wasn't even hope. *Nothing could compensate for this.*

But Passerine was fading like mist under sunshine. He wasn't flying, he was dying.

Tatters swerved. He drew an elaborate spiral in the sky, the only one he remembered from hours dancing words in the arena, the only lightborn sigil he had committed to memory: *birds who sing, who sigh, who croak, who cry.* A name. *Passerine.* He danced the name of the lightborn bound to human shape, who could never speak his own name in his own language again. The weight of Passerine leaving him, finally dispersing in the blue sky like clouds brushed away by the wind, brought a hollowness that might have been relief.

Tatters finished his sigil as the baina arrow hit its mark.

It didn't harm him, flying through his light, but it forced him back into human shape. He dropped. He landed on something soft and warm and muddy, half-body, half churned-up earth from the battlefield. A soldier kicked the side of his head, blurring his vision. Maybe they had only been running past. Tatters had time to feel wet grass under his cheek, to taste soil in his mouth, to glimpse the outline of a nail-studded boot – then something hit his face again, and he was unconscious.

* * *

Isha bit down on her cheek until it bled. The adrenaline was such that even she couldn't have explained how she did it. She guided her squadron of mages, growing smaller by the second, with her in the centre, and brought them to the doors, overstepping the bodies lying on the ground, sliding on guts and gore, most of it not their enemies'. She kept her eyes wide open, but she could hardly see the people in front of her, the hair matted with grime, the bobbing shoulders and heads ducking and retreating. She was concentrating on the gates, now only wide enough for a set of three horses, soon too narrow for them to push through.

Around their knot of order, other mages, who could have been on their side, were running into their blades in an effort to reach the entrance, to escape the Renegades closing in on them.

We're getting there, she said.

It nearly worked. It could have worked, maybe, had the Nest understood Isha's efforts and slowed the doors long enough for the last fighters to make it through. A few people from her retinue made it to safety, then more, and she stood with the last ones, shield half-held above her head, hoping no-one would stab her legs.

But the path to safety was thinning and the meagre discipline Isha had managed to muster fell apart. It was clear not everyone would make it.

People turned to run. She vainly tried to mindlink and shout them in place.

'Stay fast! Hold the line!' Her voice was lost in the howling, yelping, crying.

Someone shoved against her shoulder. As she struggled to regain her footing, someone else bumped into her legs. She tripped, planted the shield into the ground for balance, and only just had time to lift it above her again to avoid a sword aiming for her skull. The shield snapped, a small chunk still hanging from the leather buckle around her forearm.

No weapon, no shield. Isha felt her mind go blank as the panic she had fought off, in others and in herself, at last rooted itself in her thoughts. She tried to get inside the Nest. But as she stumbled backwards, hefting her shard of shield in front of her just in case, she felt studded wood behind her. This was it, then. The doors were closed. She was going to die here. She hardly knew if the people running beside her were friends or foes, making for the gates or for her throat.

Here, Isha! Mindlink like a lifeline thrown her way. She would recognise that sharp voice any day – Caitlin. Isha turned, and a pale arm shot out of the crowd, from the sky, it seemed, and gripped her shoulder. Isha held on tight and found herself dragged against the steaming side of a horse. It was kicking, but it was higher than the mob, like a piece of debris on a troubled sea, and she gratefully grabbed the saddle, put her foot in the already-full stirrup. As she hauled herself onto its croup, Caitlin turned the horse around, pulling at the reins fiercely, clicking her tongue in encouragement all the while.

'Go, go, you stupid beast,' she hissed.

The horse broke into a half-canter, half-jump. Mages screamed as they went underhoof. Caitlin ignored them and pushed towards the slim slit of the open doors, which Isha could see now, a couple of feet away, still large enough for a horse, or for three people at once. She would never have made it through the mess of bodies by herself, not when mages shoved both in the right direction and away from it, scattering in front of the Renegades' swords. In the confusion, some stragglers were pressing against the wood, drawing the doors together faster.

For a moment, Isha thought they wouldn't make it. She saw someone throw a javelin, the high arc of its metal tip, maybe because a horse was too tempting a target. She lifted onto the saddle, one hand on Caitlin's shoulder to stabilise herself, and parried the javelin with what was left of her shield. The shock of it slamming into her forearm nearly threw her off-balance; Caitlin swore as Isha put sudden weight into her back.

But then they were beyond the doors, and Caitlin was spurring her horse to the side, behind the tall shadow of the Nest's rampart.

Isha was stunned. She let herself fall back behind Caitlin. Her arm, she realised, was bleeding where the javelin had gone through the broken shield, through the vambrace, and speared her wrist. The shaft had snapped at both ends: the metal tip and long body of the weapon were nowhere to be seen, but a piece of wood still stuck out of her forearm. She had been run through, but she felt no pain. The vambrace might have slowed the javelin enough to prevent it from going beyond her arm – she would never know. The gates of the Nest closed with an ominous thud, shutting off the pleading from the other side. Yet she could still hear muted battlefield sounds, and knew the remaining mages were being picked to pieces by the Renegades.

But she had made it through alive.

Inside the courtyard, men and women were collapsing, while others rushed to help from the arches. Under her, through the fabric of her trousers, the horse was soaked through with sweat, burning hot against her thighs. It had been as scared as her.

Caitlin whipped her head around, still astride the horse, the reins held more loosely now that they were in the courtyard – now that they were safe.

'You're an idiot,' she snapped. Her cheeks were flushed with emotion, fear or rage or both. 'You wanted to get yourself killed out there?'

Before Isha could try to justify her actions or protest that her choices had been limited, Caitlin kissed her.

It was a fierce, furious, bless-the-skies-you-are-alive sort of kiss. It was all bite and push and relief. Caitlin broke away from it as brusquely as she had started it.

Isha found herself staring at Caitlin's face, the short brown hair hastily hacked off, the mud and oil from the chainmail along her cheeks and neck, the shape of her lips, wetted by spit and blood. She was beautiful. Despite the scar, despite the way her eye seemed to bleed into the scab, despite her frown. When was Caitlin anything but beautiful?

Isha couldn't help it: she laughed. Happiness crushed her lungs until she couldn't speak.

'What are you laughing at?' Caitlin grumbled, guiding the horse towards the stables, more softly now that there was no urgency.

'This. Us. Being alive.'

She sensed Caitlin was even angrier now.

'Hey, hey, wait.' Isha passed her good arm around Caitlin's

waist. She gently nudged for her to dismount; they both slid off the horse. Even on foot, Caitlin didn't let go of the reins. 'Let's try this again,' Isha said. She couldn't care less about the dull ache in her wrist.

She leant forward and placed a kiss on Caitlin's lips, as tender and deep as she could. The horse sighed as the hold on its bit loosened.

Their fingers knotted; their knees bumped gently. Isha hugged Caitlin against her. She was faintly conscious that the wetness across her fingers was blood, but Caitlin didn't seem to care. They both squeezed tightly, as if, were they to let go, they might never be able to touch again.

People ignored them. The Nest had more urgent matters to deal with. Around them mages came and went; healthy ones brought bandages to wounded ones, helping them limp towards the healers. Archers ran back and forth over the fortifications carrying bunches of arrows; high mages shouted orders. Their horse went to settle near its stables, nuzzling the floor for some stray hay, still gulping for air after its exertion.

Oblivious to everything happening around them, Isha and Caitlin forgot to breathe.

Chapter 12

'We have to surrender,' Isha announced.

Lord Leofric let out a polite scoff. He had been summoned to a meeting with Lord Daegan, to discuss their next steps. Passerine was missing; he had last been seen on the bridge, and the chances that he had survived were slim. The reduced triumvirate would be discussing how to organise the siege. Hawk would have trouble attacking the Nest without suffering severe losses, so she would most probably attempt to wait them out.

'A siege is our best option,' Lord Leofric said, as condescending as if she were a child, not his second-in-command. 'We can hold at least a month or two.'

He continued ambling down the corridor, towards the spiral staircase leading up to the council room. Isha dogged his every step.

'While Hawk waits,' Leofric went on, 'we will call upon the nearby towns for reinforcement.' Not that there were many people left to enlist, by now. Isha kept that opinion to herself. 'The Renegades will have to lay a siege to the Nest while holding the city against our soldiers coming through the Sunpath.' He smiled at the thought. 'Both besieged and besieging.'

The fortified villages along the Sunpath could, conceivably, serve as a last resort. But a lot of their soldiers were already maimed, courtesy of Leofric stealing their best fighters for himself. It would require a long, drawn-out, no doubt brutal battle. The mages who lived in those towns would have a tough choice before them: whether or not to abandon their homes to the Renegades' mercy in order to lift this costly siege.

'If we drain the Sunpath towns to attack the city,' Isha said, *our own city*, she didn't add, 'and we lose, what then? We're back to step one, only with more dead.'

Leofric shrugged. 'It may not come to that.'

Hawk could use ungifted within the city, if she decided to resort to manipulating them, growing her army by another couple of thousand soldiers. The Renegades didn't control ungifted, as a rule, because they were striving to prove themselves better than the Nest, with only volunteers in their army. Still, who knew what Hawk would do, if pushed? She could invade the Nest through its underground tunnels. Off the top of her head, Isha could think of more than one way it could *come to that*.

'Hawk will be hard to uproot,' she pointed out. 'She may have more surprises in store for us.'

He didn't seem to hear her. Her patience was wearing thin. When she closed her eyes, she could see the javelin aiming at her, cutting through the sky. In her nightmares, she lifted the shield too late. It went through her chest, through Caitlin's back, and they slumped together on the horse, bound by iron and death. They never kissed. They never lived.

As it was, her wound was bad enough. A doctor hadn't been available, so rather than removing the shaft, the worried mage in charge of the healing ward had hastily bandaged Isha's wrist, leaving the wood inside. He'd first cut off the vambrace, the decorated leather ending up torn and filled with blood, ruined. After the excitement had dropped, the pain had come. Her hand was swollen. When she moved, the bit of javelin sticking out of her flesh jiggled like a loose nail. If she brushed against anything, or tried to lift anything, the agony was sharp enough to force a gasp out of her.

'By now, Hawk's either killed or recaptured Tatters. Passerine is dead.' *Skies, I hope not.* But could she afford to believe anything else, to hold on to happy delusions? No. She would grieve later. But she would assume she had lost them both. Starling was alive, still by Lord Daegan's side, but she had proved unable to defeat Hawk. 'Don't you think that makes it clear enough that we've lost?' she said, through gritted teeth, adding a belated: 'Sir.'

Isha was seething. She could still taste blood on the roof of her mouth. Every inch of her ached with bruises, with cuts, with the painful joy of being alive.

'If we accept the Renegades' terms, Hawk has no reason to fight us,' she insisted. 'Mezyan told us as much.'

'Are you a fool?' Leofric asked, with polite disinterest. He had reached the staircase. He paused at its foot. 'She will hang us all if we surrender.'

The high mages might be at risk. So would Isha. But this war was about more than a few of them.

'Think of the ungifted lives that will be saved!'

It was the wrong plea. Something in his face hardened. 'You forget your place. And you forget that it is not so secure without your infamous protector.' Each word resonated with the clink of hollow bones. His amused, coy façade was eroding fast. 'You will obey me, girl, or you are of no use to me. Have I made myself clear?'

She cleansed her thoughts and features of emotion he might use against her. 'Clear as a lightborn through crystal, sir.'

He nodded, satisfied, his ambiguous smile flitting across his lips. Then he disappeared up the stairs.

Once he had left, Isha clenched her fist to punch something.

She used her good hand, the right one, but even then, when she lifted it too brusquely, her left wrist sent a flash of pain up to her shoulder. She sucked in her breath, annoyed with the world, with herself. She didn't hit anything.

It was time to regroup.

The meeting point was in the main healing ward, but Caitlin caught up with her before that, in the web of corridors around the high mages' quarters. When she saw Isha's expression, her smirk was neither pleasant nor pleased – it was the expression of someone who's been proven right.

'I bet Lord Leofric was thrilled with your proposition,' Caitlin said, not bothering to turn it into a question.

'How did it go with Daegan?' Isha asked, halting in the empty passageway.

Caitlin shrugged. 'As well as expected.' Her smile took on a vicious edge. 'He threatened to slap me.'

Isha was shocked. After all they had done for the Nest, both of them, all the fighting and protecting and putting their lives on the line, she had expected more from the high mages in return. Obviously, that had been naïve. Beside her, against the wall, the blue-and-gold heraldry of the Nest stood in faded colours, dust clinging to the hem of the tapestry. It had aged. Or maybe she had grown.

'He didn't dare, in the end,' Caitlin said, and the victorious glint in her gaze was hard as flint. Her bad eye shone as brightly as the one that hadn't been maimed. 'We don't need that kind of leadership, Isha. The Nest doesn't, either.'

'Before anything else,' Isha said, trying to clear her thoughts, 'I want to check on Kilian.'

They headed for the healing ward. Originally, it had been the male apprentices' dorm. The appointed doctors had built a fire far from the mezzanine, directly onto the stone floor. It cast a golden light and exhaled heavy smoke, which didn't seem to want to go out through the open windows. Pots of boiling water to clean cloth were hanging above the flames; racks to dry the bandages were placed nearby. The room was comfortably warm – every stone in this area of the building was tepid to the touch. This was Passerine's doing. No doubt, given time, he could find many useful tools hidden within the Nest. *Could have found.* She didn't want to dwell on that thought.

'Kilian's bed is over here,' Caitlin said.

She guided Isha across the room. Healers and patients alike were coughing, their lungs filling with smoke. Herbs and balms and glasses of liquor were being passed around or brewed. Nearly everyone had gathered here, maybe because of the warmth, maybe because of the desire to be close to a loved one. Isha knew mixed groups were also mingling in the female dormitory, repurposed to welcome those with lesser injuries.

Kilian was in a corner of the room, against one of the giants' high windows. He was as pale as the dead, lying under several layers of sheets. His brow was slick with sweat. Isha took in his bagged eyelids, his half-open mouth. The covers had been pulled up to his chin.

'What does it look like?' she asked.

'As good as it can,' Caitlin answered, delicately lifting the end of the blanket.

Underneath it was Kilian's arm. Or rather, the stub of his arm. They had cut it above the elbow.

Isha wondered if her sudden dizziness was due to the smoke or the sight. Bile filled her mouth. She wasn't sure whether they would need to do the same to her, cut the rotting flesh above the joint. The javelin sticking out of her wrist seemed to taunt her. She glanced down at her aching hand and, despite the pain, flexed her fingers. She could still move the inflamed knuckles.

319

Kilian hadn't been as lucky.

'Has he woken up yet?' Isha asked.

'They have stuffed him with poppy tea,' Caitlin explained. Isha knew that most of the brews above the fire would be poppy seeds soaked in water, their juices extracted to be used as a painkiller. 'He won't be coming to just yet.'

Caitlin leant over, pushing the damp curls out of Kilian's eyes.

'He wasn't taught how to be tough,' she said. 'Maybe the Nest was cruel to us, but it was cruel to him too, in its own way. It also told him lies.'

Isha's throat was knotted. 'He's going to have a hard time when he wakes up.'

'If,' Caitlin said automatically.

That was it. It was those words, the casual despondency, the way Caitlin's face was set with a dulled, stunned sort of grief, that decided Isha. She would put an end to this. She wouldn't turn into a creature who watched friends die and found themselves helpless because too much had happened, too many people had been killed, and they had lost the will to be outraged.

'We're surrendering,' she said.

Caitlin looked up at her.

'We're surrendering, and convincing people it's the right solution, and if the high mages say no, we're throwing them out.' Isha was speaking louder than she had intended; a couple of mages glanced her way. Rather than lowering her voice, however, she strengthened it. 'We're the ones who fought. We're the ones who got bloodied. We're making this decision.'

She had been expecting resistance, a list of reasons why what she was saying was foolish. Instead, Caitlin leant forward and took Isha's good hand in her own, squeezing.

'I think the Nest is ready for this,' Caitlin said. 'The war has

pushed everyone to the brink. And Daegan isn't Siobhan.' Isha
noticed she'd dropped the honorifics.

To her surprise, Caitlin pulled her close and hugged her. She
kissed the top of Isha's head.

'Should we be doing this? Shouldn't we be mustering the
mages?' Isha asked, trying to resist melting into Caitlin's arms,
and failing. She couldn't help it. She needed the human warmth,
the familiar smell, the feeling she wasn't alone to face this. When
she was close to Caitlin, the dull throbbing in her wrist seemed
to recede.

Caitlin shrugged, flicking her head to one side, in a gesture so
achingly familiar Isha's heart squeezed at the sight. Her auburn
locks, too short, didn't follow her movement.

'If the Renegades don't kill us,' Caitlin said simply, 'the
supreme mages might. Give me this, at least. It might be our
last time.'

Isha softened, but still squirmed in Caitlin's embrace.

'We are doing this,' said Isha, breaking away. 'I'm serious.'

'I know.' Caitlin planted a quick kiss on her mouth. 'You're
always serious.'

Isha clenched the fingers of her left hand. The pain cleared
her head. This was what she needed to focus on. She sat beside
Kilian, watched his wan face one more time, to gather courage,
to remember what she was trying to avoid, who she wanted to
save.

Let's assemble in the main hall, she mindlinked widely around
her. *You see the state of this place? You think we can survive a siege?*
She listened to the thoughts echoing around her in response,
mostly anguish, or worry for loved ones; harassed, depressed
minds that had worked day and night to save lives. *We need to
discuss terms of surrender. We need to decide, together, what to do
next. Not follow the high mages who led us straight to this massacre.*

Beside her, Caitlin's mindlink joined in. *This is Isha. Lord Passerine's follower. The woman who held the gates. Who assembled the armies after Lord Leofric fell.* Attention turned to Caitlin.

She was such a perfect Duskdweller mage: tall, slim, golden, young, white teeth, hazelnut eyes, a younger Lady Siobhan – before she had grown old and hairless and toothless. It shouldn't matter whether someone who looked like a Duskdweller and a mage stood up for her, but Isha knew it did. With her tattoo and Sunriser skin, she could pass as a kher, as a foreigner. But there was no doubting that Caitlin belonged.

I don't know about you, Caitlin mindlinked to the crowd, *but I want to stand beside the person who fought for me. Who would have died for me.* On the side of her head, the scar served as a reminder. *Not the one who was hiding in his tower, locking the doors on me.*

She shared images with her words, and Isha saw herself from the outside, screaming orders on a battlefield before the Nest, the uneven moorland trampled by too many horses. She saw herself in the Overgrowth with Starling flying behind her. The lightborn the same colour as the setting sun. The paint on her shield the same colour as the sky. She looked nothing like herself. In those memories, she was a young woman full of energy and fire, her tattoo as distinctive as a banner, a sign to rally people together. A warrior whose dirtied armour only enhanced her sharp features. She had never been thin, but it worked to her advantage, making her seem solid, unbreakable.

She looked like Hawk.

Caitlin finished her message, a smug smile on her lips. 'They'll come. They'll listen.'

Isha swallowed. Her throat was dry. She had turned into her mother, and it was too late to back down.

'That's good,' she said. 'Let's get the apprentices from the female dormitory too.'

They went across the Nest, sharing their message as widely as they dared, asking everyone to gather in the main hall while the supreme mages, the official leaders, were perched high in their towers that giants had built, that ungifted maintained, that apprentices defended.

Isha knew they had a good case. And Caitlin was right: the mages were sick of leaders who wouldn't risk their lives for them. Even the high mages were in a state of shock, stunned by the violence, doubtful of their superiors. Everyone wanted to hear that there was a solution in sight, one that would spare them more brutality. The closing of the doors had left a sour taste in everyone's mouths. They remembered the woman who had helped them return to safety, who had struggled until the bitter end against the Renegades. They knew her face. They recognised her name.

How has this happened? she thought. *When did I become an idea, rather than a person?*

After the two dormitories, they checked the mess. Isha insisted they invite the ungifted too, so they visited the servants' quarters. In the stables, the grooms were patching up the horses as best they could and, in some cases, were skinning the dead animals to smoke the meat.

At last, the gathering in the main hall was impressive enough that, even without ringing the bells, Isha could tell they had managed to assemble the majority of the Nest. Her faintness had returned; she felt light-headed and sick.

Caitlin escorted her up the steps leading to the balcony. Here, Lady Siobhan had mindlinked to crowds of followers while Mezyan had jumped onto the balustrade and shaken the mages to their core. Isha had never seen the main hall from this viewpoint before. It was different from this angle: wider, composed of pillars and white arches, a swarm of tiny faces at her feet.

As Isha gathered her wits, before she could officially start mindlinking with everyone, Caitlin brushed against her arm.

'You can do this,' Caitlin said confidently. 'It can't be worse than trying not to get killed.' She lowered her voice. 'And you are not your mother. At least, as long as you decide not to act like her.'

So she had read some of Isha's insecurities. Isha gave her a strained smile.

'Thank you for the half-reassurance, half-threat there.' She was trying to joke, but her throat was knotted.

Caitlin's smile was as cutting as it always had been. 'Don't count on me for reassurance. I'm here to watch you do the right thing. If you don't, I am going to be furious.'

'No pressure,' Isha said.

Caitlin shoved her chin towards the crowd waiting below. 'No pressure,' she confirmed.

Isha opened her mind and her mouth, and took a step forward.

* * *

Tatters woke up aching all over. He could tell he was bruised from the fall but, judging from the absence of acute pain, he hadn't broken anything. He could see mud, which had hardened into ridges during the night, which was softening again in the morning light. He could smell rot.

I thought they'd killed us, Lal said, as she resurfaced.

There's still time, Tatters answered.

He pushed himself to his feet. His body screamed from the abuse it had been through: the cut on his shoulder smarted, his ribs pulsed, either bruised or cracked, and the side of his face felt bloated, swollen. The view wasn't any better from higher up. He had fallen close to the chasm. The earth was upturned from hooves and feet and siege weapons. The bodies, lumpy shapes, could be glossed over as moorland, as long as one didn't stare too closely.

It was impossible to ignore the smell, though.

The giants were pacifists.

He knew what he had to do.

Tatters had run for years. Even now, he wanted to run. Yet he headed towards the Renegades' camp.

The main encampment had been set up on the city side of the bridge, although a few soldiers milled about on the Nest's side, out of the archers' range, sorting through the dead. The bridge itself had been cleaned with buckets of water, sloppy work that had left long, sinuous stains. Tatters limped across.

He approached without drawing notice, maybe because people assumed an injured man with no weapons and no armour would only be heading towards allies. He listened to the camp life as he grew closer: people walking, talking, laughing. Familiar scents: horses, smoke, peas being boiled. The ashes of old firepits. The whisper of red cloth.

Hawk, he mindlinked broadly. *Let's talk.*

That got their attention. Someone cried in alarm, shouting something about a collarbound. Before Tatters could take another step, Renegades swarmed him.

A soldier grabbed him from behind, drawing both their arms under his armpits, clenching their hands at the nape of his neck. The person was a kher: Lal was snuffed out. The open gash across his shoulder stung as skin was pulled taut. It wasn't a hold he could break out of; it was intended to overpower. A foot pushed against the underside of his knee insistently, forcing him to bend his legs until he was kneeling.

A deep male voice was giving orders. People stepped away. Tatters stayed crouched in the dirt, feeling the stronger, sturdier person clasping him. A line of red fabric drooped in front of his face, the long scarf dipping where the soldier was bending over. A lot of Renegades wore red, but something about the grip, how firm it was, yet how gentle, helped him guess who might be restraining him.

'Mezyan?' he asked. 'I have surrendered, you know.'

'Don't struggle.' His voice had lost its kindness, gained hardness. Any indulgence that might have lingered was gone.

Yet he still wore Tatters' scarf.

'I suppose we lost, then.'

Mezyan mellowed somewhat. His military demeanour relaxed enough for Tatters to sense some leeway in his hold. 'You lost the city. The Nest still stands, for now.'

Tatters let the sounds of the camp wash over him – men and women sharpening swords, unrusting mail with sand, nailing leather into shields. The banging and clinking and scratching noises of the past.

'For what it's worth, I'm glad you didn't drown,' whispered Tatters.

Mezyan laughed, but he didn't answer.

Tatters could hear Renegades discussing him, closing in. Her steps. How could he tell it was her? His head was forced downwards, preventing him from seeing anything but his knees. Still, he didn't doubt it. She was drawing near.

'Let me talk to Hawk,' he said.

Immediately, Mezyan's grip tightened. 'I can't allow that.'

'It's to negotiate peace terms,' Tatters said.

Hawk had a soft spot for messengers. It came from being a

Sunriser, always caught in frontier feuds: killing messengers was considered a grave crime. Without them, it would be impossible to argue outside of battlegrounds.

'You're not a messenger,' said Mezyan. 'You're a prisoner.'

'I couldn't hurt her before,' Tatters insisted. 'I won't do it now.'

'He won't hurt me.' She was behind him, closer than he'd thought, within earshot. He tried not to jump at the sound of her. 'Let him go.'

Reluctantly, Mezyan obeyed. Tatters ignored the searing pain down his shoulder, where Hawk's knife had left him raw. As he got to his feet, he noticed Mezyan had a new scar. A deep slash, not yet sealed, cutting the eyebrow in half, then running along his brow before disappearing into his hairline. His hair was as short and as grey as before.

Around them stood men and women in armour, their faces set in frowns, watching, waiting.

He berated himself for being such a coward.

Just turn and look at her, said Lal. *It won't be as bad as you think.*

He took a deep breath as he lifted his gaze.

Hawk had grown older, as he had, no doubt, but he remembered the lines of her face, the web of scars; the black of her hair, matted down by the helmet; the half-cut eyelid on the left side; the way her mouth twitched when she was thinking. Even the armour was familiar, the nails planted in leather, the glistening white of the circular plate across the front of the brigandine – everything, down to the sickly scent of oiled iron. She had cut her hair, that long hair she had so often plaited with red silk and been so proud of, and that was what he stumbled on, the fact that her curls now barely rose above her skull.

She was so ... human. He had expected a monster, a myth. She was tall, stout, no-nonsense. A grizzled woman.

There was a silence. It was an old silence. It had grown and aged and matured and died, this silence, without either of them breaking it.

Hawk spoke first.

'May you grow tall.'

If she hadn't taken the lead, maybe Tatters would have stayed there, tongue glued to the roof of his mouth, for the rest of his life. He cleared his throat.

'May you grow tall,' he answered.

He thought she would say that it had been a long time, because it had been. He thought she would say she was surprised to have the chance to speak with him, because it was clear she was. He even thought she would say he wasn't dead, though it was obvious. They weren't only staring straight into the eyes of their past – they were each staring at a ghost. The ghost of who they had each been stared back.

But Hawk had never been one for stating the obvious.

'Why did you give yourself up?' she asked.

Maybe the only way out of this conversation was forward. Otherwise there would be no end to their talk, like there would be no end to this war.

'I want to discuss terms of surrender,' he said.

She shook her head, not quite laughing, not quite coughing. Around them, a circle of Renegades like a noose was listening to their every word. Mezyan was not openly threatening, but close enough to become so, should he decide to restrain Tatters again.

Despite her chuckle, Hawk was serious. 'I'm listening.'

'You've already won,' he said. 'The Nest will surrender. Promise that you won't kill anyone within, and you can take it without a struggle.'

He would have to convince the supreme mages. *I'll beg them, if need be.*

We'll fight them, Lal answered. *If that's the cost of peace.*

Hawk didn't even hesitate. 'You know I can't do that.'

He had always asked her to stop – when she had conquered her convent, when she had freed the Red Belt kingdoms, when the Sunrisers were united under her rule. She had never listened, always expanding, her ambition and power growing with her. She was a threat to the Nest now, this woman who had fled her convent, pregnant, on foot, in dishonour. She would never have got this far without blood.

'The Nest is filled with innocents,' he insisted.

'The Nest is filled with criminals,' she answered, her voice hard.

Tatters couldn't hold her eye. The prisons below the Nest came to mind, their tunnels like roots, the suffering below feeding the castle, allowing it to grow. Not everyone slit the khers' throats, but everyone drank the blood. Everyone paid with baina.

She is right, Lal thought. *Maybe she was always right.*

No. That Tatters refused to believe.

Out loud, he said, 'A new crime doesn't unmake the crimes already committed.'

Before, Hawk would have argued with him. But today she spread out heavy, withered hands, marred by fighting and age. 'I cannot make that promise. That's all.'

He noticed the way Hawk held the pommel of her sword, her grip relaxed but firm, as if about to unsheathe it. He wondered if she feared he would attack her after all. Around him, the Renegades were leery, quick to assume he was a threat.

When she spoke, it was louder, with the tone she used to address her army. Maybe she was talking to her soldiers as much as to him.

'I tolerate some evil because I want to change the world. You abide evil because you won't.'

Ah, there she was. It was that voice, deep, entrancing. It was that certainty, so solid one could touch it. It was that fire, all-consuming, unstoppable – the kher god Timessi, who had to be kept in check, else he would eat the world.

'That's the only difference between us.'

The legend behind the woman. With that aura, that posture, that tone, she could lead thousands of souls over the Edge, if she so willed.

'I will change the world.'

The Renegades agreed, mutters rising in waves behind Tatters. They smelt of iron or blood. The conversation hadn't changed in all those years. Maybe they had become old. Maybe they had forgotten how to change.

'Through pain, to victory,' Hawk concluded.

She was staring at him with the expression she bore when he had begged her to remove the collar, with the expression she had, no doubt, when Passerine had screamed himself voiceless as she burnt his books. He might as well try to stop the tide with his bare hands. He'd failed.

I'll be with you whatever happens, said Lal.

'What are you waiting for?' Tatters asked. 'Reclaim your power. Call upon the collar. Let's see which one of us breaks first, me or the gold.'

Hawk glanced at the collar shining around his neck. He felt it warm around him, like a strangling hand. Beside him, he was conscious of Mezyan. He hadn't stopped this from happening before and he wouldn't prevent it now.

But we have fought it before and we will fight it now, Lal thought.

'I relinquish any power I ever had over you,' said Hawk. 'It was a mistake.'

Tatters studied her face carefully. She looked tired. She looked old. She looked like someone who had learnt to live with her mistakes.

Yet the collar stayed around his neck, cooled, but unchanged.

Harm done is not so easily undone, said Lal.

Or we broke it too thoroughly in the Shadowpass, he said.

Still, he had never considered that Hawk might regret her decision. She had changed, then, after all, as he had, as they all did. She was a person, not a nightmare. Briefly, he remembered them before the collar – how friendly they'd been, how trusting. Fearless. They'd been sure they'd take over the world, together, and that nothing would come between them. They would have laughed at anyone implying they could ever be pitted against each other.

And he remembered how soured everything had been, after.

'This, too, is a mistake.' If there was something he could reach for, some hold, some leeway of mercy, he would take it. 'You should accept the Nest's surrender. There is nothing to lose, except avoiding a costly siege. You'd be a fool to refuse it.'

Hawk's following words had something unexpected: a glimmer of hope.

'Maybe you're right,' she said. He had never thought to hear those words from her. She sighed through her teeth. Although well-protected, he could perceive the movements of her mind, her hesitation. 'I have a message for the Nest,' she decided. 'And for the eyas.'

'Her name is Isha,' Tatters interrupted. She was more than Hawk's daughter. She'd proved that, by now.

Hawk paused. In the silence, Mezyan noted, noncommittally, 'Tough kid.'

Tough mother, Lal answered.

'If the Nest surrenders, and my daughter is unharmed, I will only take the lives of the guilty.' Tatters thought that would be all, and he was already stepping back, when Hawk added, so quietly it was a whisper, 'Tell my daughter she is loved.'

You think she'll believe that? Lal scoffed.

We'll carry the message, thought Tatters. *It's not up to us to believe it or not.*

Out loud, he said, 'I will tell them. Give us some time to bring you an answer.'

Tatters gritted his teeth as light, reluctant, slow as water, covered his fingers. Hawk tensed, but didn't unsheathe her weapon. Tatters alighted slowly, like a phoenix whose feathers of fire had to grow before he could fly.

He lifted above the camp which, from the sky, might have been nothing but a colony of ants, a tide of black and red figures clustered around a stone. He flew towards the Nest, that place of spires and mirrors and arches too wide for humans. He crossed the rusting gates, wishfully pulled shut, already eaten away by time, soon to be beaten down by battering rams.

In the main hall, an impromptu meeting was taking place – mages were gathered, the wounded and the healthy sitting on the steps, on the floor, leaning against the walls. Isha was addressing the crowd, Caitlin by her side. Tatters landed beside them, interrupting the speech.

'Where have you come from?' Isha asked, startled. 'We were expecting the worst.'

'I have a message from Hawk,' he answered. He could explain what had happened later. 'If we surrender, she will only take the lives of the guilty.' Whatever that meant.

A murmur lifted from the crowd, the sound of hope. Caitlin smiled grimly, the smile of someone who can see a solution, but isn't yet sure they believe it will work.

Isha turned back to the mages. *This is our chance to end this without fighting pointlessly, without dying for men who will never put their lives on the line, and never thank us for our sacrifice.*

When she turned to Tatters, her smile had the severity, the firmness, of Hawk's face. Without the tattoo twisting the lines of her brow and mouth, she could have been mistaken for her mother.

'I'm sorry, Tatters, but you're going to have to speak to the triumvirate. They're at the council meeting, and they're being... obtuse. I talked to Lord Leofric, and Caitlin tried to persuade Lord Daegen, but they wouldn't listen. Maybe you can convince them to surrender. We couldn't.'

Isha took a deep breath.

'And I'll talk to Hawk. We need to be the ones to choose the guilty, not her.' This she said louder, for the people assembled around them. The sounds from the hall swelled. Encouragement and approval filled the room, from the men and women who feared for their lives.

Only Caitlin's face stayed sour. 'Don't get yourself killed.'

Isha nodded. Dark, childish curls bobbed around her face, and for a moment Tatters was struck by how youthful she was. A child with a warrior's features. 'I'll try.'

That was when Tatters noticed her fear, which she'd been striving to hide. At first, he hadn't wanted to say more, because Lal was right, it was misleading. But because of Isha's expression, he mindlinked.

Isha. He hesitated, even then. *Your mother says she loves you.*

She shivered, and he knew she had heard him.

But don't take her word for it, Lal added.

No point in dithering any longer. Tatters closed his eyes. With each inhalation, warmth filled his veins, light replaced his blood. With each exhalation, the heaviness of the world fell behind, like skin being shed. He flew upwards, through the ceilings, corridors and floorboards, through the thick stone of giants, the flimsy, worm-ridden wood of mages. He reached the sky, and it was achingly wide, the width of freedom, the blue of paradise.

Now he had to win over the council.

Convince them, or force them.

* * *

From the balcony, Isha continued to encourage the crowd. They were warming up to her. Seeing that she had a lightborn on her side had reassured them. The fact that both Isha and Tatters were acting together seemed to convince Passerine's followers she was carrying out his will, because they agreed to what she said without a fuss. Some mages – lawmages, notably, or older mages who had been spared being sent to the front – weren't as taken. But everyone wanted the war to end, so they listened.

It is wrong for the supreme mages to use us, Isha said, while Caitlin sent images of the ranged battle against the Renegades, the troops losing control and visibility as they only received orders, not support. *And it is wrong for the mages to use ungifted like puppets.* This she mindlinked widely, to the ungifted who were at the margins of the gathering, trying to draw them in. *We have done it, even I have done it, because we had no choice. But I want us to make a world where we do have a choice – and ungifted do, as well.*

She took a deep breath. This was the unpopular part of her speech.

I will talk to Hawk, as I promised. But I already know one demand she will make, and one we have to agree to, if we are to ever make peace with the Renegades. We have to apologise for the wrongs we've caused. We have to make up for them. And we've wronged the khers most of all.

The feedback from the crammed hall was a low grumble, from minds who didn't understand what the problem was, or who found khers off-putting, or who were scared of them.

Isha rested her hands on the balustrade, without putting weight on her bad arm. She tuned out the background thrum of mages. *Let me show you.* She closed her eyes, turning inwards, to memories of her time at the Pit, with Ka, right back to the first time she had seen a butcher rip horns out of a dead man's forehead.

She shared her memories. It was intimate, giving these strangers a part of herself – how she had felt seeing Ka in the pillory; the heavy weight of his father, whom she had helped carry inside his tiyayat to be mourned; the sound of Yua's laughter, and the stricken circle of faces when her family had heard news of her death. But she ploughed on, conveying the emotions linked to each event, the friendliness of the Pit, the fact that these were people, with children, sisters, mothers, brothers, and that their lives mattered, and of course they would fight against those who wanted to grind them underfoot.

As she did so, a sense of exaltation, of liberation, filled Isha. Maybe this was what mindlink was for. It wasn't a good way to keep secrets – but it lent itself to giving. One mage could learn from an experience, and grow as a person, then pass on their memory, leading other people to learn and, maybe, to grow.

Their true power was sharing.

She opened her eyes, slowly letting go of her mindlink. The hall was quiet, buzzing with thinking minds. Rather than feeling diminished, bared, Isha blazed with strength. Everything she had gone through, everything she had learnt, she could give to others, without losing anything herself. How many paths could they tread together? They could live a thousand lives over, in a thousand places, and all partake in them.

'That's impressive,' Caitlin whispered.

Isha didn't trust herself to speak; she nodded. Laughter bubbled up in her throat, at the rush of possibilities coursing through her.

Before Isha could check the effect she'd had on the assembled minds, she heard a click behind her. It was a stark sound, meant to draw attention to itself. She turned.

Behind the balcony there was a spiral staircase, encased in stone, that led to the council room. It was one of the Nest's spires, needle-thin when compared to the thick body of the castle. Descending the tower, his bone cane announcing his arrival as it hit the steps in front of him, was Lord Leofric.

His reptilian eyes settled on Isha.

'Well, well, well,' he said, and his smile was like the flash of a forked tongue. 'What is going on here?'

If Caitlin had hackles, Isha would have seen them rise.

'We are talking,' Isha said. She was stunned she managed to keep her cool. 'It is not illegal, I believe.'

'That depends on what you were saying,' said Lord Leofric. 'Why, are you worried it might be unlawful?'

His voice was, as always, smooth and friendly. His posture was, as always, that of a predator who has spotted prey.

'No,' Isha lied. She wondered if he could smell fear. His smirk made her believe he could.

Lord Leofric surprised them all by waving this away with a flick of his cane. 'No matter. You are needed upstairs. Follow me.'

No matter? Isha tried to push down the foreboding that clamped around her heart. Even outside of a crisis, power was the most valued currency of the Nest. Anyone exciting mages to rebellion should be the lawmages' first target. She stood frozen; she couldn't bring herself to move. Behind her, she was conscious of the uncertain mass of mages and apprentices, waiting to see what would happen, unsure what had broken the spell. Beside her, she was aware of Caitlin, nervous, poised.

'Are you deaf, girl?' Lord Leofric asked. 'Come here.'

'Why?' said Isha.

When he wanted to, Leofric had the still features of a statue. He could have been carved in precious stone, so little did his smile change, his eyes waver.

'I do not owe you explanations,' he said.

Isha made an impulsive decision. If she found herself alone with him, he could force her to submit. He was the stronger mage. She wouldn't have the choice of fighting him, but she might have the choice of battleground.

'I do not owe you loyalty,' she answered.

The moment she finished her sentence, before she could raise her mental defences, before anyone around her could intervene, Lord Leofric mindbrawled. His mouth didn't twist, his posture didn't change. He attacked with the suddenness of a snake.

Here is your explanation, mongrel. He hit her with a wealth of images, herself beside Hawk, Daegan handing her over in chains, as a hostage, to a figure who was half-truth, half-nightmare, a tall, armoured woman with an ogre's set of teeth. Reflexively, Isha translated the scene into iwdan, as a defence mechanism. Before she could disentangle herself from his mindlink, however, Leofric was sending the image of Isha on a rack, being flayed by her mother, to retrieve the tattoo from her face and make it into a banner of dried skin.

It was excruciating in every detail. It wasn't so much about psychological shock, as mindlink most often was. It was about pain. The agony of having skin pulled from your still-living face. Pain has no language. It has no voice. Isha's technique of swapping the words being used to deflect the blow didn't work.

It was a textbook takedown, as clean as any lawmage could wish for. She fainted.

She was only unconscious for a minute, at most. But she had passed out, Isha knew, because she woke up on the floor, her jaw bruised where it had hit the stone, her left wrist aching, hot with blood from the reopened wound, her bandage soaked. She could tell it hadn't been for long, because Caitlin and Leofric were still fighting.

Their mindlink filled the air with visions, all of them unpleasant, clashing in the air above them. As Isha struggled to her feet, wincing at the throbbing in her arm, she realised there were more than two people brawling. Leofric was being attacked by at least seven or so mages, as far as Isha could make out: Caitlin, of course, but a couple of others. The ones who had been most impressed by the way Caitlin and Isha had handled the battlefield, maybe; or Passerine's – Isha's – more ardent followers.

To her dismay, pockets of infighting were also breaking out in the hall, as a couple of lawmages had risen to the occasion to dismantle the gathering. The ungifted who could still do so were fleeing; the unlucky ones were being held like marionettes and forced to intervene in skirmishes they hadn't picked.

One problem at a time. Lord Leofric was radiating power, a strength that none of them had, the control that allowed him to bend whole armies to his will. *Where is Tatters when we need him?* Not here, obviously. She had to do this without hoping for his help.

Head still ringing, clouded with pain, she tried to understand how her allies were dealing with Lord Leofric. It wasn't unlike attempting to take down a boar, every hunter poking at the beast with lances, jumping out of the way when it charged. The mages harassed him, and as soon as Leofric turned his attention to them, they focused on defending, letting someone else take the offence. No-one could beat him, but they could push him to keep changing target, so no-one got crushed. As long as they weren't disabled by his attacks, they could wear him out.

But when Leofric hit his mark, he did so with such violence that people seemed to turn into lacunants on the spot: empty eyes, uncontrolled trembling and spasming, crashing to the ground unconscious.

Think, Isha exhorted herself. *You started this, it's up to you to end it.*

She spotted an opening, just as Caitlin braced herself to protect her mind from Leofric. Isha crafted an image of his betters, of people who had what Leofric craved. Envy was such a common trait in mages, it was nearly a guaranteed success. She pictured him jealous – of collarbounds he couldn't command, of spouses he couldn't seduce, of friends he couldn't coerce into liking him.

Ah, the Renegade's spawn is awake, Leofric said, recognising her.

When his mind locked onto hers, she felt like a cub held in a lion's jaws. He was overwhelming, everywhere. *The agony in her wrist only grew, climbed all the way up her arm, to the place where they would saw it off, as they had Kilian's arm, giving her only a gag to choke on as they hacked at the bone, sweaty with effort, grunting as they put their weight into the butcher's knife.*

Forced to use his mindlink elsewhere, Leofric let go of her like a hound dropping a bird with broken wings. Isha was left stunned, with precious little time to rebuild her mental barriers, or to prepare a new strategy.

It isn't envy, but it has to be something. Even Lord Leofric must have a weakness that could soulsplinter him. She crafted her next imagining in advance, waiting for an opening. Beside her, Caitlin had bitten her lower lip so hard she was bleeding down her chin. He was taking his toll on all of them. Isha heard a young man moan as he collapsed, tugging at his own hair as if to rip it from his skull. Only five of them were left fighting.

As soon as she was strong enough, Isha lunged again. This time, her angle was fear. Why be cruel to the khers, if not out of fear of retaliation? And it was happening, right here, right now. She visualised the iwdan's uprising, their bid for freedom, storming Lord Leofric's prisons, overthrowing his rule. For a moment, his mind quaked, and she felt an inch of a hold, maybe, something she could almost, but not quite, dig into.

Then Leofric was upon her again. *The walking flag*, he sneered. *We should hang you from a pole.* He sent her an image, thick with sensory information, of her being strung up a mast, the rope crushing her throat, her legs kicking uselessly beneath her. The slight pop behind her eyes as they bulged out of their sockets.

When he let go, shifting to another mage, the scene vanished abruptly. *He doesn't need to know people*, Isha realised, *or to understand what makes them tick. He's strong enough to just crush them with pain. Because everyone is afraid of dying.* Lord Leofric relied on talent, not craft. But still, he was taking them down faster than they were wearing him out. Isha would never have the knowledge to hit his weak spot, not with so little time to gather information. She wouldn't have the strength, alone, to overpower him. What was left?

She took a step back, hoping her allies could hold out without her for a while. She desperately needed to find an alternative. She let her mind expand, sensing the fight from its outlines, hunting for a pattern or a clue. On the balcony, only Caitlin and Isha were facing Leofric – but a couple of mages had rushed to help, and were standing on the top of the staircase. The hall was mostly silent, with the odd grunt or scream. Mindlink vibrated through the air; the Nest was charged with magic.

At last, Isha found what she'd been hoping for. A sliver of minds, hanging around Lord Leofric, echoing with his mindlink. A mantle of thoughts, which were not quite his own, wreathing him. It was as subtle as a reflection off a piece of metal. She squinted at him, and spotted his pendant, a small chain holding up a flask of mercury. Of course. He had collected pieces of wrecked minds inside.

Help! Caitlin's call tore Isha's heart, like the scream of a rabbit that knows it will be skinned.

She didn't have time to check it would work. Isha extended her mind towards the mercury, calling out to the shards within, the bits of memory trapped inside the metal. *Please, can you hear me?* she begged.

These people had been broken. What was left, what had been put into the mercury, were only moments – the unbearable last minutes of their lives, during which they were torn asunder. Still, some of the victims there had a stronger sense of self than others, fuelled by rage. Isha perceived someone, a woman, still spitting in anger all this time after having died. *I asked to hang, and this is what he did to me. What kind of man refuses such a small mercy?*

Relieved at having found someone who could communicate, albeit not much beyond a sense of fury, Isha coaxed the woman into sharing her experience with Lord Leofric. *Show him what it was like for you. I know it was terrible, but live it again, please, so he can go through it with you. So he can understand what he's done.* The dead didn't have much agency, only a moment they constantly repeated for themselves. Repeating it for another person wasn't so much of a stretch.

Caitlin stumbled to the floor, her knees slamming into the stone. She clutched her head with both hands, not even attempting to break her fall. Leofric spun to face Isha, his green irises bright, his pupils a pinprick inside them.

Isha ran towards Leofric, as she had seen Tatters do, as she had done against Caitlin once before. Leofric's pupils widened a fraction. Still, he braced himself, prepared for an attack he was familiar with. But Isha wasn't trying to land a hit. When she was close enough, she went to grab him. Leofric skipped out of her way, his mindlink hitting her like a spear. But as he dodged backwards, her fingers closed around his pendant. She tugged at the minds within, directing them towards Leofric.

She crushed the flask of mercury inside her fist.

For a moment, time stood suspended. The glass bit into her skin. The mercury, rather than dropping in one beady tear to the floor, split into branches, like the birth of a star. Fingers of liquid metal reached out, extending in every direction. Forming a bridge as best she could, Isha carried the trapped minds to Leofric, letting them brush through her.

Above his chest, the mercury looked like a hand trying to grab his heart.

The people he'd captured and stored shared their last instants with him. The agony. The fear. The hope, because hope died with them, but never before. Isha stepped back, aware the mindlink would break her if she were too close, as a small skiff can be torn apart by the suction of stormy waves.

The imaginings were true. They were terrible. And they touched Leofric, at last. Isha ran to Caitlin's side, hugging her against her chest to shield her, as lives ended in pain and power-lessness again and again, and the man who had orchestrated those deaths, who had found pleasure and power in them, relived them. She saw the moment he realised what it meant to be at someone else's mercy, and for it to not be given. He was a snake eating its own tail, preparing the suffering to inflict before being subjected to it. He was his own tormentor. For the first time in his life, he *empathised*, in the purest sense: he suffered with his victims. He suffered as one of them.

Only Lord Leofric could think up a torture cruel enough to harm Lord Leofric.

When it was done, the mercury dropped to the floor without a sound, like a silent, heavy, steel-grey rain.

Chapter 13

Tatters circled the spires of the Nest and the council room, where he could see the maze of panelled glass that girdled the council table. He wondered what words were carved there, what the lines of colour interweaving might be saying to those who flew above it – wait for us? Goodbye? Don't forget us?

'Leave while you still can', maybe, said Lal.

He finished his arc, skimming the crumbled steps the giants had once trodden. He transformed back into human shape, landing with a dull thump on the table. Aside from Lord Daegan, only Starling was in attendance. She was ambling through the maze, running her fingers along the panels. She was listening to the crystalline sound her nails made against the glass, with the intent focus of a child.

Tatters could have asked where Lord Leofric was lurking, but Hawk didn't have much patience, which meant he didn't have much time.

'We need to surrender,' Tatters announced.

'We'd assumed you were dead,' Lord Daegan said, not even attempting to hide his surprise.

Standing on the table in front of him, Tatters felt taller, for once, than the lords who ruled over the Nest. He looked down on Lord Daegan's skull, where the hair was already growing sparse.

'The only way to avoid a bloodshed is to give in to Hawk,' he insisted.

'What happened to Lord Passerine?' Lord Daegan asked.

Tatters snapped, 'Passerine is dead.'

He realised the moment the sentence escaped him that it was a mistake. Lord Daegan's steely eyes picked up the dullness of the collar; his demeanour pricked up like a wolf's ears at the news. He clicked his fingers. Starling lifted her face towards him, attentive, anxious. She still bore bruises from previous battles.

'Incapacitate him,' Lord Daegan ordered. 'I need him captured, for questioning.'

Starling alighted before the sentence was finished. Instinct, mixed with luck, meant Tatters threw himself backwards before she hit, alighting as he slid off the table. He hadn't transformed so swiftly in years; he gasped as the shock of the shifting rippled through him. He stayed low, sliding through stone, dipping through the floor without so much as scratching the tiles.

We need a mirror, said Lal.

Starling came crashing behind him, bigger, brighter. They cut through stone, through glass, through wood, as easily as light through air. He went through the upper chambers of the Nest, where high mages slept and plotted, hoping people would keep mirrors in their bedrooms, making the space more difficult for her to navigate, as her size would make her more prone to bumping into reflective surfaces.

When she dived for him, he changed angle abruptly, aiming upwards. Above the Nest, the sky was bright blue, without a cloud in sight.

Tatters shifted back into human form as soon as he reached the council table again. Lord Daegan watched him without flinching. His cautious step back, and the swirl of protective mindlink, belied his apparent calm.

'There's a misunderstanding,' Tatters gasped. 'I don't belong to Hawk. The collar is broken.'

Light like a thunderbolt erupted from the floor beneath him. Tatters rolled aside, off the table, dropping roughly against the floor. His knees screamed in protest. He tried to alight, to flash out of the way, but he was exhausted, and he'd lost the habit of changing mid-tussle to flee or fight. Before he could gather his wits, Starling crashed into him, human again, and her weight slammed him against the ground. He felt his ribs take in the shock as the air was knocked out of his lungs.

Tatters wrestled with his back to the cold stone, his arms flailing towards her. She punched his mouth. She cut her knuckles on his teeth, and he tasted blood – hers, and his own.

Focus, Lal urged.

Tatters slipped out of Starling's grasp as he turned to light, heading for the inside of the Nest. She followed. As she was catching up, he veered to the right, lifting above a narrow staircase. She cut his path, and they both shifted into human shape together. They flew – fell – through the air and landed on limbs that weren't made for tumbling down steps. The stairs cut into his shins; agony shot through his ankles.

Stunned, he struggled to his feet. They were close to the servants' quarters, in a staircase used to carry goods up to the high mages' rooms. Only scared ungifted were here, already scattering. Starling caught him by the front of his robes and slammed him against the wall. She moved her face close to his. He recoiled by habit, thinking she would headbutt him.

'I am so sorry,' she murmured in his ear, her face hidden by a stream of blonde hair.

Her voice was gentle. She didn't want to do this. Her pity

came to Tatters as a revelation. So many people had hit him recently, and none of them had expressed such reluctance to do him harm.

'We could escape our binds,' she said, with the soft confidence of despair, 'if you dealt me a deadly blow, and I did the same for you. Collars will not follow us in death.'

Tatters swallowed. He remembered pressing his neck against Passerine's blade and telling him to slit his throat. He remembered staring into Leofric's eyes and daring him to call the axeman.

But he thought of Yua, of a promise made in a cell so dark he couldn't see her face. He wanted to give up. He wouldn't.

'There are other ways to escape our binds,' he said.

After all, we did it once before, said Lal.

'We will both leave that council room unbound. I promise.'

Starling shook her head. 'You promised you would be back this winter.'

He alighted to disentangle himself. She transformed as he did. When their two lights mingled, he realised he didn't stand a chance. He was barely a dash of red amongst her lush yellow. He didn't colour her, but she absorbed him, integrated his light into hers. He cringed, trying to resist her tug, but as a lightborn she was greater than him. The difference in strength was the same as between a child and an adult. He could writhe and kick, but she didn't have to care.

She flashed through the slabs of carved rock as easily as if they were paper. Tatters dimly recognised the main hall from the way the walls stopped hemming them in, leaving a wide space to fly unimpeded. Isha and the others were gathered here, but their attention was elsewhere, not on the two collarbounds.

Now, said Lal, *or never*.

He changed into a human, dropping away from Starling like

lead. His stomach lurched as he shot down towards the ground of the main hall, several feet too high in the air for his body to enjoy the experience. He tried not to imagine the stain he would leave on the stones. He became light, nearly too late, and swerved, aiming for the arches leading to the courtyard.

He couldn't keep this up. Alighting was tough work and he hadn't exactly practised. He decided to get back to the council room. There must be a way to end this.

He couldn't outrun her. She caught up with him as he shot out of the council floor, and yanked him back before he could get to Daegan, throwing him in an arc of blood-red light in the opposite direction.

As he skidded to a crouch on the main mosaic, human once more, Tatters sensed his muscles trembling from the strain. His lower lip had been busted, maybe by her punch, and he could taste blood on his teeth. He was conscious of each square of the mosaic pressing against his skin.

Starling landed next to Lord Daegan. Her dress was rumpled, stained with dust and specks of blood. He lifted a hand. Obediently, she paused.

'I found Lord Passerine's notes,' Daegan announced. 'On alighting. And Lord Leofric found his pet's little secret. We have Hawk's daughter. She will do nothing as long as we hold her hostage.'

There was a manic edge to this confidence. A crack running down his mind, a sort of panic, glossed over with belief.

'You wouldn't dare use Isha,' Tatters hissed, wiping blood from his mouth. He pulled himself up by holding onto the council table.

They were both animals, growling, baring their fangs at each other.

349

'Don't tell me what I will and will not do,' said Daegan. 'But you will tell me this: how to alight.'

Ah. So that was it. Passerine's obsessive notes were contagious. What could he tell Lord Daegan, that he would accept? That there was no secret, no magic, that he would ever find useful in those hours and hours of research? Dizzy, nauseous, Tatters straightened, still leaning one arm on the table.

'If we can alight, we will be like gods,' Daegan whispered. 'We will be gods.'

His face had twisted with such hunger, his jowls had lifted into such a greedy smile, that Tatters didn't doubt for one moment that, if he could alight, Daegan wouldn't leave the human world behind. He would stay, and rule.

Tatters spread out his hands. 'If Passerine didn't find what he was looking for, I doubt you will.'

A soul like yours is too heavy, old man, Lal added. *You'll never alight.*

Bloodless lips thinned. Lord Daegan turned to Starling, who was still standing beside him, recovering her breath.

'He is of no use to me.' Lord Daegan's order sounded casual, nearly friendly. 'Kill him.'

She can't resist the collar, said Lal.

You think I don't know that?

Starling faced Tatters, letting out a long, controlled sigh. He put weight into his feet, bracing himself. He wasn't changing shape this time. He would be better off as a human. Memories of training with Hawk were kicking in at last. Lal was right: he needed a mirror.

She'll kill you. Lal was urgent, worried. *You have to hurt her.*

Great. Any ideas?

Starling alighted. She went through Tatters like a lightning bolt. She pierced him, a spear of ethereal fire – the impact nearly knocked him off his feet, but he resisted her attempt to drag him out of his body. If she succeeded in tearing him out of the corporeal world, she would kill him. She only needed to touch him to absorb him, to break down his colours into variations of gold.

Tatters forced himself to hold Daegan's eye, despite the light wreathing him. He took a step towards the supreme mage.

He gasped when Starling flashed through him again. His knees buckled; he grabbed the table for support. He wouldn't withstand a third attack. He saw Starling curve above the council room, like a rainbow of gold, before dipping towards him. Daegan's heart, no doubt, could be broken; but it couldn't be bent. He wouldn't revoke his order.

Fleshbinding, said Lal.

What?

You've tasted her blood.

Did fleshbinding even work on a lightborn? Starling veered, intent on rushing through him again, and again, as many times as necessary.

Tatters focused on his pain – the one he felt, and the one she was about to inflict. As he started fleshbinding, he had a sharp sense of her, as well-defined as desire.

When she hit him, he flung all sensation back at her. He felt nothing as he saw her light going through his stomach, his arms, with no more force than sunlight drifting in through a window.

She screamed. She fell into a crumpled heap behind him, the force of the fleshbinding calling her back to human shape. Starling whimpered on the floor, her hands slipping on the icy stones as she scrambled to get to her knees. Her collar glowed as brightly as her flight. Before she could get up, he punched the ground. He clenched his teeth, although he knew he wouldn't feel the hit. Behind him, she yelped, losing her support and

351

slipping back to the floor. Tatters hoped he hadn't broken any bones. She was the one suffering, but his body would be the one damaged.

As Starling cradled her fingers, Tatters had a few precious seconds to take down Daegan. He charged.

Tatters aimed for Daegan's thorax, hoping to knock the breath out of him. As soon as he moved, however, the high mage mindlinked. Disjointed memories crossed his mind, pages burning to cinders, Hawk lifting a banner, iron or blood in his mouth as Yua laughed her last frantic laugh, and he wasn't sure, in the confusion, whether it was his heightened emotions or Daegan's mindbrawl that summoned these images. He saw the old man grab for his hair, thought he would withstand it, and closed the gap between them. Daegan's hand ducked lower than he'd expected, and closed around the collar.

A shiver, brief and startling, like biting into ice, around Tatters' neck. The collar resonated, even now, with obedience. It stopped him in his tracks.

If I cannot fly, lightborns will carry me. Daegan's mindlink was like a knife through Tatters' temples, trying to bore a way into his head. *If my soul is too heavy, you will lift it.*

The collar flared like a fire touched by wind.

If the collar is broken, I will be its master, Daegan said.

Starling lifted above them, her flight wobbly, a bird with a broken wing. Yet she dived. At the same time, Lord Daegan mindbrawled.

Tatters felt himself lose consciousness as he might feel sleep take over after a long day. His limbs were heavy, his blood sluggish. His vision darkened. He was standing in the blackness of his mind, a void with no asperities to hang sensations onto. The only light came from a circle of fire around him, slowly closing in.

Lal stood beside Tatters, her head thrown back, her chin proud, despite a glint of fear in her expression. He took her hand.

In front of them, in the shadows, something that had the shape of Daegan, but that wasn't him – maybe it was what was left once what held a man together was broken. Panic, envy, fear, yearning, the heightened terror of someone who felt their grip slipping despite how tightly they clutched their prize. A wealth of images and well-woven traps, squirming like insects, drawing closer.

The line of fire, the circle of the collar, was reducing. It was awakening. After all these years, Tatters was still subject to its power.

Hawk, Passerine, Leofric, Daegan. It's an endless cycle, Tatters thought.

Lal squeezed his hand. When he turned to her, he saw in her eyes that she had taken a decision.

You don't belong to them, she said. *You don't belong to anyone.*

She pushed against Tatters. He staggered, taking a step over the flowing line of flames. He turned around to see Lal standing within the collar's binds, its fire growing higher, nearly as tall as her shoulder.

What are you doing? he asked.

When it happens, she said, *let go.*

She gave him a small wave, an even smaller smile. But her expression was fond.

Before he could ask what would happen, Starling struck with full force.

Minds were especially vulnerable to a lightborn's power. Tatters understood what was happening only as it unfolded: the glowing circle represented in mindlink the binds of the collar. As Starling tore through his mind, cleaving it in half, Lal and the collar and the ties that helped Lal live, that helped the collar tether his spirit, were wrenched away from him. It felt as if he were ripping at the seams, as if every inch of himself, held together by force of will, was tearing apart. Into pieces. Into tatters.

He did what his sister had asked. He let go.

It was like dodging, he supposed, if he'd decided to avoid a crossbow to the eye, only to let it shred his ear; if a blow that could have split his chest only took his arm. If he could have felt every tendon, every nerve, every fibre of his flesh being severed by the sharp end of a sword, then the pain, maybe, would have been comparable to this: every link to his sister being cut.

He opened his eyes. Daegan still stood inside his mind; Tatters still stood within the council chamber.

The collar exploded.

Shards of gold flew out in every direction. Lord Daegan was thrown back halfway across the room, crashing heavily into a coloured pane, splitting the glass into long, weblike cracks. Tatters fleshbound, letting go of the horror, of the agony of losing Lal – he gave it to Starling, betraying his sister twice.

Forgive me, he tried to convey, uselessly. He had to do this. Because he had to live, if she had died for him.

The sound Starling made was what his heart was yearning to let out; the sound of someone watching a loved one die. As she crumpled in a pile on the floor, Tatters alighted. When he reached Daegan, the old man was the colour of undyed linen. He opened his mouth, and before he spoke the order Tatters heard it on his lips. He punched the supreme mage in the face.

He heard a crack. Daegan let out a yelp, pressing both hands to his nose, gasping as blood gushed over his upper lip. As the warm blood dripped between his fingers, Tatters kept his fist clenched. He brought it to his mouth. He made sure Daegan was looking.

He licked his knuckles.

Starling stared, hugging her chest as if she could clasp the grief between her arms, ready to obey the brutal, brilliant call of the collar despite the fleshbinding still coursing through her. Tatters let his fist fall back to his side. Slowly, he let the pain return to him, the ache of losing Lal, of having his mind split in half and surviving.

Then, just as slowly, as a threat, as a promise, he shared it with Daegan. Incrementally, he increased the pressure.

'I am not interested in letting this drag on,' said Tatters. 'Unbind Starling or die.'

There was nothing but fear in Daegan's face. Tatters could feel the drop of red still on his lips, like the remainder of a kiss. Starling's cool, unflushed cheeks were ashen. She was shivering from the shock.

'I said I wouldn't let this drag on,' Tatters snarled. He pushed on the fleshbinding link, making Daegan flinch.

Lord Daegan urged Starling forward with a wave. She stepped towards him, still uncertain. The only noises were their raspy gulps for air.

Daegan placed his withered hands on her smooth neck.

'I unbind you,' he whispered.

The collar shone like a star being born. It grew and grew, until it was wide enough to encompass Starling's shoulders, until it had the width and brightness its twin, the other collar, had sustained in Tatters' mind before it broke.

Starling lifted the collar above her head, freeing herself of its influence. The circle of flame dulled and shrunk until it became a crown once more, a simple artefact forged a long time ago. The circle of gold, as fine as braided hair, seemed fragile in her hands.

'What do you want to do with him?' Tatters asked, jutting his chin towards Daegan.

Starling hesitated. 'Make sure he never harms others,' she said. 'As for me, it is enough that I am no longer bound to him.'

For the first time, Tatters realised the implications of what had taken place. When he brushed his fingers against his neck, it was naked. No gold as smooth as scales growing across his throat.

He wasn't a collarbound anymore.

Blood and saliva were drying on his fist. His mind was empty. Lal would never again whisper background advice or teasing.

She had died. He would die. The important choices of his life were behind him.

Lord Daegan's head was bowed as if tethered down by ropes. 'I surrender,' he said.

* * *

They shackled Leofric with kher horn, for safety. Isha disliked the black keratin manacles, but even she had to admit it was the only way to prevent the head lawmage from mindlinking people around him as soon as he regained consciousness. She was entrusting him to two ungifted when Tatters emerged from the spiral staircase at the side of the balcony, the one that led to the council room. Daegan and Starling were in his wake, but from the way Daegan held his head low, his hands knotted together, Isha knew who the winner of that fight had been.

'If you have another pair, I have another prisoner for you,' Tatters said. Although his words were light, his tone was grim.

'Don't worry, we have enough for everyone,' Caitlin answered.

It was only once he was close that Isha noticed. It should have been the first thing she'd seen.

Tatters didn't have his collar. There was blood on his knuckles, drying in two brown lines. Beside him, Starling was as distant as ever, and yet she was holding a crown between her fingers, letting it roll around her wrist.

Tatters turned to the crowd. Isha followed his gaze from the high arches of sandstones to the long pillars like pale fingers, down to the gathering of blue robes below. The illusion was of one piece of indigo fabric stretching from one end of the hall to the other. Or maybe a blue lightborn curled there, shimmering quietly – Byluk, the lightborn of death.

Lord Passerine is dead, Tatters announced.

Isha had been expecting it, yet it bit into her heart. She wondered what Passerine had said as he died. She wondered whose blood was on Tatters' hands.

Lord Leofric and Lord Daegan are unfit to rule, Tatters continued. *They're under arrest.*

Isha had wanted the ungifted included, and it was a relief to hear them gasp, because it meant the mages were doing their part, sharing the flock's thoughts with everyone present. Passerine had been the most liked of the three supreme mages – she sensed sorrow, the stench of terror rising.

She pushed her own emotions aside as she took her place at the front of the balcony. Before the panic could take hold, she said, *The situation isn't hopeless. We can surrender and keep our independence. I will vouch for that.*

She felt the weight of a warm hand on her shoulder, achingly familiar, like the heavy hand of a ghost. When she turned, it was Tatters. Without his collar, he burnt with inner light, as if the gold now shone from inside his chest rather than around his neck. Although he glowed, seemingly taller than before, his eyes were empty holes. His mind pulsed, raw and jagged, as if something had been ripped out of it.

She couldn't sense Lal.

'I will vouch for Isha,' he said.

The closer people heard the words; the others saw the gesture. The hall was still, as if the mages had all become statues.

Behind them, Caitlin had shackled both Daegan and Leofric to the balcony's balustrade.

'The easy part is done,' she said, making Isha's heart thump at the thought of harder trials to come. 'Now let's speak to Hawk.'

Preparing the outing took a bit of time. It was necessary to find a piece of green cloth – Groniz was the colour of life, and therefore of peace – and a flagpole to hang it from. The small door within the Nest's greater ones was tentatively opened. A retinue was put together, composed of Isha, Caitlin, the two lightborns, the kher guards who had earned the blood right, a couple of ungifted at Isha's demand, and the priest Osmund, for the same reason, so that everyone was represented.

Their eclectic group left the Nest for the muddy, churned moors beyond. Isha walked in front. Although the flag was too heavy to be comfortable, she held it in one hand, ignoring the throbbing from her left wrist, trying to forget the shaft of wood sticking out like the grotesque bind of a puppet.

At the bridge, the Renegades stood to attention, but in deference to the green flag and the small numbers being sent out, they didn't cross it, waiting for Isha to come to them.

At the foot of the bridge, above the white spray lifted by the roaring river, Isha turned to her followers.

'I will do this alone,' she said. 'If things look dire, head back to the Nest.'

'I'm coming,' said Caitlin. Her tone left no room for argument.

'I think it would be best if I were there too,' said Tatters.

The ungifted, a manservant and a coachwoman from the Nest, seemed unsure. The kher guards were probably the most ill at ease, caught between the side they'd chosen and the friends and family they'd have to face. But Osmund said, 'We came to listen and to bear witness. We cannot do that from afar.'

It was settled. Everyone stepped onto the bridge, keeping Isha in front, still holding her heavy flag. The rough wood rubbed against her palm. It was makeshift, a piece of festival cloth knotted at the top. No-one in the Nest had expected to sur-render, so no-one had prepared a gilded green banner, although there were enough dyed in crimson and blue.

The Renegades parted for Hawk. She stood at her end of the bridge, a ceremonial nasivyati of scarlet draped around her neck, mirrors as tiny as embroidered jewels threaded into the cloth. The wind tousled it, let it trail like two dashes of blood dripping from her silhouette.

Hawk stepped forward with nothing but confidence in her stride. Half a dozen Renegades escorted her. She crossed the stone bridge, above the rift in the cliff, towards the meagre speck of green cloth.

When she saw Isha's tattoo, her expression changed. When the old, damaged face showed such emotion – such vulnerability – Isha changed her speech about freedom and rights to one word:

'Mother.'

Hawk recovered from her shock faster than Isha would have thought. Her eyes were like the mirrors of her nasivyati: bright, cold.

'My eyas,' Hawk answered. She had a rough voice, but it wasn't unkind.

Isha had tied her hair with a stray strap of leather, but a black curl had escaped and lashed in the gale. She tucked it back, using all her willpower not to shake. She had to use her wounded hand to do so, and she spotted Hawk staring at the bandaged wrist.

'We are surrendering.' Even to her own ears, Isha sounded unsure and frail. Clenching her hand around the flagpole, willing herself to stand firm, she went on. 'But we have some conditions: we will adapt the Renegades' laws, blending them with our own, without adopting them all. We will remain independent. We will hold our own trials. We will choose our own guilty.'

Hawk didn't seem surprised at this, merely amused. She crossed her arms, and Isha tried not to notice the weathered armour, the way it followed her every movement, leather and metal like a second skin that she showed no sign of moulting.

'You are in no position to make demands,' Hawk said, matter-of-factly.

Isha refused to be cowed by the crowd of Renegades, by the sharp dip of the chasm, by the power that emanated, effortlessly, from Hawk. 'There must be something you want, that we can provide.'

'My wish has always been, and always will be, to break the binds that hold us down,' said Hawk.

This was, if not the truth, at least *her* truth, Isha realised. She believed those words. In her own eyes, Hawk was a hero who had led a rebel army against tyrants and prevailed. What sort of hero would back down now?

'I want to make this world a better place,' Hawk concluded. 'If to do so I must rule it, so be it.'

Isha sucked in a steadying breath. 'You should decide. Did you come to rule the Nest, or to change it?'

Hawk lifted an eyebrow. It was obvious she was only indulging her daughter, with no intention of being swayed. Well, she was listening, at least. Isha had to try to be heard, then.

'Did you come to make more binds, or to break them?' Isha ploughed on. 'If you come to the Nest as a conqueror, you will have to fight the mages every step of the way, wading through blood. I realise that's the Renegade way. But it isn't the only way. Adapting the laws, so the mages can accept them, is another solution. The first step is to let them keep their independence. If you truly are looking for change, not power, that is what you will do.'

During this speech, Hawk's attention had drifted over Isha's shoulder, to the people behind. Her gaze had settled not so much on Tatters as on his neck. She was studying the collarless lightborns, Isha guessed. Her face, like her thoughts, was guarded. But she couldn't quite hide her interest.

So here were binds that others had broken, that she had merely made. Maybe Isha could make Hawk see this.

'Your rules are the right ones,' Isha said, 'but you are not the right person to enforce them.'

This time Hawk laughed. It was a grating sound, like the screech of a bird of prey.

'And who is, then?'

'I will lead the Nest,' Isha answered.

Hawk laughed harder. Isha's head was swimming, maybe because of the pain, maybe because of the fight with Leofric. She couldn't hear her thoughts above the rush of wind and water. If Hawk refused her bid for peace, would she have to drag the Nest into a siege? Would she have to wait, gates locked, while the people she'd promised to help starved? Or open the doors, give in, and pray Hawk wouldn't punish every mage she decided to blame?

Tatters took a step forward. Isha jumped; she had forgotten she wasn't doing this alone.

'Let it be known,' Tatters said, holding Hawk's gaze, 'that a lightborn stands behind Isha.'

'Two lightborns.' Unbound, Starling had a strange peacefulness to her, an eerie sense of having already flown away. Her stark features were even more distant than usual. The elegant curve of her neck appeared naked without the collar.

But she was still here. She hadn't alighted. She had stayed to see this through.

'What Raudaz says, Gelhwos has willed.' Osmund lifted one hand in front of him and closed it, as if taking something, and placed his closed fist above his heart. He was Burdening himself with a responsibility which wouldn't lighten his soul, which was only done in times of grave necessity. 'What Gelhwos wills, we yearn for. I cannot speak for the Doorkeeper, but I will beg her to support Isha.'

Isha pictured herself as an apprentice, being refused access to the Temple, washing her hands in a pail of blood. She wondered if that had been enough – some humility, some understanding – to convince Osmund to do this for her today. She felt a connection with this man from another life, this stranger who knew her name.

'We chose our side before the battle began,' one of the kher guards said, although it was hard to decipher, from her tone, whether she regretted this decision or not.

'Mages will stand behind Isha,' Caitlin said. 'They know her. They chose her.'

Isha's head was still ringing, but hope filled her lungs with each breath, filled her to burst. Maybe they could do this.

She remembered something Tatters had said, something that had sounded impossible. Holding Hawk's quiet, closed expression, she mindlinked. *You can have the Nest, or you can have me alive, but you cannot have both.* Hawk's frown didn't soften.

If your love cannot grant me freedom, it isn't love, Isha insisted. Her mother's face was unchanged.

If you have to sacrifice those you care for to make a better world, then who are you making it for? Isha asked. *For your enemies?*

Trying to weaken that resolve was like trying to thaw stone. Isha wondered what else she could say.

'The iwdan will stand behind Isha.'

The voice was deep, and deeply unexpected. Arushi pushed to the front of the retinue of Renegades, through some protest and commotion, and joined Hawk's side. A couple of other khers – Mezyan, looking annoyed that his formation had broken due to lack of discipline; Ka, with hard eyes, watching Arushi like a hound – followed suit. For the first time, Hawk seemed impressed. Her arms uncrossed. She let her hands rest on her hips as Arushi graced her with a nod. The kher was fully armed, sword swinging from her belt, as was Ka, his crossbow strapped across his back, his arrud stained with red-brown patches.

Arushi rose from her human-like bow. First, she glanced at the guards on Isha's side of the bridge. An understanding filled the air between them – the ones who had stayed to fight for their families and the ones who had betrayed to care for their families. Then Arushi turned to Isha. 'We broke bread together. We grieved together. When a new Nest is built, let it not be on the smoking ruins of the old one. But let it be new, and let iwdan have their rightful place.'

Isha answered in iwdan: '*I will not forget the hearth I come from.*'

Or close enough. The future tense was sometimes tricky to use, so maybe she had said something more along the lines of 'tomorrow, I do not forget my hearth' but the meaning, at least, should be clear.

Ka had cut his hair short. He looked more like Mezyan than, perhaps, he realised. The armour, the crossbow, and the closely cropped hair aside, his smile was unchanged. '*I'm glad you haven't forgotten your lessons,*' he said.

Hawk studied Arushi carefully, then Ka, and her birdlike

black eyes went from one person to the next, lightborn, human, kher, as if she were choosing which prey to dive down upon and tear to shreds in her claws. Lastly, her eyes rested on Isha's. Isha stood fast. It was like gazing into a mirror, or into the water of a lake, maybe, while imagining your possible futures. Where the waters were muddied, lines of age appeared, her hair shortened, her mouth hardened. However far she'd run, Isha had ended up being who her mother had planned for her to become.

A bird of prey. A leader of the flock.

'Very well,' Hawk said. A smile broke her severe features like light brings dawn. 'I accept the conditions of your surrender.'

* * *

The first trials took place the same day. Isha may be in charge, but the Renegade laws had to be upheld for peace to be brokered. Hawk wasn't known for her patience; not before, not now. Tatters was there to watch her justice being served. He had before; he would now.

In the front courtyard of the Nest, Daegan and Leofric were stooping in the dirt. Neither of them was a lord anymore. Their hands had been bound behind their backs with kher shackles. Fear was written in Daegan's dilated pupils. Leofric ... Leofric wasn't entirely there. He had a lacunant's empty, wandering gaze.

The gathering pooled around them, into the main hall, the stables, around the gates. Hawk stood with her representatives near the front, separate from the group of mages, Isha included, who were overseeing the proceedings. Despite the symbolic distance, Tatters wondered how much of a hand Hawk would have in the new rules governing the Nest.

Hemmed in by two kher guards, who might be there to

protect her, or maybe to put pressure on her, Isha placed herself in front of Daegan and Leofric.

'For the blood you spilled in your prisons and in this court-yard, what you deserve is to be made lacunants,' said Isha, and her voice was like her mother's, when her mother had been younger, fiercer.

Isha would grow to become stouter, squarer, harder to push over, as tough on the outside as on the inside. Tatters watched her, and saw Hawk. A less damaged, less soldier-like Hawk, a Hawk when she rebelled against her convent, maybe. A hawk whose feathers were growing, still, but who would fly, just the same, one day.

'As the new leader of the Nest, I ban that practice,' Isha said. 'We will never make lacunants again.' The supreme mage who had controlled the Nest was not stupid, so he didn't show any relief. He was right. 'You will be beheaded,' said Isha.

The courtyard should have been solemn for such an important moment, but in truth, there was a lot of shuffling, people whispering for the benefit of those at the back who couldn't hear well, a kher running to get an axe, the Renegades standing in military formation behind Hawk, talking in a low rumble amongst themselves.

Hawk didn't intervene. She stood before her daughter, and if she saw what Tatters saw, if she thought of what she would have done at that age, with those foes, she didn't show it.

But when the iwdan guard handed Isha the axe, she didn't take it.

'This isn't only about humans,' she said. 'It is about all of us.'

She turned, searching for someone in the crowd. It took Tatters some time to realise she was talking to Arushi. 'Please. You are the head of guards, and the only person here who can represent justice.'

Isha lifted the double-handed axe with difficulty and presented it, handle-first, to Arushi. She was pale by kher standards, a light shade of pink across her cheeks where the blood had drained from her face.

But she took the axe. She stepped up to the two men crouching on the ground, their knees black with mud, their hair unkempt, their trimmed beards matted with spit and blood and dirt.

She picked Daegan first, maybe because it was more merciful for him to die without needing to see another man's head roll beside him and smear him with blood. Arushi wouldn't have much compassion for Leofric. Tatters didn't either. But he didn't want this. He didn't want more death. He didn't want more punishment. If everyone took revenge, for their sister, their kin, the slights endured, there would be a bloodbath.

Isha would cleanse the Nest, like her mother had cleansed the convents, and her legacy would be the smell of smoke clinging to her clothes, of the houses and corpses she burnt and left behind. Lal had been right. Picking the wrong side had been worse than staying out of the fight. Lal had been right, but she was gone, and she would not return.

Arushi lifted the axe above Daegan's neck.

'Hold straight,' she said. 'If you want it to be quick.'

Daegan didn't answer. From where he was, at the edge of the crowd, Tatters could see the mage had closed his eyes. His shoulders shuddered. The old man was sobbing.

Tatters thought of tears hitting the mud. Of the fact that, forever, he would have to remember this moment, remember he stood aside and didn't lift a hand or shout for it to stop.

Arushi was strong, at least. It was a small blessing. A slick, wet sound as the axe cut through Daegan's neck. A shock of red like spilt paint. A few drops splattered Leofric's cheek, though he didn't seem to notice. When the head fell on the floor, it stood still, flat jowls following the line of the paved stones. It didn't look human anymore.

The crowd didn't cheer. It wasn't a crowd for cheering. Most of them were mages. Tatters wondered if Kilian was there somewhere, standing amongst the people pushing and pulling, with his one arm, a cripple if he had been a soldier or a farmer, a mage for as long as the Nest survived, if Hawk didn't choose to destroy it. Could he bear letting the young apprentices he had protected kneel where Leofric knelt now? Could he bear imagining Isha asking for the axe to be done with Kilian's neck, to see the blond locks tinged with red?

Arushi went to stand in front of Leofric.

'You killed my sister.' It wasn't for the benefit of the onlookers, but Tatters heard her. He heard the words twice, as she spoke them and as they echoed inside him, in the emptiness where Lal should be. He was too numb for grief. He was too broken to step beside Arushi, to tell her no swinging of a blade would give Yua back.

But she knew that already. Leofric looked up from where he was forced to the ground, and the red across his face was like a blush. He wasn't crying.

'Did I?' he asked. He sounded confused. 'I can't recall.'

'No,' she said. 'You wouldn't.'

She lifted the axe above him. Leofric glanced at Daegan's head beside him in the dirt, nothing but polite curiosity in his features. His damaged mind couldn't quite make the necessary links: axe, neck, head. He gave Arushi a smile to hide that he didn't understand what was happening.

'You don't remember my sister's death,' Arushi said, 'but I will never forget yours.'

As the blade came rushing down, Sir Leofric straightened his shoulders, and his gaze, brilliant green, caught Tatters'. For the last seconds of his life, they stared into each other's eyes.

The chop wasn't a clean one. Maybe Leofric moved; maybe Arushi underestimated the strength to put into the hit; maybe the blade was blunted by its first kill. Leofric made a sound, a stifled scream which turned to a moan, and blood gushed from the half-broken neck, and although Arushi was prompt to lift it again and lower it a second time, cutting off both the head and the whimpers of pain, there was that unbearable moment in between, that stuff of nightmares.

Then it was over. The blade was slick with blood. Arushi gave the axe back to Isha. She wiped her hands on her trousers, distractedly, the gesture of someone who was not an executioner, who had got revenge for her sister's death and didn't know what to do with the hollowness that was left.

Isha took a step forward, holding the axe in one hand, its blade resting against the ground.

'And that,' she said, 'was the last death of this war. We will end the slaughter here. There will be trials, where there have been wrongs. The iwdan will get their say. But only hard work and time in prison will pay back for crimes committed before this day. We have had enough killing.'

'This...' She jutted her chin towards the heavy axe. '...is justice.'

She let it go. It landed heavily, lifting dust, the dirt sticking where the blood had stained it.

'But justice is only the sister of mercy. From now on, we will rely on the kinder sibling.'

Isha took a deep breath. Then she did two things at once, two things which were difficult together, as difficult as the balancing act she was trying to keep between the people who shared the

Nest: she mindlinked what she had said, for the mages, and she translated it into iwdan, for the khers.

Tatters listened to the unfamiliar tongue, spoken clearly by a human mouth, as the same words brushed around his mind, lapping at the back of his thoughts. *Justice. Mercy. The last death of this war.* He didn't remember Hawk letting go, once she had seized power. He didn't remember her ever talking of mercy.

When Isha finished her speech, the onlookers were silent. There was no shuffling. There were no whispers from people at the back, no half-mouthed translations.

The only sound came from the seagulls, who had never cared, and never would.

Epilogue

There was no body, so they couldn't conduct a funeral for Passerine.

Alone in the council room, sitting on the last step of the broken staircase, Isha couldn't get the image of vultures eating a corpse out of her head. She would have wanted to see Passerine, to confirm he was gone. She would have wanted to give him a decent flight over the Edge. He had saved her life. But she hadn't saved his, when she was needed, when she might have made a difference.

Her cheek and neck smarted. Uaza had told her it would hurt, and it would hurt more if she didn't keep the healing paste smudged over her tender skin. But Isha hadn't wanted the tattoo covered in green goop. Tomorrow, maybe. But tonight, she wanted Uaza's work to be visible. Tentatively, she ran her fingers along her face – it was hot, raw. She couldn't see the result, of course, only feel its shape in swollen skin.

'There you are.'

Caitlin emerged from the maze of glass like frozen lightborns caught mid-flight. The short auburn hair matched her beige-and-brown dress. The stitches in her scar, though still visible, had faded. The glint of white might have been bandages or bone. It

371

disfigured her, altered the symmetry of her features, yet, to Isha, she was as stunning as ever.

She paused, studying Isha. Self-consciously, Isha brushed her tattoo again.

'What does it look like?' she asked.

'Painful,' Caitlin answered.

She knelt beside Isha. Isha was on the last stable step of the staircase, which was cracked and half-hanging from the main room, as if considering whether to join the rest of the steps into crumbling to the ground. Isha was at the very end, her legs hanging in the void. She had always been afraid of heights. But today she felt no fear – she had faced much worse. She would have stepped onto thin air without a shiver.

Caitlin put an arm around Isha's waist, pulling her away from the edge. 'Don't brood. It's not your style.'

'Nobody's happy,' Isha said. 'The iwdan think I've been too soft. The mages think I've been too hard.'

'Nobody's unhappy, either,' said Caitlin. 'That's called a compromise.'

Isha didn't speak the next words; she didn't think them too loudly. *And Passerine is dead, and I still can't believe it.* This was hers to mourn.

After a while, her hand drifted back to her tattoo. She couldn't forget it, not when the pain was still so vivid. Not when all the pains, of all the recent trials, were still burning.

'Seriously, what do you think?' Isha asked.

'It's ... strange,' Caitlin admitted. 'Before it looked like the bird of prey was flying downwards, lunging, about to catch something in its talons. Now it seems ... Something about the angle of the wind, the movement of the claws. It looks like it's flying upwards. Rising. It's ...' She lifted her hand, as if to touch it, then drew back. 'It's hopeful.'

Isha smiled. 'That's the idea.' She was certain Uaza's work was skilful, an addition of a few lines around the wings, a touch of wind and movement in swirling black lines, changing the tattoo without overwriting it.

From afar, laughter and song from the festivities drifted like the memory of a dream. Isha let herself relax in Caitlin's arms.

'I would never have guessed this would happen between us,' Isha mused. 'You and me. When we met, you treated me like dirt.'

Caitlin didn't let that deter her. 'You're one to talk.' Even when being friendly, her voice could be sharp. 'You were aloof with everyone. On the day you arrived, you didn't even notice me. Whereas I went straight to Tatters to ask about you. If anything, I was the one who started this.'

'No way,' Isha said. 'You know the first thing I thought when I saw you? I thought, that girl is beautiful. I bet you weren't thinking anything nice about me.'

Caitlin pursed her lips. She nuzzled against Isha's hair, to think. 'I must have thought something like, "I'll show this puffin who's in charge".' Caitlin shrugged. 'All right, I might have been looking for a fight.'

Isha couldn't help but smile, threading her fingers through Caitlin's hair, careful to avoid touching the still-sore scar. 'Care to remind me who's in charge?'

Caitlin brought her face closer, touching her nose to Isha's. 'Who's looking for a fight now?'

But they couldn't spend the night together in the cold council room, watching the sun set, the stars rise. However much she would have preferred it, Isha was the leader of the Nest now, and she was expected.

'Kilian woke up, too, just in time for the party,' said Caitlin.

'You should have seen his face when I told him the war was over.'

Reluctantly, Isha let herself be dragged downstairs, away from the windy chambers of glass and stone, down the levels of the Nest to where the fires were roaring in the mess, food was being prepared and served by mages as much as servants, where iwdan and humans mingled, alcohol helping smooth over the conversations. It was a work in progress. At least the prisons were empty tonight.

Kilian was seated at a long wooden table, mournfully chewing an apple. He was still shaken and sickly, but at least he could stand. Isha waved to him as she came closer, and he half-turned in her direction, smiling faintly. He was wearing a blue mage's robe, and he had thrown it over his shoulder to hide the stub, but it was still obvious, when facing him, that there was only a third of an arm below the cloth. The awkward way he ate his apple, as if unused to holding items in his left hand, was also a giveaway.

'May you grow tall,' he said. There was a clumsy attempt to touch wrists while holding the apple, then putting it down, then preventing it from rolling off the table. In the end, she drew him into a hug. 'I hear our supreme mage has changed again,' he mumbled against her shoulder. 'Still saying hi to a lowly mage like me?'

'Don't be stupid,' she said. 'I am so, so glad you're all right.'

He tapped her back with his left hand and let out a choked laugh. 'Yes, well, my juggling career has been rather compromised, but I'm alive, I guess.'

'There's still time for me to join you,' she answered, lifting her wrist, bandaged properly this time, without a javelin shaft sticking out of it.

It felt strange to joke about it, but it had been the right call. Kilian smiled. 'We'll make quite the pair.'

'Let's get some more wine,' said Caitlin. 'I need it to get through the night.'

The three of them went towards the tables at the end of the mess, where people could help themselves to barrels of beer and jugs of wine, to all the food that would have supported a siege, and which could now be devoured to celebrate peace. Isha poured Kilian's drink, so he wouldn't struggle, before handing it to him. They clinked the wooden cups together in a toast.

'Come with us for a bit,' Isha told Kilian. 'I've been told by Caitlin it's bad to brood.'

He glanced at Caitlin, his blue eyes widening in mock-surprise. She only shook her head. 'I know, I know, I can be nice, who would believe it, et cetera. I've heard it all.'

'I was going to say you always liked having people around you, but whatever you say,' Kilian answered. He had more colour in his cheeks already. Talking was doing him good.

He followed them as they wandered across the room, talking to the mages they met, Isha doing her best to remember everyone's names, to congratulate them on being brave, and to remind them to be kind, to get along. Hopefully her presence was of some use.

Her meandering brought her to the area of the mess where iwdan, as per their traditions, had gathered in circles around the firepits, forming impromptu tiyayat. Ka recognised her and waved. He was with a band of younger khers, mostly male, fierce-looking, with the sullen expressions of people who had been ready to fight. He took one look at Isha, then Caitlin and Kilian standing behind her, and bared his teeth. Maybe the wine had warmed his blood, because before she could even give him a greeting, he was already snarling:

'You're not expecting me to apologise, I hope?'

From the way he glared at Kilian, Isha realised they must have met, somewhere on the battlefield. Immediately she regretted bringing Kilian along, ruining her efforts at a quiet evening. How could she have been so stupid? She should keep mages and khers apart, for now.

'Your people took the horns from our dead,' Ka went on heatedly, getting a couple of glances from his circle for raising his voice. 'I saw a mage cut off my father's horns when his body was still warm. And when I tried to say something, I was beaten for my troubles.'

Before Isha could intervene, Kilian spoke up.

'No,' he said. 'I'm not expecting you to apologise. I've come to say sorry. For everything the mages did to your people. And for not trying to stop it.'

Kilian took a deep breath.

'Sorry about your dad.'

There was a silence.

'Sorry about your arm,' Ka said, begrudgingly.

He spoke so grumpily, in such bad faith, that Kilian burst out laughing. Ka joined in, not because it was funny, but because they weren't fighting, they were alive – they were relieved. Isha didn't feel like laughing. Her eyes stung.

Kilian, she realised, was crying nearly as hard as he was laughing. He let himself slump on the floor beside Ka. Mages never touched, but iwdan did. To her surprise – to Kilian's surprise, if Isha read his expression right – Ka leant over and rubbed his shoulders. It wasn't quite a hug, but it was one person telling another that it would be all right.

'I'm a mess,' said Kilian, wiping his eyes with the back of his remaining hand, trying to make fun of his tears.

'This whole war is a mess,' said Ka. 'We'll clean it up.'

They chatted for a while, of other things, of the harvests that needed tending to if they were to give at the end of spring, of the best place to watch the stars along the Edge, of their favourite areas of the city. Ka mentioned his work hunting with birds of prey. Kilian explained he wanted to buy new shoes after the disaster-dye on the last pair. When it was clear the two men were getting along well enough, at least for the time being, Isha and Caitlin took their leave.

There was one more person Isha had to talk to. She squeezed Caitlin's hand as they drew closer.

Hawk was seated beside the giants' hearth which, for this occasion, was burning. The fireplace was huge, but the flames were human-sized. A couple of benches had been dragged close, mostly occupied by Renegades. Mezyan was telling the gathering a story, which Hawk was listening to with a smile, half-indulgent, half-teasing. They were each wearing a red scarf, although Mezyan's was faded and frayed, whereas Hawk's was more ceremonial, heavy with decorations. Because of the heat, they had both thrown the red cloth back.

They looked like old friends. Yet it was difficult to forget the sheathes hanging from their belts – daggers only, this evening – or the boots girthed with chainmail. They were relaxed, but not unarmed.

Isha cleared her throat. 'May you grow tall. Tid-idir.'

Hawk waved her over. 'May you grow tall,' she echoed, shuffling sideways on the bench to allow for more space. She gave Isha a long, pensive look. 'I see your uaza has altered your tattoo.' As to whether that was good or bad, Hawk didn't say. She had a distinctive Sunriser accent that Isha couldn't remember hearing before; maybe the wine was slurring her words.

Hesitantly, but not wanting to show hesitance, Isha took a place on the bench. She was so tense she was finding it hard to breathe. The heat from the flames stuck her shirt to her back. Caitlin sat beside her, crossing her legs.

'I was in the middle of a tale,' Mezyan said, before a hush could settle. If he recognised Caitlin, he hid it well. 'It is bad form to interrupt an uaza, especially on such an important night.'

'Don't let us interrupt you, then,' said Caitlin. Despite the fact that it was Mezyan who had mutilated her, she spoke without fear.

He flashed her a smile that was all tooth and red lips. 'That's the spirit!'

Before anyone else could intervene, Mezyan picked up his storytelling from where he had left off. Without context, Isha was struggling to follow, although she gathered this was about a kher matriarch who was leading her tribe. Every day the men went out to hunt, and when they returned in the evening, she had created a new law, which inevitably seemed opaque when it was given, but came in useful the next day to deal with whatever new crisis was afoot.

It was, she realised, be it conscious or not on Mezyan's part, the best way to spend the evening. Nobody was required to talk. Nobody was required to argue. In a way, confrontation was impossible: they were brought together by the story, they shared from the same jug and laughed at the same jokes, but they couldn't bicker, old wounds couldn't open. For now, it was enough.

Despite this, Isha had one thing she needed to say. She used mindlink, so as not to bother Mezyan. She kept it as discreet as Passerine had taught her.

Mother.

My daughter. Hawk's mindlink was slick.

I thought about what you said. Blood, or soil. Isha took a deep breath. *It's neither.*

Hawk was listening. Isha felt bold enough to add, *That was Timessi's trap: he made Itri believe that was all he could choose from. But there is another way.*

Hawk's mindlink hummed, not agreeing, not disagreeing. Her mind was warm, familiar. It was a strange sensation: that someone Isha had so often feared could feel, on some intimate level, safe. As if the smell of oil and chainmail was the scent of childhood. It was a trick, something Hawk was doing on her side of their mental connection. An openness. She was trying to show Isha her goodwill.

Maybe another chance like this wouldn't present itself.

Why did you try to capture me? Isha asked.

I wanted to spare you the war. And send her away from her foster home, from everything she knew, to live on the Sunriser side of the Shadowpass. No doubt she had been an embarrassment, to be shelved, to be set aside while her mother followed her glorious purpose. Not for the first time, Isha was grateful for Passerine. Hawk continued, *But that would have been a mistake. It forged you.*

They listened to Mezyan's rhythmic, entrancing voice for a while. The uaza's new law was about covering the dead with earth and the fire with ashes. The opportunity to understand why burying old griefs was important came, as before, the next day. A consummate storyteller, it was obvious Mezyan had picked his tale with care.

But unease was nagging at Isha. *Why did you tattoo me?*

I wanted you to do great things, Hawk answered.

She must have perceived Isha's disbelief, because she huffed in amusement. She stretched back, making herself comfortable, her mindlink smooth and unbroken.

Yes, I'm aware it's contradictory, Hawk said. *When I was young, I wanted you triumphant. When I was older, I wanted you safe.*

I suppose I wanted you to be me, without the agony. No pain, to victory.

I am not you.

No, Hawk agreed. *You are better.*

A heat spread across Isha's cheek and her arms, as if she had drawn closer to the fire, although she hadn't budged. Her mindlink faded. A warmth that wasn't linked to the flames, a certainty, a confidence, settled around her shoulders; her clothes grew heavier, sturdier, as if to protect her. For a moment Isha was confused, before she recognised this for what it was: fleshbinding.

She caught Hawk's gaze. Her mother was smiling.

Isha glanced around the table, at Mezyan deep into his story, moving his hands to illustrate it; at Hawk with her forearms resting on her knees, the scar at the corner of her mouth enlarging her grin; at Caitlin, smiling with her mouth, as usual, but also smiling with her eyes, which rarely happened.

A renegade, a mage, a soldier. A Sunriser, a Duskdweller, an iwdan. And someone who was a bit of all those things, who held them together, who had put an end to the fighting, who could see what she had been given, and knew what she would make of it. Someone whose hands would be stained with neither blood nor soil.

The eyas.

Isha.

***

To avoid meeting anyone he might know, especially Renegades, Tatters had stayed outside. In the courtyard, the festivities were messier. More drinking was involved. A couple of brawls had started and been quenched. Two khers were wrestling, their horns interlocked as they tried to shove the other person to the ground. Both ungifted and iwdan had gathered to cheer them on.

'Go on, try it.' Tatters pushed the pint towards Starling.

She scrunched her nose. Tatters assumed it was a physical reaction of disgust, something she didn't control, and probably didn't even realise she was doing.

'It smells foul,' she said.

Still, Starling put out her tongue and licked off some of the foam.

'Overrated,' she said.

'You haven't tasted it!' Tatters protested. 'That's just the top.'

He blew off some of the foam for her, spilling it over his hands. They were standing below the arches, in the secrecy granted by the shadows.

'The beer is underneath,' explained Tatters. 'It's the drink.'

Although to be fair, with how foamy this brew was, the foam was part of the drink. Undaunted, he handed Starling the glass, encouraging her to try a sip. She took a small gulp. Her expression stayed neutral, as always.

'So?'

'It's as foul as it smells.' She sounded offended, as if he had tried to trick her.

Tatters couldn't help but laugh. 'It's not so much the taste, but the feeling you get after drinking it. Light-headed.' He offered his most tempting comparison: 'Like alighting if you can't alight.'

Starling pushed the glass away. 'I can alight. I have no need for this.'

Tatters gave up. He took the drink for himself. Getting a lightborn drunk would have been a feat to be remembered for, but at least he'd tried.

'We'll get going soon,' he promised, downing her beer. 'Bear with me a little longer.'

The iwdan wrestling match concluded. An ungifted woman, whom Tatters knew to be a troubadour for various taverns in the city, clapped her hands to get everyone's attention.

He'd first seen her perform at the Coop. The memory was bittersweet – when he'd gone back to visit the tavern, he'd found it inhabited by Sunrisers. The innkeeper had been drafted for the war, they'd said, and had not, to their knowledge, returned. Not even once the siege was over. It had been a hollow moment, standing in front of the Coop, alone. No Lal. No old friends. No old life to go back to.

'Folks, we're starting,' the troubadour announced. Two musicians shuffled forward; the already-drunk crowd whistled.

The first musician had a small three-hole pipe, the other a fiddle. The minstrel stood between them, a squat figure with plump cheeks, plump arms. The man with the fiddle was stringing his instrument. The man with the pipe was pulling out a hide drum from his satchel. He sat on a stool, the drum resting on one thigh, the instrument hooked to his wrist so he could play it using only one hand. With his other hand, he held the pipe. Tatters knew both instruments – pipe and drum – could be played together. The pipe only had three holes for that purpose.

Once the fiddler had finished tuning his instrument, the drummer started a beat before placing the pipe in his mouth. A high-pitched, modulated sound filled the courtyard. The fiddler joined in. The two voices, that of the fiddle and the pipe, answered each other like two children singing together. But the true artist here was the woman.

She started singing. She had a deep voice, which served as a foundation for the lighter instruments, running as an undercurrent beneath them. She breathed loudly, singing with her mouth wide open, showing yellowed teeth and too much gum. Her cheeks puffed out, her eyes squeezed shut, until she was red in the face and anything but graceful.

But her voice made you believe she could alight.

Tatters glanced at Starling. She was watching the minstrel, transfixed. Her face was unexpressive to the unused eye, but Tatters noticed that her mouth was half-open, as if she were breathing in the music. People joined in when they knew the tune, sometimes even when they didn't, guessing at the words. A few people danced. The fiddler strolled back and forth, struggling to be heard above the ruckus, bringing his melody to different corners of the courtyard.

But the minstrel sang like the voice of the sky. She sang like rain pouring down during a summer storm, breaking the stiffness of the air, leaving behind the scent of soaked earth and a strange stillness, as if the world was born anew.

Tatters knew the minstrel had a gift. Even so, he had forgotten how touching she could be. The music echoed through his ribs, his spine, his teeth. It made his heart ache for things long gone, things he would never have again.

They waited until the end of the song.

When it concluded, Starling whispered, 'Why did no-one tell me humans could also be beautiful?'

'I wanted you to hear it for yourself,' Tatters said.

As the mood shifted to celebratory, funnier pieces, Starling and Tatters made their way out of the Nest. From there, they headed towards the Edge, following the curve of the river from a distance, staying far enough away not to trudge through mud.

When they reached the Edge, they stopped. They watched the sun setting in the distance, bleeding gold and purple. The clouds below the cliff glowed like long-lost treasure.

Tatters opened his purse – he had gathered the pieces of the collar he could find in the council room, to avoid it being recast. The fragments varied in size and length, some as long as a nail, others as long as a finger. All the bits were twisted. This broken, ill-formed thing had caused him so much trouble.

'Are you sure about this?' asked Starling.

'Lightborns can't pick these up.' So they were the best keepers of the collars. Tatters shrugged. 'And if the giants are still out there, they can have them back.'

He flung the shards over the Edge. They dropped like pebbles and were swallowed by the clouds in an instant.

Starling watched the splintered collar disappear. She weighed her own collar in her hand, took a step back, stretched her arm behind her. She threw it in an elegant arc. It soared through the sky, catching the setting lights. It burnt like the birth of a small lightborn. For a while it seemed suspended in the air beside the sun. Then it curved and dived into the clouds.

Tatters laughed, partly in relief, partly at the beauty of it.

'If I'd known this was a contest, I would have put more effort into it,' he teased.

Starling smiled. 'It wasn't a contest.' Then, as an afterthought: 'But I won.'

Tatters chuckled again. Starling arched her back, her arms and fingers spread out towards the sky. They stood in silence beside the Edge. The wind howled. They could smell the spray from the river, even from this distance. The waters foamed over the cliff, red in the sunset, gushing from the earth. The air was wet.

'I guess this is goodbye,' said Tatters.

'Goodbye,' she said.

He extended his wrist for her to touch.

'That is not how lightborns say goodbye.'

Leaning forward, she took his hand. He let her guide him, a few skips to the side, a twirl, the steps of a dance that human feet couldn't quite mimic. They moved around each other slowly, gravely, without music. When she took her fingers away, their soft, brief touch was like wings brushing against his skin.

'We were strangers to each other,' said Starling, 'yet you were kind. I will remember that.'

Tatters wiped his eyes with the back of his hands. His throat was too tight for words.

Starling pushed her long golden hair behind her face. It fell in coils down her neck, shimmering like her lightborn self. The sky was dimming. The clouds were the colour of bruises.

She alighted. She was as bright as the sky was dark. She headed upwards, away, towards the sun and the endless violet of the sky.

Then she was gone.

Tatters stayed beside the Edge. He thought about a life of boundaries and thresholds; those crossed, those he couldn't leave behind. He thought about what Lal would have said.

He stood there as the sky went from purple to blue, then from blue to black. The stars were glinting tears on a dark cheek. There wasn't a lightborn in sight. He grew cold. The river splattered and spat beside him. It was silver now, the colour of the moon, and rushing as if it hoped to fill the Edge with water.

'You're still here.'

He wasn't surprised to hear Arushi's voice behind him.

When he turned, he saw she was wearing civilian clothes. She had a cloak that he had never seen on her before, a knitted piece with the complicated patterns that iwdan favoured. Her broken horn had snapped off again during the fighting. It jutted out like a cracked tooth. She caught him staring and self-consciously touched the sharp end.

'We are both damaged, aren't we?' she said.

When she was close enough, he kissed the broken tip, careful not to cut his lips on the uneven horn. They stood side-by-side. He listened to her breathing, its rhythm as soothing as the river.

'They're having fun inside,' she said.

He nodded. 'They'll get over it. They'll rebuild. The young ones always bounce back.' Tonight, he felt old. He wasn't sure he could begin again, build something new from the ashes.

'What will you do next?' she asked.

It was the question he had been asking himself.

'I don't know.'

He watched the floor of stars below, and the ceiling of stars above, like two mirrors facing each other.

'I don't think I can live without my sister,' he said.

Arushi slid her arms around him. Her skin was warm. He shivered for the first time, and then couldn't stop; he shook until his teeth chattered.

'I didn't think I could,' she said. 'But we will find a way.'

She held him tightly. He could hear her heart as it thumped against his.

'I don't want to call you Tatters,' said Arushi. 'You're not tatters, or rags, or a slave. You are more than that.'

'You're right.' He thought of Lal, the last person who had used his true name. She wasn't there to say it anymore. 'From now on, I'll use my real name.'

He told her what it was.

Standing there, before the edge of the world, they kissed. It was the first kiss of a world at peace.

THE END

Acknowledgements

It's been quite an adventure, but this story is finished at last! It's been six years of writing, editing, polishing, and living with these characters. Thank you to Alice Speilburg and Marcus Gipps for believing in me and getting this story published; to Peter Kenny, Lara Sawalha and Laura Hanna for giving voice to the characters in the audiobook version; to Abigail for being an enthusiastic and thorough copy-editor cheering me on throughout all three books; and to the rest of the Gollancz team.

All of this wouldn't be possible without my peer group – or should I say the Interpunkt collective? Watch out what these guys are doing next, they're a talented bunch of writers! Thank you for your help with everything. I'd be a much poorer writer without you.

Last but not least, thanks to my family and loved ones, and to Nicolas, always.

Credits

Rebecca Zahabi and Gollancz would like to thank everyone at Orion who worked on the publication of *The Lightborn*.

Editor
Marcus Gipps
Claire Ormsby-Potter
Áine Feeney
Millie Prestidge

Copy-editor
Abigail Nathan

Proofreader
Alan Heal

Editorial Management
Jane Hughes
Charlie Panayiotou
Claire Boyle

Marketing
Lucy Cameron

Audio
Paul Stark
Jake Alderson
Georgina Cutler

Contracts
Dan Heron
Ellie Bowker

Design
Nick Shah
Rachael Lancaster
Joanna Ridley
Helen Ewing
Tomás Almeida

Inventory
Jo Jacobs
Dan Stevens

Finance
Nick Gibson
Jasdip Nandra
Elizabeth Beaumont
Ibukun Ademefun
Sue Baker
Tom Costello

Sales
Jen Wilson
Victoria Laws
Esther Waters
Frances Doyle
Ben Goddard
Karin Burnik

Production
Paul Hussey
Fiona McIntosh

Operations
Sharon Willis

Publicity
Frankie Banks

Rights
Ayesha Kinley
Marie Henckel